Praise for Jennifer L. Armentrout's *White Hot Kiss*

"With this first title in her new Dark Elements series, powerhouse author Armentrout delivers another action-packed, believably narrated ride... Intense, well plotted, and very readable, this title should fly into the hands of every paranormal reader out there."
—*Booklist*

"The narrative sizzles with as much tension as romance... Totally entertaining."
—*Kirkus Reviews*

"Well-paced and peppered with intriguing details that allow both Romeo-and-Juliet swoons and a zombie apocalypse to have their turns."
—*Publishers Weekly*

"A must read for fans of...Armentrout's and for those wanting an exciting book that leaves you wanting more."
—*San Francisco Book Review* (5 stars)

"Armentrout...pairs a fast-moving plot with a colorful cast and a strong-willed heroine. Fans and newbies alike will definitely love this."
—*RT Book Reviews*

**Also available in the Dark Elements series from
JENNIFER L. ARMENTROUT
and Harlequin TEEN**

Bitter Sweet Love (ebook prequel novella)
White Hot Kiss
Stone Cold Touch

Coming soon

Every Last Breath

STONE COLD TOUCH

JENNIFER L. ARMENTROUT

HARLEQUIN®TEEN

Recycling programs
for this product may
not exist in your area.

ISBN-13: 978-0-373-21134-0

Stone Cold Touch

Printed in U.S.A.

For those who never stop believing,
who never stop trying, and who never stop hoping.

CHAPTER ONE

Ten seconds after Mrs. Cleo moseyed on into biology class, flipped on the projector and turned off the lights, Bambi decided she was no longer comfortable where she was currently curled around my waist.

Sliding along my stomach, the very active demonic snake tattoo was not a fan of sitting still for any length of time, especially not during a boring lecture on the food chain. I stiffened, resisting the urge to giggle like a hyena as she cruised up between my breasts and rested her diamond-shaped head on my shoulder.

Five more seconds passed while Stacey stared at me, her brows raised. I forced a tight smile, knowing Bambi wasn't done yet. Nope. Her tongue flicked out, tickling the side of my neck.

I clamped my hand over my mouth, stifling a giggle as I squirmed in my seat.

"Are you on drugs?" Stacey asked in a low voice as she brushed thick bangs out of her dark eyes. "Or is my left boob hanging out and saying hello to the world? Because as my best friend, you're obligated to tell me."

Even though I knew her boob was in her shirt, or at least

I hoped so since her V-neck sweater was pretty low cut, my gaze dipped as I lowered my hand. "Your boob is fine. I'm just…antsy."

She wrinkled her nose at me before returning her attention to the front of the classroom. Drawing in a deep breath, I prayed that Bambi would remain where she was for the rest of the class. With her on my skin, it was like having a mad case of the tics. Twitching every five seconds wasn't going to help my popularity, or lack thereof. Luckily, with the much cooler weather and Thanksgiving fast approaching, I could get away with wearing turtlenecks and long sleeves, which hid Bambi from sight.

Well, as long as she didn't decide to crawl up on my face. Something she liked to do whenever Zayne was around. He was an absolutely gorgeous Warden—a member of the race of creatures who could look human at will, but whose true form was what humans called gargoyles. Wardens were tasked with protecting mankind, hunting what went bump in the night… and during the day. I'd grown up with Zayne and had nursed one heck of a puppy-dog crush on him for years.

Bambi shifted, her tail tickling the side of my stomach.

I had no idea how Roth had dealt with Bambi crawling all over him.

My breath caught as a deep, unforgiving pang hit me in the chest. Without thinking, I reached for the ring with the cracked stone—the ring that had once held the blood of my mother, *the* Lilith—dangling from my necklace. Feeling the cool metal between my fingers was calming. Not because of the familial bond, since I really didn't claim a relationship with my mother, but because, along with Bambi, it was my last and only link to Astaroth, the Crown Prince of Hell, who had done the most undemonic thing.

I lost myself the moment I found you.

Roth had sacrificed himself by being the one to hold Paimon, the bastard responsible for wanting to unleash an especially nasty race of demons, in a devil's trap meant to send its captive to Hell. Zayne had been doing the honors of keeping Paimon from escaping, but Roth...he'd taken Zayne's place.

And now he was in the fiery pits.

Leaning forward, I propped my elbows on the cool table, completely unaware of what Mrs. Cleo was droning on about. Tears burned the back of my throat as I stared at the empty chair in front of me that used to belong to Roth. I closed my eyes.

Two weeks. Three hundred and thirty-six hours, give or take a few, had passed since that night in the old gymnasium and not a second had gotten easier. It hurt as if it had happened an hour ago and I wasn't sure if a month or even a year from now would be any different.

One of the hardest parts was all the lies. Stacey and Sam had asked a hundred questions when Roth hadn't returned after the night we had located the *Lesser Key of Solomon* (the ancient book that had the answers to everything we'd needed to know about my mother) and had been caught by Abbot (the leader of the Warden clan in D.C. who had adopted me as a young girl). They'd stopped eventually, but it was still another secret I was keeping from them, two of my closest friends.

Despite our friendship, neither of them knew what I was— half Warden, half demon. And neither of them realized that Roth hadn't just been out with mono or changed schools. But sometimes it was easier to think of him that way—to tell myself he was just at another school instead of where he was.

The burn moved into my chest, much like the low simmer in my veins that was always present. The need to take a soul, the curse my mother had passed on to me, hadn't diminished one bit over the past two weeks. If anything, it had seemed to increase. The ability to draw the soul out of any creature that had one was why I hadn't ever gotten close to a boy before.

Not until Roth had come along.

Given that he was a demon, the pesky soul problem was a moot point. He didn't have one. And unlike Abbot and almost all of the Warden clan, even Zayne, Roth hadn't cared that I was a mixed breed. He had...he'd accepted me as I was.

Scrubbing my palms over my eyes, I bit the inside of my cheek. When I'd found my repaired and cleaned-up necklace—the one Petr, a Warden who turned out to be my half brother, had broken during his attack on me—at Roth's apartment, I'd clung to the hope that Roth wasn't in the pits after all. That he'd somehow escaped, but with each passing day, that hope flickered out like a candle in the middle of a hurricane.

I believed more than anything in this world that if Roth could've come back to me, he would have by now, and that meant...

When my chest squeezed painfully, I opened my eyes and slowly let out the breath I'd been holding. The room was a little blurry through the haze of unshed tears. I blinked a couple of times as I slumped back in my seat. Whatever was on the slide projector made no sense to me. Something to do with the circle of life? No, that was *The Lion King*. I was so going to fail this class. Figuring I should at least attempt to take notes, I picked up my pen and—

At the front of the class, the metal legs from a chair scraped across the floor, screeching loudly. A boy exploded out of his chair as if someone had lit a fire under his butt. A faint yellow glow surrounded him—his aura. I was the only one who could see it, but it sputtered erratically, blinking in and out. Seeing people's auras—a reflection of their souls—was nothing new for me. They were all kinds of colors, sometimes a mixture of more than two, but I'd never seen one waver like that before. I glanced around the room and the mixture of auras glimmered faintly.

What the Hell?

Mrs. Cleo's hand was frozen above the projector as she frowned. "Dean McDaniel, what in the world are you—"

Dean spun on his heel, facing the two guys sitting behind him. They were leaning back in their seats, their arms crossed and lips curved up in identical smirks. Dean's mouth was pressed into a thin line and his face was flushed. My mouth dropped open as he planted one hand on the white tabletop and slammed his other fist into the jaw of the kid behind him. The fleshy smack echoed through the classroom, followed by several surprised gasps.

Holy granola bar!

I sat up straight as Stacey slapped her hands on our table. "Holy shit balls for Sunday dinner," she whispered, gaping as the boy Dean had punched slumped to the left and hit the floor like a bag of potatoes.

I didn't know Dean very well. Hell, I wasn't sure if I'd spoken more than a handful of words to him during my four years in high school, but he was quiet and average, tall and slender, much like Sam.

Totally not the kind of kid who'd be voted most likely to knock another guy—a much bigger guy—into next week.

"Dean!" shouted Mrs. Cleo, her ample chest rising as she rushed to the wall, flipping the overhead lights on. "What are—?"

The other guy shot up like an arrow, hands clenching into meaty fists at his sides. "What the Hell is wrong with you?" He rounded the table, shrugging out of his zipped hoodie. "You want some of this?"

Stuff always got real when the clothes started to come off.

Dean snickered as he stalked to the aisle. Chairs screeched as students moved out of the way. "Oh, I'm about to get me some of that."

"Boy fight!" Stacey exclaimed as she dug around in her bag, pulling out her cell phone. Several other students were doing the same thing. "I so have to get this on camera."

"Boys! Stop it right now." Mrs. Cleo smacked her hand against the wall, hitting the intercom wired directly to the front office. A beep sounded and she turned to it frantically. "I need the security guard in room two-oh-four immediately!"

Dean launched himself at his opponent, tackling him to the floor. Arms flew as they rolled into the legs of a nearby table. In the back of the classroom, we were safe, but Stacey and I stood up anyway. A shiver coursed over my skin as Bambi shifted without warning, flicking her tail across my stomach.

Stacey stretched up on the tips of her boots, apparently needing a better angle for her phone. "This is…"

"Bizarre?" I supplied, flinching as the boy got a good hit in, knocking Dean's head back.

She arched a brow at me. "I was going to go with *awesome*."

"But they're—" I jumped as the classroom door swung open and banged into the wall.

Security officers swarmed the class, heading straight for the melee. One beefy guy wrapped his arms around Dean, dragging him off the other student as Mrs. Cleo buzzed around the room like a nervous hummingbird, clutching her tacky beaded necklace with both hands.

A middle-aged security guard knelt beside the boy Dean had punched. Only then did I realize the boy hadn't stirred once since hitting the floor. A trickle of unease, having nothing to do with the way Bambi was moving again, formed in my belly as the guard leaned over the prone boy, placing his head near his chest.

The guard jerked back, reaching for the microphone on his shoulder. His face was white as the paper in my notebook. "I need an EMT immediately dispatched. I have a teenage male, approximately seventeen or eighteen years of age. Visible bruising along the skull. He's not breathing."

"Oh my God," I whispered, clutching Stacey's arm.

A hush descended over the room, quelling the excited chatter. Mrs. Cleo stopped by her desk, her jowls jiggling silently. Stacey sucked in a breath as she lowered her phone.

The silence following the urgent call was broken when Dean threw back his head and laughed as the other security guard dragged him from the classroom.

Stacey tucked her shoulder-length black hair back behind her ears. She hadn't touched the slice of pizza on her plate or her can of soda. Neither had I. She was probably thinking along the same lines that I was. Principal Blunt and the guidance counselor I'd never really paid attention to had given all the students in the class the option to go home.

I didn't have a ride. Morris, the clan's chauffeur, handyman and all-around awesome guy, was still on the no-ride list with me since, the last time we'd been in a car together, a possessed cabdriver had tried to play chicken with our vehicles. And I didn't want to wake up Zayne or Nicolai—for the most part, full-blooded Wardens slept deeply during the day, entombed in their hard shells. And Stacey didn't want to be home with her baby brother. So here we were, in the cafeteria.

But neither of us had an appetite.

"I'm officially traumatized," she said, taking a deep breath. "Seriously."

"It's not like the guy is dead," Sam replied around a mouthful of pizza. His wire-frame glasses slipped to the tip of his nose. Curly brown hair flopped over his forehead. His soul, a faint mixture of yellow and blue, flickered just like every-one else's had since this morning, winking in and out as if it was playing peekaboo with me. "I heard he was revived in the ambulance."

"That still doesn't change the fact that we saw someone get punched in the face so hard that they *died* right in front of us," she insisted, eyes wide. "Or are you missing the point?"

Sam swallowed the bite of pizza. "How do you know he really died? Just because a wannabe police officer says that someone's not breathing doesn't mean that's true." He glanced over at my plate. "You gonna eat that?"

I shook my head at him, sort of dumbfounded. "It's all yours." A second later, he snatched the pizza with the little pepperoni cubes off my plate. His gaze flickered up to mine. "Are you okay?" I asked.

He nodded as he munched away. "Sorry. I know I don't sound very sympathetic."

"Ya think?" Stacey muttered drily.

A dull ache flared behind my eyes as I reached for my soda. I needed caffeine. I also needed to figure out what the Hell was up with everyone's auras doing the wonky thing. The colorful shading around a human represented what kind of soul they were rocking: white for an utterly pure soul, pastels were the most common and usually indicated a good soul, and the darker the colors got, the more questionable the sta-tus of one's soul became. And if a human didn't have that tell-tale halo around him, that meant he was on Team No Soul.

I.e., he was a demon.

I wasn't doing much tagging anymore—another nifty abil-ity I had thanks to my mixed heritage. If I touched a demon, it was equivalent to sticking a neon sign on their body, which made it easier for Wardens to search them out.

Well, it didn't work on Upper Level demons. Not much did.

I didn't stop because of what had happened with Paimon and then being forbidden to tag. Abbot had ungrounded me for life after the night in the gymnasium, but it felt wrong to randomly tag demons, especially now that I knew many of them might be harmless. When I did tag, I went for the Posers, since they were dangerous and had a habit of biting people, and left the Fiends alone.

And truthfully, the change in my tagging routine was all thanks to Roth.

"It's just that those two idiots were probably messing with Dean," Sam continued as he finished off the pizza in a nanosecond. "People snap."

"People usually don't have fists that could be considered lethal weapons," Stacey retorted.

My phone chirped, drawing my attention. Bending, I pulled it out of my bag. The corners of my lips tipped up when I saw it was from Zayne even though the pain behind my eyes steadily increased.

Nic is picking u up. Meet me in the training room when u get home.

Ah, training. My stomach did a funny little twist, a familiar reaction when it came to training with Zayne. Because at some point during the grappling and evasive techniques, he'd get sweaty, and inevitably his shirt would come off. And, well, even though I was hurting something fierce over the loss of Roth, seeing Zayne shirtless was something to look forward to.

And Zayne…he'd always meant the world and then some to me. That hadn't changed. It never would. When I'd first been brought into the clan, I had been terrified and had promptly hidden in a closet. It had been Zayne who'd coaxed me out, holding in his hands a no-longer-pristine teddy bear that I had dubbed Mr. Snotty. I'd been attached to his hip since then. Well, until Roth had come along. Zayne had been my only ally—the only person who knew what I was, and…God, he'd been there for me, my rock these past couple of weeks.

"So…" Sam drew the word out as I sent Zayne a quick okay and dropped the phone back in my bag. "Did you know that when snakes are born with two heads, they fight each other for food?"

"What?" Stacey asked, brows furrowing together like two angry little lines.

He nodded, grinning a little. "Yep. Kind of like a death match…with yourself."

For some reason, a bit of stiffness went out of my posture when Stacey choked out a laugh and said, "Your capacity for useless knowledge never ceases to amaze me."

"It's why you love me."

Stacey blinked and heat infused her cheeks. She glanced over at me, as if I was somehow supposed to help her with her recently discovered crush on Sam. I was the last person on the face of the Earth to help when it came to the opposite sex.

I'd only kissed one boy in my entire life.

And he'd been a demon.

So…

She laughed loudly and brightly as she picked up her soda. "Whatever. I'm too cool for love."

"Actually…" Sam looked as though he was about to explain some kind of random fact about love and temperatures when the pain in my head flared.

Sucking in a short breath, I pressed my palm above my eyes and squeezed them shut against the red-hot stabbing sensation. It was fierce and quick, over as soon as it started.

"Layla? Are you okay?" Sam asked.

I nodded slowly as I lowered my hand and opened my eyes. Sam stared back at me, but…

He cocked his head to the side. "You're looking a little pale."

Dizziness rose over me as I continued to stare at him. "You…"

"Me? Huh?" Frowning, he glanced at Stacey quickly. "I what?"

There was nothing surrounding Sam—not a single trace of robin's-egg blue or the soft buttery yellow. My heart tripped as I twisted toward Stacey. The faint green of her aura was also gone. That meant that neither Sam nor Stacey had—no, they had souls. I *knew* they did.

"Layla?" Stacey said softly, touching my arm.

I twisted around, scanning the packed cafeteria. Everyone looked normal except there was no halo around any of them. No soft shade of color. My pulse picked up and I felt sweat dotting my brow. What was going on?

Searching out Eva Hasher, whose aura I was all too familiar with, I found her sitting a few tables back from ours, surrounded by what Stacey lovingly referred to as the bitch pack. Beside her was Gareth, her on-and-off-again boyfriend. He was leaning forward, arms folded on the table. Staring off at nothing, his eyes were red and glazed over. He liked to party, but I couldn't remember a time when I'd seen him high at school. There was nothing around him.

I shifted my gaze back to Eva. Normally there was a halo of purple surrounding the überhot brunette, meaning she'd been slipping into questionable soul status for quite some time. The need to taste her soul was always great.

But the space around her was also empty.

"Oh my God," I whispered.

Stacey's hand tightened on my arm. "What's going on?"

My gaze flitted back to her. Still no aura. And then to Sam. Nothing. I couldn't see a single soul.

CHAPTER TWO

The rest of the afternoon went by in a daze. I hated to think that Stacey and Sam were used to my random mood shifts and disappearing acts, but they were. Neither of them pushed me about my odd behavior.

When I saw Nicolai waiting for me in front of the high school, I knew my superspecial-demon-sniffing abilities had gone to Hell. The Wardens all had pure souls—a beautiful white glow that I knew tasted like heaven. Even Petr had a pure soul in spite of the fact he was the worst sort of male and had tried to kill me.

But Nicolai, a Warden I knew was as good as Zayne, didn't have his usual white glow today. I climbed into the black Escalade, eyes wide as I pulled the door shut behind me.

He passed me a quick look. Nicolai rarely smiled since he'd lost his wife and his only child during childbirth. I used to get more smiles than most, but not since the night the clan had caught me with Roth.

"Are you okay?" he asked, his blue eyes identical to Zayne's. All Wardens had the most brilliant blue eyes that looked like the summer sky before a storm. Mine were the palest gray, as if they'd been leached of all color, a product of the demonic blood in me.

When I did nothing but stare at him like a goober, his handsome face slipped into a slight frown. "Layla?"

I blinked as if coming out of a trance and fixed my gaze on the people crowding the sidewalk. The sky was overcast from the recent cold rain and the clouds looked fat with more, but there were no traces of a soul to be found. I shook my head. "I'm okay."

We didn't speak again during the unnecessarily long drive to the compound just over the bridge. Traffic was always a pain. When Morris drove me, he didn't talk—he never talked—but I'd pretend to have a conversation with him. With Nicolai, it was just about seven kinds of awkward. I wondered if he still thought I'd betrayed the clan by assisting Roth in finding the *Lesser Key of Solomon,* if he'd ever smile at me again.

It seemed as if it took thirty minutes and ten years before the Escalade rolled to a smooth stop in front of the compound. As usual, I grabbed my bag and threw open the door. I'd done it so many times I didn't look where I put my foot. I knew the curb of the sidewalk leading to the porch steps would be there.

Except as I hopped down, my booted foot met nothing but air. Caught off balance, I threw my hands out as I toppled forward. My backpack was flung to the side as I went down palms first. Bambi shifted without warning, curling along my waist as if she sought to somehow not end up squished if I went down.

Real helpful there.

I caught myself before I kissed the pavement, sliding on the slippery, broken stone. Skin tore across my hands, sparking little bites of pain.

Nicolai was out of the Escalade and by my side in record time, swearing loudly. "Are you all right, little one?"

"Ouch," I moaned, rocking back on my knees as I lifted my battered hands. Other than feeling like a three-legged gazelle, I was okay. Cheeks red, I bit my lip to stop a flood of curse words from coming out. "I'm fine."

"You sure?" He curled his hand around my upper arm, helping me stand. Bambi shifted positions the moment he came in contact with me, and I felt her crawl up the side of my neck, reaching my jaw. Nicolai saw it, too, jerking his hand back. He cleared his throat as he fixed his stare on my eyes. "Your palms are scratched."

"They'll heal." And they'd heal within hours. Hopefully Bambi would slither back to somewhere less visible in that time. None of the Wardens liked to see her for a crap ton of reasons. "What happened to the curb?"

"No idea." Nicolai frowned as he stared at the crumbled gray stone. "Must've been all the rain."

"Odd," I muttered, spying my bag in a puddle. I sighed as I stomped over to it and wrenched it out of the muckiness.

Nicolai followed me up the steps. "Are you sure you're not hurt? I can get Jasmine to take a look at your hands."

I had no idea why Jasmine, a member of the New York clan of Wardens, was still here. Not that I had any problems with her. Her younger sister Danika, the beautiful, full-blooded gargoyle who wanted to make babies with Zayne, was another story. Then again, considering all that Roth and I had shared, I really had no room to be jealous.

But the bitter burn was there every time I saw the dark-haired beauty. Double standards sucked, but oh wellsies.

"Really. I'm good," I said as we waited for Geoff, hidden somewhere in the belly of the compound, to unlock the doors. "I'm just obviously not very graceful."

Nicolai didn't respond and—thank baby Jesus and cuddly angels—the front door opened. Careful not to step through an unexpected hole in the floor, I set my bag down just inside the door and hurried upstairs to my bedroom.

Good news. I didn't fall down the stairs and Bambi had decided to get off my face and was now back to curling around my body.

Traffic and my impromptu face-plant outside had made me late to meet Zayne, but as I toed off my boots, I wasn't sure how focused on training I'd be considering there seemed to be a wire suddenly missing in my brain.

Why couldn't I see souls? And what did that mean?

I needed to tell someone—I would tell Zayne, but not his father. I didn't trust Abbot so much anymore. Not since discovering that he'd known all along who my mother and father were. And I was pretty sure he didn't 100 percent trust my rosy-red behind either.

I dragged a pair of sweats and a T-shirt out from my dresser and tossed them on the bed. Padding around my room in my socks, I unbuttoned my jeans and pulled my sweater off over my head. Static crackled in my loose hair, causing thin wisps to stand up around my head. Zayne would know what to do. Since Roth—

My bedroom door flew open and Zayne burst in. "Nicolai told me—*holy Christ*."

I froze by the bed, my eyes increasing to the size of spaceships. Holy balls. My sweater was still wrapped around one arm, but I was wearing nothing else but my bra—my black bra—and my jeans, which were half-unbuttoned. Not sure why the color of my bra made a difference, but I stood there, my mouth gaping.

Zayne had come to a standstill, and like with Nicolai, I saw no pearly glow surrounding him. But at the moment I was more preoccupied with what Zayne *did* see: me, standing in front of him in my bra—my black bra.

His beautiful blue eyes were wide, the pupils slightly vertical. His wavy blond hair, which he'd chopped off recently, was still long enough to frame broad cheekbones. His full lips were parted.

For ten years, I'd grown up with Zayne by my side. He was four years older than me and I'd idolized him like any little sister would, but nothing I'd felt for Zayne, at least not in the past couple of years, had been sisterly. I'd wanted him ever since I was old enough to appreciate rock-hard abs on a dude.

But Zayne had been and would always be off-limits to me.

He was a full-blooded Warden and although I couldn't see his soul right now, I knew he had one and it was pure. And while he'd had no problem getting überclose with me in the past, a relationship with anyone with a soul would be too dangerous considering I'd turn them into a soul-flavored Slurpee.

And his father expected him to mate with Danika.

Blech.

Right in that moment though, his potential baby-making future with Danika seemed far removed from this room. Zayne was staring at me as if he'd never truly seen me before, and I honestly couldn't think of a time he'd seen me in even a bathing suit, let alone a bra. I tried not to think about the red polka-dot undies peeking out from behind the gap in my jeans.

And then I realized what he was staring at.

A flush raced across my cheeks and then followed his gaze down my neck and lower. I could feel Bambi's tail twitching along my spine. She was curled around my waist, with her long neck stretched up between my breasts. Her head rested on the swell of my right breast as if it was her own personal pillow, right below where my necklace hung.

Zayne's gaze tracked the length of the tattoo, and I cringed as the flush deepened. What must he be thinking at the sight of Bambi so blatantly on display, a blunt reminder of how different I was from him? I didn't want to know.

He took a step forward and stopped again as his stare traveled up with enough intensity to feel like a physical caress. Something shifted in me, and the embarrassment faded into heady warmth. A heaviness settled in my chest, and muscles low in my stomach clenched.

I knew I needed to put my sweater back on or at least attempt to cover myself, but there was something in the way he stared at me that held me immobile and I...I wanted him to see me.

To see I wasn't the little girl hiding in the closet anymore.

"God," he said, speaking finally in a voice that was a deep, low rumble. "You're beautiful, Layla. A gift."

My heart did a backflip, but my ears had to also be on the fritz, because I know that wasn't what he'd just said. In the past he'd called me pretty, but never beautiful—never a gift. Not with my hair so pale it could be considered white or the fact that I sort of looked like a demented Kewpie doll, my eyes and mouth way too big for my face. I mean, I wasn't fugly or anything, but I wasn't Danika. She was all glossy black hair, tall and graceful limbs. She was stunning.

I'd just *fallen* out of a car minutes ago and could seriously pass as an albino from a distance.

"What?" I whispered, folding my arms—sweater and all—over my stomach.

He shook his head side to side as he walked—*no, stalked*—toward me, each step full of purpose and with an inherent grace a dancer would be envious of. "You're beautiful," he said, eyes a brilliant, luminous shade of blue. "I don't think I've ever told you that."

"You haven't, but I'm n—"

"Don't say you're not." His gaze dipped once more to where

Bambi's head rested, and air leaked out between my parted lips. For once, the demonic familiar didn't move. "Because you are, Layla. You're beautiful."

Thank you formed on the tip of my tongue, because it seemed like the right thing to say, but the words died when he lifted a hand. The strap of my bra had slipped down my upper arm and he scooped two fingers beneath it. His skin grazed mine, and a fine shiver coursed throughout my body.

A strange surge of possessiveness hit me. A need to claim him, so deep and so hard that it made my knees weak and my breath catch in my throat. As he slid the strap up my arm, his fingers brushed over my skin, and the yearning was so entrenched that I knew it was mine, but something about it was foreign. A hunger that I felt, but...

His gaze collided with mine, and now his pupils were completely vertical. My mouth dried and for a wild second, I thought he might kiss me. Every muscle in my body tensed, causing Bambi's tail to flicker over my spine. A thousand fantasies, and I'd had many of them when it came to Zayne, couldn't have prepared me for this moment. Zayne...he meant the world to me and before Roth—

Roth.

Air hitched in my throat at the thought of the golden-eyed demon. The image of him formed easily in my mind—hair as dark as obsidian, cheekbones high and angular, lips curved in a knowing smirk that had infuriated and excited me.

How could I be standing here with Zayne, wanting him to kiss me—because I did want that—when I'd just lost Roth?

But I never really had Roth and kissing Zayne was impossible.

With what appeared to be a great effort, he tore his gaze away and glanced over his shoulder. Dear Lordie Lord, the door was open. Anyone could've walked by and seen me standing there. In my bra—my black bra.

Heat swamped my face again as I stepped back and hurriedly dragged my sweater back over my head. I turned away, smoothing my hands over my static-filled hair. My face felt as though I'd been basking in the sun during a solar storm and I had no idea what to say as I fixed my jeans with shaky fingers.

Zayne cleared his throat, but when he spoke, his voice was still deeper and rougher than normal. "I guess I probably should've knocked, huh?"

Counting to ten, I turned around and forced a casual shrug. He was still staring at me as though I hadn't put a sweater on. "I do that all the time to you."

"Yeah, but…" His brows rose as he scrubbed his hand down his jaw. "Sorry about that and the…um, the staring."

Now I felt as if I'd smushed my face against the sun. As I sat down on the edge of the bed, I bit my lip. "It's okay. Just a bra, right? No big deal."

He sat beside me and tilted his head toward me. Thick golden lashes shielded his eyes. "Yeah, no big deal." He paused, and then I felt his gaze move away from me. "I came up here because Nicolai said you fell outside."

Oh God. I'd forgotten about my humiliating spill.

"Are you okay?"

I lifted my hands. The palms were scratched and pink. "Yep. I'm fine. But the curb isn't. You have any idea what happened to it?"

"No." He reached over, taking my right hand. Gently, he smoothed his thumb over the blemish. "It wasn't like that this morning when I came home from hunting." His lashes swept up. "Did you get Jasmine to look at your hands?"

As nice as his holding my hand was, I pulled it free with a sigh. Jasmine had a natural talent when it came to working with healing herbs and all that jazz. "I'm fine. You know these marks will be gone by tomorrow."

He watched me for a second and then leaned back on my bed, resting on one elbow. "That's why I came up here. Thought you were more hurt than you were saying and that's why you hadn't made it down to the training room."

I twisted toward him, watching as he reached up with his other arm and snagged Mr. Snotty. He plopped it between us, sitting it up, and I grinned.

"Nicolai also said you were acting strange in the car," he added after a beat.

Wardens were like gossiping old biddies at their weekly bingo meet-up, but they did have reason to be suspicious of me. I tucked my hair back behind my ears. "Something happened today."

His large hand stilled on the teddy bear and his eyes met mine. "What?"

Pushing the whole bra and half-naked thing to the side to obsess over later, I scooted closer to him and lowered my voice, mindful of the still-open door. "I don't know how or why it happened, but in bio class, my vision started to get a little wonky."

His brows knitted. "Details."

"It's the souls. In bio class, I noticed that the auras seemed to…blink in and out, then at lunch, they faded away completely."

"Completely?"

I nodded.

Zayne sat up in one fluid motion. "You can't see any souls?"

"No," I whispered.

"Not even mine?"

"I can't see *any* soul." My pulse kicked up as it really settled in. "No one's. It's like with demons. Nothing around them."

He curled his leg up as he leaned toward me, voice low. "And this just happened. They were blinking in and out and then nothing?"

I nodded again as my stomach twisted up in little knots. "At lunch, I got this really sharp pain behind my eyes and I closed them. When I reopened them, all the auras were gone. Just like that."

"And nothing else happened?" When I shook my head, he rubbed a spot over his heart. "You didn't come into contact with...with any demons?"

"No," I said quickly. "I would've told you that right away."

A tense look flickered across his face for a moment, and there was a twisty motion in my chest. Of course he wouldn't expect me to tell him right away. I'd lied to him about Roth for two months.

"You don't have reason to believe that and I...I've lied to you before." I swallowed hard when he looked away. A muscle thrummed along his jaw. "And I am sorry for that, but I thought..."

"You thought what you were doing was right by not telling us about him and looking for the *Lesser Key*," he said quietly, not saying *his* name. "And I get that. I'm trying not to hold it against you."

Pulling my legs up, I tucked them against my chest. "I know."

He glanced over at me, expression softening after a few moments. "Okay. So nothing else happened? Right." He blew out a deep breath as he shook his head. "I don't know. There really isn't anyone to ask. There's no other..."

"Demon?"

"Yeah, that. There are no other demons around that can do what you can, so that leaves us very little to work on."

My mother could see souls, or at least that was what Roth

had said. Wasn't as if I could ask her, though, since she was currently chained in Hell.

"Maybe this is just temporary," he said, reaching over and brushing back a lock of blond hair so light it was practically as white as my face. "So let's not freak out until we know for sure. Okay?"

I found myself nodding, but I was already starting to freak out. "I won't be able to tag."

Zayne tilted his head to the side. "You haven't really been tagging recently, so that's the last thing to worry about, Layla-bug."

"You won't tell Abbot, right?"

"Not if you don't want me to." He paused. "But why don't you want him to know?"

I shrugged, not really wanting to talk about his father. Zayne loved and trusted him.

Zayne watched me for a few moments and then stretched out on his side. Offering his hand, he smiled up at me. "Want to skip practice?"

Training was important. It kept me from getting my butt handed to me when I did run into demons, but I nodded. Taking his hand, I let him tug me down beside him. We lay there for a few moments, me on my back and Zayne on his side.

He held on to my hand, careful not to push against the torn skin. "How have the cravings been lately?"

I sighed. "The same."

There was a pause. "Have you been eating normally?"

Brows furrowing, I tilted my head back to see him. "Why are you asking that?"

He didn't answer immediately. "You've lost weight, Layla."

I shrugged. "That's probably a good thing."

"You didn't need to lose any weight." A small smile appeared on his lips but didn't reach his eyes. "I know these past two weeks have been hard on you."

Pressure clamped down on my chest and a ball of emotion formed in my throat. The past two weeks had seconds of warmth and light, but endless hours of darkness and loss. I'd never lost someone I'd been close to before or remembered. I didn't know how to grieve or move on. Missing Roth was like watching a door to a life you hadn't dared dream of slam shut in your face.

What was happening to him right now? Was he being tortured? Was he in any way okay? I'd thought those questions so many times they were a constant echo in my mind.

"I know you cared about him," Zayne said, threading his fingers through mine. "But don't forget about me. I'm here for you. I always will be."

My breath caught around a sob.

He lowered his head and, after a second, his lips brushed my cheek. Only Zayne, who knew what I could do to anyone with a soul, would dare to get that close. "Okay?"

"Okay," I whispered, closing my eyes against the familiar burn. "I won't."

CHAPTER THREE

By lunch the following day, I still wasn't seeing any souls, but an idea occurred to me as I pretended to pay attention in English class while the teacher lectured on the consequences of reckless love in *Romeo and Juliet*.

I hadn't seen a demon in days and maybe something would be different about them, too. Made sense. Sort of. If humans were suddenly absent their souls, maybe I'd also see some difference in demons, who didn't have souls to begin with.

While Stacey organized her broccoli into a demented smiley face, I sent Nicolai a quick text letting him know to pick me up at Dupont Circle. He'd get it when he woke up and since he wasn't aware of what was going on with me, it wouldn't seem strange to him. To Zayne, it would be a different story, but I'd fill him in when I got home.

"No excitement in bio class today?" Sam asked, spearing his broccoli with his plastic fork.

Stacey shook her head. "Nope, but Mrs. Cleo wasn't there."

"The poor woman probably had a stroke." I pushed my veggies around the slop of mystery meat. "We had a sub today—a Mr. Tucker."

She grinned at me. "And he was hot and young."

"Really?" Sam asked. Before she could respond, he leaned across the table, smoothing his thumb along the top of her cheek.

Stacey stilled.

I froze.

Sam grinned as he brushed his finger along her cheekbone again. "Got it." He sat back.

"Got it?" Stacey murmured.

I started to smile.

"Eyelash," he explained, his gaze fixed on her. "Did you know lashes keep dust out of your eyes?"

"Uh-huh." Stacey nodded.

He chuckled. "No, you didn't."

"Yeah," she whispered.

Catching Sam's look, I laughed. I loved that Sam was finally starting to show some confidence when it came to her. It was obvious that he'd been crushing on her hard for the past two years.

Which gave me another idea. Wonky demon abilities aside, it would be good to get out and do something…normal. "What are you guys doing this weekend?"

Stacey blinked as she pushed her thick bangs off her forehead. "Baby-brother duty both Saturday and Sunday. Why?"

"I thought we could catch a movie or something."

"I'm free most of Thanksgiving break." She slid Sam a surprisingly shy smile. "What about you?"

Sam toyed with the cap to his water. "I'm free whenever." His dark eyes flicked to me. "Why don't you invite Roth?"

My heart dropped into my belly and my mouth opened, but there were no words. Well, that offer of fun times had bitch smacked me right back in the face.

He glanced at Stacey. "Um, I'm thinking I said something

wrong. You guys aren't hanging out anymore? I just assumed he was going to a new school or something."

God, how I wished that was it. "I haven't…talked to him in a while."

Sam cringed. "Oh. Sorry." He fixed his gaze on his empty plate.

Stacey quickly reverted conversation back to movie plans and after we left for our next class, she leaned against the locker beside mine, sympathy pinching her lips. "Sam really isn't that great at social skills, you know?"

I snorted as I pulled out my history text. "He seems like he's improving."

"Baby steps." She giggled, but it quickly faded. "I've been hoping you'd tell me what's up, but I've waited as long as I can. What happened with you and Roth by the way? You guys were all hot and heavy. You were supposed to spend the night with him, got busted and—"

"I really don't want to talk about it," I said, closing my locker door. All around us, students milled about. It was odd seeing them without their shimmery souls. I smoothed my hands down my black tights. "I don't mean to be whatever about it, it's just…"

"Hard? Too soon? Got it." She cocked her head to the side and took a deep breath. "So Sam…?"

On safer ground, I smiled. "Yes?"

"Okay." She leaned toward me. A wave of hope crashed into me, coming out of nowhere. It was so strong that I stepped back. The anticipation faded as Stacey's dark eyes lit up. "Okay. Is it just me or was Sam trying to hit on me?"

I shook my head, dispelling the weird feeling. "I think so."

"Smooth call with the movie idea." She fell in step beside me. "Proud of you on that one."

"I don't know why you don't just ask him out." I slowed

down as I neared history. "You've never had a problem doing that before."

"I know." She kicked her head back and scowled. "But he's different. He's Sam. He's interested in things like computers and books and nerdy stuff."

I laughed. Sam was pretty nerdy—cute nerdy. "And you?"

She sighed and then smiled broadly. "I'm interested in him."

"Then that's all that matters, right?"

"I think so." Glancing at herself, she tugged down the red tank top she wore under her long cardigan, exposing the swells of her breasts. "And in art class, he will discover that he's interested in boobs. Wish me luck."

"Good luck." I eyed her cleavage. "Not that you need it."

She winked. "I know."

As Stacey bounced away, I turned on my heel to head into the class and stopped. My brows climbed up my forehead. By the bathrooms, a boy and girl were going at it. As in I couldn't tell who they were or where one began and the other stopped. They were pressed against the wall. The girl had her leg curled around the boy's waist and his hips were…whoa.

I think they were about to make a baby.

They were so going to get in trouble. PDA was totally off-limits. Even holding hands earned an evil eye from the staff.

But…but Coach Dinkerton, esteemed leader of our winless football team, strolled right past them. Didn't bat an eye. Not even when the couple slipped into the girls' bathroom.

What in the world was going on?

After class, I hunched deeper into my thin turtleneck as I hoofed it down the crowded sidewalks near Dupont Circle. A jacket would've been a smart idea. The denim skirt and tights really didn't block the chill and damp wind, but I hadn't planned on being out.

All around me, people meandered to and fro. None of them had visible souls. Two hours into my impromptu experiment and I'd declared it a giant fail. I thought I'd spotted a few Fiends hanging around a telephone pole—Fiends loved to mess with things; electronics, construction sites, fire—but it was tough to tell for sure. They hadn't caused any active trouble and there was nothing setting them apart from the crowd. They could've just been humans waiting to cross the street.

Night was already creeping into the city, causing the streetlamps to flicker on, casting unfriendly shadows across the mixture of new and old buildings lining the roads.

Clutching my bag close to my hip, I hurried toward the park, keeping close to the storefronts. I hated to admit it, but paranoia was a friend walking beside me. Before, I could always rely on my soul-spotting ability to root out demons and I'd never honed the natural instinct other Wardens had when it came to sniffing them out. Every so often a weird shiver would dance across the nape of my neck, but I didn't know if that signified the presence of a demon or not. It was more the sensation one got when being watched.

Everyone I passed could have been a potential Poser or Upper Level for all I knew. Maybe I simply couldn't sense demons like other Wardens. God, it would suck if that was the case. I needed to figure out if that was an issue, stat, but where could I find a bunch of demons that hopefully wouldn't try to kill me?

I tripped as another winner of an idea occurred to me.

Roth's apartment building along the Palisades. The whole place was bursting at the seams with demonkind, but could I go back there? Could I face all the emotions being so close to where he'd lived would bring forth? I wasn't sure, but I'd have to try. Maybe tomorrow after school I could get Zayne to go with me. He wouldn't be thrilled, but he'd do it…for me.

Or maybe tomorrow I'd wake up seeing souls again.

God, how many times had I wished I were normal by Warden standards? And now that I was closer to being so, I was giving myself an ulcer and—

The form came out of nowhere, nothing more than a thick shadow snaking out from the alley, moving too fast for me even to get a scream out. One second I was walking down the street and the next, I was hauled sideways into a dark, narrow alley. A burst of aggression lit me up from the inside and then faded into stark, icy terror as the strong grip let go. I flew backward several feet. My backpack smacked into a garbage bin as I hit the cold ground on my butt.

Stunned, I looked up through a sheet of pale blond hair to see two vibrant blue eyes with vertical pupils staring down at me.

"Demon," he hissed, raising a jagged knife in one hand. "Prepare to go back to Hell."

CHAPTER FOUR

Holy mother of God.

For a moment, I couldn't move. It was a Warden in human form—barely in human form—one I'd never seen before. I knew where he planned to put that knife. A stab to the heart was how Wardens sent demons back to Hell.

Knocking off the heads of demons worked, too.

The moment of paralyzing fear gave way to instinct. All the hours of evasive training kicked into gear. I sprung to my feet, ignoring the ache in my backside. The wicked sharp blade arced through the air as I darted to the side.

"Wait!" I said, jumping back as he swung at me. "I'm not a demon."

The Warden sneered. He seemed young and his face was unfamiliar to me, which meant he wasn't a part of the D.C. clan. "Do you think I'm stupid? You stink of their kind."

I smelled? Resisting the urge to sniff myself, I edged around the green Dumpster, hoping I could reason with him. "I'm *part* demon. My name's Layla Shaw. I live with—"

He shot forward, and I spun around. The knife swooped down, carving through the sweater and slicing open the skin of my upper arm. I cried out as fiery pain burst along my nerve endings.

It happened so fast there was no stopping it.

The inherent urge to shift took hold and my skin stretched tight as Bambi unfurled herself from her resting spot on my skin. She spilled into the air, a mass of tiny black dots that hung between the Warden and me.

Déjà vu smacked me in the face.

The dots dropped to the alley floor and spun together, forming a thick mass that rose into the air, taking the shape of a snake.

I'd never seen Bambi so big before.

Taller than me and as wide as the Warden, Bambi hissed like a steam engine as she drew back, preparing to strike.

The Warden cursed as he stepped to the side, dropping into a crouch. His body began to shift, splitting the shirt straight up his broad chest. "*Part* demon? You have a familiar."

"Yes, but it's not what you think." Blood dripped down my arm as I stumbled toward Bambi. My heart pounded as she opened her mouth, revealing fangs the size of my hands. I glanced at the mouth of the alley. Any second someone could come back here and while the Warden wouldn't be too hard to explain, the snake the size of a Humvee was another story. "Please. Let me explain. I'm not a bad guy."

"This is hardly the first time a demon has said that." The Warden circled Bambi as his skin darkened to a deep gray.

Bambi struck, and the Warden narrowly avoided a direct hit. "Bambi! Don't!" I ordered.

The snake drew back once more, her powerful body curling and tensing. "Don't eat the Warden!" I said, breathing heavily through the pain. "We all need—"

The Warden launched forward and spun out from under Bambi as she shot at him. He popped up, half in his human form and half gargoyle. I saw the knife swinging through the air. I pushed off the ground, lurching toward him. I ducked under his arm as he swung the knife down. I spun around, planting my foot in his back. The Warden went down on one knee.

"Please stop," I gasped, still trying to put an end to this hot mess of a train wreck. "We're on the same—"

The Warden wheeled around and went for me again.

He didn't make it.

The snake shot at him like a bullet heading straight for the head. "Bambi!"

Too late.

Like a wimp, I squeezed my eyes shut at the first high-pitched yelp. My stomach turned as a sickening succession of crunching noises filled the alley. I pivoted around, facing the mouth of the alley. People strolled in both directions, having no idea what was going on in here.

There was a loud swallowing sound and there was a good chance I was going to hurl. Looking down, I wrapped my hand around my left arm and winced as pain shot through me. My sweater was dark, masking the blood, but it was dripping onto my hand. Biting my lip, I closed my eyes as a wave of dizziness washed over me.

Criminy, I had bad luck when it came to alleys.

Bambi nudged my hip with her nose. Taking a deep breath, I faced her. Her red, forked tongue wiggled in the air and she nudged me again. My gaze lifted to the shadows of the alley. Besides the rats, we were the only two things there.

"Oh my God," I breathed, patting Bambi's head awkwardly. "You seriously just ate a Warden."

And my life seriously had just gotten a lot more complicated.

I managed to find an old silk scarf in the bottom of my bag. Using it to wipe the blood off my hand, I then balled it up and kept it handy just in case I started dripping all over Nicolai's leather seats.

I didn't say anything to him, because what could I say? A Warden tried to kill me. I might be bleeding to death over here. Oh, and by the way, Bambi ate said Warden for dinner. Yeah, that was going to go over like a ton of bricks laced with dynamite.

So I focused on not passing out from the moment Nicolai showed up. As soon as I got home, I'd find Zayne and…God knows what after that.

I needed KWWRP—Killing Wardens Witness Relocation Program.

Clenching my jaw hard to keep from moaning every time we hit a pothole, I felt a bit out of it by the time we reached the compound. The cut couldn't have been that deep. At least I hoped it wasn't, but damn if my entire left arm didn't feel like a cold piece of meat.

I hurried inside and skidded to a stop in the foyer. Deep male voices rang out from every corner of the home it seemed. I looked into the living room, disoriented.

Jasmine stood there, her arms around a tall male Warden with thick, wavy auburn hair. He was holding their daughter, Izzy. The two-year-old was in her human form, but two dark-colored horns parted her red curls and her wings were poking out the back of her pink shirt. Drake, Izzy's twin brother, was clambering at the male's legs, grunting each time he jumped.

Dez was back.

Which meant Jasmine and Danika would be heading home soon since the members of their clan were back and it was no longer necessary for them to be kept here for safety reasons. Yay.

A strange look pinched his handsome features as his gaze scoured his surroundings. When his eyes landed on me, his shoulders relaxed a bit, but the odd tension on his face remained.

"Layla," he said, smiling as he handed Izzy off to Jasmine and bent, picking up Drake, holding him close to a massive chest. "It's good to see you."

I blinked slowly as I dropped my bag beside the small table in the foyer. Still holding the scarf, I forced a smile. "Hey. How…how are you?"

"Good. You look…"

Voices neared and the doors to Abbot's library swung open. As if moving through a fog, I turned. Another unfamiliar Warden stepped out, drawing to a halt when he saw me. Like the one in the alley and like Dez himself, he was young. Probably in his mid-twenties.

"What the…?" he said, reaching behind him.

Oh, for the love of God, if he pulled out a knife, I was going to give up on life in general.

"Maddox." Dez stepped forward, clutching Drake as the toddler grabbed a handful of hair with chubby fingers. "This is Layla."

There was a heavy layer of warning in Dez's voice that caused Maddox to straighten as though steel had been poured down his spine. He nodded curtly and then stepped around me, giving me a wide enough berth that one would think I was carrying some kind of vicious disease.

"Have you seen Tomas?" Maddox asked, watching me from the corners of his eyes. "He went into the city. Has he come back?"

"No," Dez said, hoisting Drake up. Behind him, Jasmine frowned as she eyed me. I was sure her "there's a wounded bird nearby" senses were firing. She was a Hell of a healer. Something I was in desperate need of, but I needed to get out of here. "I'm sure he'll be back soon," he finished.

With a sinking feeling, I had a real bad idea about who Tomas was…or used to be. Oh dear. I started to shuffle toward the stairs, but Zayne's deep, husky laugh drew my attention.

He was in the library with Geoff, our resident techie and gadget gargoyle, and his father. Some of our other clansmen were there. Abbot sat behind the desk, rolling a cigar between his fingers. It was unlit. He never smoked them, just seemed to like handling them.

Zayne was standing with his back to the door, next to a beautiful dark-haired female Warden—the kind of beauty that made me feel blah on a good day. Danika was leaning into him and smiling as one of the clansmen told a story.

I didn't know what kind of story. I was never included in the tales. And the only times I'd been in Abbot's library recently were when I was getting lectured about one thing or another.

My feet felt funny as I stood in the hallway. "Zayne?" My voice also sounded weird. The handkerchief seemed wetter.

Turning around, the smile on Zayne's face froze. "Layla?"

I knew I probably looked like death chewed up and spit back out. I nervously glanced at Danika, not daring to look at Abbot. "C-can I talk to you for a second? Alone?"

"Yeah. Hold on just a sec." He twisted back to Danika and then his father, who was most likely giving him *that* look. The look that said *don't you dare walk away from Danika, your future baby mama.* "I'll be back."

She nodded, nibbling on her lip. "It's okay. Are you?"

That question was directed at me, and I think I said something in the affirmative. I hobbled past where Dez and the new guy stood with Jasmine, not waiting on Zayne. If I didn't sit down, I was going to fall down.

With my good hand, I clenched the banister as I started

up the stairs. Zayne was right beside me, head bent low as he spoke. "Are you okay?"

"Uh…" A few more steps. A few more steps. "Not really."

Moving closer to me, he sucked in a breath. "I smell blood. You're bleeding."

"Kind of," I squeaked. As he started to turn back around, no doubt to sound the alarm, I said, "Don't say anything yet. Please."

"But—"

"*Please.*"

Zayne swore under his breath, but kept coming up the steps. "How bad?"

"Uh…"

We rounded the second landing, and once we were out of sight, Zayne bent and gathered me up in his arms. Any other time, I would've pitched a fit, but the whole "bleeding and being in pain" thing kept me quiet.

"I need a little detail," he said, heading straight for his room—not mine—*his*. I was a little distracted by that as he shuffled me against his chest and opened the door. "Talk to me, Layla. I'm starting to freak out."

When he toed the door shut behind him, I forced my tongue to work. "I think I might've been stabbed."

"You think?" he shouted.

I flinched. "Okay. I was."

"Jesus." He sat me down on the edge of his bed. Over his shoulders, the wall-to-wall bookcase was overflowing with books. "Where? Where is it?" But he was already searching with his eyes and hands. When he reached my upper arm, I yelped. "Shit." He pulled back his hand and his fingers were smeared in red. "Why didn't you tell Nicolai?"

"It's not that bad, right?" I looked down, but the black material hid the damage.

Zayne took the soaked scarf from me and dropped it on the wood floor. "I don't know. I need to take your top off."

I raised my brows at that.

He shot me a bland look as he brushed his hair back with his forearm. "And you need to tell me how this happened."

"I was near Dupont Circle and—do you really need to take my top off?" I asked as he reached for the hem of my sweater.

Zayne looked up, his blue eyes bright with determination and his normally golden skin a shade or two paler. "Yes. It's in the way."

"But—"

"I saw you in your bra just yesterday. Remember?" When he pointed that out, it wasn't as though my argument for modesty was valid. "You were around Dupont?"

I nodded, swallowing hard as he lifted my sweater. "I was out trying to spot a demon. You know, to figure out if I could see anything different around them."

"Dammit, Layla, you could've asked me. I would've gone with you."

The sweater being tugged over my head and off my good arm hid the face I'd made. "I wasn't going to engage the demon."

"Yeah, that's a moot point when a demon obviously engaged you." He didn't even check out my lacy pink bra as he gently eased the sweater down my left arm.

I sucked in a breath when he reached the wound.

"Sorry," he grunted.

"A demon didn't engage me." The wound was angry looking and bloody, and I forced myself to look away, focusing on Zayne's bowed head. "I'm not even sure I saw one."

He was quiet as he worked the sweater completely off. Reaching over, he grabbed a quilt, draping it over my front. "Then who did this to you?"

I reached up with my uninjured arm, wrapping my fingers around the necklace. "A Warden."

His head swung toward me and his lips parted. "A Warden did this?"

"Yes. I've never seen him before," I said, breathing in deeply as he gently inspected the wound. "He grabbed me as I was walking to meet up with Nicolai. I did nothing to instigate it. He just came out of nowhere and I tried to get him to understand I wasn't a threat, but he came at me."

"Shit. This was an iron blade." Tension radiated off Zayne as he pulled back, fingers covered in my blood. "Did you shift?"

"I started to when he got me with the knife, but...Bambi came off me then and...oh God, Zayne, I tried to stop her, but the Warden—he wouldn't listen."

He stilled as his gaze flicked up, meeting mine. "What happened to the Warden?"

I shook my head slowly, not wanting to say it. My stomach roiled. "Bambi...she ate him."

Zayne stared at me. "*Ate* him?"

"Whole. Like gobbled him right up." A choked laugh escaped me as I ducked my chin. Strands of hair slipped forward over my shoulder. "Oh my God, this is so bad. I think it's the Warden from the New York clan. Tomas? The one they were talking about downstairs. I mean, how many unfamiliar Wardens would just be roaming around D.C.? And that means Dez knows him and is probably his friend and I like Dez. He's always been nice to me and now my pet demon snake ate his friend and I—"

"Whoa, slow down, Layla-bug. Okay? It might have been him, but there's nothing we can do about that. He came at you and Bambi defended you. Enough said."

"Yeah," I breathed, knowing the other Wardens wouldn't see it like that.

"Stay here."

Like I was going anywhere bleeding and shirtless?

Zayne disappeared into his bathroom and returned quickly with two damp towels. He soaked up the blood in silence and the act…ah, it reminded me of when Roth had cleaned me up in his apartment, which made my chest ache as badly as my arm and this whole situation about a thousand times worse.

"How badly does this hurt?"

"It stings." I watched the array of muscles moving under his shirt.

"Where's Bambi now?" he asked, glancing to where the quilt covered my chest and belly.

"On me."

He arched a brow. "Is she invisible now?"

I cracked a smile. "She's wrapped around my leg at the moment. I think she's hiding."

"Maybe she has an upset stomach."

A partly hysterical laugh burst free and a small grin stretched his lips. None of this was funny, but if I didn't laugh, I'd probably start screaming. "I tried to stop her. And I tried to get the Warden to understand. I swear, Zayne. He just wouldn't. He said I smelled like a demon. Do I smell like a demon?"

His mouth opened and then he clamped it shut. Tossed the bloodied towel to where my sweater lay. "The cut's not healing up and it's not going to with an iron blade and that's damn…"

"Dangerous to demons. Great. That's perfect." I stared up at him, holding the quilt to my chest with one hand. "Do I smell like a demon?"

"Let me get Jasmine—"

"No. She'll tell Abbot and that Warden probably belongs to the New York clan. Abbot will blame me."

"No he won't."

A ball of unease formed in my belly. "I came to you because I trust you. You can't tell your father. Please."

Zayne's shoulders tensed. "Then let me get Danika. Don't look at me like you just swallowed cat urine."

"Ew," I groaned.

"She won't say anything and she's as good as Jasmine when it comes to these kinds of things." He leaned in, placing his hands on either side of my legs. "We can trust Danika."

I bet my face looked as though I'd also swallowed hamster pee.

Zayne got really close, pressing his forehead against mine. I tried to edge away, but he followed and he was too close. I closed my eyes, clamping my mouth shut as the urge to—to feed rose above the pain and the icy feeling of panic.

"I'm not going to let anything happen to you," he said, his hands curling around my knees. "I'm going to get your arm fixed up and then we're going to figure this out. But if you trust me…"

I started to look away, but he placed his fingers on my cheeks, stopping me. "Zayne."

"If you trust me, then you have to trust that this will be safe with Danika," he continued. "I can't do this—stitch your arm. Not by myself. Okay? I got you."

Holding my breath, I nodded. I was unsure if I agreed just to get him to back away before I latched onto him or if I was actually willing to dump my trust in Danika's—of all people's—hands.

Zayne lifted his head and kissed my forehead, causing my heart to tumble over itself. "I'll be right back."

It took about two minutes for him to return with Danika. During that time, I'd convinced myself that Zayne had been waylaid by his father and forced to spill the truth. The sick sense of dread was like rotten food in my tummy.

Zayne stepped in, closing the door quietly behind Danika. She carried a small bag that looked like a sewing kit. Oh God. They were so going to sew my skin. I turned wild eyes on Zayne.

He sat beside me, drawing my wide stare. "I've told her everything."

"I'm not going to say anything," she said, placing the bag beside me and immediately starting to rummage through it. "Just that I'm glad you're sitting here and Bambi got a good meal in."

I gaped at her.

She shrugged one elegant shoulder. "I don't like judgy people or judgy Wardens and if it was Tomas, then he'd be the kind to be judgy."

"Y–you knew him?"

Nodding, she turned to my arm and made a clucking sound. "This was definitely iron," she said to Zayne. "See how the edges are kind of burned?"

My skin was burned?

"Even if she had shifted, this wouldn't heal. She'll be fine once she's stitched up," she went on, and I saw something out of the corner of my eye that looked like thread. "If she was a full-blooded demon…"

"She's not," Zayne said, and I almost laughed at the needless reminder.

"I know," she replied quietly. "I can understand why you don't want Abbot to know. You must've been so scared."

I couldn't look at Danika and I wasn't sure what to do with her sympathy at that moment. I knew she was threading a needle and I was about to lose my shit, but then she picked up a jar.

"This is a mixture of camphor and *Spilanthes*. It will help numb the skin, okay?"

Clenching my teeth, I nodded.

Danika spread some minty-smelling gunk all over my arm. I jerked a little when it stung, but within seconds, the mixture turned cold, seeping beyond the skin and into the muscle. Placing the jar back in the bag, she picked up her instruments of unimaginable pain and she looked up. Her striking face—perfect high cheekbones, straight pert nose and full lips—was leached of all color.

That wasn't very reassuring.

"This is still going to hurt," she said quietly to Zayne. "You should probably...um, hold her in place."

I gulped.

Zayne wrapped an arm around my waist and guided me down onto my side and he curled up, throwing his leg over mine. My eyes widened and for a moment I was too stunned by how close he was to me. Roth and I had lain like this after...

He moved one hand to the back of my head, guiding my face to his chest, and wrapped his other around the hand attached to my injured arm. "I can feel your heart pounding," he said, his voice muffled in my hair. "Try to take a couple of deep breaths."

My heart felt as if it *was* going to come out of my chest, a mixture of our closeness and the jolt of fear that came with the touch of Danika's cool fingers.

"I'll make this quick," she promised. "It will literally only take a couple of seconds."

Closing my eyes, I took several deep breaths. "Okay. I can do this. I can deal."

"You can." Zayne's cheek slid over the side of my head. "You're so strong, Layla. You can do this."

I almost believed him.

When the needle pierced my skin, my back straightened. Fire poured through the tiny hole she created, lighting up my body as though I was touching flames.

"It's okay," Zayne murmured, curling his fingers through my hair. "It'll be over before—" He plastered my face to his chest, muffling the scream that erupted from my throat.

"I'm sorry," Danika whispered, her hands trembling slightly. "I wish I had something stronger to give you, but Jasmine would notice it was missing."

The fire had moved up my arm, and I tried to pull away, but Zayne locked me down, keeping my injured arm straight and still. A dizzying swarm of curses left my tongue, and Zayne chuckled hoarsely.

"I had no idea you had that kind of mouth on you," he said.

"I don't care. I want her to stop. Now." I tried to pull back, but his grip tightened. "Stop. *Please*."

"We can't stop, baby. It'll be over soon. She's almost half done." Zayne's body was stiff, and Bambi started to slide up my hip. The last thing we needed was for her to come off and eat Danika. But the snake stilled. Maybe Zayne was right and she had an upset belly. "And then you'll be perfect," he added.

"I'm not perfect." My entire body throbbed like one giant raw wound. God, I was a wimp. No pain tolerance whatsoever. Then again, my skin *was* being stitched back together with minimal numbing. "I s-smell like a demon."

"You don't smell like a demon." He seemed to hold his breath as I screamed into his chest again. "You smell like... like freesia."

"Freesia? I—I smell like blood and demon," I whispered hoarsely, squeezing his hand until I felt his bones as she made another loop. "Sorry," I gasped out.

"It's okay." Zayne managed to get closer, fitting his body against mine. "You don't smell like blood."

I moaned as Danika tugged on the thread. "You're a really bad liar."

"Finished," she said, letting out a ragged breath. "I'm so, so sorry."

"I–it's okay." I pressed my face against Zayne's chest, inhaling that winter-mint scent of his. My fingers ached from clenching his hand and shirt. "T–thank you."

She drew in a deep breath as she quickly bandaged the wound. "You should rest for a few minutes, let your body settle down, and it might be a good idea to take a deep sleep tonight, just so you'll feel better quicker after the loss of blood."

Deep sleep meant retreating into a shell-like form so we could rest on a cellular level, but I'd never slept like that before. Even though I probably would've shifted today if Bambi hadn't made an appearance, I hadn't shifted since the night in the gym and I didn't think I could ever sleep that way.

I didn't know how long we lay there with Danika sitting on the edge of the bed. Zayne smoothed a hand up and down my back until eventually the tremors subsided and the contents of my stomach settled a bit. He eased his leg off mine.

"You okay?" Zayne asked. When I nodded, he pulled back a little, smoothing a hand over my damp cheeks. "You want to try to sit up?"

Not trusting myself to speak yet, I nodded again. With Zayne's help, I got the quilt readjusted and sat up. My head swam a bit and dark spots clouded my vision.

"I can get her some pain relievers," Danika said, her voice slightly off as she stared at her elegant hands while wiping off my blood. "Jasmine won't notice that." Looking over her shoulder, her gaze landed on where Zayne's arm rested over my shoulders. "I can get you something to wear."

"There...there should be a hoodie on my bed."

Danika left and returned quickly with the hoodie and while both of them turned away, I carefully eased it up over my bandage. When I was done zipping it up, they faced me.

"Thank you," I said again.

"How do you feel?" Danika moved to sit beside me.

"I don't think I'll puke." At her relieved look, I tried to hide my weak grin, but Zayne saw it, and his eyes lightened. "That...sucked."

"You did good." She glanced over at Zayne. He stood in front of me, arms crossed and features stark. "What do we do now?"

My brain felt like mush, I figured because I needed sugar. Lots of sugar. It helped with the cravings. And a nap. Maybe two naps. Just because. Then I was going to bed.

Zayne sighed heavily. "I don't know. I don't think this is the time."

"She needs to know. Obviously."

Ears perking right up, I lifted my head, my gaze bouncing between the two. "Know what?"

He looked as though he wanted to argue, but instead he took a step and sat beside me. "There has been something I've sensed about you over the past couple of days."

"Okay." My arm burned something fierce, but dread pushed away the pain. "I smell like a demon?"

"You don't smell any different than usual. That...asshole never should've phrased it that way, but I do..." He exhaled deeply as he rubbed a hand along his jaw. "I have sensed the demonic side in you more."

My already sensitive stomach dropped.

"It's really no different than sensing another demon," Danika said, twisting her hands together. "But it's as though we're sensing a certain kind of demon—an Upper Level one."

Air whooshed right out of my lungs as I twisted toward Zayne and my voice came out in a pitiful whine. Upper Level demons were the most powerful, the most dangerous. "I'd rather smell like a normal demon."

He didn't say anything, but a tortured, pinched look crept across his face.

A second went by. Then a minute. I'm not even sure it had sunk in. The fact that I felt like an Upper Level demon to them was moldy icing on the cake. "Why didn't you tell me?"

"How could I? You would have thought the worst and I didn't want to bring that down on you. And it doesn't matter, because you're part Warden. You're inherently—"

A low hum reverberated through the house and steel shields slammed down over the windows, causing Danika and me to jump. Similar thumps sounded as Zayne shot to his feet. I'd never seen the windows do that before, but I knew what it meant.

Zayne whirled as Danika paled. "Demons," he said, hands curling into fists. "There are demons here. Stay here. Both of you."

He was already out the bedroom door.

Danika and I exchanged looks and, rising in mutual agreement, we followed him downstairs. What they had told me could wait. For the shields to go down on our home, we had to be under attack.

Two of the clansmen stood guard in front of the sitting room, where I knew Jasmine must've been cloistered away with the babies. The front door was open, which caught me off guard. There was steel reinforcement there, too, but for the door to be open, as if there was nothing to fear? The night air seeped in, bringing with it a certain scent.

My pulse kicked up and my mouth dried.

Maddox blocked the entrance and he turned, eyes narrowing on us. "Danika, you need to stay back."

"What's going on?" she demanded as her pupils stretched vertically. "There are demons out there. I sense them."

"We're well aware. Abbot is with them," he replied. "So are the men. This is none of your concern."

Danika stiffened beside me.

I didn't sense jack, which solved the question about *that,* but that smell—oh my God, that smell. Tiny hairs rose all over my body as I stumbled forward blindly.

"Layla." Danika rushed after me. "You shouldn't go out there."

Maddox didn't try to stop me as I dodged around him. The scent grew stronger as I stepped out into the chilly air. Goose bumps raced across my flesh. The sweet and musky aroma invaded my nostrils. My overworked heart kicked into overdrive and too much—*too much*—emotion rose swiftly through me.

I saw Zayne standing in the driveway and beside him was his father and Geoff and Dez and others, but it was the darker forms beyond them, near the lawn leading to the woods, that drew me closer. My legs shook as I picked up speed and raced down the steps.

Zayne turned halfway, holding up a hand as if he wished to stop or catch me. His jaw was set in a hard, forbidding line. "Layla—"

I didn't stop. Nothing in this world could've made me stop. Exhaustion and pain were forgotten in a rush. Zayne stepped just a few inches to the side, completely facing me.

Then I saw *him.*

Tears pricked the back of my eyes as my heart stopped in my chest and then sped up. Everything messed up about the past two weeks vanished the moment my eyes locked with that golden-colored gaze.

"Roth," I whispered.

CHAPTER FIVE

He was as tall and striking as any prince topside could ever be.

And he looked like he had the first time I'd seen him.

Lazy locks of raven-black hair fell over his forehead, brushing against equally dark, arched brows. His cheekbones were broad and high; eyes slightly tilted at the outer corners were a dazzling blend of gold and amber, giving his face a near inhuman quality. Those lips, with their fuller bottom one, were currently parted. A black T-shirt stretched across a chest that I knew was unbelievably well-defined and a toned stomach—the kind of stomach that put six-packs to shame. His jeans hung low on his hips, held up by a studded belt.

Only thing missing was Bambi and she was currently wigging out on my skin, slithering up and down, but Roth was *alive* and he was *here*.

His eyes widened slightly. Might've been my imagination, but I swore I could see the glint of the metal bolt in his tongue as he wet his lips. The muscles in his jaw tensed as an unreadable look flickered across his striking face, and I forgot about everyone else. My heart was swelling so big I felt as if I could float right up to the stars.

Someone said something, but it was lost in the pounding of my heart and the blood rushing through me.

Roth took a step toward me as his gaze swung sharply to my right. He stopped, his eyes flashing an intense amber. A hand clamped down on my upper arm, just below the bandage.

My step faltered as I swallowed a cry. Zayne moved forward at the same time Roth did, but Abbot bent his head to mine. "Mind yourself, girl. No matter what he did for us, don't forget he's still a demon."

"Actually, I'm a prince," Roth corrected him in that deep, rich-as-dark-chocolate voice that sent a wake of shivers down my spine—the voice I wasn't sure I'd ever hear again. "It's best *you* don't forget *that*."

Abbot stiffened and his hand tightened a fraction as I tried to pull free.

"And it would also serve you well to let go of her," he continued, raising his chin a notch. "So we can start waving our little white flag of friendship without spilling blood."

"Not that spilling blood would be such a bad thing." Beside Roth, a demon I recognized as an infernal ruler smiled broadly, displaying straight, white teeth. Cayman was sort of like demon middle management. I had no idea who the third demon was that remained behind the other two.

"And you will do well to remember you're on my property." Abbot did release his hold, and I would've raced forward, but the look Roth sent me warned me not to.

Confused, I drew in a deep breath and tried to calm my racing heart. I wanted to ignore his look and throw myself at him. Just so I could touch him and make sure he was real and he was okay, but I couldn't forget where I was. Half my clan was outside and although Roth had sacrificed himself— well, it had appeared that way—for the greater good, no one would be happy if I started climbing all over him like a deranged spider monkey.

But as I stared at him and it really began to sink in that Roth *was* here and he *was* okay, I couldn't understand how this was the first time I was seeing him. Better yet, how had he gotten out of the fiery pits? They were supposedly inescapable.

Or why he was here.

Abbot seemed to rise to a fuller height. "And there will never be a 'white flag of friendship' between our kinds."

Roth placed a hand to his chest. "Ouch, there went all my hopes and dreams of our kinds dancing together under rainbows."

A vein started to protrude from Abbot's forehead. He turned to me. "You need to go inside, Layla."

Like holy Hell I was, but before I could say that, Roth inclined his head and said, "No, she needs to be here. I came for a reason, although we got a little off track."

A little off track with what? How long had Roth been here? Pushing my hair back from my face, I felt as though my brain was running in slow motion. I glanced at Zayne, but he was focused on Roth as if he wanted to punt kick him back to Hell. The corners of my lips slipped down. I got that Zayne and Roth could never be BFFs, but had Zayne forgotten what Roth had done for him?

Maddox had made his way outside and stood beside a silent Dez. At some point, Maddox must've shifted, because he was in his true form. His skin was the color of granite and his wings reached out to an impressive eight feet. Nostrils flat and yellow eyes glowing fiercely, he showed his fangs. "There can be no reason why we're allowing them to stand here." He turned to Abbot, clawed hands forming fists. "Tomas is missing and I'm wagering they have something to do with it."

Uh…

Bambi curled around my stomach and then stretched, as if she were happy with the reminder of her early-evening meal.

"I have no idea who Tomas is," Roth replied, his lips—lips that had burned themselves into my memory—curled into a smirk. "Then again, you Wardens do all look alike."

Maddox hissed. "You think you're cute?"

"Nah, I think I'm sexy." The smirk spread, but it didn't reach his cool ocher eyes. "And I also think I'm hilarious."

Dez and the rest of the Wardens tensed. I guessed they thought Roth should be intimated by so many of them, but Roth...well, the more sticky the situation, the more of a smart-ass he became.

Cayman winked at me as he swaggered forward. My brows rose. All of this seemed surreal. Maybe I'd lost too much blood, passed out, and all of this was just some kind of bizarre dream.

"Can we get to the point?" Cayman asked gamely. "Time truly is of the essence."

Abbot exhaled deeply, nostrils flaring, but he nodded.

"We have a huge problem," Roth said, focusing on the clan leader. The smirk slowly slipped from his face, and a chill slithered down my spine. "A Lilin has been born."

All the Wardens stared at him as though he'd dropped his pants and done a little dance. I gaped at him, mind rapidly replaying what Roth had said. We couldn't have heard him right. There was no way a Lilin—a race of demons that could strip souls with just a touch—could have been created. They were so vile that stripping the souls didn't just kill the human or Warden in question, but turned them into vengeful wraiths—spirits hell-bent on causing destruction. The Wardens had been created to wipe the Lilin off the Earth back during the times of Eve and that damn apple.

"That's impossible," Zayne snarled. "What kind of crap are you trying to pull?"

Roth shifted his gaze to him, his expression a hard mask. "I'm not trying to pull anything and trust me, there're more interesting lies to be told."

"It can't be true," Abbot stated, folding his massive arms across his broad chest. "We know what it takes to raise the Lilin and those things didn't happen. Not to mention, Paimon was stopped before the ritual could be completed."

"A demon trying to lie to us?" Dez snorted as a cold breeze stirred his hair. "Such a surprise."

Mischief, the kind that would bring down entire cities, flared in Roth's eyes. He opened his mouth, but I stepped forward. "How is this possible? You—we know that it's not."

Roth kept his gaze trained on Zayne. "It is."

"How do you know?" I demanded.

A Warden snorted and muttered, "Can't wait to hear this story."

His lips curled up on one side. "As all of you should know, if you've read your 'when the shit hits the fan' manual, there are four chains securing Lilith in Hell."

I nodded. I knew that Lilith, my estranged mother, was chained in Hell, but didn't see how that had anything to do with this.

"Two of the chains broke when Paimon tried to perform the ritual, leaving only two chains secured," he continued. "A third—"

"Wait." Abbot raised a hand. "How exactly did two chains break? Paimon was stopped and Layla's innocence—the key to the ritual—remains in place. So this cannot be true."

Oh my God…

The whole innocence thing again. I bit back a groan as I folded my hand around my necklace. For the Lilin-raising ritual to have been completed, several things had to have taken place. The blood of Lilith had to have been spilled and that had come from the ring I still wore around my neck. My blood had to have been drawn and that also had happened, but the last two were the biggies.

I'd had to have taken a soul and would have had to have lost my innocence, like in the biblical sense. Only Zayne and Roth knew I'd taken a soul and Abbot could never know or he'd put me down. The other part? I was still a virgin, so it couldn't—

"Paimon had the blood parts down," Roth said, following my train of thought. He didn't look at me as he spoke, but there was a razor-sharp edge to his words. Knots formed in my belly. "She was cut. I saw it."

How in the world he'd seen the tiny prick during the fight was beyond me. "Yes. Paimon drew my blood and it spilled, but..." That night came back to me in a rush. After Roth and Paimon had been trapped and sent to the fiery pits, the floor had been scorched where they'd stood and there'd been a hole in the ground, right where I'd been tied down.

Abbot's brows slammed together. He opened his mouth and then turned a piercing stare on me. I shrank back from the accusation in his glare. Did he know about Petr? That I'd taken the Warden's soul in self-defense? I could already feel the noose circling my neck. Zayne shifted closer to me, and the air leaked out of my lungs.

"Your innocence," Abbot said in a low, deceptively calm voice. "You *claimed* that you were still innocent, Layla."

Claimed? "I didn't lie to you."

"Then how did the chains break?" he demanded.

"Now he believes us," Cayman said, shaking his head. "How quickly he doubts Layla."

Even though that accurate observation stung, I ignored the

infernal ruler as my gaze tracked over the demons and Wardens. Nicolai looked away when my gaze met his. Dez and Maddox stared at me with a look of dawning understanding. I couldn't even look at Zayne to see if he was also jumping to conclusions.

The only good thing I could see right now was that no one assumed I'd taken a soul. Instead, they believed I dropped my undies. My lips pursed. I was torn between denying what they were assuming, thereby revealing what I'd actually done, and keeping my mouth shut.

Zayne let out a deep breath. "Layla told us that she's…well, you know what she said. We have no reason to doubt her, but we have every reason not to trust them."

The relief that coursed through me was short-lived when Roth arched a graceful brow. "Considering I threw your ass out of that trap and took your place, I'd think you'd have a tad bit more faith in me."

I closed my eyes. This conversation was about to go downhill fast.

"And I thank you for that," Zayne responded in clipped tones. "But that doesn't change what you are or the fact that Layla is still—"

Heat swamped my cheeks. "Okay. Stop. All of you. This gossipfest about my virginity is not something I want to continue."

"You and me both," muttered Dez.

"But I was still rocking a hymen the last time I checked, which means I'm a virgin." My hands formed ineffective fists when Roth's brows climbed up his forehead. "So can we not talk about this anymore?"

"Then if what you're saying is true, the demon is lying," Abbot spat.

"The demon?" Roth scoffed. "That's 'Your Highness' to you."

"Okay." Cayman glided forward, raising his hands in mock surrender as the Wardens bared fangs in warning. "Nobody is lying—not our Crown Prince or our wittle, precious, virginal Layla."

I shot him a dirty look.

He grinned. "As always, the text in which the ritual was written does not go into detail explaining how or what it takes for Layla to lose her innocence."

"I wish you would stop saying that," I muttered, rubbing my brow. I was starting to get a headache. "It's not like you can just 'lose' your innocence or accidentally misplace it somewhere and forget about it."

Abbot's eyes narrowed.

"Good point." Cayman shoved his hands into the pockets of his jeans as he rocked back on the heels of his boots, and by the glee in his expression, I had this horrible feeling that I'd just talked my way into a corner. "The loss of innocence refers to carnal sin and it's not like you have to do the deed to experience the pleasure of sin. Correct?"

Blood drained from my face as my mouth dropped open. Oh, I had experienced pleasure with Roth. That blood rushed right back to my face as the hours before we'd gone for the *Lesser Key* played out in my thoughts. Roth and I...we hadn't done it, but we'd done other things. Well, he'd done things with his hand that I had only—oh God, I really needed to stop thinking about that right now.

Roth's impossibly long lashes lowered as what Cayman had said sank into the minds and imaginations of all those present. One by one, they looked at me like...like I'd murdered a nursery of babies and then bathed gleefully in their blood.

"What?" I said, shifting my weight from one foot to the next. I glanced at Zayne. A muscle throbbed along his jaw.

Cayman dipped his chin. "In other words, all she needed to do was have an orgasm."

"Oh my God," I moaned, smacking my hands over my burning face. I'd rather be back in the alley, about to be sliced and diced by the Warden, than where I was.

"And most likely not by herself," Cayman added. "Besides, that is the only explanation."

Someone kill me now.

Zayne swore under his breath and I thought I heard the word *whore* muttered from someone in the peanut gallery behind me, but I couldn't be sure because no one reacted to the low murmur. It didn't take a genius for anyone to figure out whom I'd experienced "the pleasure of sin" with. Wasn't like I had a lot of options considering the whole "getting too close to anyone with a soul" thing.

"Well..." Roth drew the word out. "This is awkward."

I slowly lowered my hands. "You think?"

He didn't look at me. "So now that we have this covered—"

"But what about the taking of the soul?" Nicolai demanded.

Hair rose on the back of my neck. The change of subject should've given me happy feet, but Hell, it just got worse.

Roth shrugged. "The *Lesser Key* is an ancient text, remember? That means it's not the easiest thing in the world to interpret. Clearly we all got something wrong, despite my superior intelligence. You have the *Lesser Key*. See if you can figure out what."

The Wardens seemed to believe that for the moment, but Abbot shot me a look that said we'd talk later and that was so not a conversation I was looking forward to.

"But back to the issue at hand—three of the chains broke, meaning there is a Lilin."

That again. "Wait," I said, drawing in a deep breath. "I didn't know her chains would break if the Lilin was created." Unease curled in my belly as I glanced at Abbot, Zayne and then back to Roth. "None...none of you have told me this. You all just said that if the Lilin were created, everyone would be too busy rounding them up to worry about Lilith."

"It wasn't necessary to tell you," Abbot responded in a clipped voice.

A hot and ugly emotion replaced my anxiety as I twisted toward the man I once looked upon as the closest thing to a father I'd known. I was so *sick* of the lies—about the fact that Lilith was my mom, that Elijah, a Warden who acted as if he loathed my very existence was actually my father. Abbot had kept all of that from me. "Really? Considering who she is to me, how isn't it necessary?"

"Good point," Roth acknowledged.

"You didn't tell me either," I shot back. His lips formed a hard line, and I willed him to look at me, to explain why he'd kept that major detail to himself. When he didn't, apprehension took root deep inside me. "And if the fourth chain breaks, then Lilith is freed?"

The third demon, who'd been silent up until that point, shook his head. "Lilith won't be freed. The Boss has her locked down now and I'm pretty sure Hell would freeze over before she gets out." He laughed at himself, and I arched an eyebrow.

Abbot's shoulders jacked up. "Even if Lilith is still in captivity, if there's a Lilin, we have a huge problem on our hands."

"Right now, there must be only one, because if there were more, you all would know. You'd have an overpopulation of wraiths. But even one Lilin can turn this city into its own personal soul-sucking playground," Roth said. "They can take a soul with a single brush of their hand or they can mess with people—slowly stripping away who they are, changing their entire internal moral code. The Lilin could turn a Warden if they got their hands on one."

Oh, that would be bad. Very bad.

"And they're the only ones that can control wraiths," Cayman added. "If they take a soul completely, that vengeful thing they create will answer to the Lilin. It's like...double the suck."

Wraiths were what became of any creature who once had a soul and then lost it. They didn't go to Hell. There was no in-between for them. They lingered on Earth, stuck, and bitter hatred festered within them. They quickly became dangerous and they were powerful, able to interact with humans on a not-so-friendly level. Sometimes they targeted people they'd known while alive. Other times they didn't discriminate, going after anyone who crossed their path.

"You know, with the rules and all, the Alphas—your big, bad guys in the big, bad sky—aren't going to be happy." Roth folded his arms across his chest. "So we need to find the Lilin before the Alphas decide to step in. Otherwise, we all will be at risk, including the Wardens."

Alphas were the ones in charge. Angels. My half-demon butt had obviously never seen one. "Why would the Wardens be at risk?" I asked, confused.

It was Cayman who answered. "The Alphas aren't the biggest fan of the Wardens, even though they created them. Isn't that right, fearless leader?" When Abbot didn't respond, the infernal ruler grinned. "The Alphas will see the existence of a Lilin as a sign of the Wardens' inability to handle things, making them useless. They'll wipe them out as punishment, right along with the rest of us."

Oh my God, Alphas didn't mess around.

"So we need to work together," Roth stated.

Maddox laughed harshly. "Work with demons. Are you on crack?"

"Like I've said before, the Boss frowns on drug use while on the job." Roth's expression slipped into his bland look. "And you'll have to get over your bigotry. We're in a city that has over a half a million people in it, and that's not counting the suburbs. The kind of damage even one Lilin can create is astronomical."

"So we're back to where we were two months ago?" Zayne said. "Except instead of a lovesick demon, we have a Lilin—a Lilin that can strip a soul from a human—"

"Wait." Maddox turned sideways, finally taking his eyes off the demons. "If the ritual succeeded in birthing a Lilin, then wouldn't Layla actually be the mother? The demon was born from her blood."

"Ew." I swallowed the sudden taste of blood. "I am so not referring to the Lilin as my kid. So none of you even attempt to put that on me."

"The Lilin was born from Lilith's blood, too, so…" Roth sighed, shaking his head. "It doesn't matter, you heavenly reject."

Maddox snarled. "Excuse me?"

He ignored the Warden.

"Just what we need to contend with—a Lilin or something similar," Abbot murmured mostly to himself, and I frowned. What the Hell did that mean? He shook his head. "We have to find and stop this Lilin."

"We're sure that Lilith can't be freed?" I asked, still unsure of how I felt when it came to the fact that my mother was bound to Hell.

"The Boss isn't going to let that happen." Roth watched Abbot, smiling tightly.

The tension was palpable between them, and instinct told me it ran deeper than the fact they were enemies. "The thing is, we don't know a lot about the Lilin."

I felt like I needed to sit down. "You don't?"

"No. There might be info in the *Lesser Key,* but—" Roth inclined his head at Abbot "—you have the *Lesser Key.*"

"And it will remain safe with us," he replied.

"Safety is subjective," Roth murmured.

"We already know what the *Lesser Key* has to say about the Lilin," Nicolai said.

"Care to share?" Roth grinned. "Because sharing is fun."

Abbot shifted his weight. "There's nothing new. Only vague references to the time they ruled the Earth. Nothing that we don't already know. This is serious," Abbot said after a few moments. "Serious enough that we won't hinder your investigation into the matter."

Meaning the Wardens wouldn't go after Roth and his crew, which was huge. Maddox and the other Wardens got their undies in a bunch over that, but Abbot silenced them with a wave of his hand.

"As the leader of the D.C. clan, this is my decision," he said, casting a fierce look at all of them. "The possibility that we have a Lilin topside is not something we can allow." He turned that deadly look on the demons. "But if I even begin to suspect that this is some sort of trickery, I will personally hunt each of you down."

Roth shrugged. "All we need is for you all to be extra vigilant while you're out on your...hunts."

"I can't believe we're entering into an agreement with demons," Maddox said, taking several steps back.

Neither could I, but a Lilin was a big deal.

"It's the way it is," Abbot said, dragging in a deep, heavy breath. "We will keep an eye out for any suspicious reports. Our contacts within the police departments and hospitals should prove helpful in this case."

Cayman nodded in agreement, and the fact we all were having a pretty civil conversation was monumental. "We will also keep our ears to the ground. A Lilin will most likely seek out other demons. You know, to bond and make friends. Hopefully, there will be one that it trusts."

"Good," Abbot said, shoulders squaring. "But for now, get the Hell off my property."

A misty cloud of air puffed out from between my lips as my stomach dropped. They couldn't leave yet. No way. I stepped forward, ignoring the piercing stares of the Wardens. I didn't care. They could take their bigoted ideals and shove them so far up their—

"We're on our way, but..." Roth finally turned to me. Our gazes collided, and it was like a punch to the chest. "We need to talk."

CHAPTER SIX

I almost rushed Roth right then and threw my arms around him, but a low growl rumbled from behind me. At first I thought it was Abbot's response, but when I realized it was coming from Zayne, I couldn't move.

Roth tilted his head to the side, watching me as a slow, roguish smile graced his lips. "Are you...seriously growling at me, Stony?"

"I'm about to do a lot more than growl."

He chuckled. "That's not very appreciative."

I turned to Zayne and my heart leaped into my throat, stopping whatever I was going to say. He glared at Roth in a way I couldn't understand, especially not after what Roth had done for him, as if it... I shook my head.

"It's all right," Abbot interrupted, surprising me. "Let them talk."

Wait. What? He was okay with me talking to Roth? Abbot's appeasement knocked me into motion. My heart did another leap.

Zayne opened his mouth and then clamped it shut. Our gazes held for a moment and then he nodded stiffly, resigned. "I'll wait for you."

I wanted to tell him that it wasn't necessary, but the oddity of the statement stole my words. Taking a deep breath, I turned to Roth.

"Let's walk?" he suggested.

There was a coldness laced through his words that left me unsettled. I told myself it was only because we were around so many Wardens, but my knees felt weak as I walked toward him. His unique scent invaded my senses, causing my skin to flush in spite of the chilled air. He turned as I reached his side and started toward the faint path Zayne and I had worn into the ground over the many years we'd traveled to the tree house in the nearby woods.

Skin tingling along the back of my neck, I glanced over my shoulder and drew in a tiny breath. The Wardens were still standing guard in front of the compound, but I didn't see Abbot anymore. Zayne was sitting at the bottom of the wide steps, leaning against one of the large white marble columns. Cayman and the other demon were gone. It was obvious they didn't fear for Roth's safety. Or they didn't care.

My head swung back around and my breath caught when I saw Roth's profile. A dizzying amount of relief crashed into me as it struck me once more that he was alive and he was here.

So many things bubbled up the moment we stepped past the crumbled stone retaining wall that surrounded the manicured lawn and under the thick, bare branches that rattled like dry bones in the breeze. But I couldn't speak. The clog was back, centered right in my throat.

Coherent thought clicked off, and I found myself moving around him. Roth stopped midstep as I did what I'd wanted to do since he'd shown up tonight. Like a mini rocket, I threw myself at him.

Roth stumbled back a step as my arms went around his neck. The moment my body came into contact with his, pressure clamped down on my chest. I squeezed my eyes shut against the violent tide of emotions. They were so tangled together—relief and fear, desperation and resolution, a deep craving that rivaled the need I struggled with every day, and anxiety—that I couldn't make sense of them, or understand how I was feeling so much.

As I nestled into his chest, I could feel his heart pounding fast and realized then that his arms were at his sides. A cloud of nervousness passed over me as I lifted my head, searching out his eyes in the darkness, but they were closed and thick lashes fanned the tips of his cheekbones. His face was pale in the thin slivers of moonlight breaking through the branches, lips pulled in a taut line.

Another shiver of apprehension slipped over my skin. When I started to pull back, to give voice to the near fear growing like a weed in the pit of my stomach, his arms finally— *finally*—encircled me. He pulled me tight against him, our bodies flush and pressed together in a way that reminded me of the night we'd found the *Lesser Key*. The muscles low in my stomach tightened as his hand smoothed up my spine, tangling in my hair. Bambi followed the caress, as if she sought to get closer to her true owner.

There was so much warmth in the embrace that it pushed the shadows away. I squeezed my eyes shut and soaked him up. I didn't know what his return meant, what it signified for us, but it didn't matter in that moment.

He dropped his head to mine and murmured something in a deep, guttural voice that I was positive wasn't anywhere close to the English language.

"You're hurt," he said, his voice rough.

All I could do was shake my head as I balled my hands into the back of his shirt. I was feeling too many conflicting emotions. Some of them were mine, but there was also a distant quality to them I couldn't quite understand.

He slid his other hand to my arm. When his fingers slipped under the sleeve of my hoodie, I bit my lip. "Your arm," he said, managing to curve his fingers just below my elbow. "How did it happen?"

"A Warden did it," I said, rubbing my cheek against his chest like a cat with a full belly, ready for a nap. A sigh escaped me. "He said I smelled like a demon."

Roth drew back and his chin tipped down. Dark eyebrows slashed together. "A Warden did this? Was it iron?"

I nodded, but this wasn't what I wanted to talk about. "Roth—"

"What about Bambi?" he demanded, withdrawing his hand from my hair. "She would've protected you."

"Bambi's fine." I forced a smile, but nothing about his features softened. "She ate the Warden."

His brows shot up. "Well…"

"Yeah." I drew the word out slowly. I knew I should ask him about why I suddenly felt like an Upper Level demon to the Wardens, but as bad as it was, that wasn't at the top of my priority list. "I don't know where to begin. How are you even here?"

Roth's golden eyes held mine for a moment and then he pulled away. I mourned the loss of warmth immediately. "Well, there's these things called portals and I popped into—"

"That's not what I meant." Before, his smart-ass responses had grated on my every last nerve, but now there was a relief in being irritated with him. "You were in the devil's trap with Paimon. You went to the pits."

"I did." He folded his arms and took another step back from me. "It wasn't fun, in case you were wondering."

I winced. "I didn't think it was, but I don't understand. The pits are permanent."

One shoulder rose gracefully. "They are, but I am the Boss's favorite and I'd done what the Boss had wanted—stopped a Lilin from being created. Or at least we thought I had."

"So you were let out for good behavior?"

"After a day or two. The Boss wasn't in a big hurry. No surprise there."

My heart squeezed. "But the pits had to be…" My voice cracked as I shook my head.

"It wasn't a vacation, shortie. Imagine your skin being flayed and burned off for a forty-eight hour period." He shrugged again, as though it was no big deal to be virtually burned alive, and brushed the dark hair off his forehead. "But it could have been worse. Paimon's dumb ass is still in there."

Meaning Roth could still be there. Two days had to be Hell, literally, but if he'd been let out that fast… "Where have you been?"

His gaze flicked up to the bare branches. "Around."

"Around?" The word rang with disbelief.

"Here and there, up and down." One side of his lips curled up but it lacked sincerity. "Hanging out."

I stared at him. "Why didn't you come see me?" That question came out like the anthem of every pissed-off girlfriend out there but the problem with that—I wasn't his girlfriend.

Roth arched a brow and opened his mouth, but then he didn't say anything. I reached out to touch him, but he drew back. A muscle flickered along his jaw. The unease and coldness from earlier returned.

"I've been so worried," I said, pulling my hand back to my chest. "I've missed you. I've *mourned* you. But I hoped that you were okay. This…" I pulled out the necklace. The cracked stone was a sad statement. "I found this at your apartment, on the roof. You did put it there, didn't you? After you left the pits. You—"

"I did. So?"

"So?" I whispered, feeling about as empty as an echo. "Why would you do that and then not come see me?"

He said nothing.

Ice trickled into my veins. "Do you know how upset I was? I felt lost without—"

"You were not lost without me," he cut in, his gaze suddenly fixed on me once more. "You had Zayne."

"Yes, but that's not—"

"You had him," he repeated, drawing in a deep breath. "Why do you think I took his place in that trap? So you could have him."

Maybe I was slower than normal, but I wasn't following where this was heading. "I know you did that for me and I can never express how truly grateful I am for it, but I didn't want to lose you. I never wanted to." The words kept spilling out in the worst case of verbal diarrhea known to humankind, angels or demons. "I don't know what we had, but we had something—something that meant a lot to me."

He stared at me a moment and an array of emotions played over his striking face before he shook his head. "You've been through a lot recently. I get that you're upset, but like I said, you don't need me."

Frustration burned like acid in my blood. "Roth, I—"

"Don't say it." He held up a hand. "Don't say it."

"You don't even know what I was going to say!" Hell, I didn't know what was going to come out of my mouth.

"I don't want to know." Roth thrust his fingers through his hair in a quick, jerky manner. "This is why we needed to talk. I'm back. I'm going to be around because of the Lilin, but that's the only reason I'm here. Do you understand what I'm saying?"

A part of my brain totally got what he was saying, but my heart was another story. His words didn't make sense to the stupid muscle. Things didn't add up. "No. I don't."

His lashes lowered as he muttered a curse. "Look, when I was topside before, with you? It was..." He gave a little shake of his head and then seemed to force out the rest. "It was fun, shortie."

"Fun?" I repeated dumbly.

He nodded stiffly. "And that was all. It was just fun while it was happening."

I jerked back as if I'd been slapped in the face. "It wasn't *just* fun to me."

"Of course it wasn't." Roth turned away, appearing to inspect a tree trunk as though it held the answers to life. "You had no experience in any of that. You'd never even kissed anyone before. It was only natural for you to catch feelings."

A lick of pain lit up my chest. "But not natural for you?"

"No. Not at all. For several reasons. Many of them boring, but logical. I'm the Crown Prince of Hell, not like your Stony."

"You're not just the next Crown Prince! You're more than that. So let's not start that crap again." Roth had never seen himself as anything but another prince out of the hundreds of princes that had come before him. He was even a little insecure about it, and I wanted to be more careful with those feelings, but I was losing control, anger and hurt giving way to a level of needy desperation that was embarrassing. I held out the ring. "This proves it was more than just fun to you. You fixed the necklace and you left it there for me to find."

"And that proves something?" he queried softly.

"Yes!" The cool metal bit into my palm. "Why would you do that if you didn't care?"

His shoulders stiffened. "I didn't say I didn't care, shortie."

"Then what the Hell are you saying?"

"I'm saying that what we did isn't going to happen again. That's what I'm saying."

I sucked in a breath, but it got stuck. "But the necklace—"

He twisted around so quickly I stumbled back. There was something dark about his face, the way his skin thinned over his bones. "Does it matter why, Layla? It's just a stupid necklace."

"That's bullshit! You knew how much this necklace meant to me." It was the only thing that linked me to my mother—to who I really was, and he knew that.

"It doesn't matter." He stalked forward, and I had to force myself not to move away. His pupils started to dilate. "I'm not interested in rekindling a pointless infatuation. Does that break it down enough for you? Do you understand now? I'm a demon, Layla. A full-blooded one who isn't ashamed of what my kind does. And you are only half demon. You want to be like your precious Wardens and Stony. Being in my presence should fill you with disgust. Why would you want to be standing here, let alone be with me?"

The pain spread from my chest, settling in my bones. "So this has been, what—a game to you? I don't believe that!" I held my ground, hand shaking around the ring. "You want me to believe that you're nothing more than a demon, but the way you kissed me, what you said to me before you were taken in that trap, proves otherwise."

"You're so naive. A kiss? A few sentimental words uttered before I thought I'd spend eternity being tortured? You can't judge me for a couple of momentary lapses, Layla. It's who I am that matters." He was an inch from me, his hands curling into fists at his sides. "I am the Crown Prince, whether you want to hear it or not."

"That means nothing," I cried, squeezing the ring—the proof that there was something in him. Evidence he had a conscience...and a heart. "You're lying and there has to be a reason."

He turned his head, dragging both his hands through his hair this time. "You know what I am. I *told* you. I covet pretty things. I like to take things that aren't mine to have." Then he looked at me and smiled. The chill of it sent shivers dancing over my skin. "You really thought I cared for you, didn't you? I wanted you, Layla. You eased my boredom. That's all."

I staggered back, wanting to stop his words from meaning anything to me, from hurting, but there was no stopping it. In an instant, I realized I should've known better. This whole time, I should've known better. After all, he was right. I had no experience with these things—with guys and relationships. If I...if I had meant something to him, he would've come to me before tonight: because if it was the other way around, his would've been the first place I went.

And that was just sad.

"I really don't know what I was thinking. I usually don't go for virgins. They are so very messy. Someone like your classmate Eva is far more entertaining and skilled in that department. Is she still around?" He sighed, shrugging casually, but a muscle ticked along his jaw. "Like I said, I should've realized you'd catch feelings, shortie. My bad."

I felt the blood drain from my face. His endearment seemed unnecessarily cruel, paired with what he was saying. "Don't call me that."

"Whatever you say." Roth spun away. The line of his spine was unnaturally stiff. "Bambi will remain with you."

I blinked back the tears, refusing to let them fall. "I don't—"

"I don't care if that's not what you want. She stays with you."

I stared at his back, feeling choked from the inside out. "You're a bastard."

He glanced over his shoulder at me, expression stark in the moonlight. "Goodbye, Layla."

And then he was gone.

CHAPTER SEVEN

I didn't remember much of the short walk back to the house. There was an ache in my chest that rivaled what I'd felt when I'd seen Roth in the devil's trap. It was cold and hot at the same time, burning and icing over my insides. A knot had formed in the back of my throat and the dampness behind my eyes increased with every step.

What Roth had said did more than just sting, and the horrible weight of the pressure settling between my breasts warned that something might have been broken in there, even if I hadn't acknowledged how deep my feelings for him had run.

I usually don't go for virgins.

God, had I been that foolish, that wrong about him? My cheeks felt scalded as his words replayed themselves. Each one had been barb-tipped, spoken with the intent to maim, and they had. My hands trembled as I folded my arms across my chest, ignoring the pain of my stitches pulling. But that hug... the way he'd held me close? It had meant nothing to him? I couldn't easily accept that. Or the fact that those tortured words he'd cast at me before the trap had taken him—words I'd held on to—had been spoken so carelessly. But maybe I was just that naive. Catch feelings? He'd been right. I'd caught them and I had hugged them close. And now look.

Under the pain, a different kind of anguish formed in the back of my throat—a scorching thirst took root. I could feel it in every cell, even in the ends of my teeth. The need to feed rose swiftly and without hesitation. My emotions were all over the place, fueling the illicit desire.

I wiped at my cheeks angrily as I reached the driveway. Wardens were milling around the entrance, in their true forms with their wings tucked close to their backs, but none paid me any attention as I hurried past them. I couldn't see their souls, but I could taste their pureness on the tip of my tongue. For a moment, I let myself imagine what it would be like to feel that warmth slipping down my throat, easing the coldness and ache Roth had left behind. It wouldn't be hard either. They didn't trust me, but they didn't expect me to outright attack one of them. And once I had a hold of a soul, there would be no stopping—

I cut the thought off, horrified to find that I'd stopped walking. I was just standing there, staring at Zayne's bowed, golden head, and my mouth was watering. The voracious need to follow through with the fantasy caused my stomach to cramp.

Elbows propped on his knees, he lifted his chin, and in a second, he was standing, hands open at his sides. "Layla?"

"I'm tired." My voice didn't sound right to me. It was too strained, too tight. I couldn't be near him, near anyone right now. "I'm going…going to bed."

The brilliance to his skin tone faded as he turned. He followed me through the door, closing it quietly behind us. The overhead foyer light was off and the small wall sconces cast a soft glow across the floor. Jasmine's voice floated out from the sitting room, and I picked up my pace. Each step up the staircase sucked the energy right out of me. By the time I reached the landing on the second floor, I wanted to turn and latch myself to Zayne in the worst possible way.

Zayne edged around me, blocking the bedroom door. "Talk to me."

Slowly, I lifted my gaze, and I didn't know what he saw in my expression, but he reached out a hand. I stepped back, avoiding his touch, too close to breaking down and doing something I could never forgive myself for. Heart pounding, I shook my head. "I don't want to talk."

He cocked his head to the side. "You're not okay."

I held my breath.

His jaw locked down. "He hurt you?"

"No," I forced out, exhaling through my nose.

"I don't mean physically. He's hurt—"

"I can't do this right now. Please," I whispered, and his eyes widened in understanding. "I need to be alone."

Zayne's nostrils flared as he stepped aside. His chest rose sharply. "Do you need anything?"

My stomach was sick from how fast my pulse was pounding. "Orange juice?"

He nodded and quickly slipped down the hall. I went into my bedroom, leaving the light off. Not that I needed it. I spent so much time in here that I could navigate it blind. I walked to the large windows, wishing I could open them to let the cool night air in, but they'd been nailed shut during my "grounded for life" phase. I guess Abbot thought I'd sprout wings and fly off to rendezvous with my demon horde.

Squeezing my eyes shut, I realized that was what I wanted to do. Not the hanging out with a demon horde part, but Hell yeah to the flying-off part. I'd almost shifted earlier tonight. Maybe I could do it again. A rush of tingles spread across my flesh. The skin along my back tightened. I opened my eyes, letting out a slow, low breath. I could almost feel the night air caressing my skin. I wondered how high I could go and if it would feel as good as taking a soul did.

Abbot would freak if I left the compound tonight, and it wouldn't be safe for me to do so. Not because there was any danger posed to me, but because of the danger I posed to other people right now—innocent people.

Zayne's presence filled the room. I turned and for the first time since I'd lost the ability to see auras, I was glad I couldn't see his right now. He placed a large glass of OJ on my desk, between the notebooks and printer paper. He glanced over at me, concern etched into his handsome face. "If you need anything, call or text me."

I nodded.

"Promise me." He didn't come closer, but his stare never left mine.

"I promise," I swore, swallowing the even bigger lump in my throat. Sometimes—no, all the times—I didn't think I deserved him. "Thank you."

His lashes fluttered shut briefly. "Don't thank me, Layla-bug. Not for this." His eyes were a deep shade of blue as they locked on to mine again. "You know...you know I'd do anything for you."

Tears raced to my eyes as I nodded blindly. His lips curved up at the corners, into a tiny smile, and then he left the room. I headed straight for the OJ, downing the contents as I held the cool glass. The acidic burn eased the cravings and when I set the glass down, movement out of the corners of my eyes snagged my attention. I turned, wiping my damp hands along the thighs of my denim skirt.

The white curtains billowed out from the closed window, trailing softly in the empty air.

My brows rose.

There was no wind in the room. The central air hadn't kicked on. I'd have heard that mammoth beast cranking up, and besides, it was too cold outside for air-conditioning.

As I started toward the window, the curtains drifted back down, settling slowly against the wall. Okay. That was strange. An odd chill raced down my spine. All right. It was actually kind of creepy, but Bambi stirred to life, distracting me as she wound her way up my left leg. Her movement was still a painful reminder, but it served a different purpose now.

You eased my boredom.

I sucked in a sharp breath as the blow hit me below the knees. Turning away from the window, I unzipped my hoodie and carefully slid it off. I let it drop to the floor. Glancing down at my arm, I winced when I saw the dark splotch on the white bandage. What a terrible night.

Biting my lip, I stripped off my clothes and changed into a pair of sleep shorts. Before I could pull on a long-sleeve shirt, Bambi drifted off my skin. In the darkness, she was nothing more than a shadow as she pieced herself together. Instead of leaving to hunt or running back to Roth like a forgotten pet, she slithered up to the dollhouse Abbot had built for me when I was a child.

I'd gone all badass on the poor thing while I'd been grounded and Roth had disappeared. About a week ago, it had reappeared in my bedroom, the roof and sides reassembled. I assumed it had been Zayne, and I didn't know why he did it or why I'd been relieved to see it. Obviously, I had problems with letting go of things.

Bambi managed to get all six feet of her coiled into the top floor, her head resting on the miniature bed. She looked... comfy. And it looked weird.

Minutes passed as I stared at the demonic familiar. A chill

formed in my chest, replacing the god-awful burn. Why had Roth given her up to me? Bambi was his familiar, not mine, and he'd always seemed fond of the snake. It didn't make sense, but it probably also didn't matter. Long ago, he'd admitted there were things he did without any reason.

And as it turned out, I was just one of those many *things*.

It hurt something bad as I climbed into bed, lying on my uninjured arm. It wasn't even late as I squeezed my eyes shut, but it felt like forever since this morning. Everything seemed to have changed in the span of a few hours.

I smelled like an Upper Level demon. Roth was back and he was relatively unharmed. A Lilin had been born. Apparently an orgasm was apocalyptic. And Roth...he'd never cared about me.

I'd just been a job to him.

And nothing more.

My head ached as though I'd spent the night banging it against the wall, which would've been more fun and fruitful than staring at the ceiling, replaying all the moments Roth and I had shared. I'd been looking for a fatal flaw in our wannabe relationship and that had been as productive as drilling holes in a bucket and trying to carry water in it.

Roth was a demon.

A male demon.

A male demon who liked to *covet pretty things*.

And I was as inexperienced as a nun, so of course, I'd attributed a lot to what he'd said to me, to the way he'd looked at me, to every touch and kiss. I'd thought it all meant something and the hurt was intense, tasting like bitter grapes in the back of my mouth. Strangely, as much as my throat and eyes burned and for all the tears that built in my eyes, those tears didn't fall. I wished they would. It felt as though there'd be something cleansing in the act.

When it came time to rise for class, I snuggled down under the heavy, warm comforter. I waited for someone to come and tell me to get out of bed, but all that came were the footsteps of Nicolai around the time he'd leave to take me to school. He didn't open the door to check in. After a few seconds, his steps faded down the hall.

I closed my eyes, unsure if I should be grateful that no one seemed to care or if I should be hurt by that. Before Roth... before the clan knew of him and our relationship, Abbot or someone would've been in here, dragging me out of the bed or at least making sure Freddy Krueger hadn't snatched me. Now? Not so much. More than ever before, I was a permanent guest in their home, one that had outstayed her welcome.

As I drifted back off, my brain wandered in every direction. An old plan resurfaced, one I hadn't given much thought to in a while. My sleepy gaze drifted to my desk. The empty OJ glass rested on top of the stack of college applications. Those papers were nearly forgotten and it was probably too late to seriously consider enrolling for next fall, but maybe that was what I'd do.

Screw all of this—the Lilin, Roth and all the Wardens. I could go to college far away from here and pretend to be... pretend to be what? Normal? I could do it. I'd been doing it for so long. Blend in among the humans and make this all into a distant memory. It was a selfish decision, but I didn't care. I wanted to be selfish and I didn't want to be here, in this body any longer or stuck with these problems.

One good thing was I wouldn't see him at school. There was no reason for Roth to return there.

At some point I drifted off again, awakening when I felt the bed shift under sudden, unexpected weight and the stirring of the covers. Disoriented, I blinked open my eyes. Heart kicking in my chest, I glanced over my shoulder.

Two cerulean eyes met mine.

CHAPTER EIGHT

Zayne stared back at me, momentarily obscured by a length of blond hair. I held my breath as he eased down on his side and tugged the covers up to his waist. My gaze dipped. He was wearing a gray cotton shirt and it stretched taut over his shoulders as he reached under the comforter, finding me in the bundle of blankets. With his arm around my waist, he snagged me back against his chest. Every muscle in my body tensed as he settled in behind me, curving his body around mine with a natural ease that scattered my senses. There was virtually nothing between us but our thin sleep clothes, which were no shield from the heat he radiated.

And that warmth...*oh*. It seeped into my muscles, easing out the knots and all the sore spots. Within seconds, the rigidness flowed out of my spine and my cheek returned to the pillow. The bed turned into a cloud and I felt as if I was in one of those cheesy mattress commercials Stacey and Sam always made fun of, but Zayne had the power to change an ordinary mattress into something wonderful. I closed my eyes, letting my body sink down. In the moments that followed, I wasn't thinking about anything and that was *great*.

He lifted his hand from my waist long enough to brush

strands of my hair out of his face and then I felt his warm breath against the back of my neck. A series of shivers danced over my skin. A different kind of tightness formed in my lower stomach as I focused on breathing normally and not as though I'd just attempted to run up and down bleachers.

It had been a long, long time since Zayne had done this— climbed into my bed to rest instead of taking a deep sleep. Not since we were much, much younger, when sharing a bed was harmless and innocent, and no one could get the wrong idea about it. Shock flickered through me. Especially after last night, I didn't expect this from him. He'd sensed that I'd been close to caving to the need. Truthfully, he was in constant danger when he was around me. At any moment, I could roll over and our mouths would be *centimeters* apart. And it would be so easy to take his soul.

"How's your arm?" he asked.

When he spoke, his voice rumbled through me. I cleared my throat and then winced at how abrasive it sounded. "It's okay."

"We should check it out later." He shifted his arm and his hand ended up on my belly, just below my navel. I jerked back in surprise, but he didn't pull away or move his hand. "It's not why you didn't go to school, then?"

Swallowing a sigh, I pried my eyes open. On the nightstand, the neon green lights showed 9:01 a.m. I should be on my way to bio at this point. "No."

"Do you want to talk about it?"

Talking about Roth while lying in bed with Zayne was the last possible thing I ever wanted to do. "No."

Silence fell between us as his chest rose and fell against my back in an even, deep rhythm. As relaxed as I was, my body was still hyperaware of his, of every breath he took and every tiny spasm of muscle. In the quiet, an ugly thought crept in.

Had he lain like this with Danika? I had no right to the caustic burn of jealousy that invaded my blood, but it was there and it was wrong, because they were able to share more than I'd ever be able to share with him.

"I'm sorry," he said, speaking the words so quietly I wasn't sure he'd said them at first.

I closed my eyes. "Why?"

There was another long stretch of silence and then he said, "I know you're hurting and I want to kill the son of a bitch for that."

My heart turned over heavily. There was no hiding anything from him. Zayne knew me better than I liked to acknowledge. I didn't know what to say. I wanted to strangle Roth and spin kick him in his junk, but I also had a sneaking suspicion that Zayne really, *really* wanted to act on his desire, and because I was a girl, I'd cry if Zayne did manage to kill him.

"He's a demon," Zayne said. "It doesn't matter that there are moments when he'll pull off acts of great compassion, because underneath it, he is what he is."

I sucked my bottom lip in. "But that's what I am."

"No." Zayne rose slightly, causing his hand to drag across my stomach to my hip. "You're not just a demon, Layla. You're also a Warden. It's not like you can't be both things and…"

"And?" I turned onto my back, resting on my elbows, and his hand ended up on my belly again, his long fingers reaching the band on my sleep shorts. Our gazes met. "And what?"

He didn't answer immediately. Instead his gaze drifted over my face and then down, beyond the collar of my shirt. The blanket had slipped below my chest. He swallowed hard as he returned to lying on his side. His voice was thicker than normal when he spoke. "And why can't you have the best of both worlds? Like the best qualities, you know?"

"Best qualities of both?" I murmured slowly. "You're saying there are good qualities in demons?"

"In you." The hollows of his cheeks flushed, and I blinked a couple of times, but the blush was slow to fade. "You're part demon. Like I said that night at the ice-cream shop, we shouldn't have made you hate that part of you."

I remember him saying that. Those words had been lost in what else had happened that night—Paimon and the devil's trap—but I *remembered*.

"Every part of you is good—even the demon side." He paused. "And I saw you that night."

Lying back, I drew in a deep breath. "What do you mean?"

He leaned over me and several locks of hair glided over his cheeks. "You didn't look like us when you shifted, but you didn't look like a demon either. You were a mixture of both."

"So I looked like a freak?"

"No." His hand moved and his fingers curved around my waist. "Your skin was black and gray, like mottled marble. It was beautiful. Best of both."

A pleasant heat crept into my cheeks and I fought not to lower my gaze from the intensity in his. "You've been saying that a lot lately."

"What?"

"The 'beautiful' thing."

His lips curled up at the corners in a small smile. "I have been."

"You need your head checked?"

He rolled his eyes. "Anyway…" His thumb moved in slow, idle circles along my lower stomach. He seemed unaware of it, but then he chuckled softly. "I have no idea what we were talking about."

I smiled. "We were talking about how awesome I am."

"Sounds about right." He settled back down and he seemed

to be closer than before. The tops of his legs were pressed to the sides of my thighs. And his thumb was still tracing that unseen circle under my belly button, creating a languid warmth that was familiar.

"I was thinking," I said finally, watching him. His eyes were closed and in that moment, he looked much younger than twenty-one.

There was a beat of silence. "About what?"

"About filling out those college applications and trying to see if I could get in for late admission."

One eye opened and his thumb stilled. Several seconds passed. "Is it because of him?"

I opened my mouth.

"You know I've always supported you when it comes to going to college." Both eyes were open now. "I think it would be great for you, but don't make a huge decision like that because of what you're feeling right now."

I wanted to deny the assumption that my sudden interest in college had anything to do with Roth, but it would be a pitiful lie. Who was I kidding? Wasn't like I hadn't seriously considered leaving here and attending college before, but right now the idea was circling in my head for all the wrong reasons.

Zayne was staring at me now, eyes as bright as midday during the summer. Unrest made me twitchy. "Do you...?" He took a deep breath, and I held mine. "Did you love him, Layla?"

Oh God. My eyes widened and I could feel the heat in my cheeks grow. The question totally knocked me right off the planet.

He looked away and shook his head. "Shit, Layla-bug."

"No!" I blurted out, and when his head swung back at me, my heart jumped in my throat. "I don't know how I feel," I rushed on, speaking the brutal truth. "I don't know, Zayne. I care about him a lot and he…" I ached at the sudden knot in my throat. "I don't know."

And I really didn't.

Love is a strange creature one thinks one has a grasp on and understanding of, only to discover later that it was only the barest taste of the real thing. And there were so many different kinds of love—that much I knew—and I didn't know where Roth fell in all of that.

Zayne held my gaze for a moment longer before nodding. "Okay. I get that." His hand left my stomach and before I could feel the pang of confused disappointment, he found my hand and threaded his fingers through mine. "I really do."

He squeezed my hand and I returned the gesture obediently, but I wasn't sure how he could get any of this when I didn't.

Zayne had slept the day away with me, leaving my bed as the other Wardens began to stir in the house. I'd watched him leave, cheeks flushed for no good reason other than it seemed wholly intimate watching him sneak out of my room as if we…as if we'd done something naughty.

I'd remained in bed after that, trying to sort through the odd tingling in my chest. There was a slight smile on my lips, because Zayne…well, he'd made my day, but then I'd remember what Roth had said to me the night before and the smile would wash away as if it had never been there.

I probably needed to get used to the whiplash mood swings.

It wasn't until after dinner that I decided to scrub a day's worth of gunk off myself. Gingerly, I peeled the bandage off, happy to find that the cut in my arm was healing as expected. I didn't need to cover it anymore. The arm was still tender, but the Warden blood in me was quickly undoing the damage from the iron.

After changing into fresh pj's, like a total hermit, I padded over to my desk, where I'd left my cell phone. It had been on silent all day and when I tapped the screen, I wasn't surprised to see a slew of texts from Stacey.

Where r u?

R u skipping, u ho?

A minute later: Your locker misses u. Guess u sick with the herp?

Oh my God. I laughed out loud, grinning as I thumbed through her texts.

Our bio sub is still hot. U r missing this.

Bio is lonely.

My boobs miss u. How weird is that?

That was notably weird and yet not surprising.

If I get my cell taken from me, it's ur fault.

Holy shit, Layla, where r u?!?

Air punched out of my lungs as I read the next text and the several following them.

U have no idea who just walked into bio!!!

Roth is here!

Holy canola oil, why aren't u here to witness this?

Ok. He says he had mono. Srlsy? Do people still get mono? And who in the duck was he kissing?

A second later: Duck? I didn't mean duck. That's SO not what I meant, autocorrect.

Another text had come in about fifteen minutes after the last one.

He asked where u were. I told him u joined a cult. I laughed. He didn't.

Finally, the last text was to call her if I wasn't dead.

"What in the Hell?" I tossed my cell onto the bed, mouth hanging open.

Anger blasted through me like a door being kicked open and I welcomed it because it was so much better than the damn hurt and the confusion and that...that *lost* feeling.

Roth was back in school? That...that was unacceptable. He had no reason to be there. None whatsoever even though he easily passed for an eighteen-year-old. It wasn't as if school seriously interested him or like he'd get a lot of Lilin hunting done there.

What if he wasn't there for the Lilin? Hadn't he asked about Eva?

The moment that question entered my thoughts, a curse burst out of me and I spun, leaving my bedroom. I had no idea where I was going, but I had to go somewhere. Maybe hit something.

Hitting something sounded good.

Because him being there was just *unkind*.

I reached the lower level, stalking past the library and I would've kept on going to God knows where in my polka-dot pajamas when I heard *his* name.

My little feet stopped on a dime and I turned, inclining my head toward the cracked-open door.

"What about Roth?" That was Dez.

"Needless to say, we cannot fully trust him," Abbot responded, and I could practically see him in my head, sitting behind the desk, rolling a cigar between his fingers. "We need to keep an eye on him."

"Done," replied Nicolai.

There was a pause and then Abbot said, "We also need to keep an eye on Layla."

I snapped my mouth shut as my hands curled in. Keep an eye on me?

His voice had dropped low and then picked back up. "You know what we could be dealing with. All of you. We have to be careful because if it's what I suspect, we have to de—"

A rush of icy wind blew down the hall, stirring my damp hair and sending it flying around my face. Sucking in a startled breath, I spun as a loud crack reverberated through the compound. The boom echoed like thunder, rattling the pictures of angels.

Directly across from me, the large picture-frame windows in the atrium cracked right down the middle. I took a step back as the glass splintered and then exploded.

CHAPTER NINE

Shrieking, I whipped around and covered my head before I was pelted with glass. Tiny shards bounced off me harmlessly, clanging off the floor like wind chimes.

"Holy crap," I whispered, jumping as the library door slammed off the wall and Wardens poured out in the hall.

Abbot was first. "What the Hell happened out here?"

"I don't know." I straightened and turned. Three large panes of windows had been obliterated. "Wow."

"Are you okay?" Dez asked, coming to my side. Not too close, but enough that I could see that his pupils had dilated.

I glanced down. In my bare feet, walking would prove tricky. Glass covered the floor, twinkling like little diamonds in the foyer light. "Yeah. Not even a scratch."

Nicolai and Geoff approached the blown-out windows. Being our resident security expert, Geoff looked disturbed as he leaned out the window and with good reason. "These windows are reinforced glass. It would take damn near a rocket to break them and nothing or no one is down there. None of the motion detectors have gone off or any of the charms."

"Or in here." Nicolai turned around, frowning. "There's no bricks or anything."

Abbot turned to me and the taut line his jaw formed told me he was not happy. My gaze dipped to his hands. In one he held a small vial of milky-white liquid. "What happened in here, Layla?" he asked before I could question what he held.

"I don't know. I was walking down the hall and the windows—they just cracked and then exploded." I shook my head and pieces of glass wiggled free from my hair, clinking off the hardwood floors. Great. It would take forever to get all the glass out. I carefully stepped to the side.

Abbot arched a brow. "So you did nothing?"

My head jerked up. "Of course not! I didn't do anything."

"Then how did the windows get broken if there's nothing here that could have done it?"

I forgot about the glass as I stared up at Abbot. Cold air rushed in through the windows, but that wasn't the cause of the sudden chill skidding down my spine. "I don't know, but I'm telling the truth. I didn't do anything."

Geoff faced us, crossing his arms. The dimple in his chin was all but gone. "Layla, there's nothing in here that would've broken the windows."

"It wasn't me, though." My gaze darted among the men. None of them, not even Dez or Nicolai, wore expressions that said they believed me. "Why would I break out the windows?"

Abbot raised his chin. "Why were you in the hallway?"

"I don't know." Irritation pricked at my skin. "Maybe I was walking to the kitchen or the living room. Or one of the many rooms down here?"

His eyes narrowed. "Do not take that tone with me, Layla."

"I'm not taking a tone!" My voice rose a notch. "You're blaming me for something I didn't do!"

"The windows didn't break themselves." The hue of his eyes burned a brilliant blue. "If it was an accident, I'd rather you tell me the truth. No more lies."

"No more lies? That's real nice coming from you," I shot back. The words were out of my mouth before I could stop them, and well, it was like having one foot in the grave already. "Especially when you're telling them to keep an eye on me."

His chest rose in a deep breath as he stepped forward, towering over me. "So you were out here eavesdropping when the windows were broken?"

"No!" Not really. At least that's not why I was originally down here, but that wasn't the point. "I was just walking by and heard my name. The door was cracked open. It wasn't like you all were trying to be quiet about it."

Dez stepped toward us. "Layla—"

Holding up a hand, Abbot silenced the younger Warden. "What did you hear?"

I folded my arms, silent. Unexpected stubbornness filled me. I didn't say anything even though I'd only heard the one part.

He lowered his head and the act seemed to symbolize how unafraid of me he was, and for some reason, that relieved me. When he spoke, his voice was low and frighteningly calm. "What did you hear, Layla?"

Summoning courage, I kept my mouth shut and forced myself to meet his stare. "Why? What do you think I heard?"

His nostrils flared with a heavy exhale. "Girl, I raised you as one of my own. You will speak to me with respect and you will answer my question."

A quiver of fear shot through my muscles. There was a huge part of me that wanted to tell him that I hadn't heard much, wanted to make him happy, because he was the closest thing I had to a father. His approval was something I constantly sought, but this—*this* wasn't fair and I wasn't going to be a doormat for him.

Or for anyone.

Tension filled the atrium and the rest of the Wardens shifted uneasily. "Just tell him," Nicolai said softly.

Resolve built steel around my spine as I continued to hold Abbot's stare.

"What's going on?" Zayne came down the steps, three at a time. Drops of water clung to his wet hair and patches of his black shirt stuck to his body. Fresh from the shower, his winter-mint scent filled the air. His gaze was trained on us and then moved to the windows. His brows rose. "Father?"

Abbot held my gaze a moment longer and then straightened, addressing his son. "The windows magically exploded, according to Layla."

"I didn't do it," I said, resisting the urge to stomp my feet and end up with glass as shoes. "The windows did explode. I don't know how it happened, but it wasn't me."

"If she says she didn't do it, she didn't." It was that simple to Zayne. He believed what I said, and for the love of all things holy in the world, he was my hero in that moment. His gaze flickered to the floor. "Jesus, be careful. You don't have shoes on."

I started to smile or launch myself at him, but Abbot moved. He stalked past us. "Go to your room, Layla." Glass crunched under his boots. When I didn't move, he stopped and his angry glare pierced straight through me. "Now."

"I didn't do anything!" I exclaimed. "Why do I have to go—"

"Now!" he shouted, and I jumped again.

Zayne caught my arm, keeping me from stepping on glass. He shot his father a look.

Abbot turned to the Wardens. They started toward him, but he stopped them. "Just Geoff. The rest of you are excused."

Geoff exchanged looks with the others, but followed Abbot

into the library. The door slammed shut behind them, and my shenanigans sensor went off. I looked at Nicolai and Dez. "I didn't do it," I said yet again.

Both of them looked away, and the unease inside of me spread like wildfire as Nicolai left the atrium.

Dez sighed. "I'll find Morris and get him to help me with this mess. And the windows." Then he was gone, too, leaving me alone with Zayne.

"He's in a bad mood," Zayne reasoned quietly as he helped me navigate the path of destruction. "He has been ever since Ro—the demons showed up last night."

Maybe that was why he was acting as if he'd sat on a nail, but it was more than that. At the bottom of the stairs, I spoke. "He was in the library with the other Wardens. I overheard him saying something."

Zayne was staring at the floor. "Are you sure you didn't get cut with all this glass?"

"No. Pay attention to me," I said, tugging on the sleeve of his shirt. He looked at me, brows raised. "He was telling the other Wardens to keep an eye on me."

"Okay," he said slowly.

"Okay? Hello. He told them to *watch* me."

Zayne took my hand, leading me up the stairs. "With... well, you-know-who being back, of course he's going to want to make sure you're safe."

That hadn't even crossed my mind. "It wasn't like that, Zayne. He said something else, but it was too low for me to hear. And then he was talking about something being what he suspected."

"What?"

"I don't know." Frustrated, I pulled my hand free. "I couldn't hear all of it and then the stupid windows blew up."

I glanced down the stairs. Glass shone like rain on the floor. "I really didn't do it."

"I believe you."

My gaze found his. "And I don't trust your father."

"Layla," he sighed, stepping back. "There're obvious issues between you two, and I totally get it. He's kept a lot of stuff from you."

"No shit," I muttered.

He shifted his weight. "But if he's asking any of the guys to watch over you, it's because he's worried about you."

"And because he doesn't trust me."

"That, too," he admitted. "Hey, you have to understand that. You—"

"Lied. I know. But he's told more lies."

Zayne stared at me as if he was about to explain how two wrongs don't make a right, but then he sighed again. "Come on. I snagged some fried chicken from dinner. It's cold, just the way you like it."

"I'm supposed to go to my room," I said peevishly.

He rolled his eyes and then made a grab for me. I jumped back, and he grinned impishly. "Walk or I'm carrying you."

"Geez, you're getting bossy as you get older."

Zayne winked. "You haven't seen anything yet. I'm giving you two seconds."

"Two seconds? What happened to the standard— Hey!" I squealed as he grabbed for me again. "All right. I'll walk."

His grin spread. "Knew you'd see it my way."

I stuck my tongue out at him, and he laughed, but I did follow him down the hall to his bedroom. My stomach rumbled at the thought of cold fried chicken, but my mind was still in the atrium downstairs, and for some reason, I thought of the vial of the milky-white substance.

I wanted to know what it was.

★ ★ ★

Parasitic butterflies had formed a prickly nest in my stomach and were currently trying to eat their way out. I'd never been more nervous about school in my life.

"You sure you're feeling better?" Stacey asked as she paced back and forth while I dragged my textbooks out of my locker. "You look like you're about to fall over."

"Yeah, I feel great." I forced a smile that probably came off creepy as I slung my bag over my shoulder. There was barely any pain from where the Warden had sliced me, which reminded me that, as of this morning, Tomas was still missing.

Bambi stretched around my stomach.

Bad snake.

"So are you excited?" Stacey asked, looping her arm through mine.

My throat felt as if I'd swallowed a hairball. "Excited about what?"

"About Roth," she said in a high-pitched squeal that made my ears ache. "About him being back."

The deadly butterflies started chomping away. Between the prospect of returning to school and what had happened the past two nights, I'd barely gotten a wink of sleep. I'd secretly hoped Zayne would skip demon duties and stay with me, but he hadn't and it would've been überwrong to ask.

"And please don't get mad at me, because I don't really know what went down between you two, but he looked hella hot yesterday."

My heart spasmed. Great. I guess hoping for him to get a mad case of facial herpes was asking for too much. "Not that excited," I said finally.

She was quiet as we made our way down the hall. The oddness of not seeing shimmery souls trailing after students distracted me from my impending face-off with Roth.

"Do you want me to take out a hit on him?" she asked finally. "I don't know people, but I bet Sam would be able to find us hit men on the internet."

I laughed loudly. "He probably would, but no. That's okay."

"Well, if you change your mind…" She slipped around me, opening the door to bio. I already knew, even before I walked in, that he wasn't in the room yet. "Sisters before the misters and all that jazz."

Smiling in spite of my nerves, I took my seat in the back of the class. Mrs. Cleo was still a no-show, and at the front of the class, Mr. Tucker was doing his best to ignore the adoring gazes of the girls sitting in the front row.

Stacey sat beside me as I pulled my textbook out and the class filled up. I busied myself picking out a pen from my horde, settling on a purple one that looked as though it had taken a bath in glitter…or with Ke$ha.

The scent was the first thing I noticed. That sinfully dark, slightly sweet aroma teased my senses. My fingers tightened around the pen as the entire atmosphere shifted in the class. Not with tension; I'd never noticed it before, but it was like the last day before break whenever Roth was near—that lackadaisical feeling of *who cares* followed him everywhere.

Tiny hairs on the back of my neck rose, and I knew he was near. Not just because Stacey had stiffened beside me. It was a sixth sense that was aware of him on a deep, intimate level.

I didn't look up as I heard the chair legs drag across the floor in front of our desk, but he was so close and that damn poignant ache took hold again, seizing up my throat and chest. I didn't want to hurt over him, and I wished I could fast-forward to the part when the piercing ache was just a minor annoyance.

"Good to see you didn't join a cult."

At the sound of his deep, velvety-rich voice, a series of shivers spread across my skin. I took a deep breath and immediately regretted it. His scent was everywhere, and I could practically taste him. Against my will, my head lifted and my brain jumped out the nearby window.

Roth stared down at me with those amber-colored eyes surrounded by thick, black lashes. His hair was an artful mess, caressing the arches of his brows. His full lips weren't curved in the smirk I thought would've accompanied that statement.

I didn't say anything and after a few seconds, his lips pursed and he turned, sitting down. A pang lit up my chest as I stared at his back. Under the faded blue shirt he wore, his shoulders were unnaturally stiff, and it should've given me an indecent amount of satisfaction to know he was uncomfortable. And who knew a Crown Prince of Hell could be uncomfortable in the first place? But realizing he was didn't make me feel better.

Stacey stretched over and scribbled "hit man?" on my notebook.

I smiled and shook my head. She shrugged and turned her attention to the Hottie McHotters sub. I tried to focus on how good-looking he was with his brown hair and boyish grin as he fiddled with the overhead projector, but all I could think about was that Roth was sitting in front of me as if he hadn't been sent to Hell two weeks ago or shared anything of any importance with me.

Thank God and the McDonald's down the street from the high school that today was Friday. At least I wouldn't be forced to endure two more days of seeing Roth and I'd have a break, because bio was the longest class of my life, even worse than history.

When the bell rang, I shot out of my seat like a mini rocket, shoving my books back into my bag as I walked out of class. Stacey was right behind me, and I liked to think that she wouldn't hold my hasty departure against me. Spying Sam at the end of the hall, getting a drink of water from one of the fountains, I breathed a sigh of relief as he looked up, smiling as he waved at me. I was kind of surprised that he didn't have tiny drops of water all over his hoodie like he normally would after attempting to drink from one of the fountains, but I made a beeline for him.

I only made it halfway.

The door to the chemistry classroom swung open, nearly smacking me in the face. I stumbled back a step, eyes welling up as the pungent odor of rotten eggs spilled out in the hallways.

"Not again!" another kid exclaimed, smacking his hands over his mouth.

I wasn't sure if he was referencing the horrible stench of the zombie we'd had in the boiler room a month or so ago, or from what happened to the demon Raum after Roth had turned him to a cloud of stinky smoke that night in the gym, but it didn't matter.

A teacher raced out into the hall, gagging as he waved his hands across his face. Seconds later, another teacher stormed out of the classroom. The ends of her blond hair were fried—literally scorched and blackened. Worse yet, her eyebrows were totally gone. Gray smudges covered half her ruddy face.

"Nice," murmured Roth, who had somehow, and probably as a result of the laws of the universe, ended up next to me. *Dammit.* "That's what we'd call a hot mess."

I shot him a scathing glare and then stepped around him, willing to inhale whatever carcinogens could possibly be in the smoke wafting out of the room. But he snagged my sweater, hauling me back. I bounced off his rock-hard chest and started to turn, seconds from slamming my fist into his stomach because it would've felt *really* good to do so when the no-eyebrows teacher zipped through the smoke.

Roth's hand slid up my back. "Careful, shortie, she's on a mission."

"*Don't* touch me." Yanking away from him, I ignored the flicker of emotion that tightened his lips. "And *don't* call me that." I turned just in time to see her take a flying leap at someone. "What the...?"

She tackled the other teacher.

Like jumped on his back and brought him down to his knees. Right there. In the middle of the hall, full of gaping students and faculty. Brought him down, cocked back an arm and punched the dude right between the legs.

CHAPTER TEN

"I'm beginning to think we're attending the most cray-cray school in North America," Stacey said at lunch, holding her chicken nugget between two black-painted nails. "I mean, we have teachers taking nut shots at each other in the hallways."

Sam winced as he dropped his crinkle fry back onto his tray. "Yeah, that was pretty crazy."

It was more than just crazy. Between the fight in our bio class and now this, in the span of less than a few days, something else had to be going on. And the couple I'd seen making out in the hallway without interruption? I nibbled on my nugget, hoping my suspicions weren't true, but a Lilin had supposedly been born and one of the signs of a Lilin's presence was strange behavior, right? But if it was a Lilin behind Dean's anger, the couple in the hallway and the teacher today, then that was four people that were close to becoming wraiths. The weight of that possible disaster killed my appetite.

I glanced over my shoulder, wishing once again I could see the auras. Those affected by the Lilin would have to have appeared different, what was left of their souls tainted somehow. But I saw nothing and that meant I was virtually useless.

My stomach dipped as I placed the half-eaten nugget on

my plate. Could my sudden loss of ability have anything to do with the Lilin? That would mean I'd been in its vicinity.

No. There was no way. I would know if I was around something that shared the blood of my mother and me. There had to be another reason, but as I poked the nugget around my plate, my stomach soured.

"What are you guys doing after school?" Sam asked, and when I looked up, he'd scarfed down everything on his plate. The boy and his appetite had to be legendary. "I was thinking we could grab something to eat. The three of us."

I smiled.

Stacey glanced at me with hopeful eyes. "I'm not on baby-brother duty until tomorrow, so I know I can. Layla?"

Considering how Abbot had acted last night, he probably wanted me to come straight home. Which meant it was the last thing I wanted. "Yeah, just let me text Zayne and let him know." I was so not texting Nicolai. "I don't think it should be a problem."

"You should invite him!" She clapped her hands like a seal on crack.

A brow rose above Sam's glasses and I almost pooh-poohed the idea, but I grabbed my cell and decided what the Hell. The worst Zayne could say was no. Wouldn't be the first time. "I'll ask."

Stacey shot Sam a look of surprise as I sent my text.

Stacey & Sam want to grab food after school. U want 2 join us?

I placed the cell on the table near my plate, not expecting a quick response. Zayne should be asleep now. Some days he wasn't, but who knew?

"You think he'll come?" Sam asked, fiddling with his fork.

I shrugged. "Probably not."

"Well, if he does, you can't ask him for an interview." Stacey pointed her bottle of water at him. "Or act like a fan boy. It will scare him off and he'll never come out and play with us again."

Sam chuckled. "I won't act like a fan boy."

That was doubtful. The couple of times Sam had been around Zayne in the past, he'd gawked at him in open wonder. I couldn't blame him. The Wardens didn't mingle with humans a lot. Most didn't even know that some of the very ordinary people they saw on the streets, in shops or restaurants were Wardens.

Stacey grinned. "Any idea of where—"

"I am?" came a deep voice that caused my heart to skip and my stomach to drop at the same time. "I'm right here."

No way—no way in Hell was Roth at *our* table. A wicked sense of déjà vu smacked me upside the head. It was like the first time Roth had appeared in my life, and I couldn't believe he'd had the audacity to seek us out at lunch. And here we were again.

My lips thinned as he sat down beside me without an invite or response. Instead of having one of the orange plastic trays in his hand, he carried a McDonald's bag. His mouth curled up at the corner as he pulled out a small white bag. "Fry?"

I took a deep breath. "No."

"I'll take one." Sam reached across the table and snatched up a couple of the offered fries. "Glad you're back. Mono sucks. I had it when I— Ow!" His eyes widened as he faced Stacey.

She gave him a pointed glare.

Not bothered at all by the exchange, Roth placed the bag of fries between us, near my phone, and then pulled out a cheeseburger. "Yeah, mono was Hell. Like being chained to a bed."

I almost choked.

My cell phone vibrated and Zayne's response popped up on the screen. Before I could grab it, Roth had it in his nimble fingers. "I'll pick you up and we'll head over there." He arched a brow. "Together?"

Stringing together a chorus of mental curses, I yanked the cell out of his hands. "It's rude to read someone's messages."

"Is it?"

"Yes," Stacey replied. "But I'm glad to hear that Zayne is joining us for dinner."

Roth's lip curled and a second passed. "Me, too."

Unable to help myself, I snorted.

His eyes narrowed on me.

"Dinner?" Sam frowned. "I thought we were going straight after school? And I was thinking of the Italian place down the street. Not really dinner—"

"Sam," Stacey sighed.

Roth grinned then. "Anyway, back to me. I'm all better and I am back." He slid me a sly look that made me want to punch him instead of cry into my pillow like a baby. "I'm sure I was missed." He took a big bite of the hamburger and grinned around the mouthful. "A lot."

I didn't know what happened that switched my emotions so fast. The hurt his rejection had left behind exploded into rage—like the head-spinning, spraying-green-vomit kind of rage. My brain clicked off. I wasn't thinking as I reached over and plucked the hamburger right out of his hand. Twisting at the waist, I threw the hamburger on the floor behind Roth as hard as I could. The satisfactory *splat* it made as ketchup and mayo splattered like a gruesome burger massacre brought a wide smile to my face.

Stacey let out a burst of shocked laughter.

Roth glanced down at the hamburger and then his gaze

slowly tracked back to mine. His eyes were wide. "But I really wanted that hamburger."

"Too bad." I swallowed a crazy sounding giggle. "Your fries are next if you don't remove your ass from my presence."

"Daaammmn," Stacey murmured, her body shaking with now-silent laughter.

We were locked in an epic stare-down for a couple of moments and then his lips twitched as if he was trying not to laugh. And, well, that just caused my anger to ratchet up several degrees. Then he picked up his bag of fries. "I think we need to talk."

"No, we don't."

His jaw clenched. "Yes, we do."

I shook my head.

Roth stared at me, and something...something about the way he looked at me shifted. Some of the hardness faded from his expression. "Layla."

"Fine," I replied, snatching up my bag as a really stupid idea formed. Maybe he wanted to apologize for being an ass. Unlikely. I turned to a greatly amused Stacey and Sam. "Text me the place we're meeting after school."

"Will do." She paused. "Don't hurt the fries. That would be sacrilegious."

"No promises." I started walking, not waiting on Roth, and I felt ridiculously proud of myself. The Layla from two months ago wouldn't have dared to make a scene, but I was a different person these days.

I was beginning to see that now.

As I passed the bathrooms outside of the cafeteria, the boys' door swung open and Gareth stumbled out, followed by a pack of giggling football players. *Giggling.* They reeked of pot smoke as they headed into the cafeteria.

"I'd kill for a bag of Cheetos right now," said Gareth.

One of his buds laughed. "I'd throw a baby in front of a bus for cinnamon buns."

Wow. That was some hard-core munchies. All of the guys with Gareth partied, but they weren't stoners. Their behavior was definitely off. Could they be...infected, too?

Roth caught up with me. No book bag. Just him and his stupid fries. "I'm surprised. I'll admit it. You surprised me."

"Really?" I let out a harsh laugh, irritated that he was shocked. "Did you think after what you said to me that I'd be happy to see you? Seriously?"

He popped a fry in his mouth and chewed thoughtfully, as if he really had to think about it. "Yes. I know so."

I stopped midstep at the end of the hallway, and stared at him. "You're delusional."

"Wouldn't go that far." In went another fry.

"You have an overinflated sense of self-worth."

He grinned. "I am very valuable, actually. Being the Crown—"

I yanked the bag out of his hand, spun around and tossed the remaining fries in the garbage. Turning back to him, I smiled widely. "That's what I think about your valuable Crown Prince shit."

Roth heaved a huge sigh. "I'm a growing boy and need my sustenance. I'm going to starve now and it'll be all your fault."

"Whatever." I folded my arms.

He stared at me and then tipped back his head and laughed. I shivered, unprepared for the sound. I'd forgotten how deep and rich his laughter was—how contagious. The laugh quickly faded, replaced by a surprisingly morose look. "Oh, shortie, you're already making this hard."

"Making what hard? And don't call me shortie."

He shook his head. "Come on, we need to talk for real. Where we won't be interrupted." He started toward the faded double doors and I knew where he was heading—*our* stairwell. The place where we students weren't supposed to be, where no one ever went. It led to the old gymnasium and smelled like mold, but it had been our place before.

And that's why it was the last place I wanted to be, but Roth was already stalking down the stairs. I squared my shoulders and followed him. Nothing had changed about the ten-by-ten landing. Gray paint was still peeling off the cement blocks. Rust covered the handrails. Dust floated in the light from the tiny window at the top of the steps. Time had forgotten this place.

Roth turned to me and leaned back against the wall. He raised his arms above his head and stretched. His long-sleeve shirt rose up, exposing a tantalizing glimpse of his lower stomach and the dragon tattoo—Thumper. Its blue-and-green scales were as vibrant as before. Roth had said once before that the dragon only came off if things went bad fast. I couldn't imagine what Roth's idea of bad was when he hadn't used the dragon the night with Paimon. The dragon was resting now, wings tugged close to its belly and its tail disappearing under the band on Roth's dark jeans. Considering how low his jeans hung, the length of Thumper's tail I could see caused heat to flood across my cheeks.

"Layla…"

I dragged my gaze up and sucked in a tiny breath when I saw how bright his ocher eyes were.

"Like what you see?"

My hands curled into fists. "No. Not at all."

"You lie." A smirk appeared on his lips. "And you're still a terrible liar."

Striving for patience, I dropped my bag on the floor. "Why are you here, Roth?"

He didn't answer immediately. "You want the truth?"

I rolled my eyes. "No. I want the lie. What do you think?"

A soft laugh followed. "I kind of like school. We don't have places like this down below." He shrugged a shoulder. "It's normal."

Something squeezed in my chest. It was the same reason I liked school—it was normal and I could be normal here, but I refused to relate to him on any level. "You shouldn't be here."

One brow arched. "Because of you?"

I wanted to scream yes—dear God, yes! "Because you being here is pointless."

"Not really." He finally lowered his arms, and I silently thanked God, because his stomach was no longer a major distraction. "You can't tell me that the death match in the hallway this morning wasn't weird."

I didn't say anything.

"And I doubt this is the first strange incident recently, right?" His eyes were hooded as he watched me.

Part of me wanted to tell him no, because I didn't want to see that smug look of his grow, but that would be stupid. I couldn't forget the very real, very huge problem we were facing. "There have been a few things. Dean—a kid who's never done anything—hit another boy so hard it actually killed him for a few seconds. And then I've seen couples really making out—"

"Nothing wrong with that," he replied, grinning.

I narrowed my eyes. "Except we have a strict no PDA policy and a teacher walked right past them, even as they went into the girls' bathroom." I tucked my hair back and then dropped my hand to where the ring dangled off the necklace. "So you think the Lilin has been here?"

He nodded. "It makes sense—after all, it was created here.

Which is why we need to talk. You should be able to pick out the Lilin, or at least any strange demons around here."

"Uh…" I looked away, twisting the chain around my neck. I didn't want to tell him, but he was a demon and maybe he knew what was up with it. "Well, you see, not really."

Pushing off the wall, he stood straight, all attention focused now. "What do you mean?"

"I can't see auras anymore. Nothing. Happened a few days ago."

His head tilted to the side. "Details."

I sighed. "The auras were kind of wonky at first, blinking in and out at lunch, and then I got this sharp pain behind my eyes, and I can't see them anymore. So I'm virtually in the dark. I don't sense other demons Wardens do—you know, not as strongly. I've never had to work that muscle."

"This is too much of a coincidence."

"That's what I feared," I said, dropping the ring. "I was hoping it didn't have anything to do with the Lilin."

Roth didn't respond. His gaze flickered over me, brows lowered in deep thought. The study was so intense it made me want to squirm. "So how do you think it's interfering with my ability?" I asked when the silence became too much.

"I don't know." Roth finally looked away, scratching his hand through his hair. "But we're going to have to find the Lilin the old-fashioned way."

"We?"

His lashes lowered and the demure look was almost laughable, except it was incredibly sexy, which I kind of hated him for. "Yes. We. You and I. Us. Two peas in a—"

"No." I held up a hand. "We are not working together on anything."

"Haven't we had this conversation before?" He took a step

forward, and I backed up. "And remember how that ended up. We made the perfect team."

I kept retreating, until my back hit the cool wall. "That was before you said I eased your boredom."

The tip of his tongue moved over his upper teeth, showing off the ball holding the bolt piercing in place. Supposedly it wasn't his only piercing—I stopped that thought. I so did not need to think about that.

"That was a jackass thing to say. I admit it. I tend to…say stupid things. I'm an ass."

"I have to agree."

His lashes rose and he moved so fast I didn't track it until he was right in front of me, totally up in my personal space. "I didn't mean what I said about Eva either."

Something inside me—something stupid that needed to be stabbed to death—opened up like a blossom seeing the sun for the first time. I tried to quash it. "I don't care."

"Yes. You do." He lowered his head, his lips dangerously close to mine. I locked up, the air freezing in my lungs. His head tilted, and my heart pounded in my chest. "It hurt you."

"Why do you even care if it did?"

Roth said nothing, and my lips tingled from how hard he was staring at them. He placed his hands just above my hips; the touch light and barely there. I wrapped my fingers around his wrists and started to remove his hands. "Don't," he said, voice low.

"Then why?" I whispered, caving to the tiny spark of hope. "Why did you say all of that? If you didn't mean—"

"It doesn't change anything." He pulled back, moving several feet in a blink of an eye. "We need to be friends. Or at least get along to the point where you aren't destroying perfectly good fast food when I open my mouth."

Just like that, he was a different Roth. Not the guy who'd

held me weeks ago or done all those wonderful things to me. The question burst out of me before I could stop myself. "Did I mean anything to you?"

"It doesn't matter," Roth said, voice flat as he turned to the steps. He stopped with his hand on the rusted-out railing. "It never did, Layla."

CHAPTER ELEVEN

It took a lot to push past what Roth had said and finish out the day. I didn't get him, and it would be a long time before I could stop trying. Throughout my afternoon classes, I was torn between wanting to find Roth and do to his face what I'd done to his hamburger, and just wanting to stare at him.

Being a girl sucked sometimes.

I dragged myself out of school and to the street corner. The site of the old Impala brought a tired smile to my face. I'd almost forgotten about Zayne joining us for food, and while I'd been dealing with Roth, I hadn't had a chance to give much thought to the fact that Zayne had agreed to hang out with us.

Which was so rare.

Deciding to forget about a certain fickle demon for the next couple of hours, I opened the door and slid into the passenger seat. I smiled as I dropped my bag in the back. "Hey," I said.

Zayne grinned. He was wearing a ball cap and it was pulled low, shielding the upper part of his face. Some guys couldn't pull off a baseball cap, but Zayne did and he did it well. "Where we heading to?"

"Little Italy—the one two blocks down."

"Cool." He checked the side mirror and then after a few seconds, he eased out.

"Thank you for coming," I said, resting my head back on the seat. "I was surprised that you said yes."

"You shouldn't have been. I wanted to come." He reached over, tugging gently on a strand of loose hair. "How was school?"

I turned my head toward him, studying his strong profile. "Nothing I want to talk about now." Because if I told him about the Lilin suspicions, I would inevitably have to tell him about Roth and I wanted to enjoy this little outing. "After we eat?"

He glanced at me and was quiet for a moment. "Should I be worried?"

"No." I liked the way the ends of his hair curled out from under the cap. "What did you do today?"

"Slept." He laughed as he drove past the eatery, looking for a parking garage. "Last night was boring. Streets were dead. For some reason that makes me more tired the next day."

"Is it odd that it was so dead?" I thought about the Lilin.

"Depends. If it continues, then yes." After finding a spot on the ground level—he had mad luck—he killed the engine and turned to me as he pulled the keys out. "Hold still," he said, and I obeyed mostly out of curiosity. He reached over, smoothing his thumb along my lower lip. "You had a tiny piece of lint there and I think…"

His words trailed off, ending in a ragged inhale. At first I didn't realize why—what I'd done, and then things began to register—the gut-wrenching sensation that caused my insides to coil into tight springs, the dilated look to his pupils, the sudden vibrancy of his blue eyes, the way his chest rose sharply and the salty taste of his skin as my tongue glided over the slightly rough pad of his thumb.

Oh God.

Oh my God.

I was licking his thumb. Like really *licking* his thumb.

And my body responded to the illicit, wholly forbidden taste of his skin. A heaviness settled in my breasts and heat flowed through me. He didn't pull away. It seemed as though he was straining forward, his upper body already over the gearshift between us.

Blood burning for two very different reasons, I jerked back, breaking the contact between us. My cheeks were on fire—my entire body was on fire. I didn't know what to say or do. Zayne stared at me, his chest rising and falling out of rhythm. I didn't know what he was thinking. I didn't want to.

Mortification replaced the simmering heat that was turning my insides into lava. What in Hell's bells was I thinking? Needing air and space, I quickly unbuckled myself and all but threw myself out of the car.

My eyes stung. There was no way I could sit through this early-dinner thing after doing whatever I was doing. I'd have to hail a cab or walk home or move to Alaska or sew my mouth—

As I rounded the hood of the Impala, Zayne was suddenly in front of me. The baseball cap was turned backward and his eyes were wide. No doubt he thought I was a freak. I *was* a freak. Like a total creeper coward, I darted to the side to get around him. He blocked my path, settling his hands on my shoulders.

"Whoa," he said softly. "Where are you running off to?"

"I don't know." My throat felt as if it was closing off. Could I be allergic to his skin? That sounded stupid. Maybe it was a panic attack. "We should go. Like now. Or we can go home if you want. I'd totally understand and I'm so—"

"Hey, no need for all of that." His hands curled around my shoulders. "It's okay. Everything is fine."

"No, it's not." My voice cracked. "I—"

"It's fine." He tugged me forward, and when I resisted, he pulled harder. I face-planted in his chest and inhaled his crisp scent. "Look, you've been under a lot of stress and crazy stuff has been happening."

True, but that was absolutely no excuse for licking someone's finger. I squeezed my eyes shut as his arms went around me. He dipped his head, resting his chin atop my head. Only Zayne could be this understanding. He was too perfect sometimes.

And I was too weird all the times.

"I don't know why I did it," I said, my voice muffled. "I didn't even realize I was doing it until…well, you know, and I'm so sorry."

"Stop." He rocked to the side, the movement soothing. "It wasn't…"

I drew back a little, daring to peek up at him. "It wasn't what? Gross? Because I'm pretty sure you'd prefer that I hadn't—"

"You have no idea what I prefer and what I don't." The way he said it wasn't dismissive. More like a statement of fact.

I searched his face for an answer to a question I wasn't ready or willing to ask. His gaze met mine, and I lowered my lashes. His hand cupped my cheek and an overwhelming feeling of fondness rose inside of me, along with something deeper, more intense.

Zayne slipped his hand away. "We should get going. Your friends are waiting for us."

I nodded, and as we headed out from the parking garage into the fast-fading sun of November, he whipped his cap around, shielding his eyes. We didn't speak as we walked the half block to the eatery, and I wasn't sure if it was due to my finger licking or something else.

The pretty college-age hostess who led us down the narrow aisle of booths and tables spent most of the trip checking Zayne out.

"If you need anything, please let me know," she said directly to Zayne as she stopped before one of the high-back booths.

He smiled. "Will do."

I resisted the urge to roll my eyes. Stacey and Sam were already inside the restaurant, sitting side by side in a booth big enough to seat six. They were cute, though. Sam with his wavy hair brushing the edges of his glasses, and Stacey sitting with her hands clasped on the table. I really hoped that whatever they were embarking on worked out.

And involved mutual finger licking.

Zayne slid in first, and Sam sat up straighter. I hid my grin as I sat down next to Zayne. "Sorry we're a little late."

"That's okay," Stacey said. "We've been munching on breadsticks."

"Probably would've been quicker to walk." Zayne leaned back, draping his arm along the top of the burgundy cushion behind us. "But there's no way I'm leaving my baby parked along the street."

The mention of Zayne's car sparked Sam's interest and he immediately launched into a conversation about the Impala. Stacey and I both stared at the boy. I guess we'd been expecting him to start hyperventilating, but he played it cool.

After the waitress arrived to take our drink orders, Sam waved a breadstick like a wand, sprinkling garlic all over the checkered tablecloth. "Did you know the reason they went with a Chevy Impala on *Supernatural* was because a body would fit in the trunk?"

My brows furrowed.

Zayne handled it like a pro. "I'm pretty sure you can stash two bodies in the trunk."

Sam grinned, but then his gaze flickered up at the same second Zayne stiffened beside me. There was a change in the eatery, a shifting of the air on an unnatural level. Beside me, Zayne stretched, craning his neck, and I knew the second I heard his swift curse under his breath. I *knew,* even though it didn't make sense.

Across from me, Stacey's brows shot up. "Um…"

I closed my eyes as I *felt* him stop beside the table.

"Fancy meeting you guys here," Roth said, and dark humor dripped from every word. "All together."

When I forced my eyes open, he was still there. He winked when he caught my gaze, and I wanted to do what that teacher had done this morning.

"Hey, Roth." Sam gave him a little wave. "You want to join us? There's more than enough room."

My mouth snapped open, but before I could say a word, Roth slid into the seat beside me. I stared at Stacey, who looked as though she needed a bucket of popcorn.

"How convenient that you find yourself here," Zayne replied. His arm was still draped along the back of the booth, but he leaned forward, dropping his other arm on the table. "With there being, I don't know, thousands of restaurants in the city."

Roth's lips curled up as he stretched out, folding his arms. Somehow, stuck between the two of them, the booth suddenly felt like a one-seater. "I guess I'm just lucky."

"The statistics of him accidentally ending up here are rather slim," Sam murmured to himself while Stacey slowly turned to him. "But it is right down the street from school, so that ups the probability."

My eyes widened. Oh no, save the baby pandas! I hadn't

told Zayne about Roth attending school. After Roth had been snared in the demon's trap and vanished, I hadn't seen the point.

"What does that have to do with anything?" Zayne asked.

No one at the table besides Roth knew any better and someone was about to blab it, so I jumped in, figuring it was better if it came from me. "Roth goes to our school."

Zayne's body locked up beside me.

I dared a peek at him. He was staring at Roth. "Is that so?" he murmured.

"You guys don't know each other?" Stacey asked.

The muscles along Zayne's forearm flickered. "We've met a time or two."

Roth smiled broadly. "Good times, too."

Oh God...

"You know he's a Warden, right?" Sam whispered, leaning forward. "I think we told you once at lunch, but I can't remember."

"Sam!" Stacey hissed.

He frowned. "What?"

"I don't know," she said, "but it seems rude to point that out."

"It's not rude." Roth's golden eyes twinkled with mischief. "I said before, I think it's epic."

Zayne smiled tightly as the hand on the table curled into a fist. "I bet you do."

I wanted to bang my head against the table.

"Oh, it is. You out there, helping fight crime and all that good stuff," he replied, and I swallowed a groan. "It's *amazing*. I bet you lay your little—er, not so little—head on your pillow every day feeling like a hero. Wait. Do you even sleep in beds? I've heard that Wardens—"

"Do you really need to be sitting here?" I interrupted, losing my patience. Goading Zayne wasn't going to help anything.

"Well, *someone* did ruin my lunch." Roth looked at me pointedly. "So I am hungry."

Sam grinned. "Yeah, you kind of do owe him a meal."

My shoulders slumped.

Zayne sat back, staring straight ahead.

"This just got real awkward," Stacey murmured, but her dark eyes glimmered with interest.

Not as awkward, surprisingly, as when I'd licked Zayne's thumb like...I didn't even know what. But dinner was painful. Roth and Zayne spent the whole time trading snide remarks, Sam and Stacey were too busy watching them as if each word they slung at one another was a tennis ball, and by the time I asked for a check, I was ready to throat punch someone.

Mainly myself.

Roth was currently asking Zayne how much he weighed, being that, according to Roth, Zayne was made out of stone. Meanwhile I stared over the back of the booth, praying our check would arrive pronto. When Sam returned from the restroom a second time, a patron at the tiny bar in the back of the restaurant fell off the stool. My eyes widened as Sam glanced over his shoulder and then looked at me, nose wrinkled. Damn, they were getting sloshed back there. Must be some good happy-hour specials.

"I weigh enough," Zayne replied. "What about you? Look about a buck and twenty soaking wet."

He snorted. "You might want to look again, or better yet, get your eyes checked. Do Wardens get degenerative eye diseases?"

I sighed as I scanned the mostly empty tables and rocked back and forth like a total mental patient. I'd already gone to the bathroom once but was considering hiding out in there until we left. The eatery didn't seem to get a lot of business, but it was right before the dinner rush. Zayne and Roth's out-snarking contest faded into background noise as my gaze slipped over an occupied table. Something drew my attention back to the two men sitting at one of those tables for two. Both were slightly older than me. I'd peg them as around Zayne's age. Both had brown hair cut in identical buzz cuts—like the kind cops or military guys wore. Their white dress shirts looked pressed, if not tucked in. From what I could see, they were wearing light-colored khakis. Obviously, there wasn't any kind of weird aura business since I couldn't see souls now, but something about them snagged my attention.

It might have had something to do with the fact that they were staring at our table, the unblinking stare of a psychopath that had you in his crosshairs.

I shivered as my gaze locked with Khaki Guy on the right. His expression was bland, cold even. A robot's.

Roth's hand landed on my thigh, causing me to jump. "What are you looking at, shortie?"

"Nothing." I went to remove his hand, but Zayne beat me to it.

"Hands off, buddy." He practically tossed Roth's hand back at him. "If you want to keep it attached to your body."

Roth inclined his head, his expression sharpening. Ruh-rohs. He opened his mouth, but the waitress finally arrived with the check and I snatched it up. "You guys ready?" I said to Stacey and Sam. They looked transfixed as they nodded. Zayne quickly took care of our tab and I all but pushed Roth out of the booth.

He bent low, his breath warm in my ear as Zayne slid out behind us. "Don't run off," he whispered. "The three of us need to talk."

Zayne's eyes narrowed and he slipped between Roth and

me, a huge barrier that caused Roth to grin like a cat that just spotted a mouse trapped in the corner of a room. I pretended I needed to use the restroom yet again to get Stacey and Sam to go ahead, giving us privacy. I figured whatever conversation we needed to have was better held here and not somewhere too remote where the two guys would likely try to kill one another.

As soon as Stacey and Sam dipped out the front, Roth took a seat where Stacey had sat, motioning us down. I sighed as I slid back into the booth. The little bit of spaghetti I did eat wasn't doing well in my belly as I hazarded a glance at the table from earlier. The two men were still there, watching us.

"You need to make this quick," Zayne said. "Because I'm not sure how much more of your presence I can stomach."

Roth faked a pout. "You're so mean, Stony. Perhaps you have something shoved up your ass that you need to remove?"

"Roth," I said, gripping the edge of the table. "Knock it off."

"He started it."

I gaped. "What? Are you guys two years old?"

He glanced at a stewing Zayne and that faint twinkle in his eyes was back. "Well, he does look like he shit himself and needs his diapers changed."

"That's it." Zayne started to rise, but I placed a hand on his arm.

"Just stop. Please?" When he blew out a breath and sat back down, I kept my hand on his arm just in case. "What do you want to talk about, Roth?"

Roth's gaze dropped to where my hand rested. "He didn't know we share classes."

I pulled my hand away, stiffening. "I never got around to telling him, and I seriously hope that's not why you wanted to talk."

He shrugged. "I just think it's interesting that you'd keep your best little stone friend in the world in the dark."

Zayne tapped his fingers along the table. "Get to the point, Roth."

Leaning back in the seat, he was the picture of lazy arrogance. "There's a reason why I'm here, other than the delicious lasagna. It's also the reason why I'm back at the school. Although I do find it amusingly normal, there's more." His gaze slid to me. "We think a Lilin was or is at the school."

"Details."

Roth explained what had happened today and then I went over the fight from earlier in the week. "I really didn't think about it until today. I was planning to tell you—"

"After dinner?" Zayne asked. "And that's when you were going to tell me about *that?*" He nodded in Roth's direction.

Roth snorted.

"Yes," I said. "I didn't want it to, you know..."

"Ruin the dinner?" He smiled at Roth. "That's understandable."

Roth rolled his eyes. "Anyway, the strange occurrences at school aren't the only reason. I think the Lilin will try to make contact with Layla," he continued, surprising the Hell out of me.

"What?" I demanded. "You didn't say that earlier."

He smiled at me. "You really weren't in that talkative of a mood."

That was true, but whatever. "Why do you think that?"

"The Lilin would be drawn to you," he explained quietly. "After all, you share the same blood."

I shuddered. My family tree was seriously screwed up. My father was a Warden who wanted me dead. My mother was a superdemon no one messed with and now there was a Lilin who could claim me as some sort of half sibling. Yay.

"Would the Lilin be dangerous to Layla?" Zayne asked, shoulders rising like he was about to scoop me up and take flight.

Roth shook his head. "I really don't know."

"That's not our biggest issue," I said, leaning forward. "If the Lilin has been messing with people at school, then that's already four people that we know of. What's going to happen to them?"

"I don't know if there's a way to stop them from losing their souls and turning into wraiths. There could be more than the four we know of. Hundreds that are...infected by it." Roth raised his brows. *Infected* was really a good way to look at it. "Really, there's no telling if the ones that are infected are the ones the Lilin is trying to take."

"Take where?" I asked.

Roth shrugged. "Remember, when Lilins create a wraith, they can control it. They are the only things that can. Think about the chaos. Not only is there a Lilin running around, but it's creating nasty, demented spirits that really do not like the living."

I had forgotten about that. Somehow. "The only way we'd know the Lilin's endgame is if..." I swallowed, unsettled. "Is if the ones at school die."

He nodded as his gaze shifted to Zayne. "So that's why I'm there and that's why I'm going to stay there. And I also think we need to do a little investigation."

I arched a brow and when he didn't continue, I sighed. "Details?"

"I think we can safely assume that Dean has been infected. We need to talk to him."

"He's been suspended for God knows how long," I pointed out.

Roth smiled slyly. "I'm pretty sure I can get his home address easily."

Not doubting that, I glanced at Zayne. He nodded slowly. "Maybe he can tell us something that points us in the direction we need to go."

"See?" Roth's eyes gleamed. "I'm necessary."

"I wouldn't go that far." Zayne met Roth's coolly amused stare. "But I'm promising you this, if you do anything that hurts Layla or even causes her to look at you strangely, I will personally destroy you."

My eyes popped out of my head. "Okay. Well, I think this little meet and greet is over." I nudged Zayne with my arm. "Let's go."

He held Roth's gaze for a moment longer and then rose. Turning to me, he offered his hand and I took it, letting him pull me up. There was no denying the fierce protective vibe he was giving off, but protector had always been Zayne's role.

"I never meant to hurt her in the first place."

We both turned to Roth, who was standing. I sucked in a soft gasp, but Zayne's lip curled up. "Whatever, man." He leaned over. While he was broader than Roth, he was not as tall, but he still got all up in his face. "You can play your little games with anyone else, but you're not going to pull that shit with her."

I squeezed Zayne's hand before an epic death match occurred. "Let's go."

A muscle flickered in Roth's jaw as we turned. I knew he was behind us and when I looked over my shoulder, I wasn't surprised to see him. But I was surprised to see the two Khaki Guys standing up. I frowned.

Roth's eyes narrowed and then he followed my gaze. His attention swung back to me, lips pressed in a tight line. It was as if he got what I was thinking—something was up with those dudes.

Outside, the streetlamps were coming on, casting light

across the rapidly darkening streets. Zayne's hand tightened around mine as we stepped around a cluster of people waiting for public transit. He sighed when he realized Roth was still with us. "Seriously? You gonna walk us to our car?"

"Actually, I think I am." Roth slowed his step, walking behind me. "We're being followed."

Under the brim of his cap, Zayne's eyes dilated as he looked over his shoulder. He turned back around, picking up pace. "Two human males?"

"Yep," Roth replied, popping his lips.

I wanted to look behind me so badly, but I figured that would be a bit too obvious. "Any idea who they are?"

"Nope. Maybe they want to get your phone number," Roth replied. "Be a part of your fan club."

He'd once said he'd be the president of my fan club, which was really stupid, but my heart twisted a little at the statement, because it meant nothing. I inhaled the crisp air. "What do we do?"

"Your car's in the parking garage, right?" he said to Zayne. When I cast him a questioning look over my shoulder, he winked. "I was following you two."

"Great." Zayne's hand slipped free of mine and landed on the small of my back. "So you're a demon *and* a stalker. Awesome."

"That's clever, Stony." Roth chuckled at the low growl emanating from Zayne. "Let's see if they follow us. What's the worst they could do? They're humans."

I didn't want to dwell on the fact that humans were capable of some pretty horrific things. I couldn't help it. I thought of the last time Roth and I were in a parking garage with those Rack demons that had wanted to play ball with our heads. Like with alleys, I didn't have a lot of positive experiences with parking structures.

We rounded the corner and my breath was forming little misty clouds. My nose was cold as I finally looked back, past Roth. Several people behind us, the two young men were there, the tails of their shirts flapping. A glint of something metal reflected off one of their waists, partly concealed by his shirt. My heart turned. "I think one of them has a gun."

"Christ," Zayne muttered.

Roth snickered. "If they try to mug us, I'm seriously going to laugh."

"Only you would laugh at that," I replied, wrinkling my nose. Mugging was not something I wanted to add to my list of messed-up things that happened this week.

"What?" he said as we reached the walk-in entrance of the parking garage. "They picked the wrong people if that's the case."

The garage was quiet and the overhead lights cast dull yellow beams over the hoods of the cars and spotted, stained cement. Not a damn thing about the place gave me that welcoming "nothing bad is about to go down in here" feeling.

At the first aisle of cars, footsteps echoed behind us. Roth drew up short as Zayne turned, moving to stand in front of me. He took off his cap and handed it over. I wondered what he expected me to do with his hat. Not get dirt on it?

One of the young men moved forward—not the one I'd seen with what I thought was a gun. Under the low light, his features looked swallowed, sunken in, as if he hadn't eaten a good meal in a while.

Roth crossed his arms, causing his shirt to stretch tight along the back of his shoulders. "What's up, home skillets?"

I rolled my eyes.

Khaki Guy in the front reached behind him, and my heart stopped. Roth's arms unfolded and Zayne started to drop into a crouch. The guy pulled out something black and rectangular—definitely not a gun. He lifted it in front of him like a shield, holding it in a white-knuckled grasp.

Roth laughed loudly and deeply. "You've got to be kidding me."

Khaki Guy held a Bible in his right hand. "We know what the three of you are," he said, voice steady as his gaze moved over Zayne to Roth, and then to where I was peering around Zayne. "God's mistake, a demon from Hell and something far worse."

CHAPTER TWELVE

My brows inched up my forehead. How in the Hell was I the worst thing out of the three of us? Not that I should be paying attention to that. It was a big deal that this human knew about Zayne, and even more shocking was he knew that Roth was a demon, considering the whole humans must be kept in the dark when it came to demons thing.

"I'm offended," I grumbled.

"The Whore should not speak in the presence of such holy text," the guy spat out.

"Excuse me?" I screeched, darting out from behind Zayne, who caught me around the waist. "Did you just call me a whore?"

The man held the Bible in my direction. "You are the daughter of one. Does that not make you the same?"

"Whoa." Roth stepped forward, hands closing into fists at his sides. "That's really impolite and kind of ironic, you know, using words like *whore* while holding a Bible."

"And that comes from a demon?" spat the other man. "You are the scourge of the Earth—a pestilence upon the people."

"I'd have to agree," Zayne muttered under his breath.

Bible Guy's wild gaze swung back to him. "And you—

you're no better. Masquerading as our protectors while consorting with our enemies. False prophets!"

"Church of God's Children," I said as realization sank in. Anger tasted like hot pepper on my tongue. Images of all those damn anti-Warden flyers that plastered electric poles danced in front of me. "You're the fanatics that have absolutely no idea about anything."

"We know more than you realize," Bible Guy announced proudly. He sneered as he looked at Roth. "We've always known of your existence, and it's our goal to reveal the Wardens for what they truly are."

"Curious," Roth murmured, shifting a foot closer. Bible Guy backed up as a little bit of his arrogance cracked like ice. "How do you know about us?"

"We have our ways," the other man answered. At his sides, his fingers twitched.

Zayne took a deep breath. "We're not demons. That's the furthest—"

"You're with a demon—two of them," he responded as he blinked several times. "Lies slip from your forked tongue."

Although I'd never been up close and personal with Zayne's tongue, I so knew it wasn't forked. "You don't know anything about the Wardens," I said, hoping to bring a dose of reality in their world. "If you did, you'd know they're helping mankind. That there is nothing to fear—"

"Shut up, whore of Satan."

My mouth dropped open and my head was about to spin *Exorcist*-style. I stepped forward as Roth cracked his neck, signaling he was ready to end this little conversation. "Call me that one more time and I'll give you something to fear." I had no idea where those words came from because, even with Zayne's training, I wasn't really a fighter, and I wasn't a badass, but my lips curved into a cold, tight smile. "That's a promise."

I felt Zayne's stare—the shock and uncertainty, because I doubted he'd ever heard me sound so threatening before, but rationalizing with fanatics was as fruitful as having a lobotomy. Twice. The simmering anger, the outrage brewing deep inside me fueled courage. Probably not the greatest combination, but I latched on to it. My skin tingled and the back of my throat burned. Bambi shifted on my skin, her tail flicking along my lower back. I bet their souls tasted like watered-down strawberry juice—tainted. "Is there a reason you followed us, other than to preach hypocritical nonsense?"

Bible Guy's cheeks flushed.

"I doubt it," I continued before he could speak. "I doubt there is a single intelligent thing either of you two have to say."

"Layla," Zayne warned softly, reaching my side.

"You should've been put down the moment you were birthed from the womb," Bible Guy said, and the sincerity in his voice was startling. "You're an atrocity."

Whatever control I had was stretched too taut and snapped like a rubber band pulled to its limits. I moved faster than I probably ever had. Shooting forward, I snatched the thick Bible out of the man's hands. Whipping my arm back, I swung it around and the sound of what had to be the most epic biblical bitch smack on Earth echoed through the garage.

Roth's surprised laugh shook me to the core. "Damn. That's getting served. In the biblical sense."

Shock buzzed through me like a thousand confused honeybees. As the man stumbled back, blood seeped out of the split in the corner of his mouth. He turned wild eyes on me as he raised a trembling hand to his mouth. My gaze dropped to the Bible I held. The edge of the top was darker—stained. Zayne's soft inhale rattled me and I dropped the Bible, expecting it to burn me.

It happened too fast.

The other guy lurched forward, his face a red mask of hate, contorted into something so ugly that it stole my breath. He reached under his shirt with his right hand, and I remembered seeing the glint of something metallic earlier. Roth cursed as the gun appeared in the man's hand, but instead of taking aim at me, he pointed it at Zayne.

"No!" I shouted.

Zayne whipped around, and my heart jumped in my throat. I launched myself at him as a popping sound exploded. Before I could reach his side, Zayne shifted. His shirt split down the center and dark gray skin appeared. Something whizzed past my shoulder and the bullet found its mark, striking Zayne in the chest. He stumbled back.

There was a blur of movement to my left as the scream froze in my throat. The silence was broken by a high-pitched yelp, followed by bones cracking, then this fleshy sound of skin giving. Bible Guy spun on his heel, taking off as if the very Devil was chasing after him. I didn't care. He could run.

I reached Zayne's side, placing my hand over his chest. He was staring down at himself, quickly shifting back to his human form, skin becoming pink. "Oh my God…"

"I'm okay," he said, but the words barely registered. Heart pumping, I ran my shaking hand over his chest, searching for the warmth and wetness of blood. I didn't stop until he grasped my wrist, pulling my hand away. "Layla, I'm okay. Look."

"How can you be okay?" My voice was thick with tears, edged with fear. "You were just shot in the chest."

He smiled when I lifted my gaze to his face. "Look. The bullet bounced off. I shifted in time. There's just a bruise. Nothing more."

"Bounced off?" When he nodded, I glanced down and saw the bullet lying on the cement. The rounded edge was flattened, as though it had smacked into something impenetrable, which it had. My brain was slow to process it, and I should've known from the beginning. Zayne had shifted. A bullet wouldn't breach a Warden's skin.

I launched myself at him, wrapping my arms around his neck and clinging to him like plastic wrap. My heart still pounded in a sickening way because, for a few horrific seconds, I'd believed that the bullet had struck true, and in human form, a Warden wouldn't survive a shot to the heart.

Zayne's laugh was shaky as he gently detached my arms from around his neck. "You're going to strangle me, Layla-bug."

"Sorry." I forced myself to step back. Trying to get control of myself, I turned around, drawing in a deep breath. It got stuck.

Roth was watching us, a distant look etched into his features, but it wasn't him that caught my attention, that doused me with a bucket of ice water. On the ground, a few feet behind Roth, was the man who'd shot Zayne.

Or what was left of him.

The man's right arm was twisted at an unnatural angle, like that of one of those creepy marionette puppets. Red stained the front of his white shirt and the gun...dear God, it was *in* the man's stomach, the handle sticking out. I tried to draw in another breath, but my lungs were seizing up.

He was still alive. I didn't know how, but his chest rose in quick, sharp and shallow breaths. His dark eyes were wide and darting from left to right. His fingers twitched on his good arm.

My feet moved of their own accord. I stopped short of the rapidly spreading pool of blood. He drew in another quick breath and when he opened his mouth, blood leaked out. "It's all...over.... We know what's happening...." His brown eyes lost their focus as the blood leaked from his mouth in a steady stream. "We know about the Lilin…."

The man shuddered once and then there was nothing—no final gurgle or deep breath. The ragged inhale just stopped as his life seeped out of him. Although he'd tried to shoot Zayne and most likely wanted to kill him—kill all of us—seeing a life extinguished—a human life—wasn't something I was okay with or even knew how to process.

I pressed my palm to my mouth as I stumbled back. A hand steadied me, but I couldn't look away from the young man. Within seconds, his skin paled, taking on the pallor of death. The life was gone so quickly. Over. Just like that. The man was dead and there was a good chance that it had been my fault. They might have walked away from this if I hadn't antagonized them.

"Oh God," I whispered.

Someone tugged me back and forced me around. Warm fingers pushed the hair off my cheeks as I strained to see the man on the floor. "Layla."

My eyes met amber-colored ones. Roth and I were so close—too close. His hands held me in place, spanning my cheeks, and his hips pressed against my stomach. "It had to happen. He was turning that gun on you and you wouldn't have shifted fast enough. And he would've killed you."

"I know." I did know that, but the guy was *dead*.

"And you need to stop looking at him. No good is going to come from that." His lashes lifted, stare fixing over my shoulder. "You need to get her out of here. I'll take care of the body."

I didn't want to know how he'd take care of it, and I wanted to not be such a wuss, so easily affected by a dead body, but my hands were shaking as his fingers slid off my cheeks. Roth's eyes met mine for a second more and then Zayne was there, steering me away from the gruesome sight.

As he led me back to the Impala, I glanced over my shoulder. Not at the body. The shadows seemed to have spread through the parking garage, becoming thicker and nearly tangible. We were only a few car lengths away, but Roth had already disappeared into the shadows.

"I'm sorry," I said, and I wasn't sure who I was saying it to, but silence was the only response.

The ride home was silent and while Zayne left to brief his father on the altercation with the guys from the Church of God's Children, I retreated to my room. I should've been present when he spoke to Abbot, but after last night, I doubted my being in the same room as him would help my current mood.

I was itchy in my own skin. Bambi kept moving around, trying to get comfortable. I wished she'd just go chill in the dollhouse, but she wasn't going anywhere.

Tugging my hair up in a messy knot, I paced the length of my room. Every time I closed my eyes, I saw the man on the dirty floor of the garage and heard his words. They knew—the church knew about the Lilin. How was beyond me. It was the same with Roth. How had they known about demons in general?

I rubbed my hands together as I passed the front of my bed again. I still couldn't believe I'd smacked the guy in the face with a Bible. That was terrible. Maybe not completely uncalled for, but my hand would've been a better choice. Then again, if I'd just kept my calm, maybe no one would've died. That was on my hands and I didn't even know why I'd done it. Yes, I'd been rocking the full-on rage face, but I wasn't typically the aggressor.

And I also didn't normally lick people's fingers.

It was something Roth would do—had done to me before. When he'd sucked off the crumbs from a sugar cookie.

Roth.

The twisty motion filled my chest.

Ugh.

Groaning, I stopped and sat on the edge of my bed, my back to the door. I'd forgotten about the whole "licking Zayne's finger" thing in light of watching someone die. It had been better that way. Flopping down, I stared up at the ceiling. Sometimes it felt as though some kind of foreign entity was invading my body. I scrubbed my hands down my face, feeling as if I needed a body cleanse.

A knock on my bedroom door forced me up. Twisting around, I cleared my throat. "Yeah?"

When the door opened and Danika appeared, my brows rose. She shifted her weight. "I was checking in—" pausing, she glanced over her shoulder "—on your arm?"

Damn. I'd forgotten about that, too. "It doesn't even hurt now."

"That's what I wanted to hear." She hesitated as she nibbled on her lower lip. "May I?" She gestured at the bed.

Okay. This was weird, but I'd had so much weird in my life recently, I was interested in seeing where this was heading. I crossed my legs. "Sure."

Her smile was tentative as she closed the door and sailed across the room, sitting beside me. For someone as tall as she was, you'd think she'd be less graceful. Nope. The girl walked on water and the water probably liked it. "Do you mind if I take a look at your arm?"

"Nope." I reached down and tugged off my sweater. Underneath I wore a tank, which gave her perfect access. The cut on my arm was nothing more than a pink mark. The skin was puckered and that would probably never change, but it was better than dying. "The stitches fell out this morning."

"Looks perfect." She raised her gaze as she tucked back a strand of dark hair. A moment passed while I expected her to get up, but she remained. "I heard what happened with those church members."

I looked away, wondering if Zayne had told his father I'd sort of instigated the violence. "Yeah."

"Abbot's worried," she said softly. "He doesn't understand how they knew what that...Roth was or about the Lilin." There was a pause as she hooked one incredibly long leg over the other. "That's not a problem he really wants to worry about right now. But I guess when it rains, it pours, huh?"

More like when it rained there was a massive hurricane. "Yep."

Danika fiddled with a silver bracelet around her wrist. "I'm not sure if you've heard or not, but we're not going back to New York. Not with the Lilin issue. Abbot wants all the manpower he can get."

Woo. I could barely contain my excitement.

"And with Tomas still missing, Dez and the guys are pretty confident something happened to him."

I stiffened, absently rubbing the spot on my chest where Bambi's head was resting.

Her eyes widened. "I promised you and Zayne that I wouldn't say anything and I won't," she insisted, her eyes as blue and bright as Zayne's. "No one even thinks you or... what is it called?"

"Bambi," I said. "I didn't name her that, by the way."

Her brows knitted. "No one thinks you or Bambi had a thing to do with that."

"That's good to know." My gaze fixed on the closed door. This was really...awkward. I was half-tempted to go find Jasmine and let her daughter chew on my toe. "Is Zayne still with Abbot?"

"Yeah. All the males are piled into the room together. No one really knows how to handle the church people without making it worse, but…I don't think that's what Zayne's most concerned with."

"No?" I asked.

She shook her head when I looked at her. "He's not really happy about…Roth being at your school. Neither is Abbot."

"Obviously." I sighed, unfolding my legs. My feet didn't even touch the floor. I was a troll sitting next to her. "He's a demon, so of course they're pissed."

"I doubt that's the only reason Zayne's not happy about Roth being at school with you."

I frowned. "What other reason could there be?"

Her brows rose as she stared at me. "You really don't know?" When I shook my head, she chuckled softly. There was a sad tinge to the sound. "Sometimes, Layla, you are so unaware that I want to pull your hair out."

I choked on a laugh. "What?"

Danika didn't answer immediately and then took a deep breath. "Okay. Let's be real with one another. You don't like me."

My mouth opened and I felt my cheeks heat. I was about to deny it, but the look she sent me said there was no reason to. "Well…this is really awkward."

"Yep." She nodded, slim shoulders rising. "Everyone in the clan—both our clans—expects Zayne and me to mate, and I wouldn't turn down that offer. I think you know that I…like Zayne."

"I'd say *like* wasn't a strong enough word."

She smiled at that. "He's…well, you know what he is. I also

know that you like him and *like* probably isn't a strong enough word for you either."

I didn't say anything, because this was a conversation I really wanted no part of.

"Anyway, since I'm going to be here for a while, I wanted to clear the air between us. I like you, Layla." She shrugged. "I hope we can be friends, and I don't want you to worry about me and Zayne."

Part of me wanted to say that I wasn't, but, apparently, I was as transparent as a window. Taking a deep breath, I decided I needed to woman up. "I know I haven't always been…uh, welcoming to you and you've been nothing but nice to me. And I'm sorry for that." Wow. That was probably the most mature string of words I'd ever said to Danika. I deserved a hand-size cookie. "I've accepted that you and Zayne will end up together." And *those* words were a bitter pill, but one I needed to swallow. "You guys are perfect for one another. Both of you are gorgeous and you're really nice and smart. And I know Zayne—"

"Stop," she said, holding up a hand. "Zayne does like me and I agree. We'd be perfect together, but that's not ever going to happen."

I stared at her, confused. "Why not?"

"Because he doesn't want me. He's not in love with me and it's obvious to everyone but you," she said, and her gaze lowered. Thick lashes hid her eyes. "Zayne wants *you*. And he's in love with *you*."

CHAPTER THIRTEEN

I was starting to regret ever letting Danika near my arm with a needle—clearly there was a good chance she was on crack.

Zayne wanted me? He loved me? Sure, I knew that Zayne cared deeply for me, but *in* love with me? That was a whole different ballpark.

I couldn't believe that, not when there were so many reasons why he wouldn't be in love with me—couldn't be. Besides the fact that everyone in his clan expected Zayne to mate with Danika or another suitable Warden to produce little gargoyle babies, he couldn't even kiss me. Yeah, that didn't mean he couldn't get close to me and we…couldn't do *other* things, but it was too dangerous.

Thinking about those things that didn't involve our lips touching kept me up most of Saturday night. Even with my limited experience when it came to those other *things,* my vast imagination was giving me lots of ideas. Ideas that involved hands and fingers and other body parts…

Oh dear.

I flopped onto my stomach and groaned into my pillow. I hadn't seen much of Zayne throughout the day and it might've been because I'd been avoiding him, but after what Danika said—and even though I really didn't believe her—there was a good chance I'd start giggling like a hyena if left alone with him.

And that was ridiculous.

I was ridiculous.

But the idea of experiencing any of those things with Zayne left my head spinning and caused my pulse to pound throughout my body. Trying to get comfortable, I curled my leg up, but it didn't help. I pushed off the blankets, kicking them down to the foot of the bed, but my skin still felt too tight, as if there was no room between my bones and my flesh.

I rolled onto my back. Placing my hand against my stomach, I wasn't surprised to find that the skin felt warm, and then a little knot formed, leaving me frustrated...and confused. My thoughts were all tangled together, because when I felt this low burn sloshing through my veins, I also thought of Roth and everything we'd shared. And when I thought about Zayne that way, I felt as though I was doing something wrong, which was stupid, because as Roth had made abundantly clear, there was nothing between us.

Too hot and too wound up to sleep, I slipped out of bed around three in the morning. Pulling on a pair of fuzzy knee-high socks that actually reached my thighs, I grabbed a heavy sweater and pulled it on over my tank top and sleep shorts.

Hair a mess and a walking fashion disaster, I crept out of my bedroom and headed downstairs. At this time of night, most of the house would be dead. Jasmine and Danika would either be asleep or off somewhere with the twins. Only Geoff would be around, monitoring cameras, and outside there'd be guards just in case something crazy happened. For the most part, I'd have the house to myself.

The cool air soothed some of the heat as I hurried down

the stairs, the edges of my unbuttoned sweater flapping out behind me like fluttering wings.

My sock-covered feet were silent as I padded into the kitchen and grabbed a small bottle of OJ. I started to close the fridge door when I reached back in and grabbed what was left of the sugar-cookie dough.

Taking my goodies and holding them close, I started toward the living areas but veered off in the direction of the library. Using my hip, I nudged the heavy wooden door open. I dropped the dough and OJ on the desk and then turned on the old-fashioned lamp. A soft glow filled the large room.

I breathed in deeply, inhaling the musky scent of old books. I'd spent many nights and days in this library when I was younger and as I scanned the numerous rows of books, I found that I'd read almost all of them. There'd been a lot of lonely days and nights. Still were.

Breaking off a chunk of dough, I shuffled around the desk and started perusing the spines, not looking for anything in particular, but as I was somewhere between bored-enough-to-read and I'd-rather-lie-in-bed-frustrated, something snagged my attention.

Methods and Practices of Herbs and Their Impact on Demons and Wardens.

Not exactly light bedtime reading or the kind of book you'd find in a human library, but I thought about the vial I'd seen Abbot carrying and my curiosity got the best of me. Tugging it out, I turned and placed it on the desk as I munched on my raw dough. Most of the book was handwritten, herbs listed in alphabetical order and accompanied with drawings.

Not even ten minutes later, the space behind my eyes started to ache. There were way too many herbs in the world and too many that were ingredients in milky-white potions.

I lifted my gaze as I grabbed my OJ and took a drink, loving the way it tingled down my throat. An idea took form. Not a smart one, but an intriguing one.

Abbot was out for the night as were most of the Wardens. Geoff was somewhere, so that was a risk, but…I was bored and curious.

The study that Abbot occupied was right down the hall. I could access it through the door in the library. It opened up into a small sitting room no one ever used and through that room I could get into his office without using the hall, which would likely be monitored. But the sitting room? Probably not.

Setting the OJ down, I hurried around the desk, my feet slipping along the hardwood floors. I burst through the door to the sitting room, relieved to find it empty and dark, and before I gave myself time to chicken out, I tried the knob on Abbot's door.

It was unlocked.

I held my breath as I turned the knob. The door creaked like old bones as I pushed it open. There was a lamp on his desk with a green ceramic shade, which cast a small swath of light over the desk and the floor.

The room smelled like Abbot—of soap, the outdoors and a faint trace of the cigars he toyed with. A ball formed in my throat as I crept toward his large oak desk. I could count on one hand how many times the Warden had hugged me, but when he had, his hugs were always warm and wonderful.

I missed them.

Swallowing down the lump, I decided to attack the desk first. There were a lot of places where he could've stashed what I was looking for—the shelves along the back walls, the cases that were surely locked and a dozen little cubbies here and there.

The first couple of drawers had nothing in them that interested me—papers and correspondences from the police and government, emails from other clan leaders. The second drawer was filled with pens, the kind that made me all grabby hands, and the third had more sticky notes than God needed.

Fourth drawer—the bottom drawer—was where I hit the jackpot. Literally.

Cushioned in a thick, dark towel, dozens of small vials rolled around harmlessly as I pulled the drawer out as far as I could. Kneeling down, I picked up one that looked like it had grapefruit juice in it and then placed it back down, carefully poking around until I found the one that looked familiar. I lifted the vial gingerly, watching the milky liquid slosh around as I stood.

Turning the vial over, I frowned as I read the scribble along the bottom. "Bloodroot?"

"What are you doing?"

I squeaked and almost dropped the vial. Spinning around, I clutched it to my chest as I breathed out a sigh of relief. "Zayne."

He stood in the doorway I'd snuck through, dressed in dark pants and a black shirt. Even though it was quite chilly outside, a full-blooded Warden's body temperature ran higher than humans' or even mine. He folded his arms and arched a brow.

"You scared the crap out of me." Heart pounding, all I could think about was the vial in my hand. Zayne wouldn't understand why I was sneaking around in Abbot's office, no matter how harmless it was. When he only stared at me, I tried a diversion as I lowered my hands. "What are you doing back so early?"

"What are you doing in my father's study?"

I wrinkled my nose. "Nothing."

"Nothing?"

Hands now hidden behind the desk, I slid the vial down my palm. I'd either have to drop it and pray to the Dalai Lama that it didn't break, or pretend to faint and put it back. Neither of those options filled me with any confidence. "Nope."

"Uh-huh."

My cheeks started to heat, and I was glad for the room's dim lighting. "You didn't tell me why you're back so early."

"And you haven't told me what you're really doing in here."

I shifted my weight, preparing to drop the vial back into the drawer I'd found it in. All I needed was the name and I'd gotten that. "I couldn't sleep so I was— Ack!"

Zayne moved incredibly fast, seeming to disappear from just inside the door only to reappear right in front of me. Before I could drop the vial, he wrapped his hand around my wrist.

"What is this?" he asked as he lifted my arm.

My fingers tightened around the vial. "Uh…"

He cocked his head to the side and sighed. "Layla."

I tried to pull free, but when that didn't work, I equaled and then topped his sigh with my own. "Fine. I saw Abbot with this vial a few days ago, and I wanted to know what it was. So that's what I was looking for."

"At three in the morning?"

"I couldn't sleep and I was down in the library when the idea occurred to me." I tugged on my arm again. "I wasn't in here photocopying Warden secrets or killing babies. Look." I wiggled my fingers until he could see the vial's handwritten label. "I'm not lying."

His gaze flicked down and he frowned. "Bloodroot?"

"You know what it is?" If so, happy me, because it would be so much better having him just explain it than going through that dusty book again.

"Yes." He let go of my arm and snatched it out of my fingers quickly, like a cat. "You shouldn't be messing with that stuff."

"Why?"

Very carefully, he placed the vial back in the drawer and eased it shut. Standing, he cast me a long look. "Come on."

Stubbornly, my feet sank into the floor. "Tell me what you know."

Zayne rounded the desk and kept going. "Layla, come on before someone else comes back, sees you in here and freaks out."

He had a point, and while I was feeling this childish urge to argue, I ignored it and followed him back into the library. Slipping past him, I made a beeline for the desk while he closed the door behind him.

My eyes widened as I spotted the OJ, the book and the… the empty cookie dough wrapper. I whirled on Zayne. "You ate my cookie dough!"

A small grin tipped his lips up. "Maybe."

I heaved out a sigh as I grabbed the bottle of OJ. "That's so wrong."

He sauntered over to the desk and placed his palms on the edge, leaning in so that we were at eye level. "I'll get a new pack for you in the morning."

"You should," I said, sounding grumpy and peevish. And I was feeling those things because he was close, and all I could think about was what Danika had said and all those dirty things I'd been thinking about that drove me from my bed. I pushed away from the desk.

A brow went up as he watched me cross the room. "You're in a lovely mood."

I shrugged as I eyed him over the bottle. Plopping down on the couch partially hidden by the shadows, I set my OJ on the end table. "You going to tell me about the bloodroot?"

"It's a herb."

I picked up a pillow and placed it in my lap. "That much I figured."

"It's actually pretty dangerous." He followed me over to the couch, sat and kicked off his boots and socks. Leaning back against the other arm, he stretched out the best he could, which meant he left me the tiny space I was occupying. "It doesn't have much of an effect on demons, other than making them sleepy. But it can kill a human and knock out and paralyze a Warden for a while."

My heart skipped a beat. "Why would Abbot have something like that?"

"I don't know. The bottle looked ancient. So did a lot of those bottles in there. He might have saved it for a Warden who gets out of hand. Like with Elijah back…" He trailed off, lowering his gaze.

I stiffened a little as my fingers tightened around the throw pillow. It was the first time Zayne has used my father's name—my absentee father. The Warden who'd slept with Lilith, and who, after discovering he'd fathered a child, had tried to have said child killed. Multiple times. That would be me. Abbot had stopped him when I was young and I could see how blood-root might've come in handy then.

"Anyway," Zayne said, watching me. "I came home early because there wasn't much going on. And I ran into Roth."

A twisty motion seized my stomach. "You did?"

He nodded. "He was doing his nightly stalking duties, I guess. Found me down by Foggy Bottom and wanted to know how Abbot took the whole Church of God's Children crap."

I schooled my features into blankness. Roth could've easily texted or called me to find that out. Then again, I'm not sure why I'd expect that from him. "Good to see that you two didn't physically harm one another."

"I wouldn't say it was the most pleasant conversation." Zayne shifted on the couch beside me, nudging my thigh with his foot. I looked at him, brows raised. "What's your deal?" he asked, brushing the flop of blond hair off his forehead.

Holding my pillow closer, I shook my head. "Nothing."

He leaned against the arm of the couch, lazily clasping the back of his neck with his hand. The muscles under his thin shirt bunched with the movement. "Something's bothering you."

Sometimes I really hated that Zayne could read me so well. That when he looked at me, like he was now, I felt as though he could discover all my secrets with his stare alone. But that didn't mean I was up for caring and sharing time.

Zayne sighed. "You avoided me all day today."

"Did not."

"Did, too." He closed his eyes, giving a lopsided shrug. "Something is up with you."

Twirling a long strand of hair around my finger, I made a face at Zayne even though he couldn't see it. "I wasn't avoiding you." Totally a lie. "That's just your insecurity talking."

One eye popped open. "Excuse me?"

"You heard me," I said, trying to hide my smile. "I wasn't ignoring you. I've been very busy today."

The other eye opened as he lowered his arm, draping it on the back of the couch. I had his full attention now. "You didn't do crap today but hang out in your room and stare at Izzy as she tried to bite your feet."

My eyes narrowed.

"Why couldn't you sleep?"

I continued to twist my hair into one giant rope. "I just couldn't."

A couple of moments of silence passed. "I'm actually glad you're up. There's something I want to talk to you about. It has to do with Roth." He said the name as if it were some new STD.

"Do we really need to talk about him?"

"Yes." He frowned. "Stop messing with your hair."

My fingers stilled and I dropped my hand, returning his frown. "What about Roth?"

"I don't trust him. Not just because he's a demon, but because of what…well, what he may or may not mean to you." His eyes still hadn't left my face. "He's… It doesn't matter. I know you're going to see him at school, but I don't want you running off with him alone."

My gaze sharpened on him. The frustration from earlier was back, prickling my skin and causing Bambi to get twitchy. "Yeah, because that's exactly what I was planning to do."

"Look, I'm not saying that you would, but I know you're going to want to find out more about the Lilin and I don't want you alone with him."

I opened my mouth.

"Only because I don't want to see you hurt more," he added, and what could I really say to that. Could it be more than that, though? God knew what Roth and Zayne had said to each other, and now that Zayne knew the full extent of what had gone down with Roth, I could only guess what he was thinking.

From underneath my lashes, I watched him stretch fluidly, like a cat with a full belly. Zayne was super protective of me, but that didn't mean he was jealous or that he was in love with me.

"Besides there's another reason why I came home early," he drawled lazily. "I was sure you missed me."

"Not likely." I tossed the small pillow at his head. He plucked it from the air a second before it smacked him in the face. "Not at all."

He flipped the pillow behind his neck, eyeing me. "Terrible liar." He couldn't know how closely his words echoed Roth's, and I wasn't about to tell him.

"I'm not lying."

His lips twitched as if he wished to smile. "Uh-huh."

I leaned forward, knocking his legs off the couch. They thumped against the floor. He kicked them back up.

"Don't be a brat, Layla-bug."

Looking away, I dragged in a deep breath, uneasy with the restlessness I was feeling. "Don't call me that. I'm not a little girl anymore."

"Believe me, I know you aren't."

I twisted toward him, about to say something snarky, but the words were stolen from my tongue. He wasn't joking. Holy crap, he was being serious. And *that* look—the way his eyes were hooded and lips parted—spoke of something I wasn't used to, but had seen on him the day he'd walked into my bedroom when I was undressing.

We stared at each other in silence. Nothing and everything changed between us in an instant. Thick tension hung in the air, settling over me like a too-warm blanket. His eyes glittered like sapphire jewels in the dim light, eliciting a shiver even though I felt flushed again.

He pushed up a little, and again, I thought of what Danika had said.

I wanted to bail.

And that's what I did. Coming quickly to my feet, I smoothed my hands over my hair, hoping he didn't notice how they trembled. "All this talking has tired me out. I'm going to bed. Good night."

Zayne cocked an eyebrow at me and remained on the couch.

I practically ran from the room and up the stairs. What in the Hell had just happened in there? I didn't know, but I recognized the heavy, breathless feeling in my chest. It had to be the lack of sleep and my overactive imagination.

Once in my room, I stripped off the cardigan and socks, forcing my mind to go blank. It wasn't easy. As I pulled back the covers, my bedroom door swung open, causing me to squeak.

Zayne walked through the door, still barefoot as he folded his arms across his chest. What if I'd been naked? My cheeks turned a deep crimson at the realization that the thin tank didn't hide much.

Struggling not to fold my arms over my breasts, I held myself still. "What do you want now?"

"Nothing." He stalked over to my bed and dropped down, stretching out his long frame. He patted the spot next to him. "Come here."

"Zayne...?" I shifted uncomfortably, wanting to both flee the room and jump in the bed beside him. "You're being annoying tonight."

"You're annoying every night." He patted the bed again, a lock of hair falling over his eyes. "Stop acting so weird, Layla."

How was I the one acting weird? Okay. Maybe I was being a little antsy. Him taking up my bed like he owned it wasn't anything new. Hell, he'd slept in it a few nights ago.

But everything seemed different after what Danika had said.

"You coming?" he murmured, watching me. Taking a deep breath, I climbed into bed. He eased down on his side, his leg brushing mine. "Nice shorts."

Of course he'd notice my Hello Kitty shorts. "Can you not talk?"

He chuckled. "You're in such a mood tonight. Was it the sugar-cookie dough?"

I rolled onto my side, facing him. There was little space between us and I closed my mouth, but the strangest thing happened when our eyes met. My breath caught as I stared at the face I knew like the back of my hand. I could close my eyes and still know every one of his expressions, except the one he wore right now. This one was something new, totally uncharted.

And it was scary—so incredibly terrifying, because I had never seriously considered Zayne returning any of my less than normal feelings for him. It was frightening because of what I *wanted* to do to him—what I *could* do to him. There was more—there was Roth and the stupid, irrational feeling that I was doing something wrong. He'd virtually sacrificed himself for me…and then told me that nothing he'd ever said or done mattered when it came to me.

Rolling onto my back, I stared up at the ceiling. My chest rose and fell in short, uneven breaths. The scent of him invaded my senses. My fingers rested against my stomach, opening and closing.

"What's going on, Layla-bug?" he asked.

"Nothing," I whispered.

"Bullshit." Zayne shifted suddenly, levering up with one arm so quickly that the air left my lungs in a harsh rush. He stared down at me, lips parted as if he was about to speak, but he seemed to lose track of what he was going to say. That was okay. I had no idea what we were talking about either.

There was barely an inch or two separating our bodies. We were so close that the edges of his hair brushed my cheeks. His gaze dipped to the neckline of my tank top. It was pulled low, revealing more than I should've been comfortable with. Bambi's head was resting on the swell of my right breast. Again.

"She really likes putting her head there, doesn't she?" Zayne's voice was rough.

"I guess it's soft for her." The moment those words came

out of my mouth I wanted to kick myself in my soft boob. "God," I groaned. "Sometimes I need to—"

Zayne placed a finger on my chin, silencing me. That slight touch packed a punch of sensations—hunger, need, a yearning so intense that it rattled me to the core. "That would make sense." Pausing, he swallowed as his gaze traced the detail of the demonic tattoo. "I bet it is a…soft place."

This conversation was…whoa. Really no words.

"Why do you keep this necklace?" he asked, lightly fingering the chain.

It was a struggle to speak. "I…I don't know."

His features tightened for a moment and then he seemed to let whatever he was feeling go. The truth about why I kept the necklace had nothing to do with my mother, but then his hand moved, trailing his finger down the center of my throat, over the rise of my collarbone and then straight to where Bambi rested, stopping a mere inch from her head.

Oh my God.

My heart fluttered so fast in my chest it was like a hummingbird about to take flight. A heaviness settled in my chest, the pressure demanding yet pleasant. Then his finger moved again, gliding across the edge of Bambi's head.

She moved slightly, turning into the touch like a pet seeking more comfort. I dragged in a breath as I wet my bottom lip. Should I be more shocked that he was touching me so intimately or that he was touching Bambi? Or that Bambi wasn't peeling off my skin and trying to eat him? It really didn't matter because every nerve ending in my body was tingling.

He traced the delicate scales around Bambi's nostrils, and when I shivered, his gaze lifted, snaring mine. There was so much heat and intensity in those cobalt eyes that there was no mistaking how he was looking at me.

Like he had the night he'd seen me in my bra.

One side of his lips tipped up, and my heart jumped in my chest. His gaze returned to where Bambi rested, to where his finger was idly tracing her scales in smooth strokes. "It doesn't feel like I thought it would. The skin is just slightly raised, but it's really like a tattoo."

Mouth dry, I closed my eyes as his finger moved over her head, nearing the tiny lace that decorated the hem of my tank top. I wasn't wearing anything under the tank and he was so, so close.

"Does she like it?" he asked, breath warm in the space between our lips.

I nodded, assuming she did, because she wasn't trying to kill him.

"Do you?"

The question whipped through me with the force of a destructive hurricane. My eyes snapped open and my breath came in short little pants. He was still so close, his hair tickling my cheeks and his finger trailing farther south, following the curve of Bambi, under the lace of my tank top.

His lashes swept up again and his gaze collided with mine. I had no idea how we'd ended up here. His hand stilled and he waited, and there was no denying the driving force behind the question. If I said no, he would move away. And if I said yes, then... I couldn't even wrap my head around those possibilities.

If I said yes, everything would change—change in ways I couldn't even fathom, ways I never truly believed could happen between us. My heart was beating too fast, and a strange kind of heat pooled deep in my body.

"Yes." The word came out barely a whisper, but Zayne heard it.

He inhaled sharply as he moved his hand to the thin strap

of my tank top. His eyes never left mine. "Can I see the rest of her?"

My heart rate kicked into cardiac territory. Was I dreaming? Did I fall down the stairs and crack my head open? Seemed more likely than this happening. Seeing the rest of Bambi meant seeing the rest of *me*. Or at least half of the rest of me.

I opened my mouth, but nothing came out. My gaze focused on the outline of his mouth, fixating on the way his lips parted, and I couldn't help but wonder how they felt—how they tasted.

Only in the distant part of my mind did I realize that I wanted to taste him and not his soul.

Bambi flicked her tail along my waist, as if she was impatient with all of this and wanted to be shown off. Unable to find the courage to speak, I nodded again.

Zayne's feverish gaze lowered as he slipped the strap down. The top was so loose and thin that it took the littlest effort to move. Within seconds, the straps ended up on my wrists, the material pooling where my hands were clasped together on my stomach.

I felt his stare as he drank in the detail of Bambi and everything else—every part of me that was exposed. It was like a caress as his gaze tracked over the long, elegant stretch of her neck between my breasts, to the way she coiled just below my rib cage.

"Layla," he rasped, and the sound curled my toes.

I stopped breathing as his hand followed Bambi's path, and the yearning and hunger I was feeling rose until every part of my body felt like a live wire. Everything outside this room ceased to exist—every problem, concern or issue. It was all gone as his hand moved again and my back arched off the bed. A breathy sound escaped me, mingling with Zayne's ragged breath.

His touch was light, reverent as he explored the layout of my body. He did so with such delicacy it was as though it was his first time, though I knew—at least I thought—that that couldn't be the case. With his looks and his personality, there had to have been times when he was out hunting—there had to have been girls.

But it didn't matter as he shifted down, his head lowering close to where Bambi's head rested. There was a good chance this could go horribly wrong, but my hands fisted together and I bit down on my lip so hard a metallic taste filled my mouth at the first whispered touched of his lips against—

The bedroom door swung open, slamming into the wall with a force that rattled the room like a clap of thunder. Zayne sprung off me and onto the floor in seconds. He whirled around and I sat up, tugging up my shirt with my heart in my throat. We were so busted, and we were going to be in so much trouble.

But when I lifted my gaze, there was no one in the doorway, nothing behind the door except the long, dark hall and all the shadows of the night.

Zayne crossed the room, grasping the edge of the door as he peered out into the hallway. As he straightened and closed the door, he shook his head. "Nothing's here."

I shivered as a cold, almost icy breeze wafted over my skin. I glanced around the room, seeing nothing abnormal. "That's..." I cleared my throat. "That's weird."

He thrust his fingers through his hair—fingers that had just been touching me. He turned back to me, his chest rising and falling heavily. He started to take a step toward me, but halted. The way he looked at me...my entire body flushed. "I...I should probably leave."

I didn't want him to. I wanted him to come back to me, but it wouldn't be smart and the most intelligent thing would be to let him walk away from this room. Tugging the blanket up, I force myself to nod.

Zayne stared at me a moment longer and then swallowed hard before he turned and quietly slipped out of the room. I stayed where I was as the cold reality of the situation came back. No matter how I felt for him or him for me, pursuing anything with Zayne was dangerous.

And it could never be.

CHAPTER FOURTEEN

"I knew it!"

I stared at Stacey as she peered into the tiny mirror attached to her locker door and combed her fingers through her bangs. The need to talk to someone about what went down with Zayne had led me to practically tackle Stacey first thing Monday morning. I'd told her everything as quietly and as quickly as possible, starting with Danika and ending with all the bared-chested goodness. Minus the tattoo part.

"How did you know it?"

She passed me a knowing look. "Well, the way he treated Roth, it was pretty obvious that the guy isn't into you being with anyone else."

I stepped out of the way of a girl hurrying down the hall. "He just doesn't like Roth."

Stacey rolled her eyes. "And it makes sense why he'd finally make a move. He's got competition."

My lips formed an O. I hadn't really thought of it that way. Could it be that Zayne was finally seeing me as something other than the little girl hiding in the closet because of Roth? Or had he always seen me differently and was acting upon it now that he thought someone else was in the picture?

I told myself it didn't matter because we couldn't be together. Abbot would stroke out and we couldn't even kiss, but still, it occupied my thoughts as we started toward biology.

"It shouldn't be so hard for you to believe that Zayne is attracted to you. You're a really pretty girl, Layla. The kind that guys—"

"Don't say the kind that guys want to be in their pockets, because that's just weird."

Stacey laughed as she bumped me with her hip. "Okay. I'm just saying that this thing with Zayne isn't rocket science. It's not as if Danika is setting you up or something and Zayne—" she lowered her voice "—he *touched* you in a totally nonplatonic manner. It's simple. Go for it."

Go for it.

I shook my head even as my heart started pounding. "It's complicated."

"No, it's not." Stopping in front of the bio door, her eyes widened. "I have the most perfect idea ever in the history of ideas."

I arched a brow. Coming from Stacey, that was kind of scary and probably involved the potential for jail time. "What?"

"You know how you totally set up Sam and me for the movies over Thanksgiving break?" Her eyes glimmered with excitement. "You should invite Zayne and make it clear—a movie date."

"Movie date?" drawled a deep voice. We turned to see Roth smirking down at us. "How cute. Who's going to be paying for popcorn?"

Irritation pricked at my skin as I stared into his mocking amber eyes. The fact that I hadn't noticed that he was near was testament to how discombobulated I was. Heck, I was so out of it that I was using words like *discombobulated*. "Eavesdropping is rude."

He shrugged a shoulder. "Blocking the door to class is also rude."

"Whatever." I turned, ready to usher Stacey inside, when he stopped me.

"Actually, I want to borrow you for a second," he said, glancing at Stacey, who was in the process of giving him a very scary evil eye. "If that's okay with you?"

Stacey folded her arms. "I doubt she wants to be borrowed by you."

"Truest thing ever spoken," I said, smiling tightly.

"I think she'll change her mind." Roth stared at me meaningfully. "It's *important*."

Which meant Lilin or demon or Warden or something else I really didn't want to deal with. I sighed as I stepped to the side. Stacey gaped at me, and I winced. "It's okay."

She narrowed her eyes at Roth. "Don't make me hate you more."

Roth's brows rose as she stalked into bio class. "What did you tell her about me?"

I shrugged. "Actually, I didn't tell her much of anything. She must've put two and two together all on her own and come up with you being a jerk face."

His gaze slid back to me and he grinned. "Ouch, shortie."

"Yeah, like that really bothered you." I glanced back through the small window in the door that led to bio. Mr. Tucker was already at his desk—was Mrs. Cleo ever coming back?—and we only had a minute, tops, before the tardy bell rang. "What did you want?"

Reaching into his pocket, he pulled out a thin slip of yellow paper, waving it in my face. "Guess what I found?"

"Obviously not a better personality," I remarked.

"Ha. Funny." He brushed the edge of the paper across my

nose and smiled when I smacked it away. "I got Dean's home address."

"Oh. Wow. That was quick."

"It was."

I didn't want to ask how he'd gotten it. I was sure it involved him waltzing into the main office and doing something unsavory. I reached for the address, but he snatched his hand away. I frowned. "I need the address so Zayne and I can go check it out."

"You and Stony?" Roth laughed as he slipped the paper back in his pocket.

My eyes narrowed. "Yes."

"You think you're going to have fun without me? Think again. We're going to have a threesome." He grinned wickedly when I rolled my eyes. "Today. After school. You and your gargoyle boy toy can meet me outside."

I wanted to say no, but he winked at me and patted his pocket as he turned and headed into bio.

This should be real fun.

From the moment Roth climbed into the back of the Impala, I knew that this little impromptu trip would end badly. Even if the two of them could agree that we all needed to work together, no one was going to make it easy.

It wasn't as if they were expected to join hands and sing "Kumbaya" together.

It was already awkward between Zayne and me. Adding Roth into the mix just made it about ten times more painful. If Zayne thought I'd been ignoring him on Saturday, there was no doubt that I had been Sunday. I didn't know how to even look at him without every square inch of my body blushing.

"We have about three more blocks to go. He lives in one of those old brownstones," Roth said, an arm resting on the back of each of our seats. "But that is if you could, I don't know, drive at a speed that doesn't take us the rest of the *year* to get there."

"Shut up," Zayne replied.

"Just saying," he went on. "I'm pretty sure the kid Dean pile-drived into the floor with a punch can walk faster than we're driving."

"Shut up," I said.

I caught his narrowed gaze in the rearview mirror and smiled widely at him. He sat back, a petulant pinch taking over his features. Roth remained quiet the rest of the trip. Zayne found the brownstone and we were able to squeeze into a parking space a few doors down.

Brown and golden leaves swayed softly in the breeze as we made our way down the sidewalk. The steps leading up to the stoop were weathered and cracked, as was the facade of the brownstone.

Zayne stepped around Roth and picked up the iron knocker, ignoring the disgruntled look the prince sent his way.

"Knock it off," I murmured to Roth as the door opened.

An older woman appeared. Her thick red hair was pulled back, but several shorter curls were sticking up all around the crown of her head. Fine lines surrounded her brown eyes and pale pink lips. She looked tired, haggard really, and as her gaze moved between Zayne to Roth and then back again, she smoothed a hand over her gray cable-knit sweater.

"Can…can I help you?" she asked, finally settling weary eyes on me.

"Yes. We're…um, friends of Dean's and we wanted to see if we could talk to him for a few moments," I told her.

She folded her hands over the edges of the sweater, tugging them close to her body. "Dean is not able to see anyone right now. I'm sorry, but you'll have to come back when he's not grounded for life."

"See, that's problematic for us," Roth replied smoothly as he edged Zayne out of the way. The moment Mrs. McDaniel locked eyes with Roth, the strained lines of her face relaxed. When he spoke again, his voice was as smooth as chocolate syrup. "We need to talk to Dean. Now."

Zayne stiffened as he glanced at Roth, but he didn't say anything, because unless we were planning on bum-rushing the house, a little demonic persuasion was needed.

And it worked.

Nodding slowly, she stepped aside and when she spoke, her voice was soft and reedy. "He's upstairs. The second bedroom to the left. Would you like something to drink? Cookies?"

Roth opened his mouth, but I stepped forward. "No. That won't be necessary."

His face fell.

Mrs. McDaniel nodded once more and then turned, drifting off through a doorway, humming "Paradise City" under her breath.

My stomach landed somewhere near my knees at the familiar tune. I hadn't heard Roth humming since he'd been back, and for a moment, all I could do was stare at him.

"I really would've liked a cookie," Roth muttered, taking the stairs two at a time.

Zayne rolled his eyes. "Too bad."

Snapping out of it, I followed the boys up the stairs. The hall was narrow and dimly lit. Old beige wallpaper peeled along the white molding. As we neared the second door on the left, a feeling of unease curled along my spine and an odd pressure circled my neck, choking. There was a heaviness to the air, like a suffocating wool blanket on a steamy summer day. I glanced over at Zayne and saw that by his tense shoulders, he was feeling it, too.

The feeling was that of evil, pure evil. There was no other way to describe it.

When Roth opened the door without even bothering to knock, the feeling increased. The Warden part of me was itchy to get away from this stink or to eliminate it, but the demon part? It was curious.

Both guys stopped in front of me, blocking my view of the room. I had to peer around Zayne to see anything. The room was one giant contradiction. Half of it was tidy. Books stacked neatly, papers tucked away in binders that looked as though someone had gone a little crazy with a label maker. A small stool sat before a telescope pointed toward the window. The other side of the room looked as if a hurricane had whipped through. Clothing was strewn across the floor. Half-eaten cartons of Chinese were thrown haphazardly in a moon chair. A pile of Mountain Dew bottles nearly reached the edges of the bed.

And on the bed was Dean McDaniel.

He was lying on his back, wearing only his plain socks and blue boxers. Headphones covered his ears and his feet moved to a beat we couldn't hear.

Dean was aware of us. His heavy-lidded gaze slid toward us and then back to the ceiling, outright dismissing our presence. I followed his stare and I gasped.

There were…holy crap, drawings in marker—circles with stars through them. Lines joining to form shapes I'd seen in the *Lesser Key of Solomon*.

Roth eyed the ceiling for a moment and then strolled over to the bed. He whipped the headphones right off Dean's head. "Ignoring us is rude."

The boy on the bed—the boy who'd always been quiet and

had held doors open for other students—smirked as he folded his arms behind his head. "Do I look like I care?"

"Do I look like I won't rip your head off your shoulders?" replied Roth.

"Whoa," I said, shooting him a look. "That's not helping."

Dean looked over at me and sat up. He reached down between his legs and did something that made my ears burn. "You're more than welcome to stay in here, honey. These two tools can hit the road, though."

My mouth dropped open. "Okay. Commence with ripping the head off."

Roth smirked.

"We've never met before." Zayne stepped toward the edge of the bed, apparently trying to be the voice of reason. "My name is—"

"I know what you are." Dean flopped on his back. *Magnam de cælo, et tu super despectus.*"

"And now he speaks Latin?" This was going nowhere fast. "What did he say?"

Roth chuckled. "Something that won't make Stony happy."

"And I know why you guys are here. You ain't getting shit from me. So you know where the door is." He looked at me. "But like I said, you—"

"Finish that sentence, and you'll be limping for the rest of your life," I warned, and Zayne smiled. As I stared at Dean, I tried to see the quiet boy from class, but he leered back at me like a forty-five-year-old man who'd had too much to drink. "Are you still in there, Dean?"

"I think we know the answer to that," Roth said, kneeling down beside the bed. Dean turned his attention to him. "Whatever piece of humanity is left in him, I sure as Hell don't see it."

I couldn't believe that. The thought of this boy slowly being stripped of his soul sickened me. Maybe it hit too close to home. I wasn't sure, but I didn't want to believe it was hopeless. I stepped around Zayne. "Do you know who did this to you?"

Dean was still for a moment and then he sprang from the bed, so fast that he was nothing but a blur for a moment. I wasn't sure if he was heading for me or not, but Zayne intercepted him, catching the boy by the shoulder. One hard shove and Dean hit the bed on his ass. "Try that again and you're not going to like what happens."

Dean drew in a ragged breath and then a great shudder rolled through him, shaking his slight frame. He lay on his side, tucking his knees under his chin. His entire body quaked as if someone was shaking the bed.

"It's constant," he said, raising his hands to cover his ears.

My pulse kicked up. "What's constant?"

"*It*. I hear *it* all the time." His fingers curled into his hair. "It never stops. It never gives me a break."

"What is it?" Zayne asked.

The boy's face scrunched up and his cheeks paled. "*It* doesn't stop."

"I think he's in pain." I looked to Zayne for help. "What can we do?"

Zayne's brows rose. "He's not possessed. You can tell by looking at his eyes."

"What's wrong with him is that he's missing a good chunk of his soul and that probably feels like a gunshot wound." Shaking his head, Roth rose fluidly. "Dean, we need you to tell us what happened to you."

"I don't understand," he moaned.

He was still rocking in a way that made me want to gather him up and hold him, despite his earlier behavior. Roth asked him the question again and then Zayne repeated it. Neither of them got a coherent response.

I edged closer to the bed. "When did it start, Dean?"

Dean didn't respond at first and then, "Days and days ago."

Roth glanced at me and nodded for me to continue. "Where did it start? School?"

"Yeah," Dean croaked. "It started there."

Zayne moved back, coming to stand beside me. "Did someone make it start?" I asked.

Dean's rocking slowed as he lowered his hands, revealing a bleak stare. I shifted my weight, uncomfortable as he continued to stare in my direction. He looked at me as if I should already have known, but that didn't make any sense to me.

When he didn't answer, Roth placed a hand on his bare shoulder. Dean jerked on the bed as if he'd been branded with a hot poker. His mouth dropped open and he howled loudly, like a wounded animal.

"What did you do?" demanded Zayne.

Roth snagged his hand back. "I didn't do crap."

I turned as the bedroom door opened. His mom came in, obviously out of whatever trance Roth had placed her in. "What are you all doing? What have you done to my son?"

"Shit," Roth muttered as he stalked to Dean's mother. Clasping her cheeks, he cut off her tirade of questions. "Shh, it's okay. Your son's fine."

Mrs. McDaniel trembled. "No he's not," she whispered, the broken sound tugging at my heart. "He's a good boy, but he's not okay. He's not okay at all."

"We're here to help him," I said, relieved to find that Dean had stopped howling.

Roth stiffened, but he kept his gaze locked on her. "Everything is fine. You just need to go downstairs and start dinner. Chili dogs would be great."

After a tense moment, Mrs. McDaniel pulled away and left the room, once again humming Roth's song. Letting out the breath I was holding, I turned back to Dean. He was holding his headphones.

"Dean—"

"Get out," he said, and when we didn't move, he lifted his gaze and a cold chill skated over my skin. There was something empty in his stare. "Get out."

Zayne held his ground. "We need—"

"Get out!" Dean was on his feet and he cocked back his arm, throwing the headphones straight at Roth's head. "Get out!"

Roth's hand snapped out, catching the headphones before they smacked his nose. The plastic was crushed in his grip and then tossed to the floor. "I seriously hate it when people throw things at my face."

The boy didn't seem to care. He whirled on Zayne and charged him. Zayne must've seen something in his stare because he shifted. The shirt ripped right across from back and chest. Granite skin replaced human flesh. Wings unfurled, seeming to take up the whole room. Zayne caught Dean and spun him around, curling a massive bicep under his neck.

Dean went crazy—kicking and clawing at the air as he wailed a steady stream of Latin.

"Show off," Roth said, rolling his eyes. "Like you needed to shift."

Zayne ignored him as the muscles in his arms flexed under Dean's neck, cutting off the inhuman sound emanating from the boy. Quickly, Dean settled down, his arms and legs going lax. He was down for the count.

Shifting back into his human form after carefully placing Dean on the bed, Zayne glanced down at his tattered shirt. "Sorry, but I don't think we were going to get much out of him after that."

"We didn't get much out of him anyway," Roth responded,

lip curling as he stared at the unconscious boy. "All he did was confirm that he came into contact with the Lilin at school."

"That's something, right?" I said.

Neither of the guys responded. As we left the McDaniels' residence, I couldn't help but feel a little defeated. I didn't know what I'd expected from coming here, but I hadn't thought I'd see Dean like that. None of us seemed to have a clue as to what Dean could be hearing.

Once we were inside the Impala, Roth leaned forward and tapped my shoulder. "You shouldn't have said what you did up there."

I caught Zayne's frown as I twisted toward Roth. "What do you mean?"

"When you told his mom we could help him," he said, an oddly serious glint to his amber eyes. "You shouldn't have said that."

My stomach took a little tumble. "Why?"

"I don't think we can help him. At all."

CHAPTER FIFTEEN

"I have an idea."

When Roth spoke those words at the beginning of Tuesday's bio class, I was immediately prepared for any amount of cray-cray, especially after our visit with Dean.

"Okay?"

"Since we didn't get anywhere with Dean yesterday, I've been thinking." He lowered his head and spoke quietly. "No one's really checked out the old gymnasium, have they?"

"Not since that night as far as I know. So?"

His eyes shone brightly. "Who knows what kind of evidence we'd find down there since it was where the Lilin was kind of born. Doesn't hurt to check it out. Thought you'd be interested in scoping it out at lunch."

I opened my mouth, but snapped it shut. This was exactly what Zayne had asked me not to do. Granted, checking out the gymnasium in the bowels of school wasn't exactly running off with Roth.

"I know you don't want to sit around and let us take care of it," he cajoled, tilting his head to the side. "At least, the Layla I remember was more of a get-involved kind of gal, not someone who'd rather sit by the sidelines."

My eyes narrowed. "I know what you're doing. You're goading me into going with you."

"Is it working?"

I sighed. "Yes."

"Perfect," he replied, twisting toward the bio door. He held it open for me. "It's a *date*."

When he laughed, I knew there was a good chance I was going to kill him and stash his body behind the bleachers.

Instead of going to lunch like a normal person, I left my bag in my locker and headed in the opposite direction. I'd spent the vast majority of the morning telling myself I wasn't doing anything wrong, and as soon as I saw Zayne after school I'd tell him that we'd checked out the gymnasium.

The hall was empty and the conversations behind closed doors muted. Overhead, the red-and-gold banner rippled softly as the heat kicked on. As I passed the computer lab, the door opened and Gareth stumbled out.

His legs and brain seemed to not be connected. He staggered to the side, leaning into a locker. Bending at the waist, his chin dipped to his chest.

I stopped, biting my lower lip. By no means were Gareth and I friends, and I'd been shocked that he'd even known my name when he'd invited me to watch football practice not long ago. According to Stacey, Gareth probably knew my bra size, which creeped me out a bit.

His body shuddered as he dragged in a deep breath.

But he was in trouble—perhaps the Lilin kind of trouble.

Taking a quick breath, I walked over to him. "Gareth? Are you okay?"

Gareth folded an arm across his waist and when he didn't answer, I touched his shoulder lightly. He jerked up, knocking my hand off his shoulder. Bloodshot eyes met mine.

I took a step back, shaken. Like with Dean, behind the red veins and hazel irises, there was something empty in there. Something gone.

"What are you staring at, freak?" he asked, and then laughed. "Freak-a-deek-a-deek…" he mumbled, giggling as he shuffled slowly off toward the cafeteria.

Good God…

Hurrying to the stairwell, I leaned against the wall down there and lifted my head as I heard the door above me open. A second later, the space that was empty in front of me was filled with six-and-then-some feet of Roth. Gasping, I jerked back.

"God! Why do you do that?" I pressed my hand to my chest. "You could've just used the stairs."

He grinned as he rocked back on the heels of his sneakers. "What fun is there in that?"

"I don't care. Stop popping in and out."

"You're just jealous you can't do that because you're not a hundred percent, full-blooded awesome demon like me."

I rolled my eyes, but there was a little part of me that was envious of that ability. God knows it would come in handy every time I found myself in a situation I wanted to pop myself out of.

Ignoring the comment, I focused on the important. "I think Gareth is infected."

"Can't say I'm too torn up over that prospect."

My eyes narrowed.

"What? Like I said before, Gareth and his daddy are well on their way to spending an eternity clawing out their eyes or some messed-up crap like that."

"Gareth may be a crappy person, but he doesn't deserve to lose his soul." When Roth looked unfazed by the statement, I sighed. "Does human life mean nothing to you?"

"I'm a demon," he replied. "Should it?"

I knew better. His words may be cold and brash, but I *knew* Roth was more than just a demon. I wasn't going to start that conversation again, though. I headed down the final flight of stairs. I didn't want to hang around in the stairwell with him and end up poking memories loose. He followed behind me, quiet as a ghost.

"The door is locked," I said, motioning toward the chain wrapped around the handle. "You can break it?"

Stepping forward, he grinned devilishly over his shoulder. "Easily."

All it took was for him to put two hands on the chain and pull. The metal gave way with a clank. The ease with which he broke the chain gave me pause. Roth was dangerous, something I couldn't afford to forget.

Musty, cold air seeped into the hallway as he pushed the heavy door open. Stepping into the abysmal darkness, he searched for a light switch while he hummed softly under his breath.

Pressure clamped around my heart, squeezing it dry as I realized he was humming "Paradise City." The song made my chest achy, and I wished I could plug my ears.

Roth found a switch, and a low whirr reverberated through the room. A few large dome lights flickered along the ceiling before clicking on. The light was dull and it took a few seconds for my eyes to adjust.

He'd already moved forward, heading for the area near the hoopless basketball pole. All the occult and satanic stuff had long since been removed, but there was an evilness that still lingered in the cold, dank gymnasium. The place gave me the creeps.

Wrapping my arms around myself, I trailed after Roth, noticing where the Rack demons' claws had scored thin slices into the flooring. There had been many of them that night.

The area where I'd been tied down was scorched black from the fire that had claimed Roth and Paimon. Lifting my gaze, I stared at Roth's back, wondering if being here made him feel anything.

He knelt, running his hand along the floor, brushing aside dirt and dust. "So...you and Stony?"

Sighing, I edged around him and the faint white line that marked where the pentagram had been drawn. Scanning the area, it wasn't hard to see myself there. Chilled, I took a deep breath.

"You guys doing a movie date?" he asked, undeterred by my silence.

I crouched down near where my arms would've been tied. Burnt, frayed rope remained, lying forgotten. "I'm not talking to you about Zayne."

"Why not?"

Compressing my lips, I lifted my gaze and met his. He arched a brow, and I shook my head. Returning my attention to the floor, I surveyed it intensely.

"You and Stony have been getting close, I imagine," he continued, straightening. "Getting food together. Maybe going to the movies..."

"We live together, Roth. Going out and grabbing food isn't that unusual."

He made a clicking sound with his tongue bolt against his teeth. "Ah, but it's more than that, isn't it? Especially from the way Stony warned me off you—twice now."

"Twice?" I ran my fingers over the floor.

"Once at the restaurant, which you were there for," he said, his voice close. When I looked over my shoulder, he was standing behind me. I hadn't even heard him move. "And then Saturday night. We ran into each other."

"I know." I turned back to the floor, ignoring the shiver of awareness that came from how close he was.

"Oh, so he told you?" Roth scooped up a handful of my hair, gently tugging my head back. I narrowed my gaze as I snatched my hair free. He grinned at me. "Did he tell you what he said to me?"

"I really don't want to know."

Roth knelt beside me, so close his thigh pressed into mine. "He said that I needed to stay away from you."

"Really," I murmured.

"Yes." His breath danced over my cheek, and I stiffened. "And he also told me that you don't belong to me."

My chin jerked toward him, and I found that we were face-to-face. "Well, the last time I checked, I don't."

The smile kicked up a notch. "And do you know what else he said?"

"If you tell me, will you drop the subject?"

He dipped his chin. "Sure."

I didn't believe it for one second. Leaning back, I forced myself to hold his gaze. "What, Roth?"

"He said that you—" he tapped the edge of my nose "—belong to him."

My mouth dropped open as I stared at him. "I don't be-lieve you."

He shrugged his shoulders.

"Something like that would never come out of his mouth." Frustration spread across me like a heat rash. "Ever."

Roth's lips pursed. "You can believe me or not, but I no-tice you're not denying it."

My first inclination had been to deny it, but as we con-tinued to stare at each other, anger took hold. "Why are we even talking about this?"

"Just curious." He rose fluidly, rubbing a hand across his

Pink Floyd shirt. "I just think it's...*great* how quickly you've moved on."

I blinked once and then twice, thinking I hadn't heard him right, and when I realized I had, I wanted to slam my fist between his legs. "Are you serious?"

Roth's brows knitted. "Do I look like I'm not serious?"

"You think it's great that I moved on so fast. Right? From what?" I came to my feet. "What exactly am I moving on from? According to you, whatever we had didn't matter and never would. All I was good for was easing your boredom, remember?"

"I apologized for saying that," he countered, eyes flashing a bright yellow. "Do you want me to apologize again?"

"No!" I stepped forward, breathing heavily. "Let me ask you a question. Do you want to be with me, Roth?"

His pupils dilated as he took a step back. "What?"

"Answer the question."

He backed up again, away from me, his chest rising deeply. "It's not about what I want."

"Whatever, Roth." Stalking forward, I shoved my finger into his chest. "I liked you—really liked you and when you were gone and I thought you were being tortured in a fiery pit, it *hurt* me."

"Layla—"

"I know we were never really together, but I hardly ate or slept after you left, and the only person who kept me from going crazy was Zayne and you knew that! You even said that was why you took his place. Then you come back and *you* tell me that everything between us never meant a damn thing to you. You even threw Zayne in my face, basically telling me to get with him and now you're saying it's *great* I moved on so fast. Well, you can go fu—"

"Layla."

"What?" I shrieked.

His eyes brightened into golden pools. "You're sexy when you're pissed off."

I gaped and reacted without thinking. Making a shrill sound, I slammed my hands into his hard chest. Caught off guard, he stumbled back. "You are so freaking annoying."

Roth tipped his head back, laughing loudly. When he finally settled down, the grin was slow to slip off his face. "But on a serious note, if I did want you…" He was suddenly *right* in front of me and his fingers spanned the sides of my face. The slight touch rooted me to where I stood. So much pent-up frustration exploded like a cannon blast, rocking me. "If I did want you, would you still want him?"

I stared at him for a moment and then jerked away, breaking the contact between us. That question…well, it pissed me off and it also floored me, because how could I answer that? I *couldn't*. It wasn't a fair question, because I never really got to have Roth and I'd known Zayne practically my whole life. When it came to the two of them, everything was tangled up.

"That's so wrong to ask," I whispered, my voice shaking. "Cruel, even."

A fierce and stormy emotion flickered across his face and then was gone as quickly as it appeared.

Disgusted with him and myself, I refocused, returning my attention to the floor, and found what I was searching for. The quarter-size hole. The edges were jagged, as if acid had burned straight through the floor. Kind of disturbing considering it was my blood that had done that.

"There's nothing up here." Roth looked around, brows raised. "Except for the stink of lost dreams and wasted potential."

I frowned at that. "But what about down below?"

His gaze dropped to me. "Good girl. That's where we need to head."

"I'm not a dog," I grumbled, standing as I wiped my hands on my jeans. "Why didn't you just suggest that in the beginning?"

Roth didn't reply as he strode off, walking toward one of the side doors. I fantasized about drop-kicking him in his head as I followed behind him. Neither of us spoke as we entered another old, forgotten stairwell that led into an ancient, outdated locker room.

The scent of mold and something…*crusty* assaulted me. I didn't even want to breathe the combination in. Though different from the rank stench of a zombie, this smell was every bit as nauseating.

He found another light switch and only a handful of fluorescent lights kicked on. Row after row of gray, lonely looking lockers greeted us. Half the benches were broken or rotted out and odd shadows were cast upon the lockers, but as Roth neared them, he groaned.

"Slime," he said, lip curling in distaste.

I neared one of the benches. A gunky white substance ran down the metal legs. Across the board, the matter dripped onto the floor, thick and slow like honey or syrup. I swallowed. "Is this ectoplasm?"

"Yeah, and a whole lot of it." Roth sidestepped quickly, almost planting his boots in the puddle of grossness. "I think we're onto something."

"Really?" I murmured drily.

He snorted. "It's amazing that no one at the school has seen this." Scanning the slime-covered walls, he laughed without humor. "It would be kind of hard to explain."

"No one has any reason to come down here." I moved forward, careful not to step on anything that might be considered sticky. "What does all of this mean?"

Roth blew out a low breath. "Really don't know. There are a few critters that leave behind ectoplasm. Nothing that should be in a high school."

Walking forward, I tried to get an idea of where the blood dripping down from the ritual would have landed on this floor of the building. After a few seconds, I realized it would have landed somewhere in the vicinity of the showers.

I eyed the doorway that led to them. The light in there flickered sporadically. Steeling my shoulders, I forced my feet to move and cautiously entered the open showers. Most of the faucets and showerheads had been torn from the wall, leaving behind gaping holes. More gunk dripped out, sliding down the wall.

This...this was really gross.

"The smell is definitely worse in here...oh, and there's your reason." Roth placed a hand on my back, and I turned toward what he was staring at.

"Holy moly," I said, eyes bugging.

At the back of the shower stalls, a mess of...*something* hung from the ceiling by thick whitish-gray tendrils that reminded me of a spiderweb. Except it would have to be a spider on steroids to spin something that massive. From the strings was a wrecked cocoon, its white carcass split open down the middle. The pod was hollowed out, the color of faded newspaper with a dark, oily substance splattered throughout.

It looked like something straight out of a science-fiction movie.

Lifting my gaze, I realized the web would be approximately where the hole in the floor above was—where I'd been tied down and that drop of blood had hit the floor.

"That's what my blood is capable of?" I asked.

"I'm guessing it is under certain circumstances." Roth walked forward. "Pretty cool if you think about it."

I wrinkled my nose. "There is nothing cool about my blood creating a pod that looks like something straight out of *Alien*."

"Great movie, by the way. Not the sequels, though." When I groaned, he sent me a wicked grin over his shoulder that, in spite of everything, made my tummy flop. "Obviously, this is where our whittle baby Lilin grew."

"From a pod?"

He nodded. "No one knows a lot about the Lilin. How it matures, what it looks like or anything like that. But what else could this be?"

"There has to be something out there that can tell us." I didn't walk closer because being in the room with this thing was bad enough. "What about the Seer?" I asked, thinking of the kid we'd met before who communed with Xbox and angels...or something.

Roth chortled. "This time, I think it'll take more than a Perdue chicken before he gives us that kind of information."

"Then what does he want?" Frustrated, I shifted my weight. "We don't know anything. Again. And all this little field trip proves is that my blood had the ability to create a gross-ass pod."

He turned, head cocked to the side. "What it does prove is that the Lilin came from here—that the Lilin *was* here, shortie."

I raised my hands. "Didn't we already know that?"

There wasn't a response as he turned back to the cocoon. "*This* has to be proof of the Lilin, because I don't know—"

"Who's in here?" A voice boomed throughout the shower, whipping me around. "Who's down here?"

My eyes widened as I whirled back toward Roth, who shrugged. Real helpful there. Before I could even decide what to do, a shadow fell across the wide doorway and my breath caught as a man stepped into the room.

He was middle-aged with coppery hair and a smattering of freckles. I didn't recognize him, but the dark blue uniform and ring of keys around his belt gave him away. He was a janitor.

As his gaze flicked behind me, I felt Roth move close. Without looking, I knew when he'd walked to my side it was with pure, predatory grace that would make any human or nonhuman wary.

The janitor folded his arms across his chest.

Roth dropped his arm over my shoulders and hauled me up against his side. I stiffened as he slid his hand up my back, balling his fist in my hair. "We were looking for a private place… you know, so we could be alone." He dipped his head to mine, sending raven-colored locks across his forehead. "Then we saw all of this and kind of got distracted by the weirdness. Isn't that right, baby?"

My jaw ached from how hard I was squeezing it. What Roth was doing was totally unnecessary. I'd seen him get in people's heads and send them scurrying in the other direction with a few well-placed words. Hadn't he just done exactly that with Mrs. McDaniel? Touching me wasn't needed.

But since he'd started this game…

I slipped my arm around his waist, digging my fingers into his side. When a low rumble of warning radiated from his chest, I smiled brightly. "Yes. So right, *honey*."

The janitor snorted. "Yeah. Okay."

Not exactly the response I expected. I started to pull away, but Roth's hold tightened. As the janitor unfolded his arms, I finally saw a name stitched onto the front flap of a wide pocket. Gerald Young.

"No need to make up stories." Rolling up his sleeve, he revealed a tattoo in black ink—four loops joined by a small circle. It reminded me of a pinwheel, and something about it was vaguely familiar. When he looked back up at us, his eyes were the color of warm cherries. "It's about time someone checked out the mess down here."

Roth sucked in a breath and muttered, "Witch."

CHAPTER SIXTEEN

Witch.

I gaped at the janitor. If my ability hadn't gone all wonky, I might've known that something was different about him because the auras of witches—real, honest-to-goodness witches—had to be different. Because a real witch was capable of some really rad things—spells, healing charms, creating fire from air and general badassery that made me envious of, well, all that badassery. But I'd never seen a witch before. The likelihood of seeing one in this day and age had to be equal to winning the mega-jackpot lottery or actually spotting the Loch Ness monster.

"You're really a witch?" I said, sounding kind of stupid. "I thought most of your kind had died off." Like during the Middle Ages...

A wry smile formed on Gerald's lips. "We're still kicking." Rolling down his sleeve, his gaze shifted to Roth. "But we're careful."

"Understandable," replied Roth. He finally removed his arm, and I put about a foot of space between us. "Wardens have never looked too kindly on witches, now have they?"

I frowned, and it intensified when Gerald nodded and said, "No, sir."

"Why?" There wasn't much known about witches. Or at least I hadn't put the effort into discovering more about them.

"Witches aren't rocking all-human DNA." Roth eyed Gerald with a measure of respect. "Although they don't claim their other half, witches have demonic blood in them."

My head swung toward him sharply. "What?"

Roth nodded. "Witches are the offspring of demons and humans, shortie. Not that they're exceptionally proud of that little fact. Sometimes they're first generation, and other times, they had a demon in the family somewhere way back. The blood might not be as strong, but it's there. How else do you think they get such awesome magical abilities?"

I blinked rapidly. "Did not know that."

"How about you?" Roth leaned forward. "Gerald? Are you first generation or was it a great-grandpappy dipping the quill where he wasn't supposed to?"

I thought it was strange that Roth didn't automatically know what Gerald was with all his awesome demon greatness.

Gerald must've read my mind, because his grin went up a notch. "Demons can't sense us. We have charms preventing that, because we really aren't on Team Demon. More like Team Mother Earth, but to answer your question, it was a grandmother—a Fiend. Had a child who was a witch. That witch was my mom."

Roth rocked back as he folded his arms across his chest. "Cool. Anyway. Back to the whatever this is." He jerked his head toward the creepy cocoon. "I'm assuming you realize that ain't normal?"

He laughed drily. "Far from it. I've been keeping an eye on it since I found it—about two and a half, three weeks ago."

His gaze landed on me, and my shoulders slumped. "Not sure what it is. No one in my coven knows either, but that's not all."

"It's not?" murmured Roth. "Oh, goody."

"Nope." He turned. "Follow me."

I glanced at Roth and he nodded. Deciding to see this through, I followed Gerald back into the main room. It was a little odd that Gerald knew what we were—what I was. It shouldn't make me feel weird, but I'd always had the upper hand before when it came to sniffing out the not-so-normal.

Gerald stepped around the slime coating a bench and stopped in front of a closed locker. "All this ectoplasm can't be good, right? At first I thought it had to do with that thing in there, but I'm not so sure now."

Roth stepped forward, straining his neck. "Why not?"

"Easier to just show you." Stepping to the side, he reached into his back pocket and pulled out a red hanky. Using it, he carefully and very slowly opened the door.

"Hell," muttered Roth.

Being incredibly short, I couldn't see around either of them. Sighing, I moved to Roth's other side and immediately wished I hadn't.

Crammed into the locker was a *thing*—a creature I'd never seen before. Its body was the color of spoiled milk—off white and sort of lumpy looking. No visible hair or definition on its slender and tall frame. Looked to be about six feet tall and no wider than two feet. Arms were folded across its chest and its head was bowed down. No facial features at all. We'd found the source of the slime. The gunky white liquid dripped from barely formed feet.

My stomach turned. "What in the Hell is that?"

"Good question." Gerald closed the door quietly. "It's not the only one. Almost every locker down here has one in it."

"Oh…" My eyes widened. "And you didn't think about saying something?"

"To who?" Gerald turned to us, eyes sharp. "The Wardens would likely kill us on the spot for the blood we carry and demons would likely kill us for sport. And I have no idea what these things are. Neither does anyone in our coven. We're not about indiscriminately killing things."

"Tree huggers," muttered Roth, which earned him a hard glare. "What's in that locker isn't Santa Claus or the damn Easter Bunny."

A shiver danced down my spine. I had a really bad feeling about this.

"And maybe if you knew what that cocoon was, then you'd understand that this—" Roth continued, waving his hand at the lockers "—isn't something you want infesting a school full of humans."

Gerald's shoulders stiffened.

"That cocoon is from a Lilin being birthed."

When those words left his mouth, the blood drained from Gerald's face and he looked faint. "The Lilin?"

"You know of the Lilin?" I asked, jumping on that. "Any specifics?"

He nodded eagerly. "Some of the covens, the more extreme ones—not ours, but others—believed that Lilith got the crappy end of the deal. That she is the mother of us all."

I arched a brow at that.

"We don't worship Lilith—not us, but…" He glanced back through the doorway leading to the shower stalls. "A Lilin here?"

"We believe so. For obvious reasons, we'd like to find it." Roth's eyes narrowed. "But what, Gerald? You were going to say something else."

He swallowed, suddenly nervous. "There is a coven near Bethesda that worships Lilith. If anyone knows of a Lilin…"

"Or if a Lilin has sought refuge…" My heart jumped with excitement. "It'd go to them, because maybe they'd sympathize with it."

Gerald started to sweat. "But you don't understand. They aren't like me or like my coven."

I glanced at Roth and he smiled, flashing a row of white teeth. "In other words, they're the wicked witches of the west."

"Yes, and I know what you're thinking—about going to them. I wouldn't advise it. They'd welcome *him*." He nodded at Roth. "But you? You're part Warden. I can tell. They'd skin you alive."

I started to tell him that I was also Lilith's daughter, so they should totally love and hug me, but Roth shot me a look of warning. "How would we find this coven?"

He inhaled deeply. "They have a club near the Row Cinema. You'll know which one by the symbol." Gerald pointed at the mark his sleeve now concealed. "Who you need to speak to—their crone—will be there during the next full moon. And don't even think about bringing a Warden in with you guys. She'll be bad enough."

Roth's lips curled up in a delicious smirk as he turned golden, dancing eyes on me. "That's perfect."

Grrreat.

"But back to those things in the lockers?" All serious-faced again, Roth pinned Gerald with a hard look. "They're Nightcrawlers in metamorphosis, and I hate to think how many of them might be ripe."

My stomach dropped as horror punched straight through my stomach. Nightcrawlers, like Hellions and Rack demons, were demonic creatures that were created in Hell and forbidden to be topside. Besides the obvious fact they didn't look human by a long shot, they were extraordinarily dangerous. Like Hellions, they were strong and ferocious, but even worse was the venom they carried in their saliva, which could paralyze their victims.

So that the Nightcrawler could feed on them while alive. That's what they did down below, torturing their prey for an eternity in Hell.

And they weren't biters like Poser demons were. They had this impressive projectile-spitting thing going on, like those creepy little dinosaurs in the *Jurassic Park* movies. If their saliva got on your skin, stuff went downhill fast.

Gerald glanced over his shoulder. "I didn't know. None of us knew what these things were."

"Obviously," Roth muttered. "We need to seal this area off and—"

A loud crash startled us. Spinning around, my breath caught as I sought out the source of the noise. The sound had echoed, making it difficult to determine where it was coming from.

"Could anyone else be down here?" I asked, already fearing the answer.

"No." Gerald wiped the back of his hand across his forehead. "No one comes down here. I only did by accident when I discovered this."

Roth frowned at the sound of metal creaking, a *tick-tacking* of old hinges. A shudder worked its way through me. There was a beat of silence, and then the sound of heavy, even footfalls.

"You got any superspecial witch powers we should be aware of?" Roth asked.

Gerald shook his head. "I'm just good with charms and spells—like love and fortune stuff."

Love spells? That perked my interest for some weird reason, but now really wasn't the time to investigate that further. The footsteps drew closer, tracking down the other row of lockers, and Roth dropped his chin. "Then you better get your ass out of here."

I took a step back, avoiding the slime on the floor. His eyes glowed a fiery amber as they met mine. "And you need to leave, too."

"No," I said, drawing in a deep breath. "I'm trained, you— *Whoa*."

The thing had rounded the end of the lockers, and it was completely, buck-ass naked. Not like that was the most disturbing thing about the creature.

It was shaped like a man, standing nearly seven feet tall. Muscles rippled under shiny, moonstone-colored skin. Two thick horns jutted from the top of its head, curving inward. The points were sharp, and I had no doubt that if this Nightcrawler head-butted someone, it wouldn't end prettily. Pupils shaped like a feline's were set in irises the color of blood. And it smiled, flashing two razor-sharp fangs.

Roth was so damn fast.

Whipping down, he pulled two long, slender instruments out of the sides of his boots. Iron blades. I had no idea. Wow. The fact that he carried something so deadly to his own kind... was really sort of badass.

He slammed into the Nightcrawler, shoving his blades into its midsection. The Nightcrawler roared, knocking Roth to the side. He hit a locker with a grunt. Metal gave way, and he dropped the blades. One landed in the gunk, the other skidded across the floor.

"Blessed be," muttered Gerald, backing up.

Pushing down the bitter fear that was useless, I darted across the floor, swiping up a blade. Roth had wrapped a black cloth along the handle, but I could still feel the heat of the iron as I rose.

Roth shouted at me, and my adrenaline kicked my senses into high gear as the Nightcrawler whirled on me. It cocked its head to the side, sniffing the air through bull-shaped nostrils, as if it couldn't figure out what I was.

Charging the Nightcrawler, I came up short when it simply vanished and then reappeared behind me. I spun around. Two puncture holes in its heavily muscled stomach bled a white substance.

I swung on the Nightcrawler, and it popped out of existence, reappearing a few steps to the left. Dropping down like Zayne had taught me, I went for the creature's legs, remembering just then that the thing was really, legitimately naked.

Yuck.

Before my kick could connect, the Nightcrawler dipped to the side, opening its mouth. I lurched to the right as a stream of white acidic-smelling liquid shot from its mouth. Momentarily distracted by that, I didn't move quickly enough when it swung out with a heavy, clawed hand. I jumped back, but its claws ripped through the front of my sweater, snagging me. The air went out of my lungs as my eyes locked with the thing. There was a quick burning sensation, and then the Nightcrawler stumbled to the side.

It spun on Roth. Moving disturbingly fast, it caught the other blade Roth now held in his hand and snapped it into two.

"Crap," muttered Roth.

Then it had its hand around Roth's throat, lifting him off the ground. Its body vibrated as it cocked back its head, baring lethal fangs, preparing another venomous spray. Gripping the meaty wrists, Roth pulled his legs up and used the Nightcrawler's chest as a springboard. The action broke the creature's hold, and Roth hit the floor, springing back to his feet.

I rushed around the rotted bench, hitting the stunned Nightcrawler in the back with the kind of kick Zayne would've been proud of. I swung back the hand that held the blade, prepared to deliver the jerk back to Hell with a direct stab to the heart.

The Nightcrawler popped out, and I hit the floor, catching myself at the last second before I face-planted in a bunch of muck. Reappearing above me, it grabbed me by the scruff of my neck and lifted me right off my feet.

Bambi shifted across my stomach as pain exploded down my spine from the tight grip, but I swung my leg back, connecting my foot where it counted. Howling, the Nightcrawler dropped me and bent over, cupping itself.

I landed on my feet and swung around, seeing Roth coming up behind it. Not wasting a moment of having the upper hand, I slammed the iron blade into its chest, jerking back quickly. White mist streamed out of the wound, fizzing in the air. The Nightcrawler's howl ended abruptly as it burst into flames. Within seconds, nothing remained but a patch of scorched floor.

Breathing heavily, I staggered back a step as I lowered the blade. My eyes met Roth's. He looked shell-shocked as he stared at me. "What?" I huffed out.

He shook his head slowly. "I forgot you could fight. And I forgot how incredibly hot that is."

My eyes met his for a moment and then I glanced at the lockers, then over to where Gerald had plastered himself against a wall. A look of abject horror filled his expression. "You said almost all of these lockers are full of those things?"

Gerald nodded.

Stomach tumbling, I swiped the fine sheen of sweat off my forehead. "That's problematic."

"I could clean them out," Roth suggested.

"What if there are more about to wake up? There's no way you can take on more than one of these things at a time."

He frowned at me.

I sighed. "Don't be an idiot. It has nothing to do with your skills. We barely took one of them out together." I flicked my gaze to Gerald. Some of the color was returning to his face. "Sorry, but we need to bring the Wardens in on this. I won't tell them about you, but I'd make sure you stay hidden while they're here."

Gerald nodded again.

Roth slipped his now-broken blade back into his boot and then stalked across the room. Without saying a word he held his hand out, and I forked over the other blade.

"Why would so many be down here? It has to do with the Lilin, right?"

"Has to be." A troubled look pinched his features. "Unless the cocoon isn't actually from a Lilin."

A dull ache picked up in my temples as I stared up at him. "I thought you were confident it was from a Lilin."

"I was, but..." He looked at the lockers for a moment and then his brows furrowed. Turning back to me, he frowned as he leaned in. Too close.

I stepped back, putting a space between us.

Roth followed, his lashes lowering for a moment. When he looked up again, his eyes were crystal bright. "Are you hurt?"

"No. Yes." I glanced down at myself, seeing the tears in my chunky sweater. My stomach didn't hurt though. "I'm not sure."

His intense regard strengthened. "Shortie..."

As he reached for me, I stepped back. "I'm fine. Remember? I just killed a Nightcrawler."

I felt as if he should be more focused on that. I kind of felt like a ninja.

"You need to let me check you over." He got all grabby hands again, this time managing to wrap his fingers around the hem of my sweater. The material was pulled taut, reveal-ing the three jagged tears.

He let out a harsh curse. "Did it claw you?"

"Hey!" I smacked at his hands, but no more than a second later, he revealed the off-white tank top I'd worn underneath the sweater. It was dotted with red just above my belly button.

"Layla," he whispered, going for that piece of material next.

"Stop!" I snapped free. "I've had enough of you, Gropey McGropers! I'm fine. My stomach doesn't even hurt. It's just a scratch."

Gerald was still plastered against the wall.

Roth's jaw tightened as he glared at me. "You need to stop acting like a fool. A Nightcrawler's—"

"None of its venom got on me."

"But it *clawed* you." He spoke as if I was a five-year-old that didn't understand logic. "I need to get you back to my place where I can—"

My obnoxiously harsh laugh cut him off. "Of all the nerve! You really think I'm going to fall for that?"

"Layla—"

"Shut up, Roth. Seriously." I stormed around him and headed for the stairs, stopping long enough to address a pet-rified-looking Gerald. "I'll get the Wardens down here as soon as possible."

Swallowing hard, he exhaled harshly. "I'll make sure no one else comes down here."

Praying that I could actually rouse all the Wardens and they could get down here pronto without causing a stir, I hur-ried up the steps. By the time I reached the last one, my skin felt clammy and I was out of breath. Had to be the adrena-line from the fighting. It couldn't be my stomach because it didn't even hurt.

I pushed open the doors and walked across the dank, smelly gymnasium when Bambi started slithering up my leg.

"Layla! Stop right now!"

The authority in his voice, the audacity to issue me an order spun me right around, but when I stopped…the room kept spinning, a kaleidoscope of grays and blacks. "That's not right."

"What?" Roth's face blurred.

The edges of my vision darkened. "Oh crap."

I was vaguely aware of Roth shooting forward as my legs just stopped working. They folded underneath me and then there was nothing.

CHAPTER SEVENTEEN

When I opened my eyes, I was staring at the stony profile of Roth, and he was focused straight ahead, hands white-knuckling the steering wheel. I was curled in the front seat of his Porsche.

I dragged in a breath. My thoughts were murky. "What...?"

He glanced at me and something like concern radiated from his golden gaze. "We're almost there, shortie."

"How...?" I swallowed, but my throat felt parched. I remembered what happened but had no idea how I'd ended up in his car. "How did...you get me out of school?"

One side of his lips curved up as he returned his attention to the road. "I've got skills."

There was a good chance the school would call home since I was missing my afternoon classes, and my heart pounded sluggishly. More so because of wherever he could be taking me. I tried to sit up, but all I managed to do was slide further into a ball.

"You've got to take me back to school," I gasped out. "I can't go to your apartment."

"Don't be illogical," Roth replied evenly. "A Nightcrawler's claws are infectious, and I really can't treat you in the middle of the hallway, can I? It's bad enough that I have to drive. Too risky to take flight during the day."

"I can call Zayne," I reasoned, squeezing my eyes shut as my stomach muscles cramped.

He didn't respond, and I groaned. "I think I'm going to vomit."

Instead of Roth telling me not to do that in his pretty little Porsche, I heard the engine rev and felt the car push forward.

"We're almost there," he said, voice tight.

I didn't want to go to his apartment, but other than diving out of the car, I wasn't in the condition to put up much of a fight.

Things were a blur for a little while. Concentrating on not hurling all over myself, I kept my eyes closed. I felt the car stopping and registered the change in light behind my closed lids. I didn't really follow the whole process of Roth getting me into his apartment building, which was a good thing, because I was sure it involved him carrying me.

"This is familiar," announced a smooth, cultured voice as a door swung shut behind us and the faint scent of apples teased my nose.

"Shut up, Cayman."

A deep chuckle irritated me, and I tried not to think about the first time I'd been here, sort of in the same position. "Look, I'm just pointing out that this is becoming a habitual behavior and we should—"

The slamming door jarred me and cut off whatever else Cayman was saying. A second later, I was laid down on a bed—Roth's bed. I peeled open my eyes and immediately wished I hadn't.

Seeing the familiar white walls lined with the DVDs and books that had been there before…the piano in the corner… even the macabre paintings that bordered on the disturbing…

it was a punch to the chest and didn't help with the sensitivity of my stomach. My feet dangled an inch off the floor, and I thought of the little vamp kitties who'd been both tattoos and pets. I wondered whether they were back now, hiding under his bed, prepared to sink their little fangs into any exposed skin.

I couldn't be here.

As Roth backed off, I started to sit up. He shot me a look of warning. "Sit still. The more you move, the more the infection will spread and this won't be an easy fix."

My chest rose and fell heavily as I watched him go to the black fridge in his small kitchen. Opening the door, he reached in and pulled out a water bottle that had been stripped of its label. I watched him warily as he approached the bed.

"Holy water." He shook the bottle slightly. "The demonic equivalent of peroxide."

"You normally keep holy water in your fridge?"

He stopped in front of me. "You never know when you'll need it."

I couldn't foresee a lot of situations when a demon would be in need of holy water. "Am I supposed to drink it?"

His face contorted in disgust. "You're part demon, Layla. You drink this and you'll be spewing vomit like a possessed chick. Since it's normally used against demons, it can heal an injury inflicted by another demon, depending on the wound and all that good stuff."

"Then what am I supposed to do with it?"

A small grin appeared. "Take your shirt off."

I stared at him.

His brows rose. "I'm being serious. I need to put this—" he shook the bottle again "—on the scratches."

It took me a second to respond. "I'm not taking my shirt off."

"Yes, you are."

Rising onto my elbows, I met his determined gaze with my own. "You're on crack if you think I'm removing a single stitch of clothing."

"Like I said before, crack is whack." He grinned while I glared at him. "Your shirt needs to come off, shortie. The reason your stomach doesn't hurt is because you've got some venom or blood soaking through your sweater. It's numbing your skin and having venom all up on you isn't really going to be conducive to healing. The top needs to go."

I glanced down. With the darkness of my sweater, it was impossible to see if there was demon blood on it.

Roth came closer, crouching by the bed. "No need to be shy."

"It's not that," I sputtered, forcing myself into an upright position. The room tilted a little and I closed my eyes.

"It's not like I haven't seen you before."

"Oh my God," I moaned. "That is not the point."

Roth sighed. "Look, we're wasting time. You're going to get sicker and this holy water won't work. It's as simple as that, so stop being a girl and take off your sweater."

Prying my eyes open, I struggled with my erratic pulse. I saw it in his steady gaze then. If I didn't take off the sweater, he was going to and that would be worse. I could do this. He felt nothing for me. Fine. I felt nothing for him now. Great. I was a big girl.

I muttered a curse under my breath and reached down, carefully taking off the sweater and tank top in one pull. As I dropped the oh-so offending material onto the floor, I cast my gaze to my stomach.

It really didn't look that...bad.

The claws had just grazed me, but the three marks were a

dark, angry red and tiny little lines were branching out from the cuts like veins.

After a few tense seconds, I realized Roth hadn't moved. Where in the Hell was the whole "time is of the essence" crap? I lifted my gaze and saw that he seriously hadn't moved at all.

Still crouched by the bed, the bottle of holy water dangled from his long fingertips. He was staring at me with the same kind of intensity he had in the locker rooms, but there was a heat behind his golden eyes and his stare was fixed on my chest. At least Bambi wasn't using my boob as a pillow this time. Her diamond-shaped head was resting against my lower stomach now.

As he continued to stare, heat curled low in my belly, especially when his tongue slipped out and glided over his upper lip. Light reflected off the bolt and I felt my skin flush. I didn't like what was starting to go on inside my body. And I didn't like that he was staring at me, that he even felt as though he was allowed to at this point.

And I sure as Hell didn't like the breathlessness invading my chest either.

"Stop staring at me," I ordered.

He shocked the demon out of me by dragging his gaze up, the concentrated power behind his irises searing my skin as he rose. A moment passed and then he spoke. "Lie back."

I wanted to resist his brisk tone, but the sooner I got this over with, the better. Easing back, I stared at the ceiling as I felt him come closer.

Roth hovered over me, and I fisted my hands in the soft blanket to keep myself still. "This might sting a bit."

I gritted my teeth. "Can't be worse than being stitched up, right?"

His gaze flicked to mine and he murmured, "Right."

Holding my breath, I prepared myself for whatever brain-cell destroying pain was about to be unleashed as he unscrewed the bottle and lowered it to my stomach. The first drop fizzled on my skin and then the liquid sloshed out, covering the claw marks and running down my belly, spilling onto the bed beneath me.

Bambi jerked back, her head disappearing under the band of my jeans, avoiding the steady stream of holy water. My skin burned at the contact, turning a ruddy pink, and I bit down on my lip. It wasn't as bad as the stitches, but it wasn't exactly pleasant either.

"Sorry," he muttered, tipping the bottle once more. He did so carefully, avoiding direct contact with it himself. I imagined his reaction, given that he was full-blooded, would be worse than mine.

The cuts frothed white as the sting brought a glaze of tears to my eyes. Finally, the water was all gone, and Roth was backing away. "Stay still for a little while."

Breathing in and out slowly, I remained where I was until Roth returned with a towel. He was silent as he swiped up the excess liquid along the sides of my stomach. It was then I noticed the tips of his fingers were a deep pink.

I cleared my throat. "You burned your fingers."

He shrugged. "It happens." He didn't touch the claw marks, but as he pulled away, his free hand brushed along the fading scar on my arm, the one left by the Warden. "Keep still."

I didn't have to wait long. Roth returned to my side with a black blanket. Like the one he'd wrapped around me the night of Petr's attack, it was made of some kind of thick, luxurious material. He draped it over my chest, leaving my stomach bare, and then retreated.

"You're going to need to stay still until the fizzing stops." He sat on the bench by the piano and bowed his head. Locks of dark hair fell forward, shielding his face. He didn't say anything else.

I drew in a stunted breath. A quiet, morose Roth was a worrisome Roth, because it was a rarity, and I wasn't sure how to deal with him when he was like that. Part of me wondered at the mood shift and wanted to ask, but I didn't want to come off as being interested.

Because I was.

And I sort of wanted to punch myself in the face for that.

As crazy as it was, while I waited for the holy water to do its thing I must have dozed off, because when I blinked my eyes open again, the claw marks were no longer fizzing. I didn't feel nauseous or dizzy, just a slight soreness around the slices.

And Roth was sitting beside me on the bed.

Well, when I turned my head toward his body heat, he was more reclining on the bed beside me.

Resting his weight on one arm, his head was propped up by his hand. An odd smile marked his eerily beautiful face, a contrast to the sullen expression he was wearing before. His lips parted just slightly. "You still murmur in your sleep."

My brows knitted.

"You make these little sounds sometimes. Like a kitten. It's cute."

"What are you doing?" Heat swamped my cheeks as I sat up quickly. Forgetting about the blanket, it slipped to my waist.

His gaze followed and he grinned as I yanked the blanket back up. "I was watching you sleep."

"Creepy," I said, holding the blanket to my chin.

He shrugged one shoulder. "How are you feeling?"

"Fine." Drawing from somewhere deep inside me, I forced out, "Thank you."

"I'll add it to your tab."

I scowled at him.

Rolling to his feet gracefully, he stood and stretched. "Perfect timing for you to wake up. You don't want Stony coming in here and finding you all content and happy on *my* bed."

"What?"

"Stony. He's on his way." He folded his arms, eyeing me. "To get you."

I blinked once and then twice as tiny knots formed in my stomach.

"I used your phone," he explained. "It was in your front pocket. You were out cold when I pulled it out. Well, you did make this moaning sound that made me think you liked where my fingers—"

"You got my phone out of my pocket and called Zayne?" I shot to my feet. "Are you insane?"

"The last time I checked, I wasn't. You should be thrilled to know that Stony answered on, like, the first ring." His lips pursed as a thoughtful expression flickered across his face. "But he wasn't exactly happy to hear my voice. Or that you were with me. Or that you were currently asleep on my bed. Or that you got hurt. Or that—"

"I get the point!" I screeched, holding the blanket to my chest. "Why did you call him?"

He tilted his head to the side and the look of innocence on his face made me want to spit fire like a dragon of doom. "How else were you supposed to get home?"

"Oh, I don't know, Roth, maybe a freaking taxi?" My heart pounded in my chest. Oh God, Zayne was going to flip. He was going to flip so epically that it would break the sound barrier. "What were you thinking?"

"I was thinking that we needed to let the Wardens know about the Nightcrawlers in the school," he replied reasonably. I wanted to smack him. "Because that was your idea and you were right. I can't possibly take all of them out all by myself."

My fingers dug into the blanket. I wasn't falling for what he was saying. The real reason behind calling Zayne wasn't to alert them to the creatures in the school. Like Roth actually cared about that. He'd done it to piss Zayne off.

The little curve of his lips gave that away.

"I bet you're so proud of yourself, aren't you?"

He stared at me and then rolled his eyes. "It's not like Stony is going to run and tell Daddy that you're with me."

That part didn't matter. Not that Abbot would be anything like okay with me being in Roth's apartment, but I was more concerned about what this would do to Zayne.

Somehow I resisted the urge to go psychotic tree monkey on him. "I need my sweater. Where is it?"

"In the garbage."

Closing my eyes, I counted to ten. "I need a shirt to wear." I started toward his closet, but he appeared in front of me, blocking my path. "Come on."

His grin grew. "Sorry. I'm all out of girls' clothing at the moment."

"I need a shirt," I insisted. "Don't be a jerk, Roth."

Considering me for a moment, a spark lit up his eyes and warning bells went off. With a sly smile, he reached down and whipped off the long-sleeve shirt he was wearing.

My eyes widened.

Whoa.

I'd...I'd forgotten what Roth looked like shirtless.

Okay. Maybe not completely forgotten, but my memory didn't do him justice. At all. Roth was all lean muscle. From his chest to those indents on either side of his hips, he was hard, cut muscle.

The dragon tattoo was where it always was, curled up along the side of his abs, with its tail disappearing under his jeans. My question about the kittens' presence was answered. One was under his right pec, appearing more like a tiger crouching, and another one looked as if it was snuggling into his side.

"Where's the third kitten?" I asked before I could stop myself.

His thick lashes lowered. "I'd have to take off my pants to show you that."

I squeezed my eyes shut.

There was a deep chuckle. "Clock is ticking. And, more importantly, the longer you're standing there in just your bra, the more I'm tempted to be a very, very bad boy."

My eyes snapped open. His stare snared mine, and I took a step back from the intensity in his gaze. There was no doubt in my mind he was telling the truth there. He may not want to be with me, but he wanted me.

"Give me the shirt," I said between clenched teeth.

He tossed it at me, but I was a little slow on the uptake. The material that smelled like him, like something wild and sinful, smacked me in the chest and landed on the floor. "You better hurry. He'll be here any second."

"You're an ass," I spat, picking up the shirt.

He chuckled. "And it's a fine ass, I'm told."

I ignored that as I turned around, giving him my back as I dropped the blanket. Maybe it was my imagination, but my spine burned under his consuming stare. "Why did you even have him come here, to a building full of demons? Isn't that dangerous?"

"He'll park down the street and come in via the roof," Roth replied, voice suddenly tight. "Don't worry. Stony is completely safe."

Slipping Roth's shirt on, I was immediately swallowed by the size of it and by his scent. I turned back to him, feeling flushed. I didn't even know what to say as I sat on the edge of the bed. There was no way I could even prepare myself for Zayne's arrival.

Not that I had to wait very long.

Didn't take more than a minute before the heavy thump from the roof rattled the twisted paintings hanging on Roth's walls. I stood as Roth turned to the narrow door that led up to the roof. Without ceremony, he opened it and Zayne stormed into the loft.

His blond hair was a wavy mess, and he was dressed all in black—black T-shirt, black tactical pants. It was as if he'd dressed to go hunting.

Zayne's gaze found me first and he didn't look away for a long moment. His eyes were startling cobalt, pupils stretched vertically, and his jaw was clamped shut. I didn't need to read his mind to know what he thought of seeing me in a currently shirtless Roth's apartment, by *his* bed and wearing *his* shirt.

I started to explain why, even though it seemed unnecessary, but before I could utter a word, Roth spoke.

His smile was wide, but didn't reach his eyes. "Hey, bro…"

A muscle ticked along Zayne's jaw and then he spun on Roth, cocked back his arm and punched him right in the face.

CHAPTER EIGHTEEN

Roth staggered back a step and the transformation took hold. Skin darkened to a smooth, polished onyx and wings sprouted from his back, spanning ten feet and arcing high in the air. The arches were adorned with sharp, deadly horns, but unlike the Wardens, his skull was bare.

His lips peeled back, revealing fangs. "Do it again."

Zayne hadn't shifted, but he did look as if he was about to punch Roth in the face again. It wasn't that I doubted Zayne's ability to hold his own, but Roth was an Upper Level demon, a Crown Prince, and, more importantly, fighting over this was stupid.

I darted between them, staring up into Zayne's furious blue eyes. "Stop it."

"Don't listen to her." In his true form, Roth's voice was guttural and rough. "You know you don't want to stop, Stony."

I shot him a death glare. "Knock it off, Roth!"

His eyes, still golden, fixed on me. A tense moment passed as his clawed hand opened and closed, and I honestly thought he was going to pick me up and toss me out of the way. When he took a step back, my heart rate slowed. "Stony started it."

"Wow." I turned back to Zayne, who was eyeballing Roth.

I placed my hands on his chest and the heat of his body burned through his shirt. "You need to calm down."

"You let her get hurt," he snarled.

Roth growled as he dipped his chin, as if he was preparing to charge. "I took care of her."

"Like that makes it better?"

I pushed Zayne back. "He didn't *let* me do anything. I went down there freely and he told me to leave, but I stayed. You trained me, Zayne. I was more than up to the fight—I killed the Nightcrawler." Something everyone seemed to forget. "You can't blame him for my getting hurt—*barely* hurt. As you can see, I'm fine."

Zayne's gaze finally dropped to mine. His nostrils flared as he breathed deeply. There was another tense stretch of silence and then he jerked his chin in an abrupt nod.

Watching him for a second longer to make sure he wasn't going to change his mind, I dropped my hands and faced Roth. When I saw that he was back in his human form, I relaxed a fraction.

"Now that that's settled, did Abbot and the clan head to the school?"

"They're there, but not willing to do anything until school lets out." Zayne's tone was clipped. "We're taking care of it. No need to worry."

Roth snorted. "Not that I was worried."

A flash of anger traveled across Zayne's face, and I knew the longer these two were in the same vicinity, the more the likelihood of boy fight round two breaking out increased.

"We should go," I said quietly.

Zayne nodded. "I couldn't agree more."

I turned to say something to Roth—something like thank you, because he had helped me, but Zayne's fingers unexpectedly threaded through mine. Roth's narrowed gaze dropped to our joined hands. His mouth tightened and his features appeared starker—more skin and bone than anything else—and then a shutter slammed down, sealing away any thought or feeling.

"By the way, Zayne…" The coldness in Roth's voice sent a chill down my spine. "That is the only time you'll get to lay a hand on me and then walk away from it."

Zayne and I didn't speak most of the ride back to the house. Anytime I glanced at him, he appeared to be wearing down his molars. I knew he was angry, so angry that he was beyond the point of speech.

Guilt soured in my stomach like curdled milk, which led to a hefty dose of confusion. Zayne had asked me not to run off with Roth, and I hadn't—not really. My stomach turned over heavily, because my rationale sucked, and I knew it was more than that.

The anger Zayne was throwing off in waves was coming from a different place—the place that had been created in my bed late Saturday night. I couldn't fool myself into believing something different. As I'd known the moment he'd touched me, everything had changed between us and his current mood was a product of that change.

But I hadn't done anything wrong. In reality, I'd done something pretty awesome. I'd killed a Nightcrawler, proving that I was useful for more than just my now-nonexistent ability.

As we pulled onto the private road, I couldn't take the silence any longer. "I was going to tell you about going down to the old gymnasium with Roth."

The muscle in his jaw spasmed. "Were you?"

His question stung hotly. "Yes. I was planning on calling

you as soon as I got out of the gym, but I got sick from the stupid scratch."

"That stupid scratch could've seriously injured you or worse, Layla."

"But it didn't," I pointed out gently. "Roth beat me to calling you, but I was going to."

"Roth." He hissed the name.

A heartbeat passed. "And there's more I need to tell you. I think we got a lead on the Lilin, but it's from…a very unconventional source."

His fingers tapped the steering wheel. "I'm half-afraid to ask."

"It's something you can't tell the others. I know that doesn't sound good, but I trust you. You're not crazy judgmental and you won't—"

"Okay," Zayne sighed. "Got it."

Because I did trust him, I told him about Gerald, his coven, and the other coven of witches in Bethesda. He wasn't exactly thrilled with the no-Wardens rule. "Layla, I don't want you going."

"Someone has to," I said.

"Let *him* do it."

"There is no way I trust Roth to go into any situation and not piss people off so bad that we don't get any information."

He was quiet as we circled the house, heading for the garage. "Do you know how hard it is for me to entertain the idea of you going off with him?"

Chewing on my lower lip, I didn't say anything to that.

"I know he was goading me today and I took the bait."

Well, I totally agreed with that. For whatever reason, Roth had wanted to get under Zayne's skin and he had excelled at doing so.

"But he allowed you to get hurt in the process," he continued as he eased the Impala into the garage, parking it near the fleet of SUVs. When he killed the engine, he turned to me. The conversation was back to *him* once more. "And you smell like him now. So, I want to hit him again."

"You can't hit him again."

His brows rose in doubt.

"My getting hurt wasn't his fault."

"He coaxed you down there when he could've gone by himself, and the moment he saw that cocoon or those Night-crawlers, he should've gotten you out of there. He didn't. And not just because he wanted to get at me. He wanted you there, with him."

I laughed at that. "I'm pretty sure he just wanted to mess with you because he knew I was going to tell you about everything."

He shook his head as he pulled the keys out and opened the door. "That's not the only reason, Layla." He eyed me from the other side of the car after I climbed out, leaning his arm against the roof. "I see the way he looks at you."

I closed the car door and stepped back, turning to the entrance that led to the kitchen. I'd seen that look on Roth's face earlier, but agreeing to that would do no good. Zayne was likely to sprout his wings, fly back to Roth's apartment and punt kick him this time. "You don't know what you're seeing."

I'd taken one step when Zayne was suddenly in front of me. Gasping, I stumbled back as his hand curled around my upper arm in a gentle but firm grasp.

"I know what I saw." The air whooshed out of my lungs as he pressed me against his chest. He dipped his chin so that our faces were only inches apart. The proximity froze me in place. "I know exactly how he looks at you and you do, too."

Words left me as I stared into eyes the color of the endless sky, because...oh my God, our lips were so close and the need that swelled within me had nothing to do with feeding, but everything to do with wanting to taste his lips.

His other hand curved along my lower back and slid up, tangling in the edges of my hair. "I know the look. So do you. Because it's the way *I* look at you."

My heart tripped up as the words settled over me. I didn't know what to say, and that swelling feeling inside me turned into something else, moved into my chest, and had my pulse pounding.

A deep sound rumbled from Zayne's throat and then he lowered his head, claiming the scant inches between our lips. At the very last second, common sense smacked into me and I jerked out of his embrace.

Breathing erratically, I kept backing up until I knocked into the side of his Impala. My lips tingled and we hadn't even kissed. But we almost did and that *terrified* me. Ice poured into my veins, turning my skin as cold as a February morning.

I placed my hand over my mouth as I stared at him. "What were you thinking?"

His chest rose and fell rapidly. "Layla..."

Fear seized me, panic more potent than facing down the Nightcrawler. If we'd kissed, I would've taken Zayne's soul— I would've turned him into something horrific and evil. I would've killed what he was.

Just like a Lilin would.

I lurched away from the Impala and darted around Zayne, racing into the small hallway just inside the house. I skidded to a halt as I entered the brightly lit kitchen.

At the round table, Danika and Jasmine sat with the twins. Bowls of ice cream were on the table, but the babies were wearing more of the creamy goodness than they seemed to have eaten.

A tentative smile tracked across Danika's face. Her right hand was covered with a rainbow of sprinkles. "You're back."

I willed my heart to slow down. "Yeah."

The door back in the hall banged into the wall, announcing Zayne's entrance. He roared into the kitchen, slowing like I had when he got that it was occupied. He took one look at the table and then turned a piercing stare on me.

Oh dear.

Jasmine's gaze moved from him to me and then back to Zayne. Silence of the awkward kind descended as Danika shifted her attention to her bowl.

"Would you two like some ice cream?" Jasmine offered as she cleared her throat. "I'm sure there's...some left."

Izzy broke into a giggle, tossing back her red curls as she slammed her fists into her bowl. Ice cream splattered across her bib. "More!"

"Uh, thanks, but I'll pass." I turned as Geoff strode into the kitchen. His brows went up as he got an eyeful of the table.

"Any news from the men?" Jasmine asked, sitting up straight.

He nodded as he ran a hand over his shoulder-length brown hair. "Yes. Since school is shutting down for the day, they're about to clean house. They've already taken out a few that were close to maturing." He glanced at me, and surprisingly, he smiled. "And way to go, Layla. I hear you took one out."

Finally someone recognized my awesomeness. "Thank you."

Geoff nodded, and then he turned his attention to Zayne. "Got a second?"

I took that as my cue to make a hasty exit. I needed a moment to clear my head, and also to shower, because smelling like Roth wasn't making me warm and fuzzy. I made it into the hallway when I felt a weird, cold air pass through me. Not around me, but literally *through* me, causing me to stop. And then I heard Zayne.

"It can wait."

My heart jumped in my throat as I all but flung myself toward the stairs. I made it two steps and then, suddenly, I was off my feet and tossed over one strong shoulder. Too stunned to make a peep, I lifted my head and watched the foyer spin around me as Zayne stalked straight through the living room and into the library. He kicked the door shut, turning and locking it. My stomach tumbled as my imagination ran wild.

Just as suddenly as I was picked up and tossed over his shoulder like a sack of rice, I was deposited on my feet. I backed up and then shot forward, smacking him across the chest. Hard.

"What the Hell?" I demanded.

Zayne's lips twitched as if he was trying hard not to laugh. "We need to talk."

"You need to talk to Geoff."

"Whatever he has to say can wait." He followed me as I backed up, frowning. "Why did you take off like that?"

"I…I need to shower," I said lamely.

His eyes narrowed. "Yeah, that would be nice, but you ran off like an entire army of Hellions was chasing after you."

"Did not."

He arched a brow.

"Okay. Maybe a little. What did you want to talk about? The witches and when we can go to the club?"

"No."

As we neared the couch, he sat down. I started to move away, but his hand snaked out, wrapping around my arm. "What are you—?"

He tugged me down, and there was nowhere to go but into his lap. I landed facing him, my mouth level with his throat. For a moment, I was frozen. With my legs straddling his, there was an uncharted feel to this that stretched my nerves tight. If I moved my hips forward… I couldn't even finish the thought.

"I'm not running from you," I mumbled.

"Yeah, you are. You're also avoiding me again." His hands spanned my waist as I started to climb off. "Nope. Not going anywhere."

"What…what are you doing?" I breathed out.

"Keeping you from running from me." He tugged me forward, causing me to clap my hands down on his shoulders to stop certain areas of our bodies from touching. "In case you haven't figured this out yet, I'm not into the chasing thing."

My brain emptied of all intelligent responses. Slowly, I lifted my gaze and found his. He was looking at me…yeah, like he'd said he looked at me. Stomach, meet butterflies.

I gave a little shake of my head. "Why would you chase me?"

The look that crossed his face was a mixture of fondness and disbelief—the "are you seriously that dumb" kind of look. "I don't want to, but I have been. I *am*. And I'd think after Saturday night, it would be pretty obvious."

Blood thickened inside my veins.

"Actually…" His eyes searched mine. "It should've been obvious for…for a long time. Or maybe it wasn't, but you have to know."

I'd have to be stupid to not know, especially after all of this, but… "I don't get it."

"Maybe it's not right. What do I know? When Father brought you home all those years ago, he told me it was my job to watch over you, that I'd be the closest thing to family—to a brother—that you would ever have. And I took that seriously. Ever since I was twelve years old." His dark blond lashes lowered, and I thought of Mr. Snotty. Emotion exploded in my chest and climbed up my throat. "I know I was never supposed to think of you any other way, but you got older and the past year or so?"

My hands curled around his shoulders, digging in through his shirt. Blood rushed in my ears.

"I'd find myself unable to stop staring at you, and it was hard not wanting to spend time with you. Why else did I always get up so early?" He laughed softly as the hollows of his cheeks flushed. "And when Father started bringing Danika around, I knew..."

"Knew what?" I whispered.

"I knew I couldn't be with her. Not when you're constantly in my head. Is it wrong?" His intense gaze swept up again, meeting mine. "No. Screw that—screw all of that. It's right. It's always been right."

My throat hurt when I spoke. "You can't—"

"Can't what, Layla-bug? Can't think about you? Can't tell you that you have always been the most amazing girl I've ever known? Can't stop living under the same roof with you and pretending that what I feel for you—what I want from you— is something brotherly?" As my breath caught, his hands slid up to my rib cage, leaving behind a wake of shivers. "That I can't hold you? Touch you? Because the last time I checked, I could do all those things."

"Zayne..."

"And I know it's what you've wanted. I've known for a long time." His thumbs moved in idle circles as he spoke. "Or has that changed because of him?"

This had nothing to do with *him*. To have waited years, to suffer through all my girlish fantasies involving Zayne and think it was utterly hopeless, to now hear these almost sacred words, I didn't know what to do with them. My heart was expanding in my chest to the point I surely thought it would burst, but there was a rising anxiety that whispered of confusion and fear.

"Why now?" The question slipped out of me.

"Is 'now is when I finally pulled my head out of my ass' the wrong answer? I guess it probably isn't good enough, huh?" He dipped his head to my shoulder, resting his forehead there as his fingers curled around the back of the borrowed shirt, and my breath caught again. "I almost lost you that night Paimon captured you. When I realized you could've died?" He shuddered. "That I could've died? I didn't want to deny this any longer. I couldn't."

I stared at his bowed head as I slowly brought my hands up. Was that it? Or was it more? Was it because of Roth and the fact that Zayne just didn't want me with him? Or was it because he now knew I could shift, which made me suitable in some way? Closing my eyes, I ignored the odd knot of unease. He wasn't like that and had never believed something was faulty with me. I gingerly touched the ends of his hair, and a sigh rattled through him. Zayne wouldn't lie to me.

The silky soft strands of his hair slipped through my fingers as I wondered if he could feel my heart cracking. Tears pricked at my eyes, wetting my lashes, and I squeezed my eyes shut. It was almost easier months ago, when the idea of Zayne harboring any feelings for me was nothing more than a fairy tale, than hearing this and not being able to act upon it.

"It doesn't matter," I said, voice thick. "It's impossible."

Zayne drew back, lifting his head. "How so?"

"We can't... I mean, we couldn't..." My cheeks flushed, and I ducked my chin.

"We can't?" His deep, shockingly sexy chuckle rumbled through me. "I think Saturday night proved there's a lot we can do."

Heat flowed through me, a mixture of embarrassment and

fire that had sparked to life at the reminder of what we'd done. "But it's too dangerous."

"I trust you."

Those three words sounded so simple, but they were confounding. "You shouldn't. Not like that—not with your life."

He frowned. "You've never given yourself enough credit or believed in yourself enough. As long as I've known you, I've never felt threatened by what you can do."

The tears that rushed to my eyes threatened to spill forth, and I was seconds from crying as if I'd watched a marathon of Hallmark movies.

"You're not evil, Layla. You never have been." His smile was tremendous, snaking its way through my heart. "And I believe that if I kissed you right now, you wouldn't take my soul."

I gasped as I started to lean back. "Don't you dare try it! I can't—"

"Relax," he chuckled.

My muscles were tense. How could I relax after his saying something like that? As much as I cared for and cherished him, I'd wither up and die inside if I was the cause of his demise. The very thought of that made me want to move to another zip code.

Zayne lifted a hand, running his fingers through the ends of my hair as his gaze tracked over my features. He tilted his head and before I could figure out what he was doing, he pressed his lips to my neck, against my wildly beating pulse.

My senses became hyperaware as his firm lips traced a hot, tiny path to the sensitive spot beneath my ear. My brain whirled as everything registered. I felt his hair tickling me under my chin, the softness of his lips and the tiny flick of his tongue, as if he were tasting my skin. I recognized the sudden tension in my body, the liquid heat and the force of the emotion swelling in my chest. But there was more, there was that foreign quality again. When he curved his hand around the nape of my neck, under my hair, it only grew stronger. There was a *masculine* edge to it.

As understanding seeped in, I placed my hands on his face. He lifted his questioning gaze. I couldn't figure out how, but I knew deep in my bones what was happening.

"Oh my God," I whispered, trailing my fingers over his face. "I get it."

His brows rose.

"I can feel you. I can feel *your* emotions."

CHAPTER NINETEEN

That was obviously not what Zayne was expecting me to say. He stared at me with those luminous blue eyes, confusion playing across his handsome features.

Feeling his emotions sounded crazy, but it made sense.

"What do you mean?" he asked.

I pulled my hands back, curling my fingers back into my palms, and almost immediately, that virile need faded away. "I can feel what you're feeling," I repeated, stunned by the realization. "I don't understand how and this isn't the first time, but I just didn't recognize what I was feeling before."

He leaned back against the couch. "You're going to have to give me more details."

"Every time someone has touched me—skin on skin—I get these faint traces of emotion that don't belong to me." I thought of Stacey and when she'd touched me while she'd been talking to me about Sam. I'd felt hope—hope that hadn't belonged to me. Then again with Roth, with Zayne, and even when I'd walked down the street and bumped into people the night I'd been trying to see auras… My eyes widened. "It started when I stopped seeing auras! Like pretty much immediately afterward. Holy crap."

"Damn," he said, shaking his head slightly. "So, you could feel what I was feeling when I was touching you?"

"Faintly. Like a rush of emotions. Nothing too strong."

His lips tipped up in a small smile. "Well, I'm glad, then. Because if you'd been feeling everything I've felt when we've touched? That would get really embarrassing considering all the feels I had going on."

I laughed even though my cheeks burned. "Yeah, I guess that would be awkward."

"Kind of." He swallowed, and then placed his hand on my cheek. "What do you feel now?"

"I don't know." It was hard, trying to decipher between my own jumbled emotions and what could possibly be coming from him, but there was one that I thought might be his. A constant thread that wove its way around my trepidation. "Happy?" I whispered, curling my fingers around his wrist. The warmth increased, like basking in the summer sun. "Happiness."

His smile spread, reaching his eyes. "Yeah, that's about right."

I tried to make sense of how losing my talent for seeing souls had somehow triggered the ability to feel others' emotions. I dropped my hand and started to move off his lap, but his hands moved to my hips, securing me in my place. I raised a brow at him.

Zayne's grin oozed boyish charm. "What?"

"You know what."

One shoulder rose in a shrug. "Focus on the important stuff here. The whole emotion thing. We know that a succubus or incubus feeds off emotions, right? And Lilith was considered a succubus in some texts. Maybe it's an ability that you've always had that's just coming out."

In other words, a demonic ability. "You know, why can't some Warden abilities start manifesting?"

"Does it matter?" He tapped his fingers against my hips.

"It should. To you."

That grin slipped into a frown. "It doesn't. Feeling someone else's emotions isn't evil. Probably would come in quite handy."

I supposed, but it was just another thing that made me so different from Zayne and uncomfortable in my own skin. A thought occurred as my body relaxed and I folded my hands between us. "Do you think the Lilin can feel emotions and see souls?"

"I don't know."

I didn't even know why I wondered. Maybe it was because I wanted to know how similar my own DNA was to this creature's.

Zayne shifted and I slid forward an inch. "I know what you're thinking."

"You do?"

He nodded. "You're thinking about that coven and when you can find out more about the Lilin."

As usual, he was pretty spot-on. "Well, my reasons are purely selfish. The more we know about the Lilin, the quicker we can find it."

"And the crone won't be at this club until a full moon?" he asked after a few moments. "That's still a few weeks away—December the sixth, I think."

I nodded absently. Demons, gargoyles, witches and their full moons.... "So, you're okay with me going?"

"Not really, but I figure you'll find a way to go anyway and I'd rather be supportive of it than be in the dark." Tipping his head back against the couch cushion, he watched me from behind lowered lashes. "And I'm assuming Roth is thrilled about the prospect of going to this club with you."

I didn't know what to say to that.

"I get that the witches don't want me there, especially those kind of witches, but I'm going to go with you that night— at least as far as I can go," he continued. "And, as much as it kills me to say this, going in there with Roth is a good idea."

"What?" Surprised, I stared at him. "Did you really just say that?"

"I'd like to peel Roth's skin from his bones in a very slow manner. You know, like with an orange peeler."

My nose scrunched up. "Ew."

He flashed a quick grin. "But for the most part, you're safe around him."

I continued to stare at him. "For the most part?"

"He'll protect you. Better than he did today." The reluctance in his voice was glaring. "You're just not safe *from* him."

"No matter what he wants or what you think he wants, I'm safe from him. Trust me. He made it plain and clear that there was nothing between us except…"

"Lust?"

"Yeah," I whispered.

"Asshole."

I coughed out a small laugh. "Yeah."

"I'm sorry," he said, and after everything he'd confessed, I thought the apology was possibly the strangest thing ever from him, but that goodness was so inherently Zayne.

Circling his arms around me, he gathered me close, tucking me to his chest. I curled into him, closing my eyes and listening to his heart beat steadily against my cheek. With his arms folded around me, I found the kind of comfort that I could only find in his arms—that I'd always found in his embrace.

A shaky breath shuddered through me. There was a lot

going on and a lot had happened in the span of a few weeks, but in those quiet moments, my mind drifted back to all those wonderful, beautiful things that I had only dreamed of Zayne saying to me, but that were now very much a reality. There were more important things I should be trying to figure out, but right now, this was the most important thing to *me*.

This development with Zayne was so unexpected. Lust was one thing. Caring for someone deeply was another thing, but those words…they seemed heavy with a different kind of meaning. The kind that sank into the heart, broke down walls, destroyed barriers and paved its own way.

As Zayne slid his hand up my spine, a sigh escaped my parted lips. "Comfy?" he asked.

I nodded.

He kept moving his hand, and I forced my eyes open, my gaze tracking over the dusty book spines lining the shelves. All of his words lay in the tiny space between us. I needed to say something, but speaking out loud about how I felt about Zayne had never been easy. I hadn't even admitted to Stacey how I felt about him. My near-lifelong crush on him had been something I kept close to my heart, hiding it the best I could and protecting it with lies. But Zayne had laid himself bare and I owed the same to him.

"I have a confession," I whispered.

"Hmm?"

Finding the courage still wasn't simple. "I've always dreamed of you…saying those words to me, of you wanting me." My entire being burned, but I forced myself to continue. Each word I spoke was a shaky whisper. "Probably ever since I understood the difference between boys and girls, I've wanted you."

His arms tightened around me and when he spoke, his voice was gruff. "That sounds like a long time."

"It was." A ball formed in my throat and, for some reason, I wanted to cry. "And, it was so hard, you know? Trying not to show it and not to be jealous of Danika or any other girl who—"

"There's never been any other girl, Layla-bug."

It took a few seconds for those words to seep through my thick skull and when they did, I drew back and lifted my head. "Come again?"

This time it was his face that flushed. "I've never been with anyone."

My mouth dropped to my chest.

"Do you need to look *that* surprised?"

"I'm sorry. It's just that I can't believe you haven't... I mean, you're *you*. You're gorgeous and you're kind and smart and perfect and girls check you out everywhere we go."

He smiled. "I didn't say the opportunity never presented itself. I just never acted on it."

"Why?"

Zayne's eyes met mine. "Truth?"

I nodded.

"I really didn't know at first why I didn't when...well, when I could have. It's as though I'd never been interested enough to go through with it the whole way. It wasn't until the past year that I realized why." He paused, and my heart was picking up its pace again. "It's because of you."

"Me?"

"Yeah." He picked up a few strands of my hair, twisting the length around two of his fingers. "I would get to a certain point and all I could think about was you and that seemed wrong. You know, to continue with someone else when I was picturing being with you."

Oh my God...

My heart exploded into a gooey pile of Zayne mush and

parts of my body got all kinds of excited at the fact that he'd been picturing *me,* thinking about *me* in that way for far longer than I could ever have known.

Zayne placed the strands of hair he'd been playing with on my shoulder, letting them slowly unravel. "So what are we going to do about it?"

My mind jumped right into the gutter and started playing happily with the idea of how we'd rectify our virginity issues, but I doubted that was what he meant. After sweeping the dirtier stuff out of my brain, I opened my mouth, but he placed a finger over my lips.

"You don't have to answer just yet," he said. "I know this isn't easy. Nothing between us will be easy and I know you have a lot of fears. I don't want to push you or push this, because I know…" Pausing, he nodded as if he was telling himself to say something. "I know you still care about *him*—about Roth."

I drew back. "I—"

"I know," he said solemnly. "It's not something that I'm happy to say out loud or even think, but I know you do. You shared…shared a lot with him and he was there when I wasn't."

I knew he was thinking about the night Petr attacked me, when I'd tried calling him and he hadn't answered because he'd been mad at me and he'd been with Danika. He still hadn't forgiven himself for that. "Zayne, that night wasn't your fault."

"I should've answered the phone, but that's not the point. He's been there for you and he accepted you for who you were. Something else I haven't always been really great at." He ran his finger along my jaw and then dropped his hand. "Anyway, I know you still have feelings for him, but I'm saying we can give this a chance—we can give us a chance."

My heart stuttered and then sped up. Zayne was right. As much as I hated to admit it, I still had feelings for Roth, but... but there was Zayne and there was our history together. There were all the years I'd spent idolizing and dreaming about him. There was everything he'd just said to me now.

And then there was everything *I* felt for him. The way I looked forward every day to seeing him. How he made me smile with the simplest of looks and the way I yearned for the briefest touch, to be able to kiss him. There had always been something there between us. I'd just always believed it was only on my side.

He smiled a little. "So I think we should take it slow."

"Slow?" Slower than baring my chest and sitting in his lap?

"Yeah, like let's go out on a date. How about that?"

My first response was to say no. There was too much risk... and if I was being honest with myself, I was scared—terrified of finally getting something I'd always wanted. What if it didn't work out for any of the million reasons why it couldn't? What if it ended in disappointment and destroyed our friendship? What if Zayne lost his soul because of me?

There were so many risks, but as my heartbeat skipped, I realized that half demon or not, life was full of risks and I was tired of *not* living—of not trying.

A date couldn't be bad, right? I stared at him as my lips spread into a wide smile. "How does a movie sound?"

Zayne stayed up the following morning after returning from hunting, and drove me to school. To the clan, that didn't seem out of place, and Nicolai was probably thrilled to be relieved of the duty.

Things were normal between us.

He teased me.

He made me blush.

He made me want to hit him at some point during the drive.

And when I arrived at school, the way he leaned in and pressed a sweet kiss to my cheek made me wish I could give him a worthy goodbye kiss.

I wasn't sure what our relationship was. Were we dating? Were we boyfriend and girlfriend? Nothing like that had been established, and it was probably for the best at the moment. In spite of wanting to take the risk, I wasn't sure we could pull this off.

Or if trying made me the most selfish person in the world.

Either way, there was a stupid smile plastered across my face as I entered the school. When I'd woken up this morning, all of the issues we were facing appeared to be a bit more manageable, as if all the problems had been dipped in glitter.

I giggled at that, earning a weird look from the girl walking beside me. Oh well. Rounding the corner, I'd passed the still-empty trophy case when a familiar coppery head appeared. Broom handle in one hand, Gerald motioned me over with the other.

Slipping around a cluster of girls, I headed over to him. "Is everything okay?"

He nodded and kept his voice low. "They took care of the problem in the basement of the school. Cleaned it all and even got rid of the muck."

"Great." I was relieved to hear that. Zayne had left last night to meet up with the others, but we hadn't talked about it this morning.

The skin around his eyes crinkled as he glanced around us. "I also wanted to thank you."

"For what?"

"For not saying anything to the Wardens about me," he responded, shifting the broom handle to a different hand. "I know you didn't, because I'm still standing here, and I appreciate it."

"It's no problem. I don't think they'd have a problem with you, but I wouldn't take that risk." Maybe I would've a few months back, but not now, and that realization killed a bit of my happy buzz.

Gerald's cherry-hued eyes darted around nervously again. "Are you still planning on visiting the coven in Bethesda?"

"Yes." We were starting to get some odd looks from the students. And teachers. From where we were, I could see Stacey waiting for me at my locker, standing by a perplexed-looking Sam. Her expression pretty much said it all.

Gerald's brows creased with worry. "I wish you would reconsider. There has to be another way."

"Unless you know of a handy *Lilin for Dummies* book, I don't see any other options." But that would seriously be helpful. "Look, thank you for your concern, but I have to get—"

"You don't understand." His hand snaked out and curled around my wrist. The sudden punch of fear in my gut rocked me, and now that I knew it wasn't coming from me, it was even more unsettling. "You seem like a nice girl, in spite of everything, but sometimes, child, you go asking questions, you don't like the answers you find."

Gerald dropped my hand before I could pull away. As he turned, he cast a long look back toward my locker, and then hurried back into the utilities room.

Okay. That was weird, and maybe more than typical witchy weird.

Shaking my head, I pivoted around. Stacey eyed me curiously as I made my way through the throng of students. "Hanging out with janitors now?"

"Holding hands with him?" Sam asked.

"Shut up," I said. "Both of you."

Flipping me off, she grinned when I rolled my eyes. "What happened with you yesterday? Please tell me you didn't run off with Roth."

Well… "Nah, just went home. Didn't feel good. You know how that…" I cocked my head, frowning. Something about Sam looked different. Wasn't his hair, even though the unruly waves appeared to have been brushed for once. Then it hit me. "Where're your glasses, Sam?"

"He lost them," Stacey answered as we started down the hall. "Doesn't he look hot?"

"Sure does." I grinned. "But are you going to be able to see without them?"

"I'll be fine." He stepped easily into the flow of traffic. "But why was that janitor grabbing your hand like that? Kind of creepy."

"He helped yesterday when I was feeling sick." The lie came too quickly to my tongue. "He was just shaking my hand."

The sweet, wild scent announced Roth's nearness. I glanced over my shoulder. He was coming down the center of the hall, frowning down at the cell phone he carried in his hand. He wasn't even watching where he was going, but people moved out of the way for him.

Roth looked up, his gaze colliding with mine. There was a faint smudge of blue along his jaw, a sign that a Warden packed a powerful punch. I hastily looked away, cursing under my breath for the twisting motion of guilt. Two seconds later, he was sliding around me. "Good morning, ladies and gent."

"Hey," Sam replied with a smile. "I've got to get to class. See you all at lunch?"

I watched him turn on his heel and disappear back up the hall. So did Roth. There was a weird twist to his mouth. "Is our little Sam turning into a big boy or something?"

"What?" I asked.

"I don't know." He shrugged, turning to Stacey. "No glasses. Actually dressed today as though his mom didn't lay his clothes out for him, and you're staring at him as if you want to make little bespectacled babies with him."

Stacey's cheeks turned bright red, but she giggled. "Maybe I am."

"Oh." Roth's eyes widened. "Dirty."

Other than the making-babies comment, Roth was rather subdued in class. He didn't turn around to annoy me or lean back in his chair so that his arms rested on my table.

It was...different.

As always, Bambi got antsy during class and started creating an invisible map on my body. By the time class was over, I couldn't wait to get out. The bell rang and our sub flipped on the lights.

"Remember," he said, running a hand over his head and clasping the back of his neck as he glanced down at his planner. "There's a pop quiz on the schedule—"

The muffled shriek cut him off, and he turned to the closed door. Then louder screams, shrill and horrified screams, roared from the hallway outside the classroom. As a whole, we rose to our feet, shifting nervously.

Roth started for the door as the screams intensified.

"What's going on?" Stacey whispered.

"I think we all should stay in the classroom," Mr. Tucker said, trying to intercept Roth, but he was fast and half the class was following him. "We don't know who's out there! Come on. Everyone! Back in your seats."

It was impossible.

There was a minor congestion at the door, and then we all spilled out into the packed hallway, Stacey clutching the back of my sweater. The hall had quieted to the point one could hear a grasshopper sneeze, and somehow that was worse than the screams.

I pushed through the crowds, spying Roth's back. His shoulders were unnaturally stiff. I broke through and he looked over his shoulder at me, shaking his head. My gaze drifted beyond him to the almost circular clearing amid the throng of students, an emptiness broken by two dull-gray legs slowly swaying back and forth.

"Oh my God," Stacey whispered.

Dragging my gaze up, my hand rose to my chest. At first, it was as though my mind refused to recognize what it was seeing, but the image didn't go away. It didn't change.

In the middle of the hallway, hanging from a light fixture with the red-and-gold school banner wrapped around his neck, was Gerald Young.

CHAPTER TWENTY

With the police and the trauma, school closed early for the day.

My call to Zayne woke him up, but the moment I told him what happened, he was up and out of the house. No more than twenty minutes after the officials started dismissing students, I found myself sitting in a small booth at a bakery down the street with Zayne *and* Roth.

We weren't the only people there from school. Eva and Gareth were also there. They sat at a bistro table, under a framed picture of baked bread. Gareth was hunched over a cup he held in his pale hands, his shoulders slimmer than I remembered and his hair a greasy mess.

Gareth looked strung out to the max, but I knew better than to interfere again.

I broke my cookie in half, but for once, there was nothing about the sugary goodness that called to me. I barely knew Gerald, having only seen him for the first time in my life yesterday, but it was like with the member of the Church of God's Children. Seeing death was never easy, no matter the relationship or lack thereof to someone.

"Maybe Gerald did kill himself," Zayne said, drawing my

attention to the problem at hand. "As sad as that is, maybe it's that simple."

Roth toyed with the lid to his hot chocolate. For some reason the idea of a demon—the Crown Prince of Hell—drinking hot chocolate brought a wry grin to my lips. "I don't know. Why would he do that, especially in the middle of the hallway? That's a Hell of a way to go out."

"But you really didn't know him. Neither did Layla." The boys were actually having a civilized conversation. "You both spoke to him once."

"Twice actually," I said, breaking another small chunk off my cookie. "He stopped me on the way to class today, thanking me for not telling the Wardens about him."

"That doesn't sound like something someone would do before hanging himself with the school banner," Roth pointed out as he leaned back in the booth. He threw one arm over the back. "Why be grateful Layla didn't put his life in danger if he was about to take his own life anyway?"

"Did he say anything else?"

I nodded. "He mentioned the coven in Bethesda and told me to be careful." I brushed the crumbs off my hands. "He said something along the lines of not liking the answers we'd find to our questions. It was almost as if he knew something, but was too scared to say it."

Roth frowned as he eyed me. "Could one of the coven members have gotten to him?" The question wasn't really addressed to anyone in particular. "Or could it have been the Lilin?"

"Wouldn't you have sensed a witch running around?" Zayne asked.

He shook his head. "They use charms to block us, just like they do with the Wardens. And we don't know enough about the Lilin to even figure out if I'd sniff it out or not."

I sat back, folding my arms across my stomach against the sudden chill that moved over my skin. "It was almost like it was a message."

Zayne twisted toward me. Shadows had bloomed under his eyes, and I knew he hadn't gotten much rest. "I don't like where that thought is heading."

"But it makes sense," Roth said.

"We meet him yesterday, he tells us what he is and about where we can find more info on the Lilin, gives me a warning and then not even an hour later, he's hanging." I took a deep breath. "Seems like the message there is pretty clear. Back the Hell off."

Roth's eyes flashed. "Not going to happen."

"As much as I hate to say it, the coven is the only lead we've got." Zayne draped his arm behind me, and his body heat immediately expanded. His fingers coasted through the loose strands of my hair in a seemingly absent gesture. "There's nothing on the streets. We've come up empty."

"Same on my side." Roth's gaze drifted to Zayne's hand and lingered. "Any update on possible deaths related to the Lilin?"

"Nothing out of the norm, but how do we really know?"

A muscle began to tick in Roth's jaw, and I looked away, focusing on my untouched cookie. There was a sudden loud thump from the other side of the bakery. When I looked up, I saw Gareth on his knees by the table he'd been sitting at. Eva was beside him, her arms wrapped around his upper arm. Two bright pink spots appeared on her cheeks as half the bakery stopped to stare at them.

"Come on," she said, forcing a smile on lips that were bare of any makeup. "You need to get up."

I cringed from the secondhand embarrassment. Eva was not a fan of mine, but watching this made me uncomfortable.

"The kid needs an intervention," an older man in line said loud enough that Eva heard.

Eva's cheeks flushed even brighter, but Gareth let out that giggle again; the kind that made my skin crawl.

"More like a demonic intervention," muttered Roth, eyeing the situation with visible distaste.

Gareth rose but then stumbled again, knocking into a nearby table. Drinks spilled and people scattered. A glassy sheen filled Eva's eyes. I couldn't sit there any longer.

"Move," I said, pushing lightly on Zayne.

He didn't budge. "Why?"

"This is too embarrassing to watch. Someone needs to help her."

Zayne stared at me a moment and then sighed. "Stay put. I'll make sure she gets him out of here."

"Thank you."

As Zayne headed over to help her out, my gaze drifted across the table. It was impossible for it not to go there. I could feel the intensity in Roth's stare. Our gazes locked.

"How are you holding up?" he asked.

The question caught me by surprise. I couldn't remember a time when he'd asked that. "I'm okay."

"Seeing that this morning couldn't have been fun."

Uncomfortable, I placed my hands on the table to keep from fidgeting. "It wasn't."

"And the guy that died a few nights back." A lock of black-blue hair fell across his forehead, softening his features. "How are you handling that?"

Pressing my lips together, I didn't answer immediately. Zayne had Gareth to the door. I hoped that wherever they needed to go wasn't far because I doubted they'd make it without Zayne carrying him. When my gaze slid back to Roth, he was still waiting.

"I'm really hoping you don't blame yourself," he said, angling his long body forward. "But knowing you, you probably do."

"Well, I did slap the guy with a Bible." My stomach twisted at the reminder. "I'm sure the situation could've been handled better."

"But you didn't pull the trigger. You also didn't kill the guy." His voice dropped. "I did."

"But I—"

His hands curled around mine, startling me. "Don't put that shit on your head. You have enough to worry about."

Part of the frustration wiggling its way around my core was mine, but there was a hard edge that didn't belong to me. A disturbance I couldn't fully understand that came from deep within…*Roth.* The longer he had my hands, the clearer the emotions grew, like clouds parting and revealing the sun. Nipping at the heels of frustration was another emotion…similar to one I'd felt from Zayne.

A harsh breath roared out of me and I started to pull my hands free. He didn't let go at first but finally relented. My fingers slipped out of his, eliciting a rush of shivers up my arms.

"What?" he asked, his stare piercing.

I shook my head. "Nothing."

Roth didn't say anything else.

Neither did I.

Later that afternoon, I watched Izzy shift back and forth while Drake clutched Jasmine's leg. She would bend down every so often, idly ruffling the toddler's red curls while he sucked his thumb.

Izzy was as much a natural at shifting as she was a handful. She raced around the living room at warp speed, one little wing flapping while the other drooped to the side. Several times she launched herself into the air when she neared Drake, causing him to shriek in terror.

For the most part, I was safely tucked in the corner of the couch, hunkered down in my hoodie. The house felt like an icebox to me, but probably not to Danika, who kept intercepting Izzy just as she would fling herself at me.

When it neared the hour before dinner, I left to head upstairs. Dinners had been awkward for weeks now and I'd rather scrounge for leftovers than sit through suspicious looks.

I passed the kitchen, spying Morris at the island. He was chopping up veggies with the kind of knife serial killers would covet. He glanced up and his dark skin crinkled at the eyes as he smiled. He waved the knife happily.

If it were anyone else, I would've been concerned. I waved back and then climbed the stairs. At the top landing, a weird shiver skated down my spine. I turned, half expecting to find someone giving me the evil eye from the floor below, but no one was there.

I could hear the distant laugh of Izzy and the low wail of Drake, but the feeling lingered. I shivered, shoving my hands into the pockets of my hoodie as I shook my head. Recent events had made me paranoid, rightfully so.

Turning, my attention fell to Zayne's closed door. He'd gone to sleep when we'd gotten home from the bakery, something that was much needed. I knew he'd be rising soon to get in a workout before he sat down to eat. I crept to the door, my fist hovering for a second, but for reasons I'd probably never know, I opened it without knocking.

He wasn't standing in the middle of his room half-naked nor was he where he liked to be when he entered a deep sleep, which was by the large picture window. Some of the Wardens liked to perch on the rooftop, much like the gargoyle stonework adorning churches and schools. Not Zayne. He'd liked that window since I could remember.

My gaze drifted to his large bed…and there he was. The corners of my lips tipped up. He was sprawled in the center of his bed in his human form, lying on his stomach. A sheet was wrapped around his hips and the corded muscles of his back were relaxed. One cheek rested on the curve of his elbow and he was facing the door, his lips parted. Thick lashes fanned the tips of his cheeks and those lashes had to be the envy of every mascara ad out there.

I quietly closed the door behind me and approached the bed. In his sleep, he looked much younger than he was, at ease, and, in a way, vulnerable. No one seeing him this way would believe that he could be so dangerous or deadly when awake.

Knowing I shouldn't be in here, I still sat on the edge of the bed and my gaze tracked down the line of his spine. I didn't really know why I'd come, but all I could think of was what he'd asked.

Give us a chance.

My heart stuttered. Could we really do this? I still wasn't sure if trying really was the right thing, but not doing so was like turning my back on the history we shared. As my eyes soaked in all the golden flesh on display, I couldn't help but wonder if we would've found ourselves in this moment even if Roth had never come into the picture.

At the thought of him, knots twisted in my stomach, a mixture of lingering hurt, the vapid bite of confusion…and guilt. My hands curled helplessly in my lap. I hated feeling that way—hated that I was still affected by Roth and that I could feel fault in any of this. He was the one who'd pushed me away…pushed me right into the arms of Zayne.

Which were really nice arms, I thought, staring at his biceps.

I felt like a total creeper.

Yeah, time to get moving. I started to get up, but a hand curled around my wrist. Gasping, I looked back down at Zayne.

One eye was visible and a sleepy smile pulled at his lips. "Where're you going?"

Embarrassment swept through me. "How long have you been awake?"

"Long enough to know you've been checking me out." The lopsided smile spread. "I feel like a piece of meat."

"Shut up."

"Didn't say I didn't enjoy the feeling." He rolled onto his side, and I noticed that the dark shadows under his eyes had faded. His gaze drifted over my face. "I like waking up and seeing you here."

A warm sensation buzzed through me like a happy little honeybee, and the feeling made me antsy. As I looked away, my hair slid over my shoulder, shielding my face.

"What?" he asked, dropping my wrist to reach up and brush back the blond locks.

"I don't know." I peeked at him, forcing my attention not to wander below his chin lest I find myself majorly distracted. "It's just…I don't know how to act when you're so…open about this."

His fingers lingered in my hair, slipping through the strands. "Act like you've always acted, Layla-bug. That's what I've always liked about you."

"The fact that I act like a dork most of the time?"

He grinned. "Yes."

A laugh escaped me as I started to relax. Raising my legs, I crossed them. I watched him place the arm closest to me behind his head.

"I wish I would've been more open about it sooner," he admitted quietly. "That I didn't wait so long."

I wished he had, too, because maybe things wouldn't be so confusing and complicated now.

"Better late than never, right?" When I nodded, he slid his fingers down my arm. Even through the hoodie, I could feel his touch. "What's for dinner?"

"I think some kind of stew or pot roast."

"You going to eat with the rest of us?"

I shrugged a shoulder. "I don't know. It feels awkward to do so."

"It's not as though no one wants you there, Layla."

That wasn't how it felt to me. I glanced at the clock on the wall. "I should probably get going. You need—"

Zayne caught my arm and rolled so quickly that there was nothing I could do. I was suddenly on my back, staring into eyes that sparkled with mischief. He hovered above me, supporting his weight on his arms.

"Your running off isn't what I need," he said.

"It isn't?" I squeaked out possibly the stupidest question, but I wasn't to blame. The sheet had slipped low on his hips, and I honestly couldn't tell if he was wearing anything under it.

"No." His grin tugged at my chest. "Let's snuggle for a while."

"Snuggle?" I giggled at the image of a six-and-a-half-foot gargoyle cuddling.

He chuckled. "I thought girls liked to snuggle?"

"I really wouldn't know." That wasn't true. I did love me some snuggling. All those times Zayne had slept beside me, and then there was the time with Roth, when all we'd done was lie in each other's arms and talk about nothing important.

I drew in a sharp breath as my stomach flopped. I should not—could not think about him right now.

Zayne's smile slipped as his eyes searched mine. "Sometimes you disappear on me when you're here, and I probably don't want to know where you go."

My breath caught as my lungs expanded. I wanted to tell him that I didn't go anywhere, and if I did it was nothing to be worried about, but that would be a lie and he'd know it.

One side of his lips quirked up. "But you are *here*. So that means more."

"It does." And it did.

A beat of heavy silence stretched out between us, and his gaze dipped to my lips and then below, to where my hoodie was zipped up to my neck. His grin spread. "Cold?"

"It's chilly in this house," I responded, happy for a shift in topic.

But then his gaze rose, and those eyes were electric. My chest rose with a deep breath. "I should get ready," he murmured.

"You should."

"But I sort of want to just lie around and do nothing."

A tingle started at my lips and shivered its way down to my toes. "That's very un-Wardenlike."

"If you only knew my very un-Wardenlike thoughts, you'd probably run from this room." He took note of my sharp inhale. "Or maybe not."

My fingers itched to touch him, but I kept them by my sides. He'd suggested that we take it slow and give us a chance, and that probably didn't involve feeling him up. But it was so hard.

"You want to get some training in with me tonight?" he asked.

"Yeah." My voice sounded husky. "That…that would be cool."

"Really cool. Or maybe hot. Probably hot…." He trailed off, and his head dipped.

I shrank back, pressing into the mattress as if it could suck me right through. "*Zayne,* you shouldn't be so—"

"It's okay." He kept coming, moving closer, completely unafraid and completely crazy. "You worry too much."

"You're crazy." I turned my head, but he placed two fingers on my chin and guided my head forward. My eyes widened. "Completely freaking crazy."

"No. I just trust you." He rested his forehead against mine, and every muscle in my body locked up. "See? You're not eating my soul, now, are you?"

I kept my mouth clamped shut. The faint burn was in my throat and I didn't trust myself to speak.

He shifted his head and his nose brushed mine, a totally new experience with Zayne. My heart sped up, beating so fast it was tripping over itself. A sigh shuddered out of him and into me. My eyes fell closed as his fingertips trailed across my cheek and then down, to where my pulse beat rapidly. If he lowered his body just a bit, we'd be pressed together in all the ways that made my toes curl and my knees weak, and I had a feeling I'd discover quickly if he wore anything under that sheet.

Oh God, that was so not the right thought to be having right now.

I thought I heard him whisper my name, and then I felt the barest sweep of his lips, as soft and quick as the flutter of wings, across mine.

Shock rippled through me, stealing my breath. My eyes popped open wide, and Zayne lifted his head. There was a tiny, smug smile on his lips and mine…oh, mine were tingling and humming from the brief touch.

"Hmm…" he murmured, and his tongue flicked out, smoothing over the indent in his upper lip. "I'm still here. Soul intact. Go figure."

I was absolutely stupefied, beyond the ability to speak. It

hadn't really been a kiss. My lips had been sealed tight, so you couldn't even say it was a peck, but Zayne...he had dared to put his lips against mine. He'd risked that—risked losing his soul for a brief brushing of lips.

Zayne stretched up, kissed my forehead and then rolled onto his side. "I really need to get into gear, and I need to get changed." He swung his legs out from under the sheet and stood.

He was totally naked.

Totally freaking naked and I was staring at his behind, his rather firm and— "Oh my God!"

Glancing over his shoulder, he arched a brow as his sly smile turned wicked. "What?"

"What?" I gaped at him, but then my gaze dropped and my face burned like the first circle of Hell. "Oh my God," I said again as I rolled off the bed, onto the other side. A giggle crawled its way up my throat and burst free. "You are so freaking naked."

"Really?" His response was dry as he plucked up the sheet. He turned slightly and—oh dear God, I whirled around, eyes widening.

Holy baby gargoyles, he was...

"You doing okay over there?"

"Yeah," I croaked, feeling flushed for a whole different reason. I turned slowly.

He chuckled as he wrapped the sheet around his waist, covering his...his goodies.

"I'm going to have to drop this again to get changed." His eyes danced with mischief. "Not saying you have to leave, but..."

"I'm leaving." I shot around the bed, my hair trailing out behind me. As I passed him, he reached out, tapping my behind. I jumped, shooting him a look. "You are so bad."

"Terrible." He grinned as he backed up, one hand resting on the knot of the sheet. "See you in a bit."

I meeped something to the affirmative, and then flew out into the hall. My entire body was flaming as I pressed one hand against my still-tingling lips and the image of Zayne's behind emblazoned itself into my eye sockets.

He had a great ass.

And from what I'd seen, he wasn't hurting in any other department either.

I giggled as I turned to the stairs, almost plowing straight into Maddox. He halted at the top step. "Sorry," I mumbled.

His expression was sharp, not entirely trusting, but he nodded. As he stepped to the side to let me past, a wave of irritation pricked its way up my back. Would it kill him to say something? The Warden had never spoken to me.

Not once.

Taking a deep breath, I moved my foot to the step below and a cold blast of air came from the hall behind me, stirring my hair and sending thin tendrils around my face.

I looked to my left and all I saw was Maddox's face white with shock, and then he tumbled head over feet down the steep stairs.

Screaming, I hurried down the steps, grimacing when he smacked the hardwood floor below, his head cracking off the floor. I reached his side as feet pounded from every corner in the house.

He lay at an unnatural angle, arm twisted behind him and one leg bent at the knee. I bent down. "Maddox?"

He didn't answer.

CHAPTER TWENTY-ONE

Seconds later, and I still had no idea what just happened.

Dez was the first to reach us. He placed a hand on my shoulder and gently moved me aside as he knelt. "Maddox?" he said to the pale, unmoving Warden. When there was no response, he placed a hand on Maddox's chest. "Christ."

I folded my arms over my chest. I knew that Maddox had to be alive. A fall wouldn't kill a Warden, but in their human form, they were susceptible to injury, even the severe kind.

"How did this happen?" Dez looked over his shoulder at me.

I shook my head. "I don't know. He was coming up the stairs and then he just fell backward."

Zayne came down the stairs, dressed only in a pair of loose sweats. "What the Hell?"

"He fell," I explained lamely.

"Jasmine!" shouted Dez as he rose.

Within seconds, Jasmine arrived, her eyes widening. She turned, handing Drake off to Danika. "Keep Izzy and Drake out of here," she said, turning back to Maddox.

Danika nodded, glancing to where Zayne and I stood. She

turned, quickly taking Drake back the way they'd come. A door shut softly.

As Jasmine knelt on Maddox's other side and placed slim fingers on his neck, the rest of the crew arrived. Once they heard that Maddox had fallen backward down the stairs, Abbot turned to me.

Shrinking back, I realized I was so about to be crucified.

"He simply fell backward?" Abbot asked, disbelief ringing from his voice as he stepped around Maddox's prone legs. "You expect me or any of us to believe that?"

At least he cut to the chase this time. "Yes! He just fell. I don't know if he lost his balance or— Wait, there was a rush of cold air right before he fell." And now that I said that out loud, I knew it hadn't been the first time. "It was the same with the windows. There was a gust of—"

"Of wind?" Abbot finished doubtfully. "Did the air kick on with enough force to knock out windows or throw a two-hundred-and-thirty-pound Warden down the stairs? That's *if* we used the air-conditioning this time of year, which we don't."

"Okay. I know that sounds ridiculous, but I'm not lying."

Zayne moved to my side. "She has no reason to lie, Father. If she said he fell, he fell."

"She has every reason to lie," his father spat. I blanched. "Once was enough, but this?" He gestured at Maddox. "One of our own—a guest of our clan—has been injured, and another is missing."

I stiffened at the implication, even though the latter was very much on point. Zayne stepped forward, blocking me. "What are you saying?"

"Guys," Jasmine spoke up. "I need to move Maddox to get a better look at his injuries. Right now, it looks like he's just knocked out. Maybe a broken arm or cracked skull, which will heal. But I need help moving him."

Zayne and Abbot, who were currently in an epic stare-down, didn't seem to hear her.

Dez nodded as he moved to stand before Maddox's feet. "Nicolai? Can you get his arms?"

As Nicolai did their bidding, Abbot eyed his son. "There is no way that I, or you, can believe that he lost his balance and fell."

Wardens typically were a wee bit more graceful than that, but there was no other explanation...other than that strange wind.

"Are you suggesting that Layla pushed him?" Zayne challenged as the muscles in his back rippled. "Because that's stupid."

Abbot stepped up to Zayne, going toe-to-toe, and my heart sank. "Watch how you speak to me, boy. I am your father."

I had the wild urge to laugh as I pictured Darth Vader's helmet descending on Abbot's head. Thankfully, I didn't, because that would seriously not help things.

Geoff came forward. "May I suggest something?" When Abbot nodded curtly, he continued. "Whatever happened would've been captured on video. The same with the windows."

My gaze swung to him sharply. Why hadn't I thought of that? "So you guys saw the video and what did it show?"

"The windows blowing out, seemingly by themselves," Geoff replied.

Zayne lifted his chin. "Let's go see the videos, then."

I wasn't sure how much it would help since they'd already seen one video of me not doing anything, but we headed down to the command center. Near the training rooms it was always several degrees cooler than anywhere else, but today, it seemed as if it was the same temperature as the above floors as we walked down the narrow, dimly lit hall.

I stuck close to Zayne, knowing better than to say much of anything right now. Anger radiated off Abbot in waves, clogging the hall. Even Bambi, who'd been relatively sedentary, grew restless, slithering along my stomach.

Tension was coming off Zayne as he stuck close to my side. He didn't speak as we entered Geoff's home away from home.

The command center was a circular room that quickly became crowded when we piled into it. Monitors lined half of the wall and the other sections were covered with old band posters, ranging from Bon Jovi, Pink Floyd and AC/DC to Aerosmith. Some of them looked authentic with their edges curling upward.

It was weird—the tiny glimpse of Geoff's personality mingled with the creepy, NSA-level security.

Geoff strode to one of the computers and his fingers danced over the keys. The screen focused on the now empty stairway and landing, began to rapidly back up, then stopped just as I came into view…with my fingers touching my lips.

Nice.

Exhaling softly, I glanced up at Zayne and he looked down at me. One side of his lips curved as a knowing gleam filled his eyes. Sigh.

I turned back to the video just as Maddox appeared on the screen. There was no volume, but you could see him step out of my way. Cameras didn't lie, and there was no mistaking the distrusting look he'd cast my way.

The room was silent as the monitor revealed exactly what I'd told them. From the positioning of the camera, it was clear the moment I'd felt the blast of air. My hair, which looked white on the screen, stirred as if I'd walked in front of a fan. The camera caught the widening of Maddox's eyes and the slight gape of his mouth the second before he went down. What I didn't realize when it happened was when Maddox fell, he didn't bounce off the steps. He went ass over teacup in the air, not hitting anything until he reached the bottom.

Like he'd thrown himself backward.

Or had been pushed by a great force.

"I didn't touch him as you can see," I said, raising my gaze to where Abbot stood beside Geoff. "I didn't do anything."

A muscle feathered along his jaw as he watched Geoff stop the recording.

"There's no denying it." Zayne folded his arms across his broad chest. "She didn't lie."

"But she was looking at him," Abbot replied, turning to us.

My brows shot up. "Unless I developed some supercool powers without realizing it, looking at him didn't throw him down the stairs."

His gaze flicked to me, and pressure clamped down on my chest. The way he stared at me, like I was a wolf among the poor little sheep he was charged with protecting, struck deep. There was no hiding his open distrust, and I didn't understand where it came from. Yes, I had lied to him, but he'd lied to me about bigger, more important things—like who my mother and father were for starters.

It hadn't always been like this. I hated the scalding tide of tears that drenched the back of my throat. It was weak to cry, but it hurt to acknowledge that Abbot no longer looked at me as a part of his family. That was so clear now.

Zayne had been speaking, but I hadn't been paying attention. Whatever he'd said, most likely in my defense, had angered his father.

"We don't know what she's truly capable of. I doubt she even knows," he replied.

Anger was like a shot of steel in Zayne's spine. "What do

you mean we don't know? I know what she is and isn't capable of. How can you be any different?"

The earnest and steadfast way he defended me, in spite of the obvious discontent it was brewing between him and his father, made it feel as if a hand had shot through my chest and closed around my heart.

Abbot swore under his breath, and when he spoke, it was as though I wasn't in the room or he didn't care that I was. "You need to look past your feelings, son. She is no longer the small, frightened child I brought home. The sooner you understand that, the better."

I sucked in a breath as the burn moved into my stinging eyes. Except this was a different kind of blistering provoked by a maddening rush of emotions. My skin crawled, causing Bambi to twitch along my back, and the need to feed punched me in the gut.

Geoff pursed his lips and looked away as Zayne stared at his father, his mouth slightly open, as if he couldn't believe what his father had just said.

Humiliation mingled with the soul-deep hurt. I took a breath and didn't trust myself to speak. I had to take another. "Then what am I?"

Abbot looked at me but didn't respond.

My voice wavered when I spoke again. "Why do you even let me stay here?"

There was a moment of silence and then Abbot looked away. A heavy sigh shuddered through him. "I really don't know."

I winced as Zayne stepped toward his father, his eyes flashing a bright, unnatural cobalt. "How can you even say that?"

Unable to stand here and not do something I'd regret, like burst into tears or kick Abbot in the stomach, I whipped around and headed out of the command center. My hands tingled as I curled them into fists. I was breathing too fast—

two breaths in, one breath out. When had Abbot grown to dislike me so much? It struck me as I crossed the training room, causing me to stop suddenly. He hadn't trusted me for a while, but that mistrust had been more pronounced from the moment Roth had returned and broken the news that a Lilin had been born.

"Layla."

Gripping the locker door, I bit back a groan at the sound of Roth's voice. Although I didn't acknowledge his presence, he leaned against the locker beside mine. I so wasn't in the mood to deal with him today. "What?"

"You look like shit."

I shoved my load of books inside. "Thanks."

"You also looked like you were about to fall asleep in bio."

"How is that any different from anyone else in class?"

He chuckled darkly. "Good point." He stopped as a sophomore approached his locker, which was the one Roth was currently resting his butt against. The boy stopped and Roth raised a brow. The boy turned on his heel and hurried off. Roth grinned as he tilted his chin toward me. "Didn't get much sleep last night?"

After everything that had happened yesterday, sleep hadn't come easily. I shook my head as I reached for my afternoon books.

"Did Stony keep you up late, whispering innocent and pure thoughts in your ear?"

I rolled my eyes at the derision dripping from his voice. "Uh. No."

He shifted, angling his body toward mine. "Did he keep you up whispering all the naughty things he wants to do to you?"

Exhaling deeply, I finally turned to him. Roth's hair was a

mess of raven locks and the gray shirt he wore stretched taut across his chest. His jeans hung low on his hips, ripped across both knees. He was the picture of lazy arrogance.

"I'm guessing he didn't do that either. He's too good for those kinds of dirty things." He tapped a finger on his chin thoughtfully, and I realized the nail was painted black. "He probably cuddled with you."

Zayne had sort of cuddled with me before Maddox had taken a fall down the stairs, but he'd also been not so pure about it. "What is with you wanting to know what's going on with me and Zayne? It's none of your business."

One shoulder rose. "I'm just curious." When I didn't respond, he sighed. "So what's your deal today? Is it because of what happened to our friendly neighborhood witch? Or something else?"

I cringed a little at his blasé attitude. "That and last night..." What was I thinking even confiding in Roth? Was our white flag of friendship cut out for this?

"Last night what?"

Sighing, I ran a hand through my hair. The need to give voice to what was troubling me was too strong. It wasn't as though I could talk to Stacey about these things, and I didn't want to involve Zayne any more than he was already by the simple act of defending me.

"Abbot thinks I'm evil incarnate."

His brows inched up his forehead, disappearing under his hair. "What?"

"CliffsNotes version? There have been some weird things happening at the house. The windows were blown out and then one of the Wardens fell down the stairs." I tucked my hair back, beyond tired. "Compounded with the fact Tomas—who Bambi ate—is still missing, Abbot thinks I'm behind it all."

Roth frowned. "And why does he think you're involved in any of this?"

I waited until a small group of people hurrying toward the cafeteria passed us before continuing. "Because I was present when the windows broke and when Maddox fell down the steps. Not sure how he attributes Tomas to me."

"Did you do those things?" he asked.

"What?" I threw my hands up. "No. I didn't do anything. They even have it on camera." A bit paranoid, I scowled. "Why would you ask that?"

"Why wouldn't I ask to make sure? You said you didn't. There's proof you didn't, so why would he still think you're behind it?"

And here came the part that had kept me tossing and turning all night. "Abbot thinks that they don't know what I'm capable of. That I have superpowers and did all of that with a single thought, I guess."

"That would be a cool ability—a very demonic ability. An Upper Level one to be exact," he said, grinning.

An Upper Level ability...oh my God, that's what Zayne and Danika had said about me, but with all the crazy, I'd forgotten about it.

"Hey." Roth's voice softened. "Layla, I wasn't being serious."

I lifted my gaze, meeting his, and I saw the truth in his eyes. My heart sped up. He...he was lying now. I knew it deep in my bones. The words came out in a whisper. "Abbot thinks I'm evil."

Roth drew back and straightened. The longer he was quiet, the bigger the knots of unease grew in my stomach, becoming balls of lead. "Skip with me."

I blinked. "What?"

"Skip with me," he said again.

That was so not what I was expecting him to say. "I'm going to lunch."

"Or you can go have lunch with me."

I shook my head. "That's not a good idea."

"Why not?" The devilish grin was back, giving his features a boyish charm. "Would Stony not approve?"

Uh, that was an understatement.

"Or are you worried Abbot wouldn't?" He dipped his head to mine and his breath danced over my lips. "He thinks you're evil? Screw it. Be bad."

"I'm not sure how being bad is going to help anything."

"It's going to help. Trust me." Reaching over, he slid the strap of my book bag down my shoulder and then tossed it in the locker. "Come and be bad with me."

Taking a step back, I shook my head. "That's not going to happen."

"I'm not suggesting you come and have sex with me, Layla." As I flushed to the roots of my hair, he puckered his lips. "Actually, that's not a bad idea, but not what I'm saying."

I cast a doubtful look in his direction.

Roth reclaimed the space, curving his hands around my upper arms. "I promise I'll have you back before Stony comes to pick you up. I'll work some of my awesome skill and no one will be the wiser. Boy Scout's honor."

"You were never a Boy Scout."

His lips curved up. "Ah, good point, but come on. What's it going to hurt? We're friends, right? Two demon peas in a demon pod."

The urge to laugh at him was powerful, but I resisted, because it only encouraged the jerk.

"Look, there's something that I want to show you." As I raised a brow, Roth pouted. "Not my manly bits, you little perv."

"Your *manly bits?*" A laugh burst from me. "You are so bizarre."

"But you were thinking about my manly bits."

Two spots of heat blossomed on my cheeks. Now I was. "No, I wasn't."

He grinned. "By the way, my manly bits are not bits. Just want to clear that up."

"Oh my God…"

"Come on. There's a place I think you need to see that will help put all of this in perspective. You'll see that being bad isn't bad at all. Come on, shortie," he goaded, eyes twinkling like two pieces of topaz. "Skip with me."

Skipping did sound good. And there was a healthy dose of curiosity when it came to whatever it was that he wanted to show me that could change my perspective, but leaving school with him was stupid, bound to turn ugly, and Zayne would be…well, he wouldn't be happy.

But Roth was like this little devil on my shoulder, urging me to be bad and to enjoy every freaking moment of it. Except he wasn't a little devil. He was the Crown Prince of Hell.

Common sense seemed to have belly flopped itself right out the window and face-planted in the cement below, because I found myself nodding and saying, "Okay."

CHAPTER TWENTY-TWO

I stared at the metal monster in front of me and slowly forced my gaze to where Roth stood. This "being bad" thing was already a horrible idea.

"Since when did you start riding a motorcycle?"

"This is not just any motorcycle, shortie. This is a Hayabusa, one of the fastest rockets on the road." He held out a helmet. "Here."

I eyed the silver-and-red motorcycle. There was barely any room for two people on the thing.

"It's not bad." The strap rattled off the helmet as he shook it at me, impatient. "We need to get going before the rent-a-cop decides to wake up from his nap and catch us outside, forcing me to do more unsavory demon things."

We'd made a pit stop at the school office, and I didn't know what he did in there to ensure no one would call home. Sighing, I studied the motorcycle.

It wasn't hard to picture Roth on the crotch rocket. Shirtless.

Why did my brain always take *everything* in that direction? I was going to blame the genes from mommy dearest.

"What are you thinking?" Roth asked as keen interest flashed across his face.

"Nothing." I snatched the red helmet out of his hands. It took a few seconds for me to get it on correctly, and when I was done hooking the strap, Roth had already donned a black one and was straddling the motorcycle.

I swallowed just as I realized how close we'd be on this thing, like a "one body instead of two" level of closeness. This was so inappropriate. Zayne and I weren't *together,* together, but my goodies were going up against a part of Roth's goodies.

"FML," I muttered.

Roth's head whipped around and he lifted the face shield. "What?"

Damn, he had super hearing or something. I waved him off as I approached the bike. Knowing I was most likely going to regret this like eating an entire cake in one sitting, I threw my leg over the seat and sat down. Almost immediately I slid forward, causing my thighs to cradle his hips.

Oh, this was not good.

Roth kicked the engine and the immediate roar widened my eyes. Tentatively, I placed my hands on his sides. He looked over his shoulder at me. I couldn't see his face, but he shook his head before facing the front. Then he reached down, wrapping his hands around my forearms and yanked me forward.

In a nanosecond, my breasts were smushed against his back. Before I could put some much needed space between us, he tucked my hands together against his lower stomach, folding one hand over my wrists. I felt his chuckle and then he gunned it.

It was as if the jerk face knew I'd pull away and had totally prevented it.

My heart leaped into my throat as he darted into traffic,

zooming between cars that felt as though they were at a complete standstill compared to how fast we were going.

Roth blocked most of the wind as he swerved around a cab, but the whispers of the wind lifted the loose stands of hair flowing out from under my helmet. The ends managed to sneak up under the sleeves of my sweater, skating over my skin. My pulse was somewhere in between *oh, crap on a cracker* and *Christ on a crutch*.

Up ahead, the light turned yellow and the bike pitched forward as he hit the gas. We flew through the intersection as it flicked red. A horn's blaring was muted as the bike eased to the side. He took a wicked curve and it was no longer necessary for him to hold on to me. My arms had his waist in a choke hold.

Roth navigated the crowded streets like a pro and, after a couple of minutes, the adrenaline kicking in my veins wasn't from fear of becoming a giant road burn, but from the rush of exhilaration.

This…this had to be what flying felt like.

A giddy smile broke out across my face, and I was happy that the shield hid it, because I probably looked like a dork. Loosening my hold, I leaned back and closed my eyes.

Oh, I wanted to shift again. I wanted to climb off this bike and force my skin to expand and my bones to stretch. I wanted to feel my wings unfurling and I wanted to take flight. But doing so in downtown D.C. in the middle of the day wouldn't go over so well.

After a short time, I realized we were heading toward the Palisades, to where Roth lived. Instinct fired off a ton of warnings, but there was little I could do about it at the moment. I waited until he winged a right into the parking garage and coasted to a stop on the first level. The moment he kicked his feet to the ground, I whipped off the helmet and tapped him on the back with it.

Taking his sweet time, he unhooked his chinstrap and twisted toward me, resting his helmet in his lap. "Didn't you love that?"

"Yes. It was fun, but why did you take me to your apartment? I shouldn't be here."

"Says who?"

I shot him a look.

"Stony?"

"Roth."

He rolled his eyes. "I told you I wanted to show you something. It's not my apartment. I'm a bit more creative than that."

I resisted the urge to hit him with the helmet as he climbed off the bike gracefully. Smoothing a hand over my wind-tossed ends, I mentally cursed myself out. I'd put myself in this situation...whatever this situation turned out to be and, as Roth thrust his fingers through his own hair, shaking out the mess of waves, I knew I was so going to pay the piper later.

When I started to scoot back off the bike, he muttered, "Finally."

I stopped and flipped him off.

Roth laughed as he took the helmet from me, placing it on the bike beside his. "No one will mess with them," he explained when I eyed what he was doing. He then extended his hand. "No second thoughts now."

My gaze dropped to his hand. It wouldn't be so bad if we were actually attempting to locate the Lilin or gain info on it. At least I'd have an excuse for being here other than being... bad, but it was too late now.

I didn't take his hand as I got off the bike, not nearly as gracefully as Roth. He shook his head as he stepped back, giving me some space. "So what are you going to show me?"

His low chuckle sent a shiver through me. "Lots of things, but you have to promise me what you see stays here."

My gaze met his and curiosity truly got the best of me. When he turned and strolled toward the gray windowless door, I followed behind him, worrying my lower lip. He opened the door, spreading his arm out in a grand gesture. He bowed slightly at the waist as I walked past him, into the lobby of his apartment building. The faint, pleasant aromas of tobacco and coffee greeted me.

It was just as I remembered—old-school Hollywood. Golden chandeliers cast bright light onto the brown leather couches that looked worn and comfy. My gaze lifted to the domed ceiling.

The painting was the only thing out of place—a hard-core battle scene of angels fighting with fiery swords. Angels fell through misty clouds, their beautiful faces warped by pain. This time I noticed something I hadn't before. The painted angels, the ones with their eyes open, all had blue eyes—that startling, electric-blue color that all Wardens had. I frowned as I studied them. What did Roth call the Wardens? Heavenly rejects?

"Shortie?"

I turned to where Roth waited by the elevators—elevators that only went down, and by down, I meant *waaay* down. He opened the door, and instead of going toward the upstairs, he headed to the steps leading down.

I halted in the stairwell. "Where does this go?"

"Remember how Gerald said that some covens have clubs where others of their kind can safely get together? We have the same thing." He took the steps two at a time. "When we're topside, we like to stick together in buildings like this and, in each of them, there's always something extra special in the basement."

As we went down a level, a set of bloodred doors appeared like a beacon of sin, waiting for us. Roth placed his hands on the center, flashed a quick grin, and then pushed the doors open wide.

I didn't know what I was expecting to see beyond the doors, probably something along the lines of a creepy dive bar, but what I saw was something else entirely.

The place was surprisingly bright. No seedy red lighting, no neon beer signs. Plush couches lined the walls, sectioned off by black velvet ropes. People of various ages lounged on the couches. I didn't need my wonky ability to know that I was surrounded by demons.

Heady music thrummed. The kind you could dance to, lose yourself in. The place was packed and, in the shadowy corners of the room, I could make out thicker shadows moving sinuously. It was the middle of the day, so I was surprised to see so many here, but then again, I doubted demons operated by human schedules.

Roth chuckled as he lowered his lips to my ear. "You should see the look on your face."

I shook my head, feeling out of my element and then some. "It's...different."

There was an S-shaped stage in the middle of the bar, surrounded by round tables and chairs, but it was what was onstage that caught and held my attention.

Scantily clad women danced. Women so beautiful, they could've walked the runways of New York and Milan. One in particular swayed in the middle of the S. A tiny ruffled skirt covered her lower half and she wore a bra that glittered and dazzled in the light.

"Is she wearing diamonds as a bra?" I asked.

Roth shrugged as he kept his eyes on me, catching each of

my reactions. "Probably. It wouldn't surprise me. We demons do like shiny, sparkling things."

The blonde with the diamond bra moved to the music, dipping down and slinking back up. She moved like a snake, or as if she was a part of the throbbing music. She went down on her knees, throwing her head back as she smiled faintly at the man in front of her. An odd light reflected from her eyes.

"She's a demon," I pointed out stupidly, as though I didn't already know that.

"They like to be called succubi," he explained nonchalantly. "I do believe that's the politically correct term."

I shot him a dirty look, but my gaze was immediately drawn back to the girl. I'd never seen a succubus in real life before. "How can they be here? The Alphas forbid them from coming topside."

"I'm not telling. Are you?"

Before I could respond, a man stood and leaned against the stage. The succubus in the diamond getup smiled playfully as she slunk down and bestowed a chaste kiss on the man's lips.

He immediately went stiff, hands spasming at his sides while the succubus's skin glowed. My mouth dropped open. Those reactions could only mean one thing. The man—he was *human*.

"Hey!" I cried out. "She took his—"

Roth placed his finger on my lips. "Shortie, what you see in here stays in here. You promised."

I did, but I hadn't known what was happening. I knocked his hand away. "This is wrong."

"Or it's right. Look." He turned me back to the stage. The man was sitting in his seat, a happy, sated smile on his lax face. "He's not harmed. He just gave her a little energy booster. If anything, he thoroughly enjoyed the little kiss. Just as I'm sure most would enjoy a little kiss from you."

I ignored the last part. "But how are humans in here? Do they know what's around them?" I couldn't imagine that they did, the rules and all, but I felt as if the world had been turned upside down the moment I stepped through those red doors.

"Some humans tend to find their way here, but do the humans truly know what they're encountering? The demons here don't expose what they are, but the humans here aren't innocent. If you could see their souls, you'd know they aren't." His hand curved around my waist, pulling me closer to his hip as we walked around the stage. Bambi glided toward him in response to his touch. "So the ones who come here? Well, they get what they deserve."

What could I say to that? As I searched for a condemning response, I caught sight of several gold-encrusted birdcages hanging behind the stage. There were girls in them. A busty redhead caught my eye and her red lips tipped up in a provocative smile. Her dress showed more than it covered. I looked away, feeling my cheeks burn.

In the darkest corners of the club, poker games were being played. A man in his thirties—so plain he had to be human—sweated profusely as the ungodly handsome man across from him glanced up, grinning. Light reflected off his irises, just like it had with the succubus girls on stage.

The demon showed his hand. "Flush. Yours?"

The man's hands shook as he flipped his cards over. "A straight," he replied hoarsely. He fell back in his seat, face paling.

"Are they playing for kittens?" I asked, thinking of an episode of *Buffy* I'd caught on the computer one sleepless night.

Roth looked puzzled. "What?"

I shook my head. "Never mind. What are they playing for?"

"I'm not sure I want to know." Roth steered me away from the poker tables.

"Pretty little girl, wanna dance with me?"

My head snapped up. One of the cage dancers reached through the bars toward me. When she couldn't reach me, she stood, closed her eyes and tipped her head back. Long brown hair fell down her back as she swayed her hips to the music. "Come on. Let loose. Live a little. You'll love the freedom. The way the music catches your blood on fire. You'll love the burn. We all do."

"Harpy," murmured Roth.

Her eyes opened into thin slits as she dipped, running her hands down the front of her barely clothed body. She smiled at Roth. *"Mei Domina."*

The language she spoke sounded old. "What did she say to you?"

He grinned. "Don't dance with any of the girls in here."

"Wasn't planning to," I replied blandly. "You didn't answer my question."

"Wasn't planning to," he echoed as he guided me toward the bar, his hand on my back a somewhat steady presence in the crazy world I'd stepped into.

"What happens if I do dance with one of them?" I asked after a few seconds.

He leaned in, whispering in my ear, "You'd never stop, shortie. You're only part demon, so you're susceptible to some of the demons' charms. Some of those girls up there are humans. They danced. Look at where they are now."

I shivered. From his words or his breath, I wasn't sure. "That doesn't seem right."

"If you could see their souls, I'm sure you wouldn't feel that way."

My gaze flickered over them. The girls were all beautiful in their own way. Some were supermodel thin and some larger, pale skin and darker, brunettes and blondes. "Their souls are tainted?"

Roth nodded, looking pleased. "This is sort of a waiting room and a welcoming committee all in one."

"Is this...purgatory?"

"No." He laughed. "Purgatory is nowhere near as entertaining as this place is."

I really wasn't sure what to think of that or why he wanted to show me any of this. I let him walk me to the bar. It was surprisingly sparse. Only three or four patrons, all human, sat on the stools. Roth left me on the stool at the very end of the bar next to a bowl of beer nuts.

"I'm going to go score us something to eat that doesn't involve a food that had about a hundred fingers in it. Just don't dance with anyone or allow anyone to buy you a drink."

"But—"

"I'm trusting you not to get into any trouble," he continued, his eyes meeting mine. "I know you can take care of yourself. I know you're smart. I'm not going to lock you in a room to ensure that you make good decisions."

I opened my mouth, but then it hit me. Roth did trust that I could take care of myself and stay out of trouble. There was a...a freedom in that I'd never really tasted before. My whole life had been inside a cage. Not like those of the dancing girls, but a gilded cage that all female Wardens were kept in, and although I'd been given more freedom than any of them had, the frustration was the same.

"Layla?" he queried softly.

Something else occurred to me then. Zayne would lock me in a room to keep me safe if he thought there was even a hint of danger in the air. Roth...yeah, he'd tried to get me out of the way, but he wouldn't shelter me. He would...he would just let me be.

"Okay," I said finally. "I'll be here."

"Good." He smiled and then disappeared back into the crowd.

I swiveled around, frowning as I told myself I totally had this. I was cool. Totally cool.

I fidgeted with the edge of the bar, keeping my eyes down. I doubted making eye contact with anything in this bar would be a smart idea. If there were succubi in here, what else could there be? I thought of the handsome demon in the corner playing cards.

Was the demon a dealmaker—a special kind of Duke that could be summoned from Hell to make deals? Back in the day, they were commonplace topside from what I knew, but just like other dangerous demons, they'd been banished to Hell by the Alphas.

God, if the Wardens knew that this place existed, they'd have a field day down here.

"She says I need a better job. That if I can't pay my own bills, then how can I pay hers?" said a man a few seats down from me. He was dressed in a drab gray suit. It looked like a knockoff you could buy at an outlet. "I don't know what to do. I can't lose her."

My gaze shifted to the bartender, and my mouth dropped open. It was Cayman! He glanced at me and winked as he topped off the man's glass from a clear bottle. His ice-blond hair was pulled back into a ponytail, and he wore a black dress shirt that was rolled up to the elbows.

So on top of being an infernal ruler and Roth's wingman, Cayman was apparently also a bartender.

Odd.

He set the bottle down between them and leaned his hip against the counter. "Women are such trouble, Ricky. That's why I prefer a good, honest man."

That he liked men wasn't news to me, but I seriously doubted he preferred a *good, honest* man.

Ricky ran the back of his hand over his forehead, blinking. "You'd change your mind if you met Angela. She's an angel, as angelic as her name. I love her."

"An angel that wants you to pay her bills?" The gleam in his honey-colored eyes brightened. "Doesn't sound like a heavenly creature to me."

"She's so beautiful. Heaven ain't got nothing on her." Ricky lowered his head to his hands, and, for a moment, I thought the dude would start crying. "She won't return any of my phone calls or emails. Not until I can prove I'm financially stable."

Cayman sighed. "What would you do for this gold-digging angel of yours?"

Ricky's head lifted, his eyes wide and sort of glazed over. He was drunk. "I'd do anything."

"Anything?" asked the demon. He leaned forward, eyes latched on to the mortal's.

I had a sinking feeling in my stomach.

"Anything," Ricky agreed vehemently.

"What do you think you need for this wonderful specimen of womanhood to stay with you?"

"Money," answered Ricky. "I need to win the lottery."

Cayman grinned wolfishly, topping off the man's drink again. "Then one more drink for good luck, my friend." He raised the bottle up.

My stomach sank even further.

Ricky tapped his glass off the bottle, then downed the glass. He slammed it down and the glass shone an unholy red for a brief second. A deal had just been struck.

Love in exchange for a soul.

Ricky stumbled from the bar after a few minutes, and I

hoped he didn't accidentally get on the wrong elevator or something. I turned an expectant look on Cayman.

He laughed as he made his way over to me. "Care to share your worries?" he asked smoothly.

I leaned back. "Yeah, no thank you."

He slid the bottle in front of me and leaned against the bar. "Would you like a drink, then?"

My eyes narrowed. "I'm fine."

"Smart girl," he replied. "Then again, I doubt there is any deal you could make me." He looked over my shoulder, scouring the bar. "You're looking at me like I just murdered a baby, sugar. You know what I am. You know what *you* are."

"You just let a guy trade his soul for love."

"Part of his soul—just a teeny, tiny piece. That's all." His gaze moved back to mine. "What was Roth thinking by bringing you here?"

I shrugged. "I have no clue."

"And where is he?"

"Headed off to get us food."

He laughed. "Roth brought you *here* for food? That's great. You look as comfortable as a kitten huddled in a pile of pit bulls."

I made a face. "I look that out of place?"

"You got that look that says not quite human, but that's not it." Cayman cocked his head to the side. "Frankly, when you look around, you look like you've smelled something bad, sugar."

Did I?

Cayman flipped the white towel across his shoulder. "I don't have to know you that well to know you ain't happy with what you are."

"That's not…" I trailed off. There was no point in denying

it. I still hadn't fully come to accept that I was both Warden and demon—the embodiment of good *and* evil.

He smiled again. "You know, I know why Roth brought you here. He wanted you to see this—to understand what this place is."

"A den of sin?"

Cayman chuckled. "Cute, sugar, but I'm sure he told you that a certain kind of people come here, right?"

"People whose souls are already tainted?"

He nodded as he lowered his voice. "These are the bottom of the barrel, the humans who do bad all on their own. They find their way here because it's in their nature, and we're doing society a favor with the services we provide."

My brows rose.

"We're aiding the process, getting them out of the gene pool so to speak, one little nip and suck at a time. That is what most demons do. We don't go after the innocents. We go after the sinners—and, boy, do we love them." He straightened. "That's what your Wardens don't understand. Just because there's a few bad demons in the bunch, doesn't mean what we do isn't a very necessary evil."

His words rained down on me as though I'd stepped out into an ice storm. Was that why Roth had brought me here? To show me that evil was necessary in the world and maybe not even that wrong?

I glanced around the bar again, easily spying the humans, and Roth was probably right. If I could see their souls, I'd see their sins. But what did that have to do with me?

It was so obvious that I sort of wanted to smack myself in the face.

Maybe Roth was trying to show me that somehow, some way, the demon part of me was necessary. That the demon side had been the one who'd given me the ability to see souls, and now to feel others' emotions, and it had been the demon that had forced me to shift the night Paimon had tried to free Lilith. In reality, he'd always been trying to show me the benefits of my darker heritage. A small grin pulled at my lips. Thinking of those benefits didn't lessen the blow of Abbot's obvious disgust with me, but it helped.

"So has Roth wooed you away from all common sense, yet? He's a yummy one, isn't he?"

Caught off guard by the question, I felt my smile fade. "No! No. It's not like that."

"It's not?" Cayman's eyes seemed to catch and swallow all light. "How is it ever not like that with Roth? Denying him is like not breathing air."

"Well, then, I must not be breathing. Roth and I are just friends." *Friends* sounded so lame and wasn't even particularly true considering our past.

He arched a brow, but shrugged. "Whatever you say, sugar. You want to pretend you're not attracted to a hottie like that, it's on you. Although he usually doesn't do the dark hair. I like it better than the bleached white he does sometimes. It's like Billy Idol called, wants his hairstyle back. I prefer the darker look myself."

I couldn't help it. Curiosity got the best of me. I leaned forward. "What do you mean?"

He grinned, dropping his head so we were eye-level. "He likes to change up his coloring. The facial features are always the same, and so are the piercings, but the hair is different. Now that he's rocking the dark-and-brooding look, I guess he isn't all about the 'White Wedding' or 'Cradle of Love.'"

"Huh?"

Cayman rolled his eyes. "You younglings wouldn't know good music if it hit you upside the head. Anyway, I like him when he's dark and poetic. It's rather entertaining."

"I kind of like him this way, too." I bit my lip and mentally bitch slapped myself. "I mean, I think the hair looks good."

Another man sat down in the spot Ricky left open, sighing heavily. Cayman glanced over at him and a look of pure eagerness crept across his handsome face. "Ah, duty calls, little Layla. I have another client."

"Uh…well, have fun?"

Cayman whipped the towel off his shoulder. "I always have fun. Love my job. Sit still. I'm sure Roth will be back soon with all kinds of greasy goodness."

My stomach grumbled at the thought of food as I shifted back in the stool. That probably had to be one of my most bizarre conversations, and that was saying something. Even stranger was the fact that the moment I'd crossed through the door, none of the humans in here were all that tempting when it came to wanting to suck out their soul. Maybe it was sensory overload, or all the evil kept my demon in check. Wouldn't that be ironic? The only place my demon behaved was around other demons. Totally would be my luck.

A hand curved over my shoulder. "Well, hello there."

I twisted around. A girl a little older than me stood there, her waist-length hair shiny and black, just like her skintight dress. Her eyes were dark, lush mouth painted red, and she was beautiful in a purely sinful way.

Another hand touched my other shoulder, heavier and far stronger than the female's. "Sister, what have you found for us?"

My head whipped in the direction of the voice. He could have been the woman's twin. Raven hair fell over his pale cheeks. His crisp white shirt was a shocking contrast to the dark hair and red lips. I looked for Cayman, but he was preoccupied with his latest client.

I swallowed. "I'm here with Roth."

"Did you hear that, sister?" The guy sent a provocative smile over my head. "She belongs to Roth."

"Hold up. I don't *belong* to him. I'm here as his guest."

Sister laughed softly. "Did you hear that, brother? She is only his guest."

I had a strong feeling I should've said I belonged to Roth.

"Then we must treat her like the guest she is." Brother ran his hand down my arm, threading his fingers through mine. The sudden rush of desire simmered into mind-numbing lust the moment his flesh touched mine. "We will take good care of you."

"I...I don't think you..." My eyes met his. It was like falling under water, sinking so fast I couldn't even will my lungs to breathe.

"She doesn't think," murmured Sister. "No one thinks here. This is the place for no thinking."

"Yes," agreed Brother, his eyes taking up his entire face. "This is where fun begins and fun ends. You must join us." He tugged on my hand. "Come with us."

I stood on shaky knees, my mind strangely empty of all thought.

Sister grabbed my other hand and they led me out onto the dance floor. One of them let go of my hand while the other spun me around. Brother caught me around my waist, pulling me against him. I looked up, his eyes a solid black. No white. Instead of fear and dismay, I felt nothing.

"What are you?" he asked. Brother spun me around.

Sister caught my arms, leading me through a stilted waltz. "There's a strong demon inside of you." She let go, hissing much like a spooked cat.

"But," Brother murmured in my ear, his arm snaking around my waist from behind, "There's a Warden in there, as well."

We swayed to the heavy beat of the music for a few moments, brushing against other couples that seemed just as lost as us. His hands dropped to my hips. I let my head fall back against his chest, closing my eyes. My blood did burn. The cage girl was right. He spun me around, into Sister's waiting arms.

"You're so very beautiful," she cooed, sounding childlike. She rested her head on my shoulder as we spun around again and again. "You'll taste like nothing else, but taste you I must."

As I spun, I saw odd shapes and shadows. Flesh with no faces. Faces made of skeleton and nothing more. Soft material billowed around my legs, supple and daring. For a second, I thought I wore a gown, but when I looked down I saw only blue jeans.

Brother pulled me back into his arms. I pressed against him, inhaling deeply. He had no scent, nothing at all. Our hips fit together, moving in tempo.

"We feel the same need." He placed his lips against my flushed forehead. "A taste will not hurt." He pushed me away.

"A taste will ease your burden," Sister whispered, placing a kiss against my throat. "A taste will help you see."

"See what?" I asked, breathless and dizzy.

Sister smiled. "Brother, she wants to see."

He came up behind me, flattening his hand against my stomach. "We have one for you, our lovely little sister."

I let him pull me away from Sister, turning me so that I faced the crowd, my back to his front. We were farther into the shadows than I'd realized. Everyone seemed so far away. Sister flitted away from us, spinning around the dancing couples like a mini tornado.

"Lovely," he said again, kissing my neck, where my pulse pounded, then underneath my jaw, my cheek.

I closed my eyes, leaning into him. I felt warm, wanted

and cherished in his embrace. I wasn't lonely or unwelcome. I was the most beautiful girl in his world and his world centered around me—*only me.*

"Open your eyes, lovely," he ordered softly.

I did.

A redhead stood in front of me, her dress pink with purple dots. A pretty cupcake, I thought. I liked cupcakes, especially these kinds.

Her face seemed fuzzy, though. I thought maybe she was older and that maybe I should be more concerned about this, and yet, I no longer knew myself. Sister whispered in her ear, taking a glass from the woman's suddenly limp fingers.

"Dance," Brother said.

And we danced, this girl and me. We didn't touch, but we moved in the exact same step. As if we were reflections of one another, but we were nothing alike. That much I knew. Soon, Brother joined me, whispering words I didn't understand. A language I was meant to know, I believe, but could not quite grasp. Sister did the same, and the woman seemed to grow fuzzier.

The woman stilled in front of me, head tipped to the side and blue eyes closed. Blue? She wasn't a demon. She wasn't like me. But it didn't matter. I stepped forward, because I knew I was supposed to. It was what Brother wanted. I wanted it, too.

I stood on the tips of my toes, barely able to reach her. I felt hands on my shoulders, holding me steady. We were close, close enough. I closed my eyes, waiting for a moment, a sweet moment of pure torture. Then I inhaled slowly, deeply.

I took her soul.

CHAPTER TWENTY-THREE

Warmth flooded my veins, igniting flames as it continued to my curled toes. This woman tasted of frosted sugar and bubbling wine. Every cell in my body opened up, like a flower that had been denied water and sun for far too long. Without thinking, I inhaled again.

The air moved as the woman jerked.

Oh God, why had I denied myself this?

Brother sighed, his fingers digging into my arms. The tiny spark of pain was nothing compared to the rush of this woman's essence. I kept dragging her in, filling my body with light and air. A door seemed to open in my mind. I saw her more clearly. She was a pretty woman but had a cruel mouth that said cruel words. She'd cheated her way through school and then on her fiancé. In a flash of light, I saw a brief memory of her whispering wretched words about a coworker to her boss and then laughing when the coworker was fired.

So many memories rushed me, all of them stacking the odds against her. She was mean, spiteful to the core, but I knew if I kept going, if I kept tasting her spirit, I'd see what damaged her. Something had turned her into this hateful person, something darker and more twisted than any bullshit she could pull.

Without warning, she was yanked away from me. I stumbled forward, gasping for air. I felt Brother let go of my arms and I looked up.

Roth was before me, tall and terrible. He held on to the woman's chin, forcing her to look him straight in the eye. "You will remember none of this," he said. "Leave this place. Go home and never come back here again. Do you understand me?"

The woman managed a short nod and then stumbled to the side, into the crowd. Where she went, I didn't know. I didn't even care. My eyes were trained on Roth.

Sister giggled. "You ruin all the fun. She said she didn't belong to you."

Roth leveled a stare at me. "She doesn't belong to either of you."

I sighed dreamily, swaying toward him. "Where have you been all this time? It's been hours and hours."

"I've only been gone ten minutes," he snapped, and I didn't like his tone or the way he thrust his hand through his hair, as if he were upset. "Shit, Layla... Didn't I tell you to stay put? Not to dance?"

I giggled at his stern expression. "They made me."

"We invited her," corrected Sister. "We didn't make her do anything. We know the rules."

"She just wanted a taste," added Brother, touching my arm with just the tips of his fingers. I shivered. "We didn't hurt her. Did we, lovely little sister?"

Roth shot forward, wrapping his hand around Brother's throat and lifting him off the ground until his feet dangled in the air. "What did you just call her?"

Sister hissed, fingers sharpening into deadly looking claws. In an instant, her beauty fell away. Skin thinned over sharp bones, eyes narrowed and predatory. She looked more feline than human.

"You take one step toward me, and I will snap your brother's neck," Roth warned without taking his eyes off Brother. "Do not ever touch her. You're not welcome here any longer."

"You cannot banish us," Sister shrieked. "You are no King."

Roth dropped Brother and turned around. "Maybe not, but I can rip your heart out and feed it to Hellions. How does that sound? Like a party you want to join?"

The dysfunctional siblings retreated, slinking back into the crowd. I floated away, eyeing a dancer on the stage. He was beautiful, full of ropey muscle and long, flowing blond hair. Cayman stood by the stage, smiling up at the guy.

An arm circled my waist, stopping me. "Where are you going, shortie?"

I leaned into him. "I don't know. I feel…really good."

"You do." A sigh seemed to work its way through him and, when he spoke, his voice was deep and lovely. "You almost killed that girl, shortie. I shouldn't have left you alone."

I shrugged, moving my hand back and forth. A strange pearl-colored shade followed it.

"What are you doing?"

I turned in his arms, looking up at his near-perfect face. God, he was so beautiful. Why must something so hot be so… hot, especially when I couldn't have him? I couldn't remember why exactly, but I knew there were reasons, good ones. "I think I can see my soul."

His brows rose. "Can you? Can you see anyone else's now?"

"No, but mine is white." I sighed happily. "That means my soul is pure."

Roth watched me, a slight smile on his face. "Demons can't have pure souls."

Somehow my head ended up burrowed in his chest. "Then I can't be like you."

"Oh, wow, you're so off the charts right now." Shaking his head, he moved, and the next thing I knew I was off the floor and in his arms. "Up you go."

A wild laugh escaped me, and I felt as if I could keep laughing. "What are you doing?"

"Taking you someplace you won't get into any more trouble." He started forward, easily parting the crowd.

The bar was upside down to me. "Everyone is walking on the ceiling."

His laugh was strained, reluctant sounding as he shifted me in his arms. My head now rested against his chest. "Better?"

The world was right once more. "What were those people back there?"

He shouldered open a door, walking into a dimly lit corridor. "A succubus and an incubus. I call them Sucky and Inky. I think I'm going to change their names to Dead and Deader. I can't leave you alone for ten minutes without the wolves pouncing on you."

I threaded my fingers behind his neck. "They weren't so bad."

"Guess what?" His grin didn't quite reach those eyes of his. "What?"

"You're not going to be thinking that later."

I giggled. "You're such an asshole."

Roth's laugh was lighter as he turned toward the stairs. "I kind of like you like this."

"Maybe." I kicked my feet in the air, giggling. "You can put me down. I can walk."

Instead, he carried me up a set of stairs so easily it was as though I was nothing more than a feather. He went down a hall, then up another flight of steps. "You'd trip and break your neck or fall over one of our guards. Or try to pet it."

"What guards?" I looked around the stairwell. "I don't see anything."

Roth didn't say anything as he continued all the way up. An average man wouldn't have made it fifteen floors, but he wasn't even out of breath. When he pushed open another door, I saw something that hadn't been there before. Sitting before his door at the end of the hallway were two dogs the size of Chihuahuas.

I squealed, clapping my hands together. "I do want to pet them! They're so tiny!"

He sighed. "I've been told size doesn't matter."

"Someone lied to you."

"Ah, that may be the case." He lowered me to my feet gently, keeping an arm around me. "Do keep in mind that looks can be deceiving."

I started to turn into him, but one of the rat dogs stood. "I could carry it in a purse, like…like one of those expensive purses."

"I don't think they like the sound of that."

They didn't. Both were now standing, ears back and growling. One barked. It sounded like a squeak.

I laughed. "What are they going to do? Bite my ankles?"

Roth pulled me closer, which was all right by me. I liked the warmth his body gave off, the way we seemed to fit together even though he towered over me. How had I not noticed that before? But I had. It was something I had forgotten or had been trying to forget, but I couldn't make sense of the why behind it. I wanted to admit it now, scream it from the top of the building and do stuff, lots of stuff.

Teacup dogs forgotten, I twisted and placed my hands on Roth's chest.

His dogs didn't like that.

One let out a squeak that turned into a roar. I whirled around, stumbling aside. Growling, snarling and snapping, their bodies twisted and grew. Huge paws replaced little ones. Claws rapped the floor as they prowled forward, still growling. Their flanks were thick with muscles, their tails bushy. Snouts grew long, mouths wider and ears flattened back against matted russet hair. Their teeth jutted from their mouths, razor sharp and huge. Eyes went from doe-brown to bloodred and the smell of sulfur filled the hallway.

They were the size of bears and, in the distant part of my brain, I realized they were hellhounds.

"Holy shit," I whispered, knowing I should be afraid, but I was still floating.

"Sit down," Roth ordered, suddenly in front of me. *"Vos mos non vulnero suus!"*

In unison, they backed up and sat beside the door. Their ears were still pinned back, but they no longer looked as if they wanted to eat me. I considered this a good development.

Roth glanced over his shoulder at me. "You're right. Size does matter. They won't harm you. Come on." He held out his hand.

I took it, eyeing the beasts. One smelled my leg while Roth opened the door, and the other rolled onto his back, tongue lolling out of its mouth. He swooped down, patting the hellhound's exposed belly.

"That's a good boy," he cooed. "Who's the good boy?"

"What're their names?" I asked, leaning against the door. My head felt heavy.

He looked up, grinning. "This one is Bluebelle and that one," he gestured at the one that smelled my leg, "is Flower."

I made a face. "What is it with you and the movie *Bambi?*"

He stood up fluidly. "It's an American classic."

Smiling, I closed my eyes. "You're ridiculous."

"Open your eyes, shortie."

I felt his hand in mine again, so I pried my eyes open. "Why?"

"You need to see where you're going." He pulled me into the darkness. A second later, soft light flooded the room and he let go of my hand. Heavy blinds were pulled down, blocking out the sun.

I kicked off my shoes, stumbling as I pulled off my socks. My toes sank into the plush carpet. "I think I'm hungry."

"I'll have the food sent up here."

I faced him, my breath catching as he pulled off his shirt and tossed it aside. Smooth skin stretched over hard muscle. His pants hung so low.

"I had a little bit of everything made. Hamburgers. Fries. Chicken tenders." He stopped, looking at me. A smug smile appeared as he removed his shoes. "See anything you like?"

I couldn't answer, but I saw lots of things I liked.

He prowled across the room, stopping a few feet in front of me. "Sorry. I can't stand the smell of smoke. Does it bother you?"

I knew there was a reason it should, but I shook my head and then found my voice and a healthy dose of boldness. "No."

"Then you won't mind shedding this?" Roth wrapped his fingers around the strings dangling off the neckline of my hoodie. "It reeks of Sucky and Inky."

Before I even shook my head no, he'd worked the zipper down. I held my breath as his knuckles brushed over me. Sharp tingles shot through me, clearing the haze from my brain for a moment or two. Then he slipped the "offensive" material off my shoulders, letting it fall to the floor.

"Pretty.... What is it called?" he murmured, eyes clearly not on my face.

"A…camisole." I took a deep breath, but couldn't get enough air in my lungs. "Roth?"

His gaze flicked up. "Layla?"

I started to speak, but something soft and furry brushed against my foot, drawing my attention. A tiny white kitten stared up at me with beautiful blue eyes. I bent at the waist, reaching for the little fur ball, wanting to hug it and squeeze it and love it, but then I remembered.

Frowning at the little devil, I pulled my fingers out of reach. "No. I remember you. Bad kitty."

Hair along the little darling's back rose, and it hissed before spinning around and dashing back under the bed.

"I see you've learned from your previous mistakes, but I think you've upset Nitro."

"Those kittens have rabies." I rose and then gasped as a wave of dizziness washed over me.

Roth placed a hand on my arm and there was a muted sensation of concern. "Are you okay?"

"Yeah…I'm fine. This happens after…" I trailed off as the black-and-white kitten poked its head out from under the bed, eyeing me with ears flat.

"After feeding?"

Feeding. Was that what I'd been doing? Just like the rest of the demons in the strange place in the bowels of this apartment building? Doing my part in the demonic food chain? I shivered.

"You didn't take her soul, shortie."

I cocked my head to the side. I hadn't. "She was okay, right?"

"Yes."

"And if she was down there, that meant she was bad, right?"

His warm breath danced along my cheek. "Yes."

Did that make it okay? I wasn't sure. "I don't want to think about this."

"You don't have to. Why don't you sit down?"

Because there didn't seem to be much else I could do, I made my way around the edge of his bed and sat among the king-size pillows. His scent was everywhere, and when I closed my eyes, inhaling deeply, I remembered being here before, on this bed…in his arms.

A warm flush traveled over my skin and my eyes drifted shut. When I reopened them, I saw Roth striding toward the bed with a long tray in his hands. Several plates were covered with silver tops.

I sat up straighter, confused. "Did I fall asleep?" It had felt like seconds had passed when I'd closed my eyes.

He laughed as he sat, placing the tray between us. There were two tall glasses filled with ice, sitting next to two cans of soda. It was like room service provided by a hot, half-naked, demon dude. "No. You were sitting here singing."

"I was?"

"Yep. 'Paradise City.'" He smiled as he peeked up at me through thick lashes. "I think I'm rubbing off on you."

For some reason, that didn't sit well with me, but then he started removing trays and I fell in love—in love with all the glorious, wonderful food placed before me. A buffet of meat, grease and salt.

Between Roth and me, the food was gone in a nanosecond. As he gathered up the plates and took them into his kitchen area, I lay on my back and patted my stomach. "My belly is happy."

"I bet it is." There was a sound of water running and then it stopped. Not even a second passed before he was sitting down beside me. Placing a hand on the other side of my shoulder, he leaned over me. "How are you feeling?"

My lips split into a wide smile. "Good. Great. Happy. Maybe a little tired, but I feel like—"

"I get the point," he said, chuckling. His head tilted to the right as the intensity of his stare increased until it felt as though he could see right through me. A tense look appeared on his face as he carefully picked the strands of my hair off my shoulders and spread them out on the pillow. "I wish you would feel this way later, but you won't."

My heart turned over as he lowered his gaze. "You're going to hate yourself after this, even though you didn't hurt that woman. To her, it will be like having a hangover after a bad night of partying. And she won't miss that tiny part of her soul that you took. Not that she missed any part of her soul that she willingly gave for every atrocious sin she committed." He sighed heavily, as if there was an invisible weight settling across his shoulders. His lashes swept up. "I didn't mean for you to do this when I brought you here. Sucky and Inky should've stayed away from you. I should've made sure of that."

He gave a little shake of his head. "I just wanted you to see how the other half lives. Not those two bastards. They're bad news, but not…not all of us are like that. I wanted you to see that. For you to see that what's inside you…" He tapped a finger off my stomach. "Isn't bad, no matter what that asshole of a clan leader says to you or how he makes you feel."

"Same to you."

A brow arched. "What does that mean?"

I reached up, tapping *my* finger off his chest. "You are not as bad as you like to think. You are capable of acts of great kindness."

He snorted. "You're high."

"Am not." I poked him again. "You've done things that humans with souls wouldn't do. You—"

His hand encircled my wrist, pulling it away from his chest.

"Everything I do is for a purely selfish reason. Trust me on that."

I didn't believe him. I went to pull my arm away, but somehow all I managed to do was pull *him* closer. The muscle in his arm flexed as he hovered over me, supporting his weight. The warmth of his body once again seeped into mine. Bambi stirred. I really liked that snake, I realized. She slithered over my skin, tickling me as her head reached my shoulder, seemingly compelled by Roth's closeness. A faint smile crossed his lips as he spotted Bambi, and I wondered if he missed her.

Our eyes met and that feeling from earlier was back, slipping through my veins. The words bubbled out of me. "Kiss me."

Flecks of amber darkened in his eyes. His face tensed, almost as if he was in pain, and I wasn't sure why that request would bother him so. "Layla…"

I tugged on my arm again, and he came even closer. When I spoke, our lips were inches apart. "Kiss me."

His lashes swept down, shielding his eyes. "You don't know what you're asking for."

"Yes, I do."

He shook his head as he let go of my hand. "You don't. You're really—"

I pushed Roth and he landed on his back with force, bouncing the bed. It might have been the fact that I'd caught him off guard, but, either way, I took advantage of it. I threw my leg over his hip and sat down, pressing the palms of my hands into his shoulders.

His eyes widened with shock as I moved my weight to my arms. My hair slid over my shoulders, creating a whitish-blond curtain. Sitting astride him, feeling him under me, between my legs, I felt like a goddess rising on the throne of sexy. I almost giggled at that thought, but figured that would ruin my sexiness.

"God." He kicked his head back, groaning as his hands settled on my hips. "I really, *really* like you this way."

"Then what's the problem?" I asked as I rocked back, trailing my fingertips down his flat stomach.

His fingers dug into my hips as he stared up at me through heavy-lidded eyes. "I can't really think of one right now."

"Good." I started to dip my head, aiming for his parted lips.

He caught me again by the wrists, lifting my arms and holding me back. "This...this isn't going to happen, baby."

Confused, I tried to get closer, but he held me off. A little bit of the pleasant haze faded as my heart tripped up. "You... you don't want me?"

Roth moved so quickly I didn't have a second to think about what he was doing. He had me on my back with my arms stretched above my head. "Don't want you?" he said, pressing down on me. Every part of our bodies touched, robbing me of my breath. "I think you know the answer to that."

Oh, I think I did.

I managed to get one of my legs freed from under his, and I hooked my calf around his lower leg. His hips sank in and my body tingled as if little sparks were dancing over my skin. He groaned again.

"I want you so badly it's like a hunger that gnaws at me endlessly. It doesn't go away." He dipped his head to the space between my neck and shoulder, inhaling deeply. "You have no fucking clue."

"Then do something about it," I whispered.

Roth lifted his head, and his pupils had stretched vertically. "Layla..." The way he spoke my name was like a benediction. "Please..."

My fingers curled helplessly as I stretched up, finally reaching him with my lips. Our mouths barely touched, but Roth shuddered and his grip around my wrists tightened.

And then he was on me.

It was as though the chains holding him back had snapped. Roth kissed me, and there wasn't anything soft or sweet about the way his mouth worked mine. He moved my wrists to one hand, and his other hand slid down my arm and then down my side, under the hem of my camisole. His hand left a wake of fire as he moved it up the bare skin of my stomach and then farther up. I arched into the touch, and I got lost in that kiss, lost in the taste and feel of him that was so familiar it ached.

Then the kiss deepened, and the taste of him branded me from the inside out. His heart was slamming against mine. Our bodies fit together and moved, causing every cell in me to burn for more, to demand it. And Roth gave it. His hips rolled in ways that had me gasping in between the deep, soul-searing kisses. My legs curled around him.

"You feel too good," he murmured against my mouth. A deep sound rumbled from him as he kissed me again. "You taste too good to be true."

I really didn't understand what that meant, but I wanted to touch him, to run my fingers over the ropey muscles of his back, to slip them under his loose jeans. I felt as if I was going to come out of my skin, like I had before…that night with him, which felt so very long ago, but this was right now and his body moved like sin.

Without warning, he was off me, and the bed shook when he flopped on his back. For a moment, I was too stunned to move, too caught up in the racing sensations playing across my skin.

Panting, I started to sit up and follow him. "Roth—"

"Don't," he said, raising a hand that trembled. "God, I can't believe I'm even saying this, but don't come closer. Don't move."

Without warning, he threw his legs off the bed and stood. Slowly rising up onto my elbows, I watched him stalk around the bed.

Roth thrust both of his hands through his hair and cursed low. Like a caged animal, he looked over at me. His eyes burned from a fire within.

I followed his gaze. My camisole was rucked up, past my bra. Before I could do anything to rectify it, he spun around and headed for the bathroom. The door slammed shut behind him, echoing throughout the loft.

Exhaling deeply, I fell back and squeezed my eyes shut. What just happened? It felt as though we'd both been on the same page, that we wanted the same thing. Didn't we?

I rubbed my hands down my face and then tugged my shirt down. A couple of minutes passed, maybe longer, as I willed my body to calm down and my heart to slow. Roth had still not returned from the bathroom, and my face flamed an un-holy shade of red when I wondered what he could possibly be doing in there.

The high was fading fast and all that logic and common sense I'd swept away like an annoying gnat was warring with the exhaustion creeping up on me. That little voice in the back of the head was getting louder, full of righteous humili-ation, and threatening to bitch slap me in the face, but then the three demon kittens from Hell loped up over the foot of the bed. Prowling forward, their paws sinking into the cov-ers, they eyed me as if I was a colorful, yet stupid, butterfly snared in a spider's web.

I froze as they wiggled their way up to my side, and then frowned as they settled down into little balls that purred so loudly they vibrated the bed.

Somewhat dumbfounded, I stared at them as that little voice started up again, telling me to get up and to get the Hell out of this place before it was too late. But the hum of the kittens had a lulling effect, and, before I knew it, the distance between right now and later expanded.

CHAPTER TWENTY-FOUR

I awoke to the soft flicker of candles and a pounding head-ache, slightly confused by my surroundings. It took me a few moments to realize where I was and what had happened in the strange room below the Palisades apartment.

Jackknifing up, I felt my heart race. There was a funny taste in the back of my mouth. Throwing off the covers, I was relieved to find that I wasn't naked. I remembered coming here with Roth, talking to Cayman and the evil demon twins, and then the…

Oh God.

I remembered tasting the woman's soul, the one who reminded me of a cupcake.

Oddly enough, the nausea that occupied the fading high from taking a soul was minimal. Just a slight unease of the stomach, but that was truly insignificant in comparison to everything else.

I scrambled from the bed, my eyes darting around Roth's loft. On the edge of the bed, the small white kitten stretched out on its side. When it spotted me, it hissed. The black-and-white kitten sat on his piano. It stood, idly prowling across the keys. Each note the paws stroked was jarring. Out of the corner of my eyes, a shadow rushed in front of the glass wall, momentarily blocking out the moon and lights from the surrounding buildings. I whirled around, my heart in my throat.

Nothing was there.

My gaze fell to the bathroom door. It was open and it had been closed when I… Oh crap on a cracker, *Roth*. I'd thrown myself at him. Well, technically, I had knocked him over and straddled him. I had kissed him and he had kissed me back before stopping what I would've surely continued.

I placed a hand to my temple, wincing. In that moment, I wasn't sure what was worse: molesting Roth and having him hide in the bathroom or that I'd tasted a soul.

I scanned the loft again, but I didn't see Roth. My steps felt heavy, my legs disjointed. I found my shoes and hoodie next to my bag, the three items placed on a chair by the door. I didn't even remember bringing my bag with me. I dug out my cell, tapping the screen. There were missed calls—two from Stacey and more than I could count from Zayne and my heart sank. Then I saw the time.

3:15 a.m.

"Oh shit," I screeched, startling the kitten on the piano. The crashing of keys matched the tempo of my pulse. "Oh shit, shit, shit."

I dug around for my wallet, finding it smashed between two notebooks. I'd need to get a cab. As I slid my phone back in my bag, I thought of the missed calls from Zayne. He had to have been panicked and he had to have thought… I couldn't even let myself finish that thought. My hand shook as I wrapped it around the bag strap. I needed to call him, but I couldn't focus on anything but putting one foot in front of the other.

Where was Roth?

It didn't matter. He'd brought me here and he…he let me sleep for hours. A flash of anger shot through me, but how could I really blame him for this mess? I should've listened to my instincts, but I'd come with him. Then I'd danced with Sucky and Inky and, even though they had done something to me, I'd been the one to taste the woman's soul. It was as though Roth had opened the door when he'd asked me to be bad with him, and I had bounced right on through it.

I'd gotten myself into this mess.

Walking to the door and opening it took a lot of energy. Outside his loft, the two hellhounds were sitting like sentries. Their ears perked up, but they didn't turn toward me. As I eased past them, the muscles in their backs bulged in irregular humps. I held my breath, praying they didn't eat me, until I made it to the end of the hallway and opened the door.

Half running, half sliding down the steps, I kept going until I heard high-pitched, mewling cries. Coming to a halt outside the door leading back the lobby, I froze. Wild laughter echoed through the stairwell, as did screams and moans.

What the…?

Backing up, I turned and spied the exit to the garage. Anywhere was better than going into the lobby or back into the bar, back into the madness without Roth. Or was he in the lobby, enjoying the party?

I pushed open the door, rushing through the dark garage and out into the streets. My thin sweater was no protection against the chilly air. I hugged myself and my bag close, barreling down the fog-covered streets. I suddenly thought about Jack the Ripper. Didn't he always attack his victims on foggy London nights? Not that I couldn't take out a serial killer, but still, the thought creeped me out.

I hurried on, eyes searching through the clouded streets for cabs. God, I was in so much trouble. I'd tasted a soul. My insides twisted with guilt and shame, and I told myself to stop thinking about it, because there was nothing I could do now.

But my skin crawled as I continued down the silent street. If I breathed too hard, inhaled too deeply, I could still taste her essence—frosted icing. I bit down on my lip until blood replaced the sugary sweetness. The pain did little to stop the rushing memory, the pleasure the soul had brought.

What had I done?

The withdrawals seemed not to have hit me yet and I deserved the sweats, chills, and the hunger that couldn't be assuaged. I deserved that and much more.

All the buildings lining the streets were quiet and shadowed until I crossed a street and realized that one of the shadows had broken apart from the rest. It flitted along the pavement beside me, thicker and larger that my own slight shadow. The smell of sulfur replaced the musty smell of the nearby river.

I stopped.

The shadow stopped.

Ice drenched my veins as the smell of rotten eggs increased until my eyes burned.

Beside me, the shadow grew tall and slender, taking the form of a faceless figure made of dark smoke. The shadow raised its arms high in the air and bent to the side, lifting one leg up. The heavy fog retreated, as if it didn't want to touch the abomination. Slowly, the shadow twirled around like the prima ballerina on the jewelry box that I never used.

Crap.

It was a shade—a demonic spirit. The kind that could possess weak humans and cause a whole lot of trouble.

A chilly laugh seemed to come from the shade, from the pavement and the buildings all at once. It surrounded me, raising the tiny hairs all over my body. I took a step back.

The shade stopped, lowering its leg to the ground. It placed smoky arms on what I assumed was its hips and did a happy little jig. Then it bowed, holding out a see-through hand to me. Flimsy fingers wiggled an invitation to dance.

More shades came to join the bizarre dance. Twirling and dipping around me, breaking up thick plumes of fog. They continued at dizzying speeds, beckoning me to join the melee. It reminded me of the twins and the moments I caught sight of fleshless faces in the club.

I so didn't have time for this.

"Go away," I urged. "I don't want any of what you're offering."

They stopped, misty heads tipped to the side, except the original shade. It became thicker and more solid as the seconds past, body solidifying. Specks of ash began to fall from the sky, landing on my hands and in my hair, smelling of burnt flesh and evil.

"But we have time for you," it said in a hoarse voice. "We know what you seek."

Every instinct in me screamed to get away from these things, but I held my ground. "You do?"

The shade nodded and smoke wafted into the air. "You seek the Lilin but you do not seek it in the right place."

"Gee, thanks for the clarification."

It laughed and the sound shook the windows of the building behind us. "You seek too far. You need to look closer. Closer," it cajoled. "The truth is far stranger than your wildest imaginings."

Against my will, I leaned in, drawn by the smoky voice.

The misty face before me took form, two eyes burning red. A face full of squirming, round little things appeared. Maggots.

Screaming, I jerked back and then took off, my feet pounding along the sidewalk. The shades gave chase, running alongside me, laughing as I desperately tried to put distance between us. I could see street people, homeless who'd probably seen just about everything, scuttle back against the walls and the building, trying to make themselves as small as possible.

The shade with the maggot face pulled back, spinning into the sky above me. Air rushed over me as another shot forth. In the center of a smoky face, features melted together as though the face had been made out of dripping candle wax. They kept switching out, each reveal more disturbing than the last until the one who was nearly solid looked back at me with my own face.

I stumbled to a stop.

My own round eyes stared back at me, but they were different. The gray was split down the middle, like a cat's eye—like my eyes did when I had shifted. My face hissed at me, revealing a mouth with no teeth, just maggots—more maggots.

Horrified, I couldn't look away.

The maggots wiggled free, hitting the pavement with small little smacks. The shade with my face spoke. "In time you'll see, you're just like us, and we will all be free."

The shade with my face floated back and I snapped out of it. Turning, I ran as fast I could.

The streets were empty. I darted across, daring a look back.

I slowed down, turning around. Sweat poured off me, stinging in the damp, cold air and my stomach twisted. There were no dancing shades. I looked down at my hand. Ash covered it.

Hastily, I wiped it off on my jeans as I lifted my gaze.

The shade had shown my face.

My face.

Pressure clamped down on my chest as I drew in a deep breath and flagged down an approaching white taxi.

I yanked open the back door, sparing the streets one more glance as I slid into the seat.

"Where to?" the cabbie asked.

I looked up, catching his reflection in the rearview mirror. Sleep pulled at his eyes and placed several deep wrinkles in his skin. "Dunmore Lane."

He nodded, turning back to the road. "That's a decent trip from here. You look a little young to be—"

A Warden dropped from the sky, landing in front of the taxi.

"Oh no," I whispered.

The impact shook the cab and added another pothole to the street. His wings were unfurled, spanning several feet on either side. The broad chest, the color of granite, was smooth. I didn't even have to look at the face to know who it was.

Zayne.

"Jesus!" the cabbie gasped, pressing a hand against his chest. Humans were well aware of Wardens, but I seriously doubted any of them expected to see one drop out of the sky in the middle of the night. "Where did he come from?"

Zayne placed one clawed hand on the hood of the taxi, tipping the car up onto two wheels. The cabbie clutched the steering wheel while I pushed against the back of the seat in front of me.

"Get out of the car now," Zayne ordered, slowly setting the cab back on four wheels as his piercing gaze landed on me.

The cabbie twisted around in his seat. "He's talking to you?"

I nodded.

"Then get out," he said, pointing at the door. "I don't want no trouble with them. He wants you out of this cab, you get out of this cab."

I frowned, wanting to point out that I could be an innocent girl in need of help, but that wasn't the case and I didn't want to drag someone who was innocent into the middle of this.

Opening the door, I stepped out. The moment I closed

it behind me, the cab peeled off, burning rubber as it flew down the avenue.

"You've been with him."

My heart turned over heavily as I forced my eyes to meet his. In his true form, Zayne was an intimidating mass of granite.

"You smell like him, so don't even try to lie."

"I wasn't going to. I swear." I swallowed the lump in my throat. "Zayne—"

"I've spent all evening and all night looking for you," he said, taking a step forward. His head was dipped low. "I stopped by *his* place. I couldn't get in, but he met me on the roof. He said you weren't with him."

He said what? That had to have been when I was asleep, but why would Roth lie? Probably because I'd fed off a soul and he didn't know if I was still high as kite.

"He lied obviously," Zayne snarled. "I can't say I'm surprised by that, but from you?" The anger seemed to seep out of him as he took a step back. His shoulders slumped as he dragged in a deep breath. "You spent the night with him."

The statement, not so much of a question, broke me. "No—no! It's not like that. I didn't go with him because of something like that."

He turned his head and the light from the lamppost reflected off the shiny, black horns. The fact he was still in his gargoyle form in front of me was testament to how upset he was. There used to be a time when he hid what he looked like in his true form from me.

"I skipped lunch with him. That's all! I know it doesn't seem like that, but that's why I left school with him." My backpack dropped to the ground. "I was upset today over what happened last night with Abbot and I just...I just needed to get away."

His head swung back to me. "Get away with him?"

"I didn't mean it like that." I squeezed my eyes shut, knowing what I was about to admit was going to be far worse than anything Zayne thought. "We went to this place and there was this woman there and I…"

"You what?"

I opened my eyes and saw again what that shade had shown me—my face. "There was this woman and I…I fed off her."

Zayne stared at me, eyes widening. "No."

The word sounded tortured and damn, that hurt deep. "I didn't mean to and I know that's no excuse." It didn't matter that Sucky and Inky had had something to do with it. Blaming them was pointless. "I didn't kill her. She was okay, but I did it and I got…"

"High?"

My cheeks burned with humiliation. "Yes."

"Let me get this straight. You left because you were upset over what happened last night with Maddox, who, by the way, is awake and has confirmed that you didn't push him." Before I could say that the confirmation probably did little to change what his father thought, he continued. "So you run off today with a demon and do exactly what my father was accusing of you doing?" He started to pace before me, agitated. "How in the Hell does that make any sense."

I ran my hands through my hair. "It doesn't, and I know I screwed up—"

"It's because you were with *him*."

I shook my head, knowing he hadn't even heard the worst part yet and I had to tell him. "It's not because I was with him. He didn't force me to do anything."

Zayne opened his mouth and then pain flashed across his face. He took a step back and his skin lightened until he was standing before me in his human form. Wearing only low-slung leather pants, he looked no less intimidating.

But the look on his face, those piercing blue eyes, hit me in the chest. He thrust a finger through his loose hair and then dropped his hand. "What...what did you do?"

"I...I kissed Roth," I said, forcing myself not to look away and to own up to what I'd done. "I was kind of out of it and—"

"Basically it's like getting drunk and hooking up with someone?" He laughed, but there was no humor. "Is that supposed to make it better?"

"No. It's not, but I wouldn't have done it if I hadn't been out of my head." A little voice inside of me disagreed but I shut that bitch up right quick. "It was a mistake," I whispered. "I'm sorry. I know that doesn't change anything or make it better, but I'm so sorry."

He gave a little shake of his head. "I don't even know what to say, Layla. I know you." He gripped my shoulders as he lowered his head. "I *know* you, but sometimes, you are a complete stranger to me. You do things that will only hurt you in the end and you don't even know why."

"I just..." I squeezed my eyes shut. I just what? Did I know why I did the things I did sometimes? The answer seemed too simple. It was in my nature. That wasn't an excuse. Not feeding wasn't in my nature. But none of that mattered right now, because when I opened my eyes, I saw only Zayne's hurt. "I'm sorry."

His hands slid down my arms and then dropped away as he straightened. "When I said that we should give this—this between us—a chance, I didn't think this would happen."

My insides twisted into even more intricate, painful knots. This was it. Whatever was between us was over before it even got started. Maybe it was for the best. A relationship was impossible and it would drive a wedge between him and his father. Even though I told myself that, tears slipped down my throat, burning the back of my eyes.

"There's no chance now, is there?" I asked, my voice cracking.

He didn't answer for a long moment. "I really don't know."

My chin dropped as I drew in a ragged breath. It was better than I expected, but it did nothing to ease the guilt crawling over my skin.

After a few seconds, he said, "I covered for you."

I lifted my head and when I saw that he was speaking the truth, I wanted to cut my tongue out of my mouth. "How?"

"Somehow I knew you were...okay," he said, running the palm of his hand across his jaw. "Didn't stop me from spending hours looking for you, but it wasn't hard to cover for you."

I felt about two feet tall.

"This afternoon we received word while you were out doing...doing whatever. Dean McDaniel passed away."

My hand flew to my mouth and everything else was forgotten. "Oh my God."

"You know what that means."

Besides that a life had been taken too young? I lowered my hand. "It means that he's become a wraith."

CHAPTER TWENTY-FIVE

Bad news traveled fast.

By the start of school the following morning, it seemed that everyone had heard of Dean's passing. While he hadn't been popular and most people had only become of aware of him after he'd gotten into the fight in bio, there was a pall over the crowded halls. No one smiled or laughed. The low thrum of excitement over the approaching Thanksgiving break was muted. Dean's death affected all of us. Perhaps it served as a painful, dreaded reminder that even the young could perish at a moment's notice.

"Someone said it was a heart attack," Stacey said as we made our way to class. "But how does a seventeen-year-old just have a heart attack?"

I shook my head. It was the best I could muster given what happened last night and early this morning. Oddly enough, the withdrawals that occurred after feeding, like when an addict comes down off a high, still hadn't hit me.

I knew from what Zayne had told me this morning that Dean's death had been ruled as due to natural causes, but it was far from normal.

Dean was dead, but he was most certainly not at peace.

That cloud of evil, the thick, almost suffocating blanket brimming just beneath the surface that I'd felt at Dean's house, was present at school today. It was like a shadow hiding in every corner, an invisible stalker waiting to pounce.

"Maybe it was drugs," a girl next to us said, and for the life of me, I couldn't remember her name. "He could've overdosed and they're saying it was a heart attack."

Speculation continued until the bell rang, signaling the start of class. I tensed as Roth strolled in at the last second. Hair damp and curling from a recent shower, he looked as tired as I felt. Humming softly, he took his seat in front of us and glanced over his shoulder at me. There was a wealth of secrecy in his questioning stare that I ignored as Mr. Tucker—who I was guessing was going to permanently replace Mrs. Cleo—moved to stand in front of the classroom, hands folded over the transparent slides.

My eyes met Roth's for a moment and then I focused on Mr. Tucker. I was too tired to be embarrassed over what I'd done yesterday, but I didn't know what to say to Roth. Apologize for molesting him? Sounded like fun. I could feel his gaze linger on me for a few more moments before he faced the front of the classroom.

"What's up with you two?" Stacey asked in a low voice that I knew Roth could definitely hear.

"Nothing," I replied.

Roth leaned back in his seat, letting his arms dangle at his sides.

"I call best-friend bullshit on that." She knocked her leg against mine. "You disappeared again yesterday. You were with him, weren't you?"

The lie rose to the tip of my tongue, but I was so incredibly sick of lying. I didn't respond, which was answer enough. Roth's chair rose onto its two back legs, balancing precariously in a way that only he could manage without toppling over like an idiot.

Stacey sucked in a breath. "What about Zayne?"

My heart squeezed as if someone had shoved it into a juicer. Good question. I'd screwed up last night and I'd hurt Zayne more than I probably even realized. When he'd driven me to school this morning, he hadn't spoken. Neither could I because at this point, words were cheap and useless, full of empty promises and expectations.

Roth's elbows rested on our table, and Bambi stirred restlessly on my stomach. She'd disappeared as soon as I got home last night, most likely to feed. When I'd awoken with only half an hour to get ready for school, she'd been curled up in my dollhouse.

Mr. Tucker cleared his throat. "I know we've learned very tragic news today about one of your fellow classmates."

My gaze drifted to where the boys had sat behind Dean. Lenny still hadn't returned to school, but Keith was there. Based on the way he was slouched in his seat, legs stretched out in front of him, I could tell he wasn't too torn up by the news.

"I've been advised that there are grief counselors on the premises for anyone who would like to speak with them," Mr. Tucker went on, moving the slides back and forth in his hands, causing them to wave at the classroom.

The next breath I drew in got stuck in my throat as the feeling from the hallway seeped into the classroom, like a dark, thick cloud passing over the sun. I couldn't help but shiver.

I laid my pen down on my notebook as I glanced around the room. Everything looked normal, but something was off.

Roth tilted his head to the side, and I knew he was feeling it, too.

"There's nothing to be ashamed of if you feel as though you need to talk to someone," Mr. Tucker continued. "No one will hold it against you. Death is a hard thing to deal with, no matter how old you are."

The light above Mr. Tucker flickered and went unnoticed by everyone but Roth and me. He lowered his chair to all four legs. The light above the substitute teacher stopped blinking, but the one in front of it began to—and once that stopped, another started, cutting a clear path down the middle of the aisle, until the overhead light above the desk Keith sat at flickered wildly.

Keith glanced up at it, frowning.

"So ask any of your teachers and we'll get you set up with one of the counselors..." Mr. Tucker trailed off as his gaze moved to the light in turn. The slides stilled in his hands.

There was a beat of silence and every muscle in my body tensed as an icy breeze washed over my skin. I stiffened at the familiar feeling. Something was about to happen. I knew it—I knew the feeling. The bone-deep chill that had seeped into my being was the same thing I'd felt right before the windows exploded and Maddox fell down the stairs.

I started to stand, and Stacey grabbed for my arm.

The light above Keith suddenly exploded in a shower of sparks and glass. The room filled with shrieks and the sounds of chair legs screeching across the floor as people came to their feet in surprise.

"Here we go," muttered Roth, now sitting straight.

Mr. Tucker dropped the slides as he rushed forward. "Everyone stand back. There's glass every—"

Keith bumped into the empty chair beside him, shaking his head. Tiny pieces of glass fell from his hair. I turned to move around Stacey when Roth shot to his feet as a dark blur came from the corner of the classroom, moving too fast for any human eye to track.

Goose bumps broke out across my skin.

A wraith—there was a wraith in the classroom—and I was willing to bet a year's supply of sugar cookies it was Dean.

The shadowy form, no more than three feet tall, barreled into Keith's legs, knocking him over the chair. To everyone in the class it probably looked as if he just lost his balance, but I knew better.

Keith hit the floor hard, letting out a grunt. His legs kicked into the chair and the shadow blurred as it moved again. The chair flipped up and backward, slamming into Keith's face.

"Holy shit!" exclaimed Mr. Tucker, and God, any other time I would've laughed, but nothing about this was funny.

The shadow skittered to the far corner of the classroom, lingering near the door as Mr. Tucker bent down, helping up a bloodied and shaken Keith.

Stacey turned to me, her face pale and eyes wide. "I'm beginning to think it's time to transfer schools."

"That might be a good idea," remarked Roth as he moved toward the center aisle.

I tracked the shadow as it darted toward the door. It collapsed into itself, becoming a murky puddle before it slipped under the door. The Warden in me demanded I give chase.

"What are you doing?" Stacey reached for me again, but I was already too far away.

"I'll be right back," I called over my shoulder.

Mr. Tucker and half of the class were too wrapped up in tending to Keith, who was rambling incoherently, to pay attention to what I was doing.

I slipped out the door and turned to my right, spying the wraith immediately. It glided down the hall, nothing more than a misty cloud of creepiness. Tapping into energy I didn't realize I had, I kicked off the floor and started running.

The wraith stilled for a second and then a low chuckle echoed down the hall a second before the locker doors flew open. As though an invisible spring had been released, books and jackets flew out of the lockers, joined by notebooks and loose paper.

I yelped as a particularly heavy history textbook slammed into my thigh, then pushed forward, losing sight of the wraith in the storm of books.

Out of the mess of swirling school supplies, my eyes widened as pens and pencils turned into mini instruments of doom. They zoomed through the air, plunking off the walls.

The cloud of books and pens beat at my arms. I knocked a few down only to be fighting against more.

Suddenly Roth was there, smacking a book to the floor before it knocked me upside the head. "Chasing after a wraith probably isn't the smartest idea."

"What do you suggest we do, then?" I ducked a large makeup bag. "Let it hurt someone else?"

Roth opened his mouth to respond, but the chaos stopped. Books and paper hung suspended in midair before smashing into the floor.

The hall looked like a back-to-school sale gone terribly wrong.

Staff poured into the hallway, taking one look at the mess before turning to where Roth and I stood. Looks of disbelief crossed their faces, quickly followed by suspicion.

"Crap," I muttered.

I stared at the butter-yellow slip of paper in my hand as I stood out in front of the school. My face felt frozen in a frown.

One of the doors opened behind me, but I didn't need to look to know who it was. The sweet scent gave him away. "You got suspended, too?" he asked.

Sighing, I folded up the paper and placed it in my jeans pocket as Roth came to stand beside me. "Yeah. Their 'no tolerance' policy."

Roth chuckled as he shoved his hands into his pockets. "At least it's just for the next couple of days. Thanksgiving break is next week. We're unsuspended after that."

The principal and administrative staff had taken one look at the hall and had blamed Roth and me for the mess, citing before-break high jinks or some crap like that. And what could we have said in our defense? That a wraith had done it?

Yeah, that would've gone over smoothly.

"Are you going to be in trouble?" he asked when I didn't respond.

I squinted up at the bright sun, shivering. "Probably."

"That's not good." He angled his body toward me, blocking some of the brisk wind whipping across the pavilion.

Nodding slowly, I turned my attention to the street.

"How much trouble did you get in for last night?"

I tugged the sleeves of my sweater down over my fingers and held the material tight. "Zayne covered for me. The rest of them had no idea I was missing."

"That's good, then."

Turning to him, I raised my brows. He stared straight ahead, lips pursed. "You told Zayne I wasn't with you."

"You know why I did."

"He didn't believe you."

He raised his chin. "Does that matter?"

"You let me sleep until three in the morning," I said, voice thin. "If Zayne hadn't covered for me…"

"But he did." His gaze shifted to me. "I didn't want to wake you."

"Because you were afraid I was going to throw myself at you again?" The question burst out before I could stop myself.

Roth cocked his head to the side. "More like I was afraid you *wouldn't* and that's the problem." He went down a step and turned to me. "I left you alone because if you woke up and you asked me to kiss you, I wouldn't be able to stop a second time around."

His words had a warring effect on me. A rush of molten heat coursed through my veins, causing tight little coils in the pit of my stomach, but that was wrong for a multitude of reasons.

"You don't have to worry about a second time," I told him. "I was high."

One side of his lips curled up and he laughed softly. "You are such a terrible liar."

"I'm not lying."

Roth came back up the step, crowding me. As he dipped his head so that his mouth nearly brushed mine when he spoke, I refused to back away. "I know why you say that. I even understand it, Layla. I get it. I hurt you and deserve every single one of your lies."

I stilled as his warm breath danced over my lips.

"But there is so much you don't know or understand," he said, tilting his head so that his words brushed the lobe of my ear, sending a shiver down my neck. "So don't claim to know what I really want or what I would do to protect it."

Roth spun on his heel as I blinked stupidly. He went down the wide stairs, taking the steps two at a time. I pressed a hand against my neck as I watched him walk off. There was so much I didn't know?

When it came to Roth, I was beginning to believe that was true.

I found myself in Abbot's study the moment he woke up and my name was bellowed through the house. It had sounded as if the *Cloverfield* monster was about to knock down walls or something.

Right now, Abbot kind of actually reminded me of the *Cloverfield* monster.

"Suspended?" he said, holding the sheet of paper.

I nodded. "There was a wraith at school. It attacked this kid Keith and then it went out to the hallway. I followed it and it just went crazy, tearing open lockers. What was I supposed to say when the teachers came out?"

Abbot dropped the slip of paper on his desk and pinched the bridge of his nose. He didn't say anything, but Nicolai, who'd been standing to his right, inclined his head. "Since the boy's passing, we knew there'd be a wraith created. That is what happens once a soul is stripped from a human."

I sent Nicolai a grateful look.

"I know," Abbot murmured, rubbing his brow. "The fact that the wraith went straight to the school is concerning."

Crossing his arms, Zayne pressed his shoulders against the wall he was leaning into. He'd been quiet again when he'd picked me up and hadn't said much while we spoke to his father. His gaze met mine briefly before looking away.

I sank a little in the chair. As Abbot talked about plans for scoping out the school tonight, I replayed what happened in class. Keith could've been seriously hurt and unless we got the wraith out of there, everyone was in danger. The chill that settled over my skin caused me to hunker down in my sweater—*the chill*.

The cold air I'd felt before the wraith attacked had felt familiar. How could I have forgotten that? I leaned forward in the chair. "Wait a second. Before the wraith attacked in the classroom, I felt a burst of cold air. The same thing I felt before the windows exploded and Maddox fell down the steps."

Abbot's fingers stopped along his brow as he looked at me. "Are you telling me that there's a wraith in our home?"

It sounded crazy, but it wasn't impossible. Protective wards against demonic activity *inside* the house was pretty much nil due to me being in here. And wraiths weren't technically demons anyway.

"Why would there be a wraith here?" Abbot answered, lowering his hand to the top of his desk as he studied me. "Typically they are drawn to locations familiar to them when they were alive."

Dez shifted from where he sat in one of the oversize leather chairs. A contemplative look crossed his face. He didn't speak and I didn't know what he was thinking, or if it was along the same lines of where my mind went.

A wraith was created when a soul was stripped from a human. Only certain demons could do that—Lilith, a Lilin, and…and me. Wardens also had souls, pure souls. And I'd taken Petr's soul the night he'd attacked me. It had been self-defense, because he would've surely killed me if I hadn't, but the act of taking a soul, no matter the cause, was strictly forbidden.

And something horrific had happened to him. He hadn't died like a human would when the last wisp of soul was stolen away. He had morphed into something diabolical, more frightening then an Upper Level demon. But then Roth had killed whatever he had become.

Could Petr still be here, but as a wraith?

My stomach twisted into knots as I lowered my gaze. "You're right." The words were like acid on my tongue. "There's no reason for there to be a wraith here."

When I looked up, I realized Zayne was standing straight and he knew what had really gone down that night. I hadn't admitted it to him, but he always saw through my lies.

"How will you get rid of the wraith that hurt Keith?" I

asked, hoping to bring his attention back to the problem at the school.

Abbot held my gaze, his expression closed off. "A good old-fashioned exorcism."

CHAPTER TWENTY-SIX

Time dragged by uneventfully. Probably since I hadn't left the house. Abbot hadn't grounded me, which had surprised me. Even though it was obvious that I hadn't caused the mess that had landed me in out-of-school suspension, I really had thought he'd find some way to lay that blame down on me.

I'd learned from my one brief conversation with Nicolai that an exorcism had been performed at the school Friday, after school let out, and that the wraith formerly known as Dean was no longer an issue. I was relieved to hear that the malicious spirit had been removed and there was no need to call in the Ghostbusters, but it didn't change the fact that Dean had died without a soul and was therefore in Hell.

Dean hadn't deserved that and it wasn't fair. Worse yet, there'd be wraiths. Or there could already be more and we just hadn't discovered them. The Wardens were investigating suspicious deaths, but it was impossible for them to catch everyone. We were operating in the dark, waiting for a disaster to come ashore.

At least when I had been able to go to school, I'd felt as if I could do something if anything happened, but being stuck here made me feel about ten kinds of useless.

That was it. I was *stuck*.

The only bright spot in the downtime was the phone calls and messages with Stacey and Sam. They were still under the impression that I'd be joining them for movies with Zayne, but that wasn't happening. I hadn't really seen Zayne. Not that I blamed him for avoiding me. Whenever I thought about him, a throbbing ache would light up my chest. I didn't regret telling him the truth, but it didn't make dealing with the consequences any easier.

Dinner had already been served and most of the Wardens would be getting ready to head out for the night. Before I headed down to the kitchen to see what food I could hoard, I walked over to where my cell rested on the foot of the bed.

On some kind of weird, annoying subconscious level, I reached for the phone. Stopping halfway, I drew my arm back. "Crap."

There was a time bomb waiting on my phone.

A text message from Roth that was two days old. A text message I would not, could not respond to.

The message had been innocent enough. A simple are you bored yet? But it had been the first time he'd texted me since he returned from his little trip to Hell and for some screwed-up reason, the text made my stomach decide it wanted to be a gymnast every time I thought about it. In my head, the text symbolized a clearly drawn line and responding would be like cartwheeling across it.

Roth had been right the last time I saw him.

I didn't understand jack when it came to him. I didn't know what he was about or what he was trying to accomplish with the things he'd said to me. All I did know was that his outright dismissal of what we'd shared still festered like an infection in the chambers of my heart. That was a fact—a reality. I wasn't going to allow it to happen again.

And then there was Zayne.

Drawing in a shaky breath, I forced myself away from the bed. As I left the bedroom, I tugged the hair tie off my wrist and yanked my hair up into a half-assed ponytail, which matched my half-assed attempt at dressing. My sweats were at least two sizes too big and the long-sleeve shirt was probably two sizes too small.

Hotness.

I veered away from the dining room large enough to accommodate an entire NFL team. Deep voices radiated from the room, broken up by the soft laughter of either Jasmine or Danika. I lingered for a second by the closed pocket doors, letting the ridiculous yearning to be a part of *them* take hold for a second.

Silly.

I shook my head and shuffled on toward the kitchen. Not the one that Jasmine fed her babies in, but what I liked to think of as the place where the food magic happened. The doors closed quietly behind me. House staff milled about, not surprised to see me roaming through the large, industrial space.

Morris turned from where he stood before several bowls, smiling when he spotted me. He reached over, picked up a covered plate and placed it on the island. Then he patted the spot before it.

I grinned as I hopped up on the stool. "Thanks. You didn't have to do that."

He shrugged as he handed over a fork and knife, then removed the lid from the plate with a flourish servers all around the world would envy. Pot roast and red potatoes. My mouth watered.

I dug in, chewing to the sound of water running and dishes clanking together. Somehow, over the past month or so, that had become a comforting sound. None of the staff besides Morris really paid any attention to me, but I was okay with that.

I was kind of like them. Ghosts in the house. Nothing really there to get attached to.

God. My mood was somewhere between *in the crapper* and *lying facedown in a puddle.*

Gathering up my plate, I walked it over to where the dirty dishes were stacked. Like always I tried to rinse it off, but one of the staff relieved me of the plate with a quickness that was impressive.

"You know, I can clean up my own mess," I pointed out.

The woman said nothing as she placed it with the rest of the dirty dishes. Making a face, I turned and sharp tingles radiated down my spine as my eyes locked with blue ones.

Zayne stood just inside the kitchen, his expression sheltered as his gaze dropped from my face to the knife I clutched in my hands. He arched a brow. "Should I be worried?"

I was a bit dumbfounded by seeing him in here.

Morris appeared, whisking the knife out of my hand. Eyes widening as he gave me a not-so-discreet push in Zayne's direction, I stumbled like a doofus. "I was...uh, eating."

"I gathered that much." His gaze dipped again, and this time I knew I wasn't holding any stabby weapons. He was staring at the wide strip of flesh my ill-fitting shirt was showing off. Heat flowed into my cheeks and then turned into a pleasant liquid feeling that went much, much lower. When his lashes finally rose I knew I looked like a tomato. "I was heading to the training rooms. Want to join me?"

Before I could respond, Morris passed behind me and gave yet another well-placed, strong shove toward Zayne. I shot him a look over my shoulder. *"Geez."*

He winked.

As I turned back to Zayne, I saw his lips twitch as if he was trying not to smile. Good sign or not? "Sure."

Zayne nodded and I followed him to the narrow door beside the oversize freezer. It was an entrance to the floors below that I rarely used.

"I overslept today," Zayne said as he closed the door behind us. "Didn't get in any workout before dinner."

"Did...did you have a busy night?" I trailed behind him in the dimly lit hall, but he'd stopped and waited until I was walking alongside him. "Hunting?"

"We found an enclave of Terriers over near Rock Creek Park and were dealing with that most of the night."

"Terriers?" When he nodded, all I could do was shake my head in wonder. Terriers were creatures that were a cross between an ostrich and a raptor, another class of demonic lovelies. "That's kind of abnormal, right?"

Zayne slowed as we reached the door leading to one of the training rooms. "The last time we'd seen any was right before Dez brought Jasmine down here for the first time."

"That was years ago." I stepped into the room as he held the door open.

"Yep," he said, passing me and crossing onto the blue mats, heading for the equipment laid out on benches. He picked up some white cloth and began wrapping his knuckles. "The thing is, so many of these demons aren't allowed topside and, because we don't see them often, we think they're not here. But they are. They've just gotten better at hiding themselves."

I thought of the club of sorts under the Palisades and all the demons there that weren't supposed to be walking among humans.

"Want to join?" he offered as he finished wrapping his knuckles.

"No. Ate too much. I'll just watch." I tugged on the hem

of my shirt and the moment I let go it popped back up, revealing half of my lower stomach. Probably should've revisited my wardrobe choices. After dinner, I was rocking a bit of a belly.

Zayne strode past me, settling both hands on the sides of the punching bag. "I really wish you'd reconsider eating with everyone."

"I really wish you'd stop bringing it up."

He looked over his shoulder at me, brows raised. "You don't need to feel like you don't belong in there. You do. And you're missed at the table."

I laughed at that. "By who?"

"Me."

My lips parted and I really had no response for that. I watched him turn back to the punching bag. He fell back into position and raised his arms. "How have you been enjoying your time off?" he asked, throwing a punch that knocked the bag back several feet.

"I've been bored out of mind."

Expression concentrated, he swung with his other arm. "And you have the rest of the week."

"Yeah, thanks for reminding me." I sat down on the mats and crossed my legs.

A slight smile appeared as he moved around the bag, targeting different sides with different hand techniques. Sweat dotted his brow and dampened the blond hair at his temples. "We heard back from a contact at one of the hospitals—the same one Dean had been taken to. They had another DOA brought in two nights ago—a young woman who had no previous health conditions died of a massive heart attack. Heart blown out basically, like with Dean."

I winced.

"Her fiancé will be out of town the day after tomorrow to attend the funeral in Pennsylvania, so I'm going to check out their town house," he continued. "It's the only way to see if she was infected, you know? If she's now a wraith, her house would be the most likely place she'd be."

The Wardens had been doing a lot of that lately—scoping out the recently deceased. "Can I go?"

He stopped, wiping the back of his forearm as he looked at me. A second passed. "You're starting to sound like Danika. She's been demanding to be allowed to go on hunts."

"Why shouldn't she be? The girl is trained. She's a full Warden. She can fight."

"You know the answer to that."

I frowned. It felt weird to defend Danika when I'd spent so much time hating on her. "Maybe she doesn't want to be just a baby-making machine."

He shook his head as he turned back to the bag and got back to working out. Only he could beat the Hell out of something and not be out of breath. I'd be panting, lying on the floor in a puddle of sweat at this point.

"So can I?" I asked again. "I haven't been tagging, so it would feel…good to do something helpful."

Zayne threw a couple of punches and then drew back from the bag. The front of his gray shirt was damp with sweat. "I guess it wouldn't be a problem. Sure."

A wide smile broke out across my face. "Thank you. I really want to do something that doesn't…"

I trailed off as he reached down and pulled the shirt off over his head and dropped it to the floor.

Holy hotness…

Now that was just so wrong.

My eyes roamed over his chest and defined stomach like those of a starved person looking at an all-you-can-eat buffet. Those sweats of his hung low, revealing the indents on either side of his hips. Zayne really didn't have a six-pack. More like an eight-pack.

"What were you saying?"

Each ab was tightly rolled. As if someone had carved them into his stomach. "Huh?"

Two fingers suddenly pressed under my chin, forcing my gaze up to his face. The corners of his lips curled up as I flushed. "You were talking about going with me to the town house?"

"Oh. Yeah. That." Important stuff that didn't involve touching his stomach or anything like that. "It will be really productive."

Zayne chuckled as he dropped his hand and returned to the bag. The way his muscles worked along his back and stomach as he threw punch after punch was truly fascinating.

I was sure if I sat here any longer and watched him, I'd turn into a puddle of goo on the mats, but I didn't get up. This was better than looking through Tumblr posts of hot guys.

When he was finished, he swiped a fresh towel off the rack. I was pretty much still sitting on the mat with my tongue lolling out. He lowered the towel. "So, about the movies tomorrow…"

That was like having a bucket of ice water thrown in my face.

Reality sucked. I pushed to my feet, keeping my eyes trained on his sneaks. "Yeah, about that." I exhaled slowly, working through the lump in my throat. "I guess I'll text Stacey and let her know that the movie thing is a no-go for us—I mean, for me. There's really no reason for me to go and it's probably better that way, because it's, like, Sam and Stacey's first date and all."

I started past Zayne, but he reached out, wrapping his arm around my waist. As he snagged me, the bare flesh of his arm connected with my stomach and I froze at the sudden intrusion of emotion. It was a tangled ball I wasn't skilled enough at deciphering.

"Whoa," he said, dragging me back so that I was right in front of him. He dropped his arm. "You don't want to go anymore?"

"Well, I guess...I figured that after Thursday night and stuff, you wouldn't want to go." I stumbled over my words as though I'd just learned to speak yesterday. "And I completely understand that and—"

"Did I ever say to you that I'd changed my mind about tomorrow?" he asked, frowning.

"No, but—"

"But I never said that and as far as I knew we were still going." He flipped the towel over his shoulder, watching me. "You didn't change your mind. So we're on."

I gaped at him, wondering if I'd stared at his abs so hard that I'd given myself a stroke. "But why?"

"Why?" he repeated softly.

"Yeah. I...I screwed up. Big-time." It seemed unnecessary to explain this. "Why would you want to go to the movies with me? Stacey and Sam are going to think that means something."

His hand snapped out, catching my wrist and stopping me from fiddling with the hem of my shirt. "Do you think us going together means something?"

My tongue felt tied.

He lowered his head, his steady gaze searching mine. "Do you *want* it to mean something?"

"Yes," I whispered, and there was a whole lot of truth in that one word.

His hand slipped up my sleeve, curling around my elbow. "Then we're going to the movies tomorrow."

It sounded so simple, but I truly didn't understand why he'd still want to. A small smile crossed Zayne's face, as if he seemed to know what I was thinking, and the words sort of fell out of my mouth. "I don't deserve you."

"See, that's where you're wrong." He reached up with his other hand and tucked a pale escapee from my ponytail back behind my ear. "That's where you've always been wrong. You deserve everything."

Perhaps my priorities were all kinds of jacked up, but as I applied the finishing touch in the form of lip gloss, the Lilin, the wraiths and the difference I felt inside me were the furthest thing from my thoughts.

As I leaned back from the mirror in my bathroom, I took in my outfit with a critical eye. Stacey would say I needed to show more boob. The dark jeans were tight, paired with a loose white blouse cinched at the waist with a dark blue braided belt and the black heels that made me feel taller than the Lollipop Guild.

My hair was down, falling into loose waves and the pink sweeping across my cheeks told me there'd be no need for blush. My pulse was a steady thrum as I stared at myself in the bathroom mirror. Was I really going out on a date with Zayne? Was this really happening? Excitement hummed through my blood, making Bambi all kinds of antsy, but there was a part of me that felt as if I was dreaming.

Never once had I thought this day would ever, *ever* happen.

I picked up the tube of mascara, wondering if another coat would make it look as though spiders had mated with my eyelashes.

"You look great. So stop messing around. We're going to be late."

I jumped at the sound of Zayne's voice and dropped the

mascara. The plastic tube clanged off the sink basin. He stood just inside my bedroom and the smile he wore made me feel as if I'd spotted a rainbow.

He was wearing a dark gray V-neck sweater that stretched across his broad shoulders and he made light-colored denim jeans look damn good.

"Thank you." I plucked up the mascara and placed it in its basket. "You look very...very nice, too."

Zayne chuckled as I came out of the bathroom. "Your face is so red."

"Thanks."

"It's cute."

The fact I probably resembled a chili pepper wasn't cute. My gaze wandered everywhere but his face. "Do you mind picking up Stacey and Sam at her place? I think it would be easier instead of taking two cars."

"That's fine with me."

"Good." I turned, frowning at the mess that was my room. "I just need to find my purse."

Zayne had moved closer, as silent as a shade. "You don't need it. I'm paying. That's what guys do on a date."

My heart kicked at my chest. This was a date. I couldn't wrap my head around it. Scanning the scattered books and clothing, I gave up on finding the purse I rarely used and faced Zayne.

He was closer than before, so close that I could feel the warmth from his body. Slowly, I lifted my eyes and I was left unsteady. His gaze tracked over my face and the smile he wore slipped a little.

"You really do look beautiful," he said, voice gruff. "But you always look beautiful, like something that's not quite real."

Hearing Zayne say something like that never failed to knock me into la-la land. All I could do was grin up at him like a fool.

The smile returned in full force and he laughed again. "Come on. We've gotta go."

I nodded and as we turned, we realized that we weren't alone. Out in the hallway, Danika stood with Maddox. Heat infused my body but was quickly chased away by a trail of icy fingers over my skin.

Danika was staring down the hall, her expression completely devoid of any emotion, and oddly enough, I felt a lick of pain in my chest for her. It was so weird, but I knew she liked Zayne—more than just liked him—and I felt bad. I felt as if I should put some space between Zayne and me.

But Maddox…? It was the first time I'd seen him up and walking around since the fall down the stairs. Not that he'd been out of commission this entire time, but I'd made sure to avoid him. Well, avoid pretty much all of them.

Maddox stared at Zayne with wide eyes. His jaw worked overtime, as if he was doing everything to keep his mouth shut as he looked at me.

I *really* felt as though I should put more space between Zayne and me.

Zayne reached down between us, threading his fingers through my mine, surprising all the sugar I'd consumed earlier right out of me. "What's up, guys?"

With a small smile, Danika shook her head. "Nothing. We were just heading down to the training rooms. Right?" She looked at Maddox.

He wasn't paying attention to her, his gaze fixed on our joined hands as though we were holding a grenade. Anger infused me, straightening my spine and replacing the awkwardness I felt.

"Something you want to say?" asked Zayne, his narrowed gaze on Maddox.

The Warden shook his head as he curled his lip. "Nope.

Not a damn thing." Then he turned, stalking down the hall, toward the stairs.

Danika sent us a sympathetic look that didn't seem right on her. "Sorry. Have…" She smiled, but it didn't reach her eyes. "Have fun."

Once the hall was empty, I glanced up at Zayne. "Maddox didn't look happy."

"Do I look like I care?" Zayne's grip on my hand tightened. "Now, come on. We have a movie to get to."

Twisted around in the front seat of Zayne's Impala, I stared at Sam and wondered if an alien had abducted him. Nothing about the guy sitting in the backseat next to Stacey was anything like the awkward, somewhat nerdy boy I'd known since I started school.

His usually unbrushed hair was actually *styled*. I figured he could tell all of us the year in which hair gel was created, but I'd had no idea he even knew how to use it. His curls were swept back from his forehead, artfully messy. The new look changed the whole landscape of his face. His jaw was stronger, a cut line. His cheekbones appeared higher, sharper, and without his glasses, his lashes seemed ridiculously long.

The way he sat was different. Body relaxed and legs spread apart as he stared out the window. His typical slouch was gone. He was dressed nice—a sweater like Zayne wore with a white dress shirt underneath it.

Sam looked really good. It was like seeing your son growing up or something.

And Stacey couldn't keep her eyes off him…or her hand. Right now, her fingers were curled around his forearm and his hand…whoa. His hand was resting on her thigh, like her *inner* thigh.

I whipped back around, feeling like a peeper. My gaze

shifted to Zayne. His right hand rested on his leg while his left held the steering wheel. I wanted to reach over and place my hand over his, but years of being nothing more than a friend to him prevented me from taking that action.

The worst thing ever entered my brain at that chosen moment. Would it be this hard with Roth to forget who I used to be versus who I was now? I quickly looked away, blowing out a low breath as I watched a cab stop to pick up a couple.

I will not think of him. I will not think of him. He had no place in this, in any of this.

Traffic was a beast and it took a lifetime to get to the theater in the historic district. The place wasn't a Cineplex. More like an old-school theater with only a couple of movies showing, but it was quaint and cute and once we all decided on a film, we were ready to do this.

The lobby was mostly empty by the time we got our tickets, but the smell of buttery popcorn made the fact that we'd missed the previews okeydoke.

As we walked to the concession stand, Sam moved to Stacey's other side, wrapping his arm around her waist, and I was guessing I hadn't been around for the day that their relationship went from finally acknowledging each other into touchy-feely land.

Considering how far Zayne and I had gone without really going anywhere, I wondered just exactly what Sam and Stacey had shared, and made a mental note to demand the lowdown on their current state of affairs.

But right now, I was more concerned with my own current affairs.

Still surprised that I was here with Zayne after what had happened, I looked up at him. He was watching me as I nibbled on my thumbnail.

"You doing okay?" he asked, tugging my hand away from my mouth.

I nodded.

He dipped his head so that his mouth was near my ear. "So relax."

It wasn't until then that I realized how locked up my muscles were. I forced a couple of deep breaths, willing the tension out of my body.

"That's better." He placed a hand on my lower back and whispered, "I want to be here, Layla-bug. No matter what has happened in the past, I want to be here."

Those words made the breath catch in my throat and spun my heart around like a ballerina. "I want to be here, too," I whispered back.

His lips brushed my temple. "That's what I want to hear."

When he pulled back, my smile was so wide there was a good chance it would crack my face open in a good way. If there was such a thing.

The jiggle from the door behind us announced we weren't the only ones running late. The sound drawing my attention, I looked over my shoulder and almost fell right over. Face-first into a trash can.

Walking through the door was the man I'd slapped in the face with the Bible—the member of Church of God's Children that had gotten away. He was dressed the same way he'd been that horrible day—white shirt and pressed pants, hair cropped close to the skull. He carried a bottle of water with him. It couldn't be a coincidence, but had he known we'd be here? Had he been following Zayne and me? Or my friends?

My mouth dropped open as I whipped around, grabbing the back of Zayne's shirt. He turned, gaze questioning. "Look who just walked in," I whispered.

He glanced back and he swore under his breath. "You've got to be kidding me."

"What are you guys chatting about?" Stacey asked, twisting toward us. As she did so, she leaned into Sam's arm in a way that would've been supercute if I wasn't seconds away from flipping out.

"Nothing." Zayne sent her a sure smile as he slipped his arm over my shoulders, effectively moving me so I was standing in front of him. "You guys getting popcorn or something?"

"I have a need for Skittles," Sam replied, eyeing the counter as he rested his hands on the glass countertop. The cashier, a young girl with more freckles than there were stars in the sky, was leaning toward him.

"Skittles?" Stacey wrinkled her nose. "You hate Skittles." Zayne curled his hand around my upper arm. "We're going to go ahead and—"

The man stepped right in front of us and he looked directly at Stacey and Sam. "You shouldn't be here with them."

Stacey looked over at him, blinking slowly as Sam pushed away from the counter. A curious expression marked his face. "Excuse me?" she said.

"You shouldn't be here with them," the man repeated, voice low and shaky. "They are the devil's minions."

There was a pause and Stacey choked out a laugh. "Oh God, you're one of those freaks that hates Wardens?" She tugged on Sam's hand. "Hey, you finally get to meet one in person."

Sam eyed the man. "Not impressed."

"You don't understand," he said. "It's not because of him as much—"

"Oh, yeah, we aren't doing this," Zayne cut in, his grip tightening on my arm. "Let's go."

"I'll get popcorn later." Stacey wrapped her hand around Sam's. "And I'll come back for your Skittles."

We were walking away. Not fast enough for me, but we were walking away. My heart started to slow down. We'd made it into the hall leading to the closed doors to the theater Then three words stopped us dead in our tracks.

"She's a demon."

Air flew out of my lungs.

"She's a demon," he repeated with the kind of conviction only zealots could muster. "And I can prove it."

Stacey faced him, shaking her head. "Are you nuts?"

I had no idea how he could prove it, but I didn't want to risk it. Bambi grew restless as tension poured into me. "That's not true."

He looked at me with pure hatred in his eyes. What about the rules, I wanted to scream. Humans were never supposed to know that demons existed. Something the Alphas had decreed—that humans must have faith without proof of a Hell. Always sounded crazy to me, but he had to be aware of them and he didn't care. "All you tell is lies."

Zayne dropped his arm and moved in front of me. "Don't make me do something I'm going to regret."

"There is already plenty you should regret." He moved away from Zayne.

My heart beat wildly again. He wanted to expose me, right in front of my friends. I didn't care about the greater consequences of such an action. These were my friends—friends who thought I was normal and accepted me. I couldn't let this happen.

I grabbed Stacey's arm as I sent Zayne a panicked look. "Come on, let's just go. We can—"

"She doesn't want you to know the truth," the man said, reaching into his back pocket with his free hand. Zayne stiffened, but all he pulled out was a paper that had been rolled up. He shoved it at us, showing what turned out to be a photo of an older woman. Whoever the lady was, she was wearing some kind of orange shirt, her light blond hair was greasy and stringy. Scabs covered her slack lips and heavy lines crossed her face.

Sam frowned. "You're showing us a mug shot?"

"Her name was Vanessa Owens," he said, his hand trembling causing the thin paper to flutter. "She was twenty when she worked at a state-run foster care back in the late nineties, going to school at Georgetown. She had a bright future ahead of her—a loving boyfriend, a close-knit family and friends."

Stacey cocked her head to the side, brows knitted together. "Let me guess? She found meth? Because it looks like she did. Drugs suck. Not sure what that has to do with any of this."

I stared at the picture. Nothing about her name or her face was familiar to me, but there was a growing unease that bloomed in my chest.

"This is enough," Zayne said, wrapping a hand around my arm. "Let's get the Hell out of here."

"He doesn't want you to know either—because the Wardens protect her, protect what she really is and what she did to this innocent woman."

"I've never seen this woman," I said, feeling trapped. The few people in the lobby were looking over at us, but I didn't think they could hear what was being said. "I don't know who she is."

"You may not remember her, but I'm sure she remembers you. After all, you destroyed her life," he said, lips curling back in disgust. "She watched over you while you were in foster care and you, true to your nature, fed off her and took a part of her soul, sending her into a downward spiral that ended in drugs, robbery and eventually death."

Blood drained from my face so quickly I thought I would pass out. The woman's face in the photo shifted, became younger and was replaced by vibrant blond hair, flawless skin and a warm smile.

Oh my God…

This was the woman I'd fed off when I'd been younger? The woman I'd *attacked,* which had prompted the Wardens' discovery of me? I'd known that she had been hospitalized after I'd fed off her, but this?

"Whoa," Sam murmured, rubbing his brow.

"She had been in and out of jail for ten years until recently she decided to rob a convenience store. She shot and killed one of the clerks and was killed by the police when they responded to the scene," the man said, lowering the photo. "This is what you've done. How many more lives have you stolen since then?"

Zayne said something and tugged on my arm again, but I was frozen. All these years, I'd never really thought about what had happened to the woman. I'd thought that since I hadn't taken her soul completely, she would've recovered. That she would be okay. But I'd effed up this woman like no tomorrow.

It struck me then and my stomach roiled so tightly I thought I might hurl all over the guy. What I had done to this woman by taking just a part of her soul was no different than what had happened to Dean and what was happening to Gareth and God knows how many more.

"You're a demon," the man seethed. "And the time will come when you won't be able to hide what you are."

I had no idea how the church knew so much about me, but at this moment, it didn't matter. Nothing mattered except what he'd claimed and what I'd realized about myself.

"Wow. Man, you're crazy." Stacey crossed her arms, shaking her head. "Like not even in the slightly entertaining way, but in the 'it's time to call the police and possibly think about getting a restraining order' kind of way."

"You don't believe me?" he asked.

She snorted. "Does anyone believe you?"

"You'll see." The hand holding the water bottle moved so quickly there was no stopping him. Even Zayne hadn't seen it coming. With some pretty excellent force and aim, he shook the bottle at us. Water doused Stacey and me, and hit Zayne's pants leg.

Stacey shrieked as she flung the water off with her fingers. "What the Hell!"

Water ran down my head, across my face and into my eyes, pooling in several spots on my shirt, turning the material transparent, except...except it wasn't normal water. I stumbled back a step, bumping into Stacey as Zayne shot forward, sweeping his arm across the man's chest, knocking him back several feet. He whirled back to me and the horrified look creeping across his face confirmed it.

"Oh no," he whispered.

My skin stung all along my forehead and across my cheeks. My vision blurred and the inside of my mouth smarted as though I'd swallowed hot sauce. Patches along my breasts and stomach started to throb. Bambi whirled around my body, escaping to my back.

The sting quickly escalated, turning into a fierce burn that robbed the breath from my lungs as I raised my hands. Thin wisps of smoke wafted from the tips of my overly pink fingers.

"Oh my God." Stacey's horrified voice reached my burning ears. "Layla..."

The guy stumbled to his feet, the empty bottle clutched tight in his hand, and when he spoke, satisfaction dripped from his voice as he spat out two words that changed everything. "Holy water."

CHAPTER TWENTY-SEVEN

I was only vaguely aware of Zayne punching the Church of God's Children guy into next week. He hit the opposite wall and slid down. The water bottle of doom rolled across the floor. My skin felt as though it was being burned off my bones. This was nothing compared to the tiny amount Roth had used when I'd been clawed by the Nightcrawler.

Pain rippled through me like a shock wave. Doubled over at the waist, I tried to breathe through it, but it was nearly impossible. I could hear Stacey's strained voice, but she sounded so very far away.

"We need to go." Zayne was closer and then he was gathering me to his side, steering me out of the hallway and through the lobby. The cool air from outside intensified the burn and I bit down on my lower lip. "I need to get this off her."

"Someone please tell me what's going on?" Stacey asked, closer and clearer. "I don't understand what just happened."

"I don't have time to explain right now. Drive." He tossed the keys at Sam and if I hadn't been close to keeling over anyway, I would've done so from the fact he was letting someone drive his Impala. "Your house is closer."

Sam caught the keys, but he shook his head. "We can't go to my place. My parents will freak."

A low growl rose from Zayne's throat. "I need to get her in a shower now. I don't care what your parents think—"

"No," I wheezed. "Take me...to Stacey's place. It's only a couple more blocks."

"Layla—"

"She's right. My mom isn't home and I'm only a couple of blocks away. If you take Fifth Avenue, it might even be quicker," Stacey said, out of breath. "But shouldn't we take her to the hospital? Her skin is all pink. Was it acid? Oh my God, did that freak—"

"It wasn't acid and a hospital can't help her." We'd walked about half a block before Zayne cursed and scooped me up. God knew what we looked like to people around us, but I was beyond caring. I bit back a moan as he shifted me. "Sorry," he whispered, voice hoarse.

"I don't understand," Stacey repeated, her voice sounding distant again. "It was just water. It hit me, too. I *don't* understand."

No one replied and when we finally reached the Impala, Zayne crawled into the backseat with me and tried to wipe up most of the water with an old shirt he had in the back, but it didn't help. I needed a shower. The trip to Stacey's house was pure Hell. I was vaguely aware of Zayne calling Nicolai and warning that we might have a possible demonic-level PR disaster on our hands. I followed the conversation enough to know that Nicolai would check out the theater, do some damage control. At some point, my vision cleared enough to make out Stacey's stricken face.

She stared at me as though...as though she didn't know what she was looking at, and maybe her brain was refusing to put two and two together, but it would eventually. And I couldn't deal with seeing her look at me like that. Closing my eyes, I kept them that way until we arrived at Stacey's house.

The pain deep in my core was just as bad as what was firing off across my skin. I didn't say anything as Stacey led the way upstairs and to the bathroom she used. Sam stayed downstairs, no doubt to research how holy water could burn a person. He'd been remarkably quiet through all of this.

"No one should be home for at least two hours." Her voice was garbled. "Can I...can I help?"

"Do you have anything she can wear?" She must've nodded, because Zayne said, "Leave it outside the door."

"But—"

"We'll explain everything." He opened the door, ushering me in. "I promise."

Stacey caught the door before he could close it. "Are you okay, Layla?"

"Yes," I croaked out, keeping my back to where she stood. "I'll...be okay."

Zayne managed to get the door shut then. He moved around me, turning on the shower. A second later, I was under an icy stream of water, gasping for breath. Drops pelted my face, ruining all the hard work with the mascara and eyeliner.

"The clothes have to come off," he said.

He didn't have to tell me twice. I turned sideways, nodding my agreement. Neither of us spoke and there was nothing sexual about the fact that I was standing in the shower, being drowned by a steady stream of cold water as Zayne stripped me down to my undies. Gone were the skintight jeans, the thin braided belt and my bra. Everything that had been touched by holy water had to come off.

Bambi had made her way to my lower back, where she was curled into a small, protective ball as Zayne kept turning me around and around, his arms getting soaked as he made sure all the holy water was rinsed away.

After about five years of circling the drain on the fifth circle of Hell, the burning eased off and tiny little bumps spread across my stomach as shivers coursed up and down my back. Blinking the water off my lashes, I could see that my arms, currently folded over my chest, were a lovely shade of ouch.

"I'm so sorry I didn't stop him," Zayne said finally, turning me around. "I should've stopped him. I could've stopped him."

"It's not your fault. Who knew he…was going to throw holy water on me."

He looked up. "I should've expected something."

I shook my head, shivering. "It's n-not your f-fault."

A look of doubt settled onto his face, making him appear older. "You're not burning anymore."

"N-no."

When Zayne turned the water off, I couldn't feel my face or my toes, which was probably a good thing. My skin was the kind of cold only a snowy February day could rival.

He quickly wrapped a large fluffy towel around me, tucking it under my arms.

"Hold this," he said, and I grabbed the edges, knotting them together. He picked me up out of the tub and twisted. Sitting down on the rim, he pulled me into his lap and grabbed another towel, immediately soaking up the water from my icy hair. "God, you feel like an ice cube."

"Why did he do it there, where it was just Stacey and Sam who'd hear and see, instead of in front of a large crowd of people?" I asked, teeth chattering.

"It was personal. It's the only reason." Zayne rubbed the other towel up and down my arms, chasing the chill. "How are you feeling?"

"B-better." I stared at the buttercup-yellow wall as Zayne

got the blood going in my chilled skin. I don't know how much time had passed before I spoke again. "What are w-we going to tell them?"

He didn't answer immediately. Instead, he gently rubbed the towel over my cheeks. "The truth, I guess."

"What about the r-rules?"

He curled the towel around my bare shoulders. "Well, technically they've already been broken and an Alpha hasn't landed on our heads, right? And they're your best friends. You trust them." He paused. "I also have no idea how to come up with a lie that's going to make them believe anything else."

I tried to smile, but failed. "What if S-Stacey hates me now or is a-afraid of me?"

"Oh, Layla, she's not going to hate you." He lowered his head and pressed his lips against my forehead. "She's not going to be afraid of you and she's not going to think of you differently."

What felt like ropes circled my chest. "How c-can they not?"

"Because they know you like I know you, that's why." The intensity to his words was compelling. "What you are doesn't change who you are."

I nodded.

His eyes searched mine and then he slid his arms around me, letting the towel he held fall to the floor. I folded into his tight embrace, soaking up his warmth and his acceptance. It seemed faulty, his belief in me, when I wasn't sure it was warranted.

But I needed to pull it together, because Stacey and Sam were waiting for us, and I couldn't hide in the bathroom half-naked with Zayne forever.

"I'm ready," I said, and my heart dipped a little as I pulled free and stood.

Zayne retrieved the clothes Stacey had left outside the bathroom. I changed into the sweats and sweater and then forced myself out of the room. He'd been leaning against the wall, waiting for me, eyes focused wearily on the ceiling. When he pushed off the wall and stepped in front of me, I wanted to push a rewind button on today.

"Everything is going to be okay," he assured me.

I wasn't that hopeful.

Stacey and Sam were in the living room downstairs. She stood as we entered the room, her normally dark complexion pale. Sam turned to us, his expression expectant.

"Okay," she said, clasping her hands together. "Before we talk about anything, are you okay?"

I nodded. My skin was a deeper pink than normal and a bit raw to the touch, but by tomorrow morning it would be fine. "I'm okay."

She closed her eyes and breathed out a deep sigh. "You really scared us—scared me. I thought he'd thrown acid on you or something, but I know...that's not it. First off, you didn't go to the hospital and your skin hasn't peeled off your face."

My brows rose.

"And the water hit Stacey," Sam pointed out, head cocked to the side as he studied me. Not like he would if he was afraid, but more like he was genuinely curious. "Nothing happened to her."

"But something happened to you," she said, drawing in another deep breath. "Something really strange happened. I saw smoke coming off your skin."

Well, that would definitely tell someone something was up. I glanced at Zayne and he nodded as he sat on the arm of a chair. "I don't know where to even start."

"How about with the truth?" Sam said.

That statement stung and rightfully so. "I'm sorry that I

haven't been completely honest with you two, but there are things—rules—that have prevented me from doing so."

"Are you like Zayne?" Stacey asked, looking at him. "Because if so, I don't see what the big deal is."

"I am kind of like Zayne. I'm part Warden." Hearing myself say these words to my friends was strange. I sat in the chair Zayne was perched on. "But I'm not like him. Not really. I…I'm also part demon. That's why the water did what it did. It was seriously holy water."

Stacey opened her mouth and she blinked once, then twice. Then she laughed as she dropped in the seat next to Sam. "Okay, Layla, don't bullshit me."

"I'm not."

"Demons don't exist," she said, rolling her eyes. "That guy at the theater was crazy."

"Gargoyles don't exist either," Zayne said gently. "Right?"

Stacey shook her head. "But that's different. You guys are just another species, right? Kind of like Big Foot. You're not this biblical mythical creature."

"But our kind was considered mythical at one time." Zayne leaned forward, resting his hands on his knees. "Layla is telling you the truth. She's part demon."

"Demons can't be real. They just can't be."

"Do you believe in angels?" Sam asked, watching me. "Because if you do, how can you not believe in demons? After all, weren't most of them angels at one time?"

Part of me wasn't surprised Sam was handling this so well, but I was shocked that he wasn't up and poking me like a science experiment.

"No." Stacey shook her head again, sending her bangs flying across her face as she stared at me. "There's no way."

"Okay." I stood up. "I am part demon. And here's the proof.

Bambi?" I willed her off my body, hoping she'd listen to me and not make me look like a fool. "Off."

Bambi stirred along my back and then I felt her lift off my skin. A shadow of tiny dots formed beside me. Stacey jumped to her feet, her mouth working as if she was trying to say something as the dots shot together. A second later, Bambi formed and lifted her diamond shaped head, eyeing Sam and Stacey as if it was potential feeding time.

"Don't eat them," I warned under my breath.

There was a breath of silence and then Stacey screamed like a banshee, jumping up on the couch as if she was going to crawl behind Sam. "Oh my God! Oh my God! A snake! That's a big-ass snake!" she screeched, going as white as a Warden's soul. "Where in the Hell did that come from?"

"Me," I said. "She mostly stays on my skin, like a tattoo. She's a familiar."

Stacey looked as if she was a second from passing out, so I called Bambi back. The snake hissed its forked tongue at me in annoyance but returned to my arm and then to my stomach.

"Holy shit-ball storm," Stacey whispered, slinking down the couch. "I did not just see that."

"Yes. Yes you did." I sat back down.

"How did you hide that thing all this time? It's huge!"

"Actually, she's only been a recent development. Bambi is a demon familiar, but she's not mine. Not really."

A look of understanding dawned on her face. "Wait—wait a sec. Roth has a snake tattoo."

I nodded. "Had."

Her eyes widened to the point I feared she'd burst a blood vessel. "Are you saying that Roth is also a demon?"

"Full-blooded," Zayne answered. "He's really known as Astaroth, the Crown Prince of Hell."

Stacey looked at Sam, who just stared at us, and then back to me. "I...I don't know what to even say at this moment."

"Whatever you think about demons, and despite what that bastard at the theater said, you should know that Layla isn't evil. She's good to her core," Zayne said, and I smiled a little at the sincerity in his words. "She's more Warden, more *human,* than anyone I know."

Stacey made a face. "Well, fucking duh. I know she's not evil. I've known her for years. She's like the equivalent of an evil baby panda or some shit like that."

I gaped at her while Zayne grinned at me.

"What about Roth?" she asked. "I mean, you just said Crown Prince of...of Hell?"

"Totally evil," Zayne threw out.

I sighed. "He's not totally evil. He's here doing something really important."

"Which is?" Sam asked, his gaze darting between us. "You have to tell us now."

Zayne nodded slowly and then I told them everything about me—what I could do and who my mother was. Zayne took over halfway, giving them the lowdown on the whole situation with the Lilin and what we suspected was going down at school. Saying both of them looked floored would be the understatement of the century.

"But neither of you can breathe a word of this," Zayne said, wrapping up the most epic info dump in the history of humanity and Wardenkind. "I'm serious. Our job is to keep the public from knowing that demons do exist. If you start telling people..."

"Kind of like if I tell you this, I'm going to have to kill you?" Stacey swallowed when neither of us responded. "Holy mind blown..."

When Stacey finally found the ability to speak again, she

focused on probably the least important thing of everything we'd just told her. "So that's why you've never gone out with boys before? Because if you kiss them, you take their souls?"

"I'd like to think that's not the *only* reason," Zayne muttered.

I nodded. "I'm kind of a succubus—just a very rare kind."

"And this Lilin thing is like you? Except it can take souls by touching? Wow." Stacey looked at Sam. "We seriously do need to change schools."

"Yeah," he said, nodding his agreement. "Maybe even cities. Possibly countries."

It was late by the time we finished talking and her parents were due back any moment. Neither Stacey nor Sam were staring at me as if I was a dangerous freak, but I suspected that it hadn't really settled in yet. I kept expecting Sam to make some kind of random statement about demons, but he didn't and that alone told me he was knocked off his game.

"We probably should be leaving," Zayne said, standing slowly. "But you guys—"

"We're not going to breathe a word of this. Besides, no one would believe us." She glanced at me, and I knew the friendship between us had changed. Maybe it wasn't as big a change as I'd feared, but there was a shift. "How can we help?"

Zayne stared at her.

A wide smile broke out across my face. "You're crazy." She frowned at me, and I immediately apologized. "I don't mean that in a bad way. Just that I've been petrified that you guys would hate me once you knew the truth and instead you're asking to help." Tears burned the back of my throat. "I really don't know what to say."

"Well, if I followed this crazy-pants conversation correctly, if the Lilin continues to um…take souls, the Alphas will get involved and that's bad news bears for all of you, right? So, why wouldn't we want to help?"

"We appreciate the offer, but it's too dangerous for us to take you up on it." Zayne held up his hand as she started to protest. "If you really want to help, then be extra vigilant. Be aware of your surroundings, watch for anyone acting strangely. Stay away from them and let us know."

"He's right." I said. "I couldn't deal with it if something happened to either of you two."

"Nothing will." Sam shot Stacey a look. "We'll stay out of it, but if you need our help, we'll be there for you."

"Like the Scooby-Doo gang," Stacey said with a smile. "But cooler and without the dog." She paused, wrinkling her nose. "We have a giant demon snake instead."

I coughed out a laugh, totally shell-shocked by how well both of them were dealing with this. I just hoped it didn't change once they had time to really think about everything. When I finally rose to leave, I was exhausted from the drama of today.

Stacey stopped me at the door and I held my breath as Zayne paused on the stoop, watching us warily. "I wish you would've been honest with me a long time ago, but I get why you weren't. It's not something you can easily tell someone and not expect them to flip out."

"It's not," I whispered.

She took a deep breath, glanced over her shoulder at the dark hallway behind her to where Sam waited for her inside the house. "You're still my best friend. You're just not human. And, well, I feel kind of cool that my best friend is part Warden, part demon in denial."

I stared at her a moment and felt a laugh burst free. The ropes around my chest snapped and the pressure eased up.

"Just don't keep me in the dark again, okay? Promise me."

I met her eyes. "I promise."

Then she hugged me, and in that moment I knew that the whole world could be on a verge of catastrophe, but Stacey and I would be okay.

We would be fine.

Abbot was waiting for us as soon as we returned to the compound.

The moment our feet hit the floor inside the foyer, he appeared before us, as tall and formidable as a great lion about to whip up on a gazelle. He took one look at me, didn't bother to ask if I'd been sunbathing recently or if I was okay, and then turned to his son.

"We need to talk," he said, jaw locked. "In private."

Zayne glanced at me and I shrugged, figuring he wanted to talk about the mess at the theater. Giving him a little wave, I darted around Abbot and headed up the stairs. Only a tiny part of me was disappointed that Abbot hadn't asked about me. I guessed I was getting used to the way he acted now.

Once inside my bedroom, I quickly changed out of the borrowed clothes and into my own pajamas. It was early in the evening, but I was whipped. After pulling my still damp hair back in a bun, I crawled under the covers and stared at my cell phone, wondering if I should alert Roth to the fact that Stacey and Sam now knew his true identity.

My fingers hovered over the screen. I needed to tell him. It was only fair and it was also the only reason I was going to contact him. My message was short and to the point.

Stacey and Sam know what we are.

Maybe a minute passed and then his message popped up. Do tell.

Church of God's Children. Holy Water. Me. Not a good combination. All is cool, tho.

This time his response was immediate. R u ok?

I nodded and then realized, like an idiot, he couldn't see
me. Yes. I paused and then typed, So is Bambi.

Minutes passed after my last text and I realized that Roth
wasn't going to respond. If he was mad that we'd exposed him,
I didn't know, but I had a feeling he probably really didn't
care. Just as I rolled over to put my cell phone on the nightstand, he responded.

U probably shouldn't have gone to the movies w/ Stony, huh?

I stared at the message, half annoyed and half amused that
somehow this was Roth's only takeaway. Like being with
Stony—er, Zayne—made a difference. I didn't respond because I figured the conversation would only go downhill at
this point.

My phone went off again, but this time, it was from Zayne.

U up for company?

I laughed at the fact we were in the same house and he was
texting me.

Sure.

Incoming.

Turning my gaze to the door, I watched it open no more
than a second later. I fought a smile. "Were you waiting out
in the hall?"

"Maybe." Zayne had changed, wearing black sweats and a white shirt. He sat down on the bed beside me. "Hanging in there?"

"Yeah. Just tired."

He stretched out on his side beside me, resting his cheek on his elbow. "It's been one Hell of a day."

"What did Abbot have to say about it?"

A cloud passed over his features. "Nothing much."

Immediately, I knew there was more. I rose up on my elbow. "What are you not telling me?"

"Nothing." Zayne laughed, but something about it was strained. "Relax, Layla-bug. Today has been crazy enough without adding crap to it."

"But—"

"Everything is fine. Chill. I have the rest of the evening off and I want to spend it with you. Salvage the rest of our date," he said, toying with the edge of my sleeve. "All right?"

Protests formed on the tip of my tongue, but he was right. We'd had enough crap to last us the rest of the week, which reminded me of tomorrow. "Are we still checking out that house tomorrow night?"

"Yep."

I eased onto my back, watching him. Thick lashes shielded his eyes as he ran his finger along the vein in my wrist. I wasn't picking up any overpowering emotion from him; then again, my own feelings were all jumbled together.

In the silence that fell between us, my mind wandered to what the man had shown me at the theater. "Can I ask you a question and you be honest?"

He arched a brow. "I can try to be honest."

I ignored that. "Do you think what I did to that lady is any different than what the Lilin is doing?"

His lashes swept up and his eyes were a startling cobalt. "It's completely different, Layla. You were just a kid who had no idea what you were doing. The Lilin is doing this on purpose."

"True, but…" I lowered my voice to a whisper. "But I fed off that woman last Thursday night. Yeah, it was a weird circumstance, but I did that."

"We don't even know if what that bastard said was true," he argued. "Just because he said that was the lady, doesn't mean it was really her. And even if it was her, there's no proof that you affected her life in that manner. There's no reason for us to believe that."

"You really think so?" I wished I could share his certainty.

"Yes." He paused. "Speaking of Thursday night, what kind of weird circumstance are we talking about here?"

I focused on the ceiling. I couldn't tell him without revealing what went on under the Palisades and I had made a promise.

Zayne sighed. "I thought we weren't keeping secrets anymore."

"I know. But if I told you this, you would have to tell your father and…well, what would happen would be my fault. Any blood would be on my hands."

"You think I tell him everything?"

The irritation in his voice drew my attention. "No, but I think there are some things you would want to tell him, and I'm not putting you in that position."

He rolled onto his back, the muscle in his jaw working. His fingers remained around my wrist, though. A few minutes passed. "I know what's going on in your head. You're comparing yourself to the Lilin."

I was, but it was more than that.

"You're not like that." He turned his head toward me, meeting my gaze. "Not a single part of you is."

Man, it would be nice to drink the Zayne Kool-Aid, but

when I closed my eyes, all I saw was Vanessa Owens's face and it kept switching out with Dean's. What if...? I couldn't even allow myself to finish that thought, to let the idea take root and gain ground.

He stretched out his arm, beckoning me. "Closer?"

I bit down on my lip and then I wiggled closer, resting my head on his chest. His heart was a steady beat under my cheek. His arm came around my waist, securing me to his side.

So many thoughts whirled through my head, and I latched on to one of them—a theory that I needed to look into. "Remember when we were talking about the wraiths with Abbot?" When he nodded, I took a deep breath. "I wasn't kidding around when I said the same feeling I had at school was what I felt here before those windows blew and Maddox took a swan dive. And I..." God, this was hard. "The night with Petr, I had—"

"You had to defend yourself," he cut in quietly, his hand tightening along my waist. "I know what you did, Layla. You don't have to say it."

I squeezed my eyes shut. "He could be here, you know? He could be a wraith."

A moment passed. "I thought of that, but with a house full of Wardens, you'd think we'd have caught on to that by this point."

That could be true, but crazier things had happened. "I'm sorry today was ruined," I said, deciding I really didn't want to think about Petr while I was here with Zayne.

"It's not your fault, so don't apologize."

I wanted to apologize again and keep apologizing, like I was going to turn into one of those people who constantly said they were sorry, but the feel of him cleared away some of the unpleasant thoughts.

Zayne lowered his chin and swept his lips across my forehead. My heart jumped at the tender contact, and I knew in that moment I couldn't put him in danger. No matter what he said, what he wanted to believe, we couldn't ignore reality.

I stared at the wall, feeling the soothing rise and fall of his chest in every cell in my body. A cold acknowledgment frosted up my insides. If what that man had said was true, then what the Lilin did and what I did were one and the same. We both destroyed lives and all it would take, for me at least, would be one slip up with Zayne. Just a tiny moment and he'd be in danger.

I couldn't do that to him. I wouldn't.

Even if that meant staying far, far away from him.

CHAPTER TWENTY-EIGHT

"You look like a ninja," Danika said. "Not a particularly skilled ninja, but like an after-school-special ninja."

I looked over my shoulder at where she sat on my bed. I honestly did not remember inviting her into my room. "Thanks. A lot."

She giggled. "I'm kidding. You look hot, though."

"I'm not trying to." I turned back to slipping my flats on. I got the ninja thing, though. I was wearing black yoga pants and a black thermal. I probably also looked like a ghost. All black did not do good things for my complexion.

"You never try to." She rose behind me. "That's why you're sexy."

Twisting around to face her, I had to think that hearing her say I was sexy was bizarre. Danika's looks and body rivaled that of the models in the Victoria's Secret campaigns. Humans and Wardens across the world would fall at her feet given a chance.

"Your skin looks a lot better," she said as the silence stretched out between us.

We'd made this promise to be friends with one another,

but it really was a slow go. "I slapped on a ton of moisturizer last night."

"Can I tell you something that's going to sound really weird?"

Turning back to the small mirror hung near my closet, I tugged my hair up into a bun. "Sure."

She sat back down on the edge of the bed again. "I'm jealous of you."

One eyebrow climbed up my forehead as I slowly lowered my hands and turned to her.

Her cheeks flushed. "And not because of Zayne. Well, yeah, I'm kind of jealous over that, but whatever. I'm more jealous that you get to go out and do things—go to school, go tagging if you want to. You've fought demons and you've gotten hurt."

"You're jealous because I've gotten hurt?"

"I know that doesn't make sense." She sighed. "I'm not happy that you were injured, but you've been out there. You've gotten scratched or bumped up, but you've been out *there* while I've been..." She waved her hands around the room. "I've been stuck in here."

I didn't know how to respond at first, but I got it. I really did. The females in the clan were so protected it was suffocating. For the most part, they'd probably never suffered a hangnail, and if they had, it was a national crisis.

Danika and others like her were *stuck* in pretty cages.

"I get it," I said, sitting down next to her. "You know, when I was younger, I was jealous of the other female Wardens, because they were accepted. Everyone cared and paid attention to them. They were wanted and I was...well, I was just here. But I got over that pretty quickly." I looked over at her, wishing it could be different for the whole lot of us. "I think, in a way, you guys have it worse than I do."

She nodded slowly. "It's not like I don't ever want to mate and have babies. It's just that I…"

"Want to do something else, too?" When she nodded, I bit my lip. "Then why don't you? You're trained. You can fight. Do you really need their permission? I mean, really? Who's here to stop you if you go out and hunt?"

Danika didn't respond for a long moment and then her eyes lit up. "You know, you're right. I could do it and once I got up there, what could they do to stop me? Send me home?" She laughed. "I'd like to see them try."

"Try what?"

We turned at the sound of Zayne's voice. Goodness gracious, dressed as he was in dark cargo pants and a tight Under Armour shirt, he was hot in a completely dangerous way.

"Nothing," chirped Danika. She leaned over, surprising me with a quick hug. Then she popped up and left the room, waving at Zayne as she squeezed by.

He frowned. "What's going on?"

I shook my head and repeated what she said. "Nothing. You ready?"

"Yeah." He eyed me as I made my way over to him. "Nice outfit."

"Danika said I looked like an after-school-special ninja."

Zayne laughed. "Nice."

I started past him, but his arm formed a wall as he placed his hand on the other side of the doorjamb. My eyes lifted to his and he lowered his head, almost as if he was about to kiss me, but that couldn't be it. He wouldn't dare do something so insane again. Zayne didn't have a death wish. But as his mouth drew closer, the flutter in my stomach grew. His fresh, winter-mint scent surrounded me, and then his lips brushed the curved of my cheek.

I tensed in the sweetest kind of way. My eyes closed as my

hands itched to touch him. Things...things were so odd between us. Both of us had admitted that there was something
between us, that we wanted more, but there was also a line between us, one that consisted of labels and promises and danger.

I thought of the promise I made to myself last night, the
promise that changed what we both wanted. Disappointment
swelled and crashed through me like tumultuous waves as I
abruptly dipped under his arm.

Ignoring the look of confusion, I smoothed my hands over
my pants. "Is there anything we need to get before we go?"

A moment passed before he answered. "I have everything
we need packed away in the Impala."

Everything we needed for a possible exorcism consisted of
holy water, something I was so not getting near, purified salt
and stinky, blessed incense. We had everything needed to do
one in the house, and I briefly considered doing an exorcism
here, but that would kind of be hard to explain to the Wardens. I'd have to bring up Petr, and with the way Abbot was
acting toward me, that wouldn't be smart. I had no idea what
to do about Petr, and there was a tiny part of me that really
wondered if he was here in wraith form. Either way, excitement hummed through me as we headed out to the garage. I'd
never seen an exorcism before. This should prove interesting.

"Can I yell 'By the power of Christ, I compel you' whenever we get to that point?" I asked.

"What?" Zayne laughed as he opened my passenger door.
"Hate to break it to you, but we don't have to say a word and
no one will be yelling anything like that."

I pouted. Dammit, I'd always wanted to say that. "Well,
that's not nearly as entertaining as the exorcisms I've seen on
TV."

He gave me a look as he stepped aside to let me climb in.

Just as he went to close the door, Dez came out the compound door, heading for one of the SUVs.

His gaze moved from Zayne to me. "She's going with you to the house?"

"Yeah." He leaned against the open door, eyeballing the older Warden. "You got a problem with that?"

Dez held up his hands. "Didn't say I did. Just be careful." He glanced at me and the look said he wanted to pull me out of the car and toss me over his shoulder. "She's a..."

A scowl pulled at my lips. "A demon?"

"No." Dez's brows rose. "I was going to go with 'a girl,' one who is young and doesn't need to get hurt."

"Oh." I felt like a bitch. "Thanks for pointing that out."

Zayne closed my door before I could say anything else. As he crossed paths with Dez, he said, "You know I won't let anything happen to her."

He nodded. "Still. Just be careful."

As Dez disappeared into the further recesses of the garage, I looked over at Zayne as he got behind the wheel. "Guess what?"

"What?" The engine purred to life.

"I'm a girl."

His lips curled up. "Shut up."

I giggled.

Zayne backed out of the garage as he asked if I'd heard from Stacey or Sam yet. Stacey had called me earlier and the conversation had been a little bit awkward, but all in all, it had been normal. Except that I'd told her what I was really doing tonight for the first time ever. There was something freeing in not lying about my extracurricular activates.

The drive into Alexandria, to the town house of the recently departed, didn't take long. Traffic was minimal and we were relieved to find inconspicuous parking in the back.

Zayne picking a lock was surprisingly hot.

I wasn't sure what it said about me that I got turned on by his confidence as he worked the pick until we heard the click of a lock being thrown.

"That's a handy skill."

He grinned as he straightened. "It's either that or break it. Figured a gentler touch worked best."

Roth would've broken it and been gleeful doing so. There were no two guys more different than them.

Quietly easing the door open, we waited to make sure an alarm wasn't triggered. When silence met us, we stepped into the darkened foyer. The house was full of shadows. Only a small end-table lamp was lit in the front room. Floorboards creaked as we moved farther in.

Zayne hefted the canvas bag over his shoulder, eyeing the paintings adorning the green walls. As we walked into the dining room, a small shadow zoomed out from underneath the table.

It was a gray cat.

Instead of pulling a stranger-danger dash and run, it curled around Zayne's legs and then mine. Bambi stirred in interest as I leaned down and scratched the cat's ears. Silently, I issued the snake a stern warning not to even think about eating it.

I wondered if the kitty belonged to the woman or the fiancé. Or was it both of theirs? The thought of that made me sad.

The house was tomb quiet as we entered the kitchen. A bowl of kitty chow was near the stove, along with a full dish of water.

"Everything seems normal," he said, turning to me. "You feel anything?"

I shook my head.

"We need to check upstairs."

Kitty followed us back through the house and up the stairs. There wasn't enough light to make out the framed photos hanging on the wall, but they seemed like the family sort that might've been taken over the holidays.

There were only two bedrooms upstairs and a bathroom shared by both. One bedroom was a makeshift office and in the other, another small lamp had been left on.

The kitty dashed across the room and pounced onto the bed as soon as the door opened. There, she rolled onto her back, showing off a well-fed belly.

I petted the cat while Zayne checked out the bathroom. Unlike Roth's kittens, this one didn't try to kill me as I idly rubbed its belly.

It felt wrong being in here, all up in someone's privacy. The bed wasn't made. Pillows were haphazardly strewn across the head of the bed. Dresser drawers were left half open and there was a glass of water on the nightstand, next to a framed photo of a couple. Drawn to the picture, I left the kitty on the bed and picked up the photo, holding it under the light.

A tremor ran through my arm. I almost dropped the frame. "Oh my God."

"What?" Zayne called.

I couldn't speak as I stared at the photo. A man smiled at me. He was probably in his late twenties. He had his arm draped over the shoulders of a shorter woman.

A woman I'd seen before, although briefly.

Zayne came to my side, lowering the bag. "What is it?"

I was shaking as I handed the photo to him. "This is their house, right?"

He frowned as he took it. "I guess so. It would be weird for the owners to have another couple's photo by the bed."

Panic knifed through my chest. "I know her."

"How?"

My knees felt weak. "It's *her*—the cupcake."

Confusion poured over his face. "I have no idea what you're talking about."

There was a good chance my heart was going to beat itself out of my chest. "She's the woman I fed off of Thursday night."

Zayne dropped the bag, startling the cat. His throat worked. "Are you sure?"

"Yes." I started to sit, but then I couldn't bear to be still.

"How can you be sure? You saw her—"

"It's her!" I shouted, pressing my hands against my lower stomach. Nausea rose. "Oh my God."

"Wait." He reached for me, but I edged away. "Just hold up a second. You fed off her and she walked away. Did she seem fine?"

"Yes, but you saw what happened to the lady at the foster home—to Vanessa."

"We don't know if that's true and even if it was, you didn't kill Vanessa." He thrust a hand through his hair. "And you didn't kill this one."

"She's dead. That's a huge coincidence, right?" Sweat dotted my brow. That horrific thought from the night before came back. "What if...?"

Then I felt it.

Tiny hairs on my arms rose. The stench of something unnatural crept into the room like insidious smoke. The cat's back arched like one of those Halloween cats'. Hissing, it darted off the bed and under it.

"Shit." Zayne knelt, opening the bag. "We've got a wraith."

"Of course we do," I mumbled, numb to the core.

I'd killed this woman. Somehow I'd done this and taken her soul, damning her to an eternity in Hell. How else would she have become a wraith? The likelihood that the Lilin had stumbled across her was astronomically small.

And that was if a Lilin even existed....

The temp in the room dropped severely. Puffs of misty clouds formed in front of my mouth.

"Layla."

The wraith was close—the wraith I'd created.

"Layla," Zayne snapped, at my side in an instant. "I need you here with me. Do you understand? This isn't going to be easy. I need you *here*. Are you?"

Air rushed out of me. *Pull it together.* Moving panic and horror to the back burner, I forced a nod. I needed to be in the present. "I'm here."

"Good." Zayne zeroed in on the open bedroom door. "Because so is the wraith."

A dark mass filled the doorway, roughly the same size as Dean's wraith. A shadow person. It didn't move. Appeared to just stand there and check us out.

Zayne shoved the bundle of dry incense into my hands. He lit it and the pungent odor of frankincense pillowed out in puffs of smoke. "Whatever you do, don't drop this. If you do, the whole exorcism will stop."

Seemed easy enough. "Okay."

The wraith drifted closer and the room turned into an icebox. Wind picked up, whipping around the room. Clothing blew out of the dresser. The lamp fell over. A pillow smacked my arm.

Zayne moved forward, a bottle of holy water and a small jar of salt in his hands. "Stay back. I don't want to get any of this on you."

The smoke was choking as I moved out of the way. A high-pitched wail came from the wraith, a sound that was a cross between a hyena and a screaming baby. It charged Zayne. One second, he was in front of me, and the next he was slamming into the opposite wall. He held on to the water, but the jar of salt rolled across the floor, to the other side of the wraith.

Crap.

It hissed at me, the sound feline and yet distorted, stretched out into a howl. Zayne was back on his feet, hair windblown but still in his human form. He tossed the water onto the wraith and it didn't go through the shadow. It seemed to soak the holy water up, causing it to bloat like that annoying kid in *Willy Wonka and the Chocolate Factory*.

As the wraith spun on him, I took off, heading for the jar of salt. My feet went right out from under me. I landed on my back with a grunt and somehow, by the grace of God, I held on to the incense. I turned my head, spying the jar resting a foot from me.

The wraith laughed evilly as I rolled onto my side. I snatched up the jar and unscrewed the top with one hand just as icy fingers trailed down the back of my neck. The heebie-jeebies I experienced at that moment almost made me scream as though a spider had landed in my lap.

"Toss the salt at the wraith," Zayne shouted over the pounding wind.

Twisting against the force of airstream, I knew that if I took Zayne's advice, the purified salt would just blast me in the face. The wind was terribly powerful, robbing my lungs of the ability to draw in a breath.

I pushed to my feet, holding on to the incense tightly as I forced a step forward and then another toward the wraith. Instead of throwing the salt, I shoved it, jar and all, into what might've been the creature's midsection.

The reaction was immediate.

Like a rubber band snapping, I was propelled backward as the wraith let out a scream nightmares were made of. I hit the middle of the bed. The incense slipped, and I dug my fingers in, keeping the cloying crap from hitting the bed, stopping the exorcism and most likely burning down the townhome.

The wraith exploded into wisps of smoke that quickly evaporated as if a vacuum had been placed in the room, sucking out the evil. Everything settled and the heavy presence of the abnormality eased off. The air became lighter.

My eyes met Zayne's.

He looked as though he'd gone through a wind tunnel. "You okay?"

"Yep," I squeaked, sitting up. The incense had burned out on its own. How convenient. "Wow."

"Was it everything you were expecting?"

I considered that as I saw the cat peek its head out from under the bed. "Still wish someone yelled 'power of Christ,' but it was okay."

Zayne shook his head as he hauled me to my feet. Taking the incense from me, he dropped it into the bag and then tied it up. "We need to get out of here stat before someone checks out the commotion."

Agreed.

I petted the cat one last time and then we hurried through the house. Once we were back inside the Impala, I was relieved to find that the sickly scent hadn't lingered on our clothing. Glancing at Zayne as he threw the car into Drive and peeled out of the narrow backstreet, I let everything I'd held off seep back in.

With the adrenaline still kicking around in my veins, my thoughts held a razor edge to them. As each one fell into place, it sliced and diced.

We'd reached the rural road that Zayne had taken as a shortcut to get to Alexandria by the time I found it in myself to speak. "We can't ignore what we found."

He cast me a quick, sharp look. "What do you mean?"

"Who that woman was. We can't ignore it, Zayne. I did that to her." The words cut through me. "I must've fed off her more than I thought I did."

Zayne's knuckles blanched from how tightly he was grasping the steering wheel. "You would've known if that was the case. There has to be another explanation for this."

"What?" I demanded, curling my hands into tight balls. "The only one is that the Lilin has been following me around and took her soul."

"Then that's what happened." His jaw locked down. "That has to be it."

I stared at him. Tears burned my eyes. His adamant defense of me was heartbreaking. "What if…what if there isn't a Lilin?"

"What?"

My stomach roiled, but I needed to give voice to my fear. I had to put it out there. "What if there is no Lilin, Zayne? What if we just think there is—and Hell thinks there is—but there's not."

"That doesn't even make sense."

"But it does," I whispered as the trees blurred past us. "Think about it. No one really knows what was required to complete the ritual. It's about how we perceive it. What if I needed to lose my virginity for it to work? I haven't. So if Cayman was wrong, then the ritual didn't work. It couldn't. And Abbot even said that it was a Lilin or something similar. I heard him that night. It's probably why he ordered the other clan members to watch me. He suspects it, too!"

"If the ritual didn't work, then how did Lilith's chains break?"

"I don't know, but it could be something I'm doing. I'm her kid. I probably have an impact on it. Think about it. What the Lilin can do is the same thing I can do—take a soul. We just do it in different ways." Words spilled out of me, as fast as we were driving. "And where is this stupid Lilin? How come we haven't seen it and neither has Roth? It's supposedly at the school, but no one has found it. But I'm at the school! I've been around everyone who's been infected so far and God knows how many other people."

"Then what about the cocoon in the basement and the Nightcrawlers?"

"Who knows why they were there or what was in the cocoon. It wouldn't be the first time something demonic showed up there because of me. Remember the zombie in the boiler room? Raum—the demon Roth took out?"

Zayne shook his head. "I can't believe you're even saying this stuff."

"I can't believe you refuse to see what's right in your face!"

"Shit." He swerved to the right, slamming on the brakes. I pitched forward, caught by the seat belt as we screeched to a stop on the shoulder of the road. He twisted toward me, eyes a furious shade of electric blue. "But you didn't feed off Dean! Or Gareth! You are not responsible for this, Layla."

"Maybe I don't need to feed to take their souls. Who knows?" My throat clogged with rawness. "My abilities *have* changed. I can't see auras anymore, but I can feel emotions. Maybe my ability to take souls has changed, too."

"This is absolutely ridiculous. Do you hear yourself?"

"Do you hear me?" I threw back. "What I'm saying isn't impossible and you know it."

When he didn't say anything, I unhooked the seat belt. I couldn't sit in the car. I couldn't be near him with my emotions so explosive. The need to feed was there, simmering below the surface, which was just great.

I pushed opened the door, ignoring his shout, and started

walking. I made it a few feet and he was suddenly in front of me. "You need to calm down," he said.

"You need to listen to me! You know that stuff that's been happening at the house? I thought maybe it could be Petr, because I took his soul, but maybe it isn't him. Maybe it's me." My heart was beating so fast I thought I'd be sick. "Maybe Abbot is right and I'm unaware of what I'm doing."

"No—"

"You don't get it!" Wind whipped around us, but I barely felt it. "I was mad when the windows blew out and I was annoyed with Maddox when he fell because of the way he looked at me! And both you and Danika said I feel like an Upper Level demon to you all now. You said that yourself!"

"That doesn't mean you're going around killing people and not knowing about it!" The wind seemed to toss the words in his face. "I know you, Layla."

Wetness gathered on my lashes as I stumbled back a step. "You just want it not to be this way and that's blinded you—"

"I am not blind." He lurched forward, grasping my shoulders. "I know exactly what I'm looking at when I see you. I know exactly what I'm dealing with when I touch you. And I know that no matter what, you would never hurt me. And because of that, I know that whatever is doing this, it's not you."

I shook my head. "You can't—"

He cut my words off as he pulled me against his chest and lifted me up until my toes barely brushed the ground. My eyes widened in that tiny second that I realized what he was going to do, what he was willing to risk to prove that his words were the truth, that his convictions were right, that I was just freaking out. I jerked back, but it was too late. I couldn't escape him. I never could.

Zayne kissed me.

CHAPTER TWENTY-NINE

My gasp of surprise was captured by his lips. I planted my hands against his chest and tried to push him away, but he was locked on and this...oh God, this was no innocent brushing of the lips that was over before it started.

This was a *real* kiss.

The kind that broke hearts and then patched them back together. His lips were on mine, demanding and fierce as I kept my mouth sealed. A deep sound rumbled up from his chest as he nipped at my bottom lip. I gasped again as the little bite blasted through me. Zayne took complete advantage, deepening the kiss. His tongue swept over mine, and I breathed in his taste, because I couldn't help it, and he was everywhere, in every sense, and I was burning up.

When he finally broke free, I cried out and I wasn't sure if it was from the loss of him or from what I knew was surely to come.

Zayne held on to my shoulders, his gaze locked on mine. And he was standing, not convulsing, not dropping to the ground or turning into something straight out of a nightmare.

We stared at each other, both of us breathing heavy. "You... You're okay?"

"I am." Part of him sounded a bit surprised. "I am completely fine."

"I don't understand," I whispered, staring into his eyes.

One side of his lips curled up. "I told you, Layla-bug. I fucking told you."

My heart tap-danced in my chest. "It doesn't make sense. This is impossible. Something has—"

Zayne kissed me again, effectively shutting me up and shutting down everything in me that wasn't focused on the way his lips felt against mine. He took my breath in the most wonderful way possible.

My feet were once again flat on the ground and his hands slid to my cheeks, tilting my head back. I moaned into the kiss as he slanted his head, taking it deeper and longer. I gripped his shoulders.

I didn't know what came over us. Maybe it was the fact that we'd gone forever thinking we could never share something that everyone took for granted. Or maybe it was all the wild emotions we were feeling. Maybe it was more than just a swelling of passion. I didn't care. Either way, the promise I'd made to myself last night crumbled like a dried up petal. I was drowning in him.

Our mouths didn't break contact as he gripped my waist and lifted me again, urging my legs around his hips. I didn't think we'd ever stop kissing. There was no way. Not even if an Alpha landed beside us and started to dance naked.

Zayne turned, his hands skating up my back, tangling in my hair, and then they were traveling down to my hips. The shivers drove me crazy. He was walking and the next second, my back was against the Impala.

I slid my hands into his hair, getting my fingers tangled in the softness as he shifted his weight to the side, reaching for the door. The boy had skill, because somehow he got the back door open without breaking contact.

He bent at the knees and then we were out of the cold and

inside the backseat, his long body pressed down on mine, and he was still kissing me, dragging my breath into his.

He should've weighed a ton, but the weight of him was delicious and maddening in all the crazy ways.

"God," he whispered against my swollen lips as he lifted his head. "I've thought about this for a very long time, and I had no idea it would feel like this."

My thoughts were scrambled as I placed my hand against his smooth jaw. He kissed me again, like a man starving for oxygen, taking lengthy, breathy draughts. He nibbled when he pulled back, only to come back for more, and things spun out of control.

His hand slid up my hips and under my shirt and the touch of his skin against mine, the mixing of our emotions and needs, it reached deep inside me, warming every cell, filling every dark space in me.

All the years of dreaming about being able to do this rushed to the surface in both of us and it made us greedy and crazy. My fingers clutched at his shirt and when he lifted his head this time, I tugged and he answered, letting me pull it off. My hands smoothed down his chest as he bent his head to mine. I tasted in him my own consuming desire. I felt it and I welcomed the whirl of it, reveled in it, and it was I who deepened the kiss this time.

The sound he made curled my toes as his hips pushed against mine. My heart kicked and my pulse pounded throughout my body. And then my thermal was off, disappearing somewhere on the floor of the Impala. His fingers skated over my ribs, reaching the fragile clasp. There was just a flick of his wrist, and then we both were bare from the waist up.

Oh my God, we were on the side of the road, in the backseat of a car, half-undressed, and it was so...so human and normal.

A laugh bubbled up from me and escaped against his lips.

Zayne's brows drew down, but before he could speak, I stretched up and kissed him again, simply marveling in the fact that I could kiss him—that this was happening.

"Sorry," I said. "I just never expected this. I never—"

He kissed me softly, a lazy sensual exploration that had to have steamed the windows of the car. "I never thought it was impossible. I've always trusted you."

Tears pricked my eyes for a very different reason this time. "Zayne, I..."

I couldn't finish the thought, but it was okay.

Time seemed to stop for us and what we were doing was crazy insane, but we were too caught up in each other to care. His lips trailed a fiery path over my cheek as his hand traced where Bambi was curled around my ribs. Her head was using my breast as a pillow again, and I didn't mind. Not when he followed the elegant curve of her body with his hand and then his mouth, causing mine to arch into his touch.

He lifted his head again, his gaze hooked to my face, and then it traveled down, and my breath caught. Then our bodies were flush, chest against chest and I'd never felt anything like it before. A deep groan rumbled through him and a thousand emotions erupted inside me. Our bodies moved together, against the backseat. A wildness pulsed through me. I pulled him closer, sweeping my lips over his, and he trembled. I wanted to feel more. I slipped my hand down the thick cords in his neck and back, and then lower. He sucked in a sharp breath.

And the way his body rocked against mine and the tension I could feel building in both of us told me where this was heading. It wasn't impossible, the location and all. In the back of my head, I knew I wouldn't be the first girl, and maybe not even the first with Warden blood in her veins, to do this. If there was a will—and, holy moly, there was *so* a will—there was a way.

There was something in me, though, that threw on the brakes. I didn't know what it was or if it had a name. Or maybe I did, and my heart and my brain didn't want to claim ownership of that, but confusion left my skin chilled. I wanted this. Badly. Maybe it was just nerves, but suddenly my hands were shaking. All I did know was that my anxiety had nothing to do with the stupid spell tied to my virginity. If a Lilin really had been created, my virginity was a moot point, and even if there was no Lilin, Lilith's chains were already broken, so that didn't matter. No, it was something else.

"Zayne," I whispered, breathing in his air. "We should…"

His eyes were closed when he answered. "Stop?"

I nodded.

"You're right." He rested his forehead against mine, dragging in deep breaths. "We need to stop. I don't want it to be like this…in the backseat of my car."

Somehow I flushed. Strange to be embarrassed now, when being half-naked didn't have that effect on me. I swallowed as he pressed his lips to the bridge of my nose and then lifted up, using his arms to support himself and put space between us.

The way he stared at me made me want to take my foot off the brakes and floor it. "God, Layla, I… There really aren't any words."

There weren't, and not in a bad way. Even though there was a niggle of weirdness in me, threatening to shatter this warmth, speechlessness was a bounty.

Zayne ran his hand over my skin, as if he was seeking to memorize the feel, and then he found the clothing that had ended up on the floor of the car. He helped me get back into them, and it probably took longer than necessary, because he'd stop and kiss my shoulder, then my neck and he had me wanting to undo all of his hard work.

When he pulled me out of the backseat, cool night air

washed over my blazing skin. He captured my cheeks, tilting my head back. "I don't want to hear anymore crap about you being responsible for what's been happening," he said, his eyes holding mine. "If this proves anything, it shows you that you are capable of controlling your abilities. You'd know if you were taking souls. You aren't. So that's it. No more. Promise me."

I'd been real bad at keeping promises lately, but I promised him and prayed it was one I could keep.

It was a little after six in the morning when, mostly asleep, I felt my bed dip under sudden weight. I blinked groggy eyes open and smiled a little as the blankets stirred and an arm snaked around my waist.

Warmth pressed against my back. Every morning for the past week, this was how Zayne woke me when he returned from hunting. The past couple of days...well, it had been something straight out of dreams. We spent a lot of time together, either holed up in my bedroom or his, or we'd spend time over at Stacey's place with her and Sam. Thanksgiving came and went. On Saturday, we'd left and had coffee like we used to, but this time had been different. There'd been kissing. There'd been *a lot* of kissing. So much so that my lips felt swollen a good part of the day.

My favorite part was the mornings, though. He was always extra touchy then and it was one Hell of a way to wake up. I knew eventually that this would have to stop. Someone would catch him entering and leaving my bedroom and his father would stroke out. And there were bigger reasons why. Reality hadn't really existed since my suspension. There were no issues with the Lilin, nothing from Roth except harmless texts here and there, and when I was with Zayne, it was easy to believe that I wasn't responsible for the infection.

Zayne nuzzled my neck and then chuckled as I squirmed when he hit a sensitive spot. "Good morning," he said, kissing the space below my ear before he lifted his head.

"Morning." I rolled onto my back and somehow, right into his arms. "You're back early."

"Yeah." He tugged my blanket down to my waist, grinning when he saw Bambi's head peeking out from under the low collar on my shirt. "It was kind of dead last night."

His head dipped and his lips brushed over mine in a soft, tantalizing touch. I raised my hand, placing it against his chest. The thin shirt he wore was a hindrance that annoyed me, but his heart pounded strongly against my palm.

The kiss deepened as he shifted closer. One of his legs ended up between mine and the weight of him above me did wonderfully wicked things to my insides. His hand ran down my stomach and then under the hem. When it came into contact with my bare skin, I picked up the intensity in what he was feeling. The need. Desire. Something far stronger drove him. My back arched into his touch and my toes curled.

After what felt like forever, but not long enough, he pulled back with a regretful sigh. Both of us were breathing heavily. Our chests rising against each other. One of his hands was still under my shirt, touching me. Little tremors coursed through me.

He rested his forehead on mine and the edges of his hair teased my cheeks. "I'm going to make you late for school if I keep this up."

That wasn't going to be the only thing that happened if he kept moving his thumb back and forth or if he kept kissing me. We hadn't gone beyond this, not even as far as removing clothes, since the night we'd gone to that house. I could tell by the way his body would shake that he wanted to go further. I was pretty sure I wanted to, but that step was as scary as it was exciting. All of this was something I'd truly never thought was possible with Zayne.

But school also meant back to reality and if anything was a giant mood killer, it was that. Back to being around humans other than Stacey and Sam. Back to facing the cold possibility that I could be the cause of the infection. Because even though I could kiss Zayne without sucking out his soul as if he was a Tootsie Pop, that didn't mean it wasn't me.

He sensed the moment I withdrew and he frowned. "Where'd you go?"

"Nowhere." I forced a smile. I hadn't talked to Zayne about my fears since that night because I knew he firmly believed that I was innocent and I…I wanted to keep it that way. With him, I didn't feel as if I was a time bomb waiting to go off. I felt normal. "Maybe I can skip?"

"Hmm…" He brushed his lips over the tip of my nose. "While I love the sound of that, your cute little ass needs to get to class."

I pouted.

He laughed softly and then the smile faded. Seriousness crept into his teal eyes. "You know you're not infecting anyone, Layla-bug. It's okay for you to go back to school. Deep down, you know that."

"I know."

Zayne kissed me again, and for a little while, I got lost in his lips and his intoxicating scent and taste. And for a little while, I stayed in our world, even if it seemed to be make-believe.

Stacey and Sam were waiting for me at my locker. She popped forward and gave me a quick hug, pulling back before I could push her away and look like a freak.

"Welcome back," Sam said. He was still missing his glasses. "I bet you missed school."

"I missed it a little." I opened the locker door and pulled out my bio text. That was true. School was kind of like a sanctuary…when there weren't zombies, Nightcrawlers and wraiths crawling out of the woodwork.

My high school was turning into the Hellmouth.

I giggled.

Stacey arched a brow. "What?"

"Nothing. I was just thinking of *Buffy the Vampire Slayer.*" It was a relief to be honest with them now. Closing the locker door, I turned to them. "I was thinking that our school is kind of like Buffy's Hellmouth."

She grinned. "I'm totally Cordelia. And you're Buffy."

I laughed as we started walking down the hall. Sam was holding Stacey's hands and that made me all kinds of warm and fuzzy. "I'm not Buffy. More like Willow. Sam, you're totally Xander."

"I'd say I'm more like Angel," he commented, and I expected there to be some kind of factoid about *Buffy the Vampire Slayer,* but there was none.

"By the way," Stacey said, leaning toward me and lowering her voice. "I'm assuming you told Roth that we knew the… uh, the truth."

My stomach did a cartwheel. They hadn't seen him since we'd been suspended. "Yeah, he knows, but I wouldn't make a big deal out of it. I'm going to the bathroom real quick."

Stacey stopped. "I need to go, too." Turning to Sam, she pressed a quick kiss to his cheek. "See you later?"

He nodded as he backed away and then turned, running a hand through his messy hair. I watched him for a few moments and then shook my head. "Do you really need to use the bathroom?"

"No," she giggled. "I just wanted a few seconds alone with you to ask if you've had sex with Zayne yet."

Heat bled across my cheeks. "What? No. Have you and Sam?"

Her grin spread and my eyes widened as I pushed open the door, greeted by the smell of disinfectant and the faint aroma of cigarettes. "Oh my God, you seriously had sex with…" I trailed off and then came to a complete stop inside the bathroom.

Stacey bumped into me from behind and she, too, stopped.

At one of the sinks, Eva was hunched over, hands pressed against her face, covering her eyes. Her slim shoulders trembled. Lying in the sink and on floor were tiny balls of brown rolled-up paper. A cell phone sat on the ledge above the sink.

She was crying—no, sobbing really.

"This is awkward," Stacey murmured as the door closed behind her.

Yeah, it kind of was. Eva was evil and if I hadn't known better, I'd categorize her as a demon from Hell, but she wasn't. Just a typical mean girl who probably didn't get enough love at home or whatever, but the girl code kicked in.

Sighing, I stepped forward, making a face as I tried to come up with something to say. "Uh, Eva, are you okay?"

Her shoulders stiffened and she lowered her hands. Wow. Eva did not cry pretty, which for some horrible reason made me feel better about myself. In the reflection, mascara streaked her cheeks and her face was puffy and red.

Then she crumpled—her face did. It screwed up as fresh tears ran down her cheek. "No. I'm not okay. I'm never going to be okay."

The look on Stacey's face said she was wondering if Eva was being a tad bit melodramatic, but unease blossomed in the pit of my stomach.

Eva turned to us, her hands closing into balls against her ruddy cheeks. "He's dead. Gareth's dead."

CHAPTER THIRTY

Gareth had overdosed sometime during the night. His parents had found his body in the garage that morning, when his father was leaving for work. Rumor had it that he'd been huffing alcohol.

A heavy sadness clung to the school. Dean's death had been bad enough, then Gerald's, but Gareth had been popular. Everyone knew him and, while his steady descent into drugs had confounded a lot of people, he was still the guy half the girls wanted to be with and half the guys wanted to be.

Teachers talked about it in every class, citing it as a tragic accident and turning it into an after-school special about drugs and their dangers, but I knew differently.

So did Stacey and Sam.

So did Roth.

Not that drugs weren't a huge problem, but this went beyond addiction and the stupid things we did. Gareth had been infected. His life and his soul had been stolen from him. Not only would there be another wraith, but Gareth would spend an eternity in Hell.

And that killed me, even if there turned out to be a Lilin somewhere.

Roth caught up with me as I headed toward lunch. Being alone with him had my nerves twisted into useless knots. I knew it had everything to do with Zayne and me...and everything to do with Roth.

"I haven't sensed a wraith yet," he said, hands shoved into the pockets of his ripped jeans. "Have you?"

I shook my head as Bambi started to climb up between my breasts. I issued her a stern warning not to appear on my face. Whenever Roth was near, she liked to be seen. Kind of like one of those annoying yappy dogs that needed attention.

"I guess it will only be a matter of time before it shows up. We're still on to see the coven this weekend?" I asked. When he nodded, I leaned against the wall. The hallway was virtually empty. As I peeked up at him, finding him watching me closely, I shifted my weight. "Is there anything we can do about their souls? Any way we can get them free?"

Roth turned, angling his body sideways. He shook his head. "Not unless you want to strike a deal with the Boss and that's not something I'd suggest."

I opened my mouth to protest, but he placed a finger against my lips, silencing me. Energy jolted between us and I pulled back.

One side of his lips tipped up. "I know you want to help them, shortie, but once the souls are down *there,* it's a bitch to get them out. And I'm not talking about an inconvenience. Boss likes an eye for an eye. If you ask for a soul, the Boss will ask for one in return. You don't want to make those kinds of deals, carrying that kind of weight around."

He had a point, but I was already carrying a decent load on my shoulders.

"You haven't returned any of my texts or calls," he said after a few moments, propping his hip against the wall beside me. His chin was dipped down and his dark lashes shielded his eyes. "I was worried."

My brows rose. "Were you?"

"Yeah." The corners of his lips turned down. "Why would that surprise you?"

I shrugged a shoulder. He'd reached out to me a couple of additional times during our suspension and over break, but I hadn't responded. It would've felt wrong if I had and not because being with Zayne meant I couldn't talk to other guys. It was just that Roth wasn't an "other guy"—he was a whole slew of something else.

"You're with Zayne, aren't you?" he said, as if he read my mind.

Was I? We hadn't called each other boyfriend or girlfriend, but we treated each other as if we were. "I really don't want to talk about him with you."

His lips pursed. "Tell me you're at least being careful."

My eyes widened. "Okay. This sounds like an 'are you using a condom' conversation."

"That's not what I meant and you know it," he said.

Our eyes met, and I totally got what he meant. "I am." Which was such a lie.

He tipped his head against the wall and breathed in deeply. I watched him for a moment. His arms were folded loosely over his chest. Everything about him looked tense. I hadn't even told him about the woman from the Palisades.

"Hungry?" he asked, his voice off. "We should probably head in there before Stacey and Sam start making babies on the lunchroom table."

"We found another wraith," I said in a low voice.

His eyes snapped open. "What?"

"Last week. Zayne and I did an exorcism," I explained quietly.

He was standing straight now. "Why didn't you tell me?"

"It was the woman from the club in the Palisades, Roth." My stomach dipped as his eyes flared. "The woman I fed off."

He opened his mouth, then snapped it shut as he thrust a hand through his dark hair. Tight lines formed around his lips. "You're sure?"

"Yeah, I'm sure. It was her." I scrubbed my hands down my face. "She walked away, right?"

He nodded. "She did. I swear to you, Layla. She walked away."

"But how did she end up dying? It was supposedly a heart attack, but she didn't have any existing issues. I know that doesn't mean it's impossible, but the likelihood of that? What if it was me? What if I infected her? What if I've been the one infecting all of these people?"

"Whoa, where has this come from?" Roth got all up in my personal space. "Is this something new?"

I shook my head. "No. I've been wondering about it for a while and Zayne doesn't think it's me, but we haven't found any evidence of a Lilin, nothing concrete, and everyone who's been infected has been near me."

"But how? Have you been wandering around kissing people? Because if so, I'm pretty pissed off that I wasn't included in that."

I shot him a look. Not like I hadn't kissed him recently. "Uh, no, I haven't, and I don't know how. That's the only part I can't figure out." I looked up at him and put it all out there, because I trusted him to not hold back. He hadn't before on the sucky stuff I didn't want to hear. "Do you think it's me?"

He stared at me a moment, not moving. I wasn't sure he was even breathing. Then he leaned in, placing his hands on my shoulders. His grip wasn't heavy, but there was so much in the touch. It was a comforting pressure, and I closed my eyes.

"Stop," he whispered against my hair, "asking questions that serve no purpose."

Roth said nothing more as he pulled back, his arms falling to his sides and whatever comfort he'd offered turned to apprehension. His silence was unsettling. He never answered my question.

The night we left for the club in Bethesda, there was a hint of snow in the air. It was definitely cold enough and the crispness had that wintry feel to it.

Our drive to the club was quiet. Roth was waiting inside his Porsche in the parking lot across from a school. As soon as Zayne and I pulled up in the Impala, he opened the door and stepped out.

I glanced down at myself and wrinkled my nose.

Roth was dressed as if he was about to walk into a coven full of witches. His legs were encased in leather and he wore a dark shirt. The outfit bled menace and mayhem, while my blue jeans and blue turtleneck pretty much bled Susie Homemaker.

"I should've worn something better," I commented.

"I think you look fine."

I glanced over at Zayne and smiled. "Thank you, but I have a feeling I'm going to stand out."

"You always stand out." The grin on his face faded as Roth strolled up to his window. Grumbling under his breath, he rolled it down. "What?"

Roth looked unfazed. "About time. I think I grew about a week's worth of facial hair waiting for you two."

Zayne rolled his eyes as I glanced over to where the club was. At first I didn't think we were at the right spot. It was inside a ritzy hotel. The kind of hotel that had all reflective glass walls and sculptures that looked like something a five-year-old had molded.

Or something I would make.

"I really wish I was going in there," Zayne said, pulling

his hands off the steering wheel. "I don't like you going in there alone."

"She's with me." Roth grinned as he leaned into the window. "She's not alone."

"You don't count."

It was so past the time for me to get out of the car. I started to open the door, but Zayne caught my hand. "Be careful," he said.

"I will." I hesitated, feeling as though I should kiss him goodbye, but I couldn't with the one-man peanut gallery staring at us.

"How cute." Roth pushed back from the car, his tone light, but his expression was sharp. "Don't worry, Stony. She's in good, capable hands. I think you know just how good and capable, right?"

Zayne drew back, anger flashing across his features. "Yeah, go screw yourself."

He grinned. "Well, about that—"

"Don't even finish that sentence," I snapped, slamming the door shut. His eyes met mine over the roof of the Impala. "Seriously."

Roth arched a brow and then wiggled his fingers at Zayne. Turning away, I headed toward the sidewalk. He was beside me in an instant.

"That wasn't necessary," I said.

Roth's shoulders were tense. "Whatever. It's not what we need to focus on right now."

"Focusing on that or not isn't the point." We crossed the virtually empty street, which was strange considering it was only around eight in the evening. "There's no reason for you to say stuff like that to him."

He looked at me as he reached for the door. "There isn't, Layla?"

For a moment, our gazes locked and it was as though his shields were down. Anger. Disappointment. Yearning. Helplessness. It all came through those amber-colored eyes. And then he turned, motioning me into the lobby. "Let's get this over with."

Taking a deep breath at the harshness in his tone, I shook off whatever was going on with him and went in. The hotel was nice and new. Silver ceiling lamps cast light across the main floor, but it was as though the building reached out to us, as if it was seeking comfort and light. The hairs on the back of my neck rose.

I followed Roth to the elevator and we rode it up to the thirteenth floor in silence.

I was all nerves as we stepped into a long hallway. Not just because we were about to be surrounded by a slew of witches of the unfriendly kind. A seedling of hope was burning bright in my chest. Maybe the crone would tell us something that changed what I believed and proved that Zayne was right.

Just as I was about to ask if we had the right place, we turned a corner and a restaurant or club came into view. The windows were tinted bronze, but I could make out several human forms sitting at tables. There was the loopy design above the double doors.

"You ready for this?" Roth asked.

"Sure."

He looked doubtful as he opened the doors and we stepped inside. The first thing I noticed was how normal everything was. Like totally human normal. We were stopped right in front of a hostess station. Couples sat at tables, laughing and talking. A stocked bar ran along the back, packed with people sitting and standing. Light jazz played from overhead speakers. These people didn't look as though they'd stepped off the Goth train. I actually blended it.

"What were you expecting?" He chuckled in my ear, and I wondered if I'd spoken out loud or not.

"Not this."

"Haven't you ever heard of not judging a book by its cover?" He reached down and took my hand in his and when I got all *what the Hell is up with that,* he tightened his grip. "Like I said, shortie. Don't judge a book by its cover. I need you to stay close to me."

A slender woman appeared, her hands clasped together. She wore a simple black dress cut above the knees and her hair was pulled back in an elegant chignon. "I'm sorry. We do reservations only."

Roth smiled. "How do you know we don't have reservations?" He glanced over at the hostess station. There was no book. "You don't know our names."

"I know you don't have reservations." Her chin rose as her cool gaze centered on us. "And I also know what both of you are. So if you want to leave this building without so much bad luck it would make the *Titanic* look like a Disney cruise, I suggest you leave before—"

"Rowena," the man who came up behind her said. "They are expected. Let them through."

We were? I glanced at Roth, but his expression was unreadable.

The woman didn't look happy about it, but she stepped to the side. The man nodded. "Follow me. She is waiting for you."

Well, this was only a little creepy. As we followed the man, who looked as if he was in his forties, the people—er, witches—sitting at the tables stopped what they were doing and stared. Some had forkfuls of food halfway to their mouths. Others turned around in their chairs. Out of all of their hard faces and distrusting eyes, none of them looked happy.

Suddenly Roth holding my hand wasn't such a bad thing. Even if it made me feel like a bit of a wussy. I was trained in hand-to-hand combat—not to ward off spells and charms.

The man led us around the bar, to an area of the club that was somewhat secluded. There was only one table back here, surrounded by a large crescent-shaped couch. Several women rose from where they were sitting. Each of the women, a total of six, passed by without looking at us.

Not odd or anything.

The couch looked empty until we moved to the area that was open. Then I saw her and, holy crap, I thought the crypt keeper was sitting before us. The woman was old—like, I wasn't quite sure how she was still alive and breathing.

Patches of snow-white hair fell down her tiny, frail shoulders. Deep wrinkles creased her face and her eyes...they were milky-white. The whole eye.

The old woman smiled and her faced was so crinkled I thought it would collapse into itself. "What did you expect?" For such an old woman, her voice was strong. "A young woman? You seek the crone, do you not?"

I found my voice. "Yes."

"A crone is someone who is old and wise...or just old. Either way, I've walked this Earth for many years," she said, lifting a small white hand, motioning us to sit down. "And this is the first time I've seen a Crown Prince."

Roth sat, tugging me down beside him. "It is an honor, crone."

She tipped her chin up. "I've also never thought I'd live to see a child of a Warden and our true mother, but here you are, Lilith's own flesh and blood."

I really had no idea what to say to that.

The crone leaned forward and I was worried she'd tip over and shatter right in front of us. Her heavily wrinkled face seemed to age even more, as though she would turn into dust at any moment. "What you fear, child, is wrong. Some evil, my children, is necessary."

Roth slid me a look, as if he was saying I told you so. I wisely kept my mouth shut.

"I know why you two are here." Her laugh rattled like dry bones. "I know you are here to find the Lilin."

My heart jumped and I figured it would be best for us to be honest. "Yes. We need to find the Lilin."

"Like, yesterday," Roth added. "I know ya'll love you some Lilith, but you know the chain reaction the Lilin will cause."

"Ah, yes, the Alphas." She waved her hands. "I'm surprised they haven't already arrived with their mighty swords, cutting through all things they feel are not worthy of this Earth. Have you ever seen an Alpha, children?"

I shook my head. "No. I've been…near them, but never seen one."

"I haven't," Roth replied. "Obviously."

The crone heaved out another laugh. "No. You would not be sitting here if that was the case, would you? Ah, the Alphas. They are a threat to us all. Maybe even the humans. They see only in black and white, no shades of gray. No sympathy. They are the true monsters."

I schooled my expression into blankness as she prattled on. The Alphas were literally the boogeyman of all things and while there was a part of me drawn to them, they also terrified me.

"Back to the Lilin," Roth coaxed gently.

"Impatient, young Prince? You should not be." The old crone cackled. "No Lilin has sought refuge with us, if that is what you think. There is no reason for that. You seek what is right in front of you, Prince. You know that. It's the truth behind why you rose from Hell."

CHAPTER THIRTY-ONE

Unease formed in my belly and the fear that was never too far away returned like a vise circling my throat. I looked at Roth and the muscle in his jaw ticked. "What do you mean?"

She turned those milky-white eyes on me. "He knows. You know. That is all I am willing to tell you. Your coming here was unnecessary. Now go." She lifted her frail arm and waved slender, bonelike fingers at us. "I am tired and done with this conversation. Go."

Roth didn't give me a chance to protest. Wrapping a hand around mine, he hauled me to my feet. Then he bowed at the waist. "Blessed be."

The crone hooted. "Silly, Prince, silly..."

His grin was cheeky as he turned, but the look in his eyes could freeze the circles of Hell. He held on to my hand as we headed around the tables and past the witches. They may have been looking at us once more as though they were about to dump a hex on our heads, but I didn't care.

You seek what is right in front of you, Prince. You know that.

I tried to pull my hand free as the knots in my stomach tripled, but Roth tightened his hold. "Don't, Layla."

My breath was coming too fast—two breaths in, one breath

out. I let him pull me out to the hallway and down to the elevator. As soon as we stepped inside, I pulled free and smacked the emergency button.

"What are you not telling me?" I demanded, hands curling at my sides.

Roth leaned back against the wall of the elevator. "I don't know what would make you think that."

"Don't mess with me, Roth. I want to know why you really came back from Hell. What is the truth?"

"You know why I came back. To look for the Lilin," he said, crossing his arms.

Everything in me told me there was more to this. "It seems like the crone expected us to already know who the Lilin was. Like maybe it was right in front of our faces—in front of mine. And you know what I think? I think…" My voice cracked and I looked away.

"What do you think?" he asked quietly. "Tell me, Layla."

Our eyes met. "I don't think there's a Lilin, at least not one that was born successfully from the ritual with Paimon."

He didn't say anything as he kicked his head back against the wall. Closing his eyes, he swore under his breath and my stomach dropped.

"Roth," I whispered.

He uncrossed his arms and rubbed his hands down his face. "It's not simple. I don't think you'll understand that it's not."

I took two breaths. "Try me."

Lowering his hands, he pierced me with eyes that were… that were sad, and that told me everything before he spoke. "I wasn't around when the chains started to break and I don't know if it happened before I was cast into the pit or during. The Boss…well, wasn't really paying attention. We couldn't figure it out. We knew the ritual wasn't completed."

I slumped against the wall, forcing my legs to hold me up. I'd asked for the truth and I needed to hear it.

"At least we didn't think the ritual was completed, but Cayman was right. Who knows if the carnal sin was sex or just something related to it? None of us know that, but we knew something was happening up here and we knew that either a Lilin was born or..."

"Or it was me?" I asked.

Roth closed his eyes again briefly and then he nodded. "Or it was you. Those are the only two options. All of us knew that. So the Boss sent me back up to either find the Lilin or find proof that it is you."

I pressed the heel of my hand against my chest.

"That's why I returned to the school at first. I wasn't convinced that the Lilin was really there, but I knew I needed to...to stick close to you, to see if you'd changed," he continued as he pushed off the wall. He started to pace in front of me, the elevator music an odd backdrop. "I didn't think it was you, because I know you. You may be part demon, but at your core, you're pure. Not in the bullshit way people label things pure, but you're inherently good."

My heart ached, because his words reminded me so much of what Zayne believed. It appeared their undying faith in my gooey goodness was the one thing they had in common.

"But then it was other students who were infected, people who've all been tied to you, one way or another." He shook his head as he passed in front of me. "And there was no proof of the Lilin. Still really isn't anything concrete other than a cocoon. I'd hoped that the crone would point us in another direction and not confirm what I...what I feared."

That it was me.

He stopped in front of me, his striking features strained. "From the beginning, I knew your abilities were like the Lilin's, just slightly different. Where the Lilin can take with touch, you do so by breathing the soul in. But maybe your abilities have shifted. I don't know, but I do believe you're not aware of it. That you have no idea that it's happening."

I closed my eyes. "Does that make a difference?"

"Yes."

A harsh laugh escaped me. "Not to the Wardens or the Alphas. Or to humans or—"

"You once told me that everyone has free will and I told you that free will was bullshit. Remember that?"

I opened my eyes. "Yes."

"And you were right. We all have free will. Even demons." He placed his hands on either side of my head and leaned in. "I proved that was true. And what is happening to you—if this is you—it's not something you'll freely choose to do. So to me, it makes a difference."

"What do you mean by if? We haven't found the Lilin. The crone all but said it was me. You even came back up—" My voice cracked again and I didn't know why—why knowing that the reason he'd returned to the school was that he thought I was taking souls and nothing else hurt like a stab to the chest. "You came back because you thought there was a good chance it was me. Why…why didn't you tell me at the beginning?"

He turned his head and breathed deeply. "What good would it have done?"

"You should've told me."

Roth hung his head. "I didn't want to put that on you."

Something lurched in my chest at the soft admission, but there was something else I needed to know. "What are your orders if I'm the one causing this?"

He shook his head a little.

Anger rose swiftly through me and I reached up, knocking his arms down. "Tell me."

Roth's gaze latched on to mine. "I'm to take care of you."

Hearing his words was like being smacked. "In other words, you were going to kill me?"

He swallowed. "Layla—"

"Oh my God, Roth, you...you're really here to take me out, aren't you? If you find proof or another demon or the Wardens discover that it's me, you're here to stop me."

"It would be my job to do so."

"Are you serious?" I slid along the side of the elevator, putting space between us. My stomach roiled. After what we'd shared, after he'd comforted me when I admitted my fears... "I trusted you. Jesus, everything about you—about us—has been nothing but a manipulation. Do you understand that? You were here the first time around to find Paimon and I was just a means to an end then. And now I'm literally the means and the end for you. Another *fucking* job."

He flinched.

I moved in a tiny circle, pushing the hair out of my face. My thoughts whirled and bounced from one messed up thing to another. "Is there anything else that I don't know that you want to tell me?"

There was a pause and even as he shook his head, I knew differently.

I lowered my hands, staring at him. "You're lying now."

"You don't understand."

That was it. I lost it. Who knew what exactly flipped the switch. The fact that Roth was technically topside to kill me might have had something to do with it. My arm swung back and my hand cracked across his face. The blow stunned him, but didn't move him. And he didn't retaliate. He just stared at me. Silent. Full of more secrets. I swung again and his hand snapped out, catching my arm.

"Stop it," he said.

I was beyond listening.

Bringing my leg up, I aimed my knee at a vulnerable spot, but he whipped me around before I could make contact. He crossed my arm over my front and then locked me in an embrace.

"Let me go!" I shrieked, throwing my weight back.

Roth braced himself. "Yeah, I don't think I want to get bitch slapped again."

I pulled my legs up and then swung my upper body weight down. Caught off guard, the momentum pitched us forward. He shifted, taking the brunt of the fall, but rolled quickly, forcing me onto my stomach. I started to push up, but he was suddenly on me, the entire length of his body pushing me down.

"Stop," he hissed into my ear. "I don't want to hurt you."

My heart turned over. "Yet."

Roth suddenly shifted, rolling me onto my back. Before I could raise my arms, he caught them, pinning them above my head. Raising my hips, I tried to knock him off, but that ended up having the complete opposite effect, pushing him farther down on me.

His eyes met mine and something shifted in his gaze. My chest rose and fell in ragged breaths. Roth didn't look angry as he held me down and my emotions were too much of a storm to pick up anything from him, but when his gaze dropped to my lips, the shadows that formed across his face made him look…hungry.

In spite of the billion reasons why this was wrong, the familiar wave of awareness rose between us, a connection that threaded us together.

"Please," I whispered.

He popped off me and was on the other side of the elevator in a blink. His eyes were glowing as he straightened.

Pushing to my feet and panting, I hit the emergency button again and the elevator kicked into gear. He took a step forward and I shook my head.

Roth closed his hands. "Layla…"

"Did I mean anything to you?" I knew I'd asked him that before, but now…now it meant so much more. And when he didn't answer again, I nodded, finally getting it. I cleared my throat, but it ached when I spoke. "I don't want you coming near me."

His jaw worked. "That's not possible."

"I don't care what you think is possible. You come near me and I will hurt you," I warned. And then it struck me. *Bambi*. It suddenly made sense why he'd ordered the snake to stay with me. After all, it was like having a GPS chip installed in the form of a demonic tattoo. "Bambi, off."

Roth's eyes widened. "Layla, that's not smart. Don't do it. Bambi is as much a part of you as she is me."

"I don't want anything that is a part of you." I called the snake again and she spilled into the air, forming between us. "Go to him," I said, voice thick and shaky.

Bambi cocked her head to the side, studying me. As the elevator stopped and the door slid open, she turned to Roth.

"No," he said. "Layla, you need me. You need—"

"Stay away from me." I backed out of the elevator as I reached up, snapping the chain off my neck. I tossed the necklace at his feet. "Just stay away from me."

The elevator door slid shut on Roth and Bambi as I turned and ran out of the small lobby, into the cold night.

Zayne was waiting, leaning against the Impala. He pushed off the car when he saw me. "Whoa. You okay?"

"Yeah." I slowed down, glancing over my shoulder. Roth hadn't followed me out. "We need to go."

Instead of asking a dozen questions, he opened the passenger door for me and then jogged around to his side. But the moment the door closed and the engine roared to life, the reprieve was over. "What happened?"

I shook my head, not sure where to start. "I need a minute." Leaning forward, I pressed my hands against my face.

Zayne reached over with one hand, wrapping it around my knee as he hit the roads. "I'm here."

Nodding, I closed my eyes. Those were the only two words spoken the entire ride back to the compound. Whatever Zayne sensed, he knew it wasn't the time to push. And that was good because I didn't know what to say.

For the most part, I was numb. Or maybe some part of me had already accepted the truth, gotten all up and friendly with the idea when I started putting two and two together earlier, but Roth's betrayal cut deep.

He'd known this whole entire time, since he'd come back. Every time he'd spoken with me, he could've told me, especially when I'd gone to him last time. He could've told me. But why would he? I'd trusted him. As stupid as that was, I'd trusted him and if he'd found proof beyond a doubt that I had been responsible, it would've been easy to get to me.

God, all those times I'd been alone with him. The day I'd been in the bottom of the Palisades with him, in his loft… I shuddered. He could've "taken care" of me any of those times. And that hurt because, damn, it was honesty time. Even though he'd rejected me like I was faulty brakes and there was Zayne and every wonderful thing I felt for him, I still—deep down, nestled in a part of me I held close—cared for Roth and those feelings were stitched inside me.

There was really nothing left to do but go rock in the corner somewhere. Okay. There was a lot to do. Like for starters, what next? Another shudder rocked me as I curled my fingers into the hair at my scalp.

"Layla?"

At the sound of Zayne's voice, I lifted my head and realized we were sitting in the garage at the compound. The car was off. I had no idea how long we'd be in here, but chilly air had seeped into the interior.

I looked at him and he was pale, but his gaze was steady. "Let's get inside," he said. "And we'll talk. All right?"

The house was silent as we headed in, passing Morris in the foyer. He was carrying a pot of poinsettias into one of the living rooms. Upstairs, Zayne closed the door behind us.

I turned just as he crossed the room and his arms circled my shoulders. He didn't say anything as he drew me against his chest. For a few peaceful moments, I leaned into him, closing my eyes. When I was with him, when he held me like this, I felt like I had before all of this began. But I really couldn't live in the past.

Drawing back, I lifted my head, preparing myself to tell him what the crone had said and what Roth had admitted to. I had no idea where we'd go from here, but everything had changed and I had to deal with that.

I didn't get to speak, though.

Zayne cupped my face with both hands, smoothing his thumbs along my cheekbones. My eyes fell shut again and as his breath danced over my lips, the troubles eased off, temporarily retreating into the background. Kissing him shouldn't be high on the priority list, but he was safe with me, and I needed to be reminded of that in this moment when I felt like a monster.

His mouth brushed over mine in the sweetest way possible, and my lips immediately opened to him. A deep sound rumbled from him as he deepened the kiss. I breathed in his taste, moaning against his lips as we both took the kiss deeper.

A tremor coursed through Zayne's hands, and his fingers

curled in, digging into my cheeks. The spark of pain snapped my eyes open. His were wide, unseeing and I...I felt *it*.

It gathered in the pit of my stomach, like a tight ball of energy. I grasped his wrists, hoping to break his hold before it was too late.

But it was already too late.

I could feel Zayne's essence—his pureness—and it tasted like peppermint. The tremor in his hands spread to his body. Panic dug in with nasty claws. I struggled against his bruising hold, but he was locked on.

And I was taking his soul.

CHAPTER THIRTY-TWO

The purity of Zayne's soul, the power in it, hit every cell in my body and the demon inside me soaked it up like a flower thirsting for water and sunlight.

Horror seized me as his pupils dilated until there was only a thin slice of blue. I was taking his soul—taking *Zayne's*. His body shook as his hands—his claws—dug into my cheeks. Fiery pain sliced through me as wet, warm liquid spilled down my face. I had to stop this. In an act of desperation, I slammed my knee into his stomach.

He broke free, lurching back. A ghastly shade of white replaced his golden complexion. His lips parted.

"Zayne…" I reached for him, but he went down before I could stop it.

His body hit the floor with a heavy thump and he didn't move. Not even a twitch. Terror flooded my senses, erasing the pain. This couldn't be happening. There was no way. It didn't make sense. We'd kissed before and I hadn't fed, but this time—oh God—this time there had been no hesitation. The moment his lips had touched mine, I had done the unthinkable. I wasn't latched on to him for long, but the damage…the damage had been done.

And part of his soul swirled inside me, a glowing ball of warmth and light that was almost too beautiful to comprehend.

I never felt uglier, more monstrous, than I did in that moment.

Dropping to my knees beside his prone body, I placed my hands on his chest. I couldn't feel any movement as I grasped his shoulders. "Zayne! Come on, Zayne! No. Oh God, no." His head lolled to the side as I shook him. "Zayne!"

There was no response. Nothing.

Panicking, I shot to my feet and raced to my bedroom door. Throwing it open, I wasn't even sure what I screamed, but I screamed something that was answered by pounding feet. Within seconds, Wardens crested the top of the stairs.

Dez's eyes widened. "Jesus, Layla, your face!"

That wasn't important. I whirled around, heading for my bedroom. "Please! You have to help him. Please!"

Dez followed at breakneck speed. When he saw Zayne on the floor, he turned ghost-white. "What happened, Layla?"

I dropped to Zayne's side as Nicolai and several other Wardens filled the room. Slipping my hands under his head, I blinked through the haze of tears. "I don't know how it happened. He kissed me, but—"

"Oh God," Dez whispered, placing his hand on Zayne's chest. He lowered his ear over his parted lips. "Come on, man, come on."

My entire body shook as tears streamed, stinging when they made contact with the wounds on my cheeks. "Please. You have to help him. Please." I looked up, my blurry gaze moving over the faces of the Wardens. Danika was by the door, her hands placed against her mouth, her eyes full of horror. *"Please…"*

And then Abbot was there, pushing past the Wardens. He

drew up short, his mouth dropping open. He stumbled a step, his large hand flying to his chest. "Son?"

There was no answer from Zayne, and a ragged sob rose from the depths of my soul. My heart cracked wide-open. "I don't understand…"

Abbot raised his gaze to me. "You…you did this?"

I curled my hands around Zayne's, shoulders shaking. "It wasn't supposed to happen. He kissed me—"

He shot forward so fast I didn't even see him move or feel the blow until I crashed through the dollhouse. Wood splintered and broke as I hit the floor.

"Abbot!" Dez shouted, shooting forward. As he moved to get between us, Abbot hit him across the chest with a broad sweep of his arm, knocking him into the wall.

"Stay out of my way," Abbot warned as he stalked forward. "Geoff. You know what to do."

I stumbled to my feet, pain firing through my senses as Geoff darted from the room. "It was…an accident."

"That is my son—my only son!" Abbot roared, shaking the photos on the wall. "I brought you into my home, protected you and this is how you repay me!"

Backing up, I raised my hands as if that could ward him off. "I'm sorry. This wasn't supposed…to happen."

Rage spread like blood across his face. "Elijah was right. I should've let him put you down the moment we found you."

The words stung, but I didn't have time to fully feel their effect. Abbot reached for me and as I lurched to the side, the demon inside me pushed hard against my skin and bone. Like the night of Paimon's attack, there was no hesitation. The change that came over me was too powerful to fight.

"Stop!" Danika screeched. "Please! She would never hurt Zayne, not on purpose."

Her protests fell on deaf ears as Abbot advanced on me.

Instinct kicked in. If I stayed in this room, I'd be dead. There was murder in Abbot's stare and the demon inside me wanted to live. It wanted to fight, to rip through the roomful of Wardens, but it also knew it was outnumbered.

The back of my shirt tore as my wings spread out from behind me. Fangs punched through my gums and my hands lengthened into claws. Someone in the room cursed as I crouched, kicking off the floor. I just missed Abbot's reach as I landed on the other side of him.

I spared a quick glanced toward Zayne. Nicolai was by his side and I thought—I hoped—I saw his chest rise in a shallow breath, but there wasn't time. The doorway had never seemed so far away before, so out of reach. My fingers scraped down the door just as my legs went out from underneath me. There wasn't even a second to brace myself. I went down hard, my head cracking off the doorjamb. Black bursts darkened my vision as I lay there stunned.

Maddox was on me, flipping me over, and I blinked slowly. All I saw were wings the color of the sky before a storm as he hovered over me. Two heavily clawed hands punched the floor on either side of my head. He threw his head back, muscles straining and popping out of his neck as I slammed my knees into his midsection, knocking him back.

I popped up. Wet warmth trickled down my face. Everything spun as I rushed through the bedroom, reaching out and slamming the door shut behind me. Each step felt like a spike being driven through my head. Pain consumed me but instinct drove me to overlook it.

Vaulting over the banister, I propelled myself into the air. My wings unfurled, slowing the decent. I landed with a crash in the foyer, my feet denting the hardwood floors. To my left a Warden blocked the door to the living room, where the soft cries of the toddlers could be heard.

I ran for the door and just as I reached it, Geoff barreled forward. I whipped around, preparing to defend myself. His hand shot out and a small glass jar flew from his hand. I raised my arms, but it was too late. The jar exploded against my chest in a shower of glass and a milky-white substance rained down. The liquid immediately soaked through my torn shirt and jeans, seeping in through the pores in my skin.

Confused, I lifted my head. Geoff stood a few feet from me, breathing heavily. At the top of the stairs, Abbot appeared. I had no idea what the Hell Geoff had just tossed on me, but I didn't have time to stand around and ask questions.

Turning, I reached for the door, prepared to give my wings a try and take flight, but as my hand came into view, I froze as the marbled skin tone was quickly replaced by lighter, pinker flesh.

My heart skipped a beat as my hands shrank back to their normal, ineffective size. The claws were gone. The fangs retracted and my wings folded into themselves. Twisting back to Geoff in dawning horror, I tried to walk, but my brain wasn't communicating with the rest of my body.

"Bloodroot?" I whispered, recognizing the substance now.

I thought, and maybe it was my imagination, but I thought I saw remorse flicker across his face. And then there was nothing as my legs buckled out from underneath me. I was out before I hit the floor.

When I opened my eyes again, I was surprised to find that I was still alive. Or maybe I wasn't. I was surrounded by darkness. Had my eyesight checked out? But as my senses kicked back into gear, my sight adjusted to the shadows.

The first thing I saw were bars.

Bars.

I drew in a shaky breath as my heart rate kicked up. My

stomach cramped as I opened my dry mouth, trying to get a deeper breath. A musty, dank scent was heavy in the air, as well as the pungent odor of vomit. Underneath my body was a cool piece of rigid board.

I knew where I was.

Down below the compound, I was in one of the cages used to trap demons. I hadn't even known if they'd ever been in use before. Demons never really made it close enough to the compound to end up here, but the bars would be impossible to break through. Not that I could try. I couldn't move. The bloodroot was still kicking around in my system.

A painful, tight spasm rolled through my muscles, making my breath catch. I panted through it as I lay there. There was a steady dripping sound from somewhere behind me. The only sound that let me know that I wasn't in some kind of black hole.

As I stared into the darkness, I saw Zayne's pale face and dilated eyes and heard Abbot's harsh accusation. Had I really seen Zayne's chest move before I left the room? Was he okay? The fateful kiss and its aftermath replayed over and over again in my head. I didn't understand. We'd kissed—a lot—before and he'd been fine. What had changed?

There were no answers in the blackness that surrounded me and my heart ached. Every time I thought his name, it cracked open and festered into an ugly wound. If I had hurt him, if I had changed who he was, I could never forgive myself. And no amount of punishment, nothing that Abbot or the other Wardens planned, would be truly fitting.

The sickness from feeding on Zayne's soul took hold. When it passed from my system, leaving behind the chills, I screwed my eyes shut and refused to see the part of him I stole.

Was he okay?

I didn't understand why the soul had sickened me now when

it hadn't before. There were a lot of questions, and again, no answers.

After a little while, the ache in my cheeks and sides became a steady throb. The bloodroot prevented me from shifting and had to have also affected my body's natural healing cycle. With each passing hour, different parts of my body began to hurt and then tiny pangs of hunger spliced across my stomach. The back of my throat burned. Water. I became fixated on it, obsessing over how it would feel slipping down my throat.

Finally I could speak above a whisper and I called out. And I kept calling out until my voice gave way.

No one came.

More time passed. Hours. Days maybe? Eventually I could move my legs and then my arms. I could almost sit up without hitting the bars of the cage.

And still no one came.

Tiny squeaks, along with the rasp of sharp claws against cement, joined the sound of dripping water. *Rats.* They came closer, their eyes shiny in the darkness. I curled into the back of the cage, pressing into myself.

Had they forgotten about me or had they left me down here to die of thirst and hunger? The backs of my eyes burned. I didn't want to die in the cage. I didn't want to die at all. It wasn't the demon in me fearing that. It was me. I wanted to live.

But more time passed and I couldn't feel my toes. It was so cold down there and the rats drew closer, sniffing around the bars, looking for a way in.

I'd lost track of time when a small light flared to life somewhere beyond the cage, sending the rats scurrying back into the thick shadows lining the slippery walls. Muscles cramped and weak, I forced myself to turn around.

More light flooded the room, blinding my too-sensitive

eyes. There was the sound of heavy footsteps approaching the cage and finally the light receded. I could see.

The Warden in front of me was young, only a year or two older than me, obviously one of the newest recruits, straight from the house where the mated Wardens lived with their children. But that wasn't what held my rapt attention. It wasn't even the opaque glass he carried in his hand that was probably full of much-desired water.

It was what I saw before I could pick out the Warden's features.

I saw the pearly translucent glow around him—his soul.

"I see your soul," I whispered in a thready voice.

Those words were lost on the Warden as he knelt in front of the cage. He glanced over his shoulder and I saw the other Warden's aura. When it faded, I recognized Maddox. "Are you sure it's okay to open the cage?" the younger Warden asked.

Maddox stopped by an empty cage, crossing his arms. "It's fine. She's not going to do anything."

My gaze shifted back to the newer Warden. A look of doubt crossed his features as he reached for the lock, which was unnecessary. I could barely keep my head up.

"Is she supposed to look like this?" he asked.

Did I look that bad? But then my gaze dropped to my own arm. With the light, it was the first time I could see myself. Through the torn shirt, my skin was mottled—gray, black, and pink. My eyes widened. What in the holy Hell?

I tried to speak again, but the words only scratched at my dry throat.

"She's a mutt—part demon and part Warden," Maddox explained as he came closer, kneeling down beside the other Warden. "The bloodroot is keeping her from fully shifting in either form. Give her the drink, Donn."

The door to the cage opened and Donn extended an arm

in. It took a lot of effort to reach for the glass, but thirst was a powerful motivator. The glass shook as I raised it to my lips and drank greedily. The moment the liquid sloshed down my throat, I jerked back, dropping the glass. Water spilled across the cage, seeping into torn, dirtied jeans and then through to my skin.

Maddox sighed. "The drink isn't poisonous. It's just bloodroot mixed in with the water. We can't have you shifting."

My head pounded disbelief. "Wh-why?"

"We need to move you out of here, to the warehouse," Maddox explained, and my heart stuttered weakly in my chest. I knew what those warehouses were used for. "And we want as little trouble as possible."

I wanted to point out that I wasn't going to attack them unless they gave me no choice, but the room started to swim again. Before I slipped away, I forced his name out. "Z–Zayne?"

Maddox's face blurred as he shook his head no, and my heart cracked all over again. This time, I welcomed the nothingness.

I had no idea how long I was out this time around, but when I came to, I wasn't under the compound any longer. The little bit of relief was quashed when I remembered what Maddox had said and realized just where I was.

It was one of the places in the city where the Wardens brought demons for interrogations. Fear trickled over my skin, seizing my insides. Oh, this was bad....

Part of me wasn't surprised that they'd brought me to this warehouse. They wouldn't want to take care of their...dirty work on their own premises. Why would they want that kind of reminder?

There was a chain around my neck that connected to the one that secured my wrists behind my back. Not just any chain—but iron. No demon, not even an Upper Level one, would escape these chains.

I was lying on my side. The room I was in was empty with the exception of a tall folding table. From my position, I couldn't tell if anything was on it. Knowing what happened in this place, my stomach dipped at the prospect of all the horrible instruments of torture that could be there.

My thoughts were disjointed and I wasn't sure if it was due to the bloodroot or the lack of food and the injuries I could tell still hadn't begun to heal. Each breath I took hurt and, as my head started to clear a little, I recalled the way Maddox had shaken his head when I asked about Zayne. My worst fear swamped me, threatening to drag me under. A sob worked its way up, spilling into the air.

"You're awake."

I forced my head back and saw boots and leather-clad legs. And then hands were on my shoulders, sitting me up so I was leaning back against a wall.

My head was fuzzy, as though every thought was covered in wool, and my tongue felt thick as I tried to speak. "What... Zayne...?"

The Warden backed up, coming into my line of vision. After the pearly glow faded, I saw that it was Maddox. I didn't see any other Warden. He strolled over to the table. "I'll make a deal with you, Layla. An answer for an answer."

I rested my head against the wall. The position wasn't comfortable, with my arms secured the way they were, but it was the least of my pains.

He picked up something from the table and light reflected off it in a way that caused nausea to crawl up my throat. When he turned to me, I saw he held an iron dagger in his hands.

Oh crap.

"Tell me where Tomas is, Layla."

That question? Of all questions, it had to be that? Sweat dotted my brow. If I answered the question honestly, then it implicated me and like I needed that right now, but I *needed* to know about Zayne.

Maddox knelt by my legs, which were curled in an awkward way. "Tell me what happened to him and I will tell you about Zayne."

It was crazy and would only serve to make everything worse for me, but I had no other option. "Tomas...isn't here."

His jaw hardened. "He's dead?"

I swallowed, eyes squeezing shut in concentration. "The night...you all came...he cornered me in an...alley. I tried to tell him...I wasn't a threat, but he wouldn't...listen."

"What happened?" His voice was hard.

My chest rose in a ragged breath. "He stabbed me...and Bambi—the tattoo—attacked him."

He drew in a sharp breath. "The familiar is not on you now?"

"No." My eyes opened into thin slits. "Bambi ate him... she was protecting me."

"Ate him?" The disgust in his voice was like muddied water on my skin. "That's how he died?"

Feeling a little more stable, I nodded. "What...about Zayne?"

Maddox didn't answer for a long moment, and I lowered my chin. He met my gaze. "You'll never see him again."

My world shattered. I dragged in a breath, but it didn't go anywhere. "No."

He didn't say anything as he rose at the sound of a door opening. Fresh tears swelled in my eyes and fell. Never seeing him again could only mean one thing. I hadn't just taken part of Zayne's soul.

I had killed him.

The pain that lanced through me was greater than anything I'd ever felt.

"Layla."

At the sound of Abbot's voice, I wanted to curl further into myself. "I'm so…sorry. I never wanted this…to happen to him."

There was silence and I felt him draw closer. Through the haze of tears I realized he wasn't alone. Almost the entire clan was with him. My eyesight was feeling wonky again, but it seemed as though Nicolai stared at me in horror, pale and shaken.

"Abbot," Nicolai said, shaking his head as he backed away. "This is wrong."

He looked over his shoulder at them as Maddox moved to my other side. "You know that this must be done. What we suspected is true. There is no Lilin. There is only Layla."

I didn't say anything because it was the truth. There was no Lilin. It had been me. How? I wasn't quite sure yet, but the evidence pointed to me. Even Roth knew it. The only one who hadn't known was Zayne, and look at where that got him. My body shook as another sob rocked through me. I needed to pull it together.

"We should have stepped in before she attacked my son," Abbot continued, turning back to me. "It is a miracle that he lives."

I stopped breathing.

"We have no concrete evidence," Nicolai argued while Donn frowned. "Just suspicions. She is—"

"She is not a child," said Donn, his blue eyes snapping.

I didn't care about any of this. If Zayne was alive, why was I here? "He's…okay?"

Abbot turned to me. With his hair loose around his face, he looked so much like Zayne it hurt to see him. "My son lives."

"And...h-how is he?"

Sympathy crossed Nicolai's face as he moved forward this time. "He's himself. And he's been lo—"

"Enough," snapped Abbot.

My heart pounded in my chest. Zayne was really okay? I wanted to see him, to see it for myself. "Can I...can I go home now?"

A keen emotion flashed in Abbot's eyes and then he looked away, shaking his head slightly. "This can no longer continue. Because of me, too much has already happened. Too many lives are now in my hands and some have slipped through."

"Abbot, I must protest this," Nicolai argued, and those words spurred an argument I wasn't even following.

Zayne was alive and by most accounts, he sounded *okay*. That was all that mattered. Everything would have to work itself out now. He was alive and—

Pain exploded in my stomach, deep and wrenching fiery pain that rose up, captured my breath and caused my body to go rigid. My senses fired in every direction. I didn't understand what had happened or why Nicolai and Dez were shouting. Or even why Abbot looked horrified as he stared upon me.

"There," Maddox said, and pulled his arm back. My body moved with him, in a way that wasn't normal. "It's done and over. All of it."

A fire swept through my body as I looked down. Why was there oil on my stomach? No, that wasn't oil. That was blood. A lot of blood. As Maddox walked away, the sharp end of his dagger was covered in it.

Holy crap.

The bastard had stabbed me!

I tried to pull my arms forward to cover the wound, forgetting they were secured. This was badder than bad. It was an iron blade, deadly to demons. Even though I was only part demon, this wasn't…

I opened my mouth and all I could taste was blood. "Why?" The question leaked out, and I wasn't even sure why I'd asked. I knew the answer. Maddox had only done what he was supposed to do—what Roth had also been ordered to do: stop whatever was taking the souls of innocent people, thereby ensuring that the Alphas wouldn't intervene. But the question came again. "Wh-why?"

Then chaos reigned.

A window shattered and there was Roth standing just inside the room, the silvery rays of moonlight at his back forming an aura of their own. He let out a howl of rage.

And then another.

The wall of the warehouse shuttered and a second window blew. Shards of glass splintered in every direction. And then Roth wasn't alone. Cayman landed in a crouch, looking surprisingly human with the exception of his eyes. They glowed like topaz jewels and the pupils were stretched vertically.

And Dez stood beside Cayman. What was he doing with them?

The Wardens immediately shifted, shedding their human facades as their wings unfurled and the skin turned a deep granite.

Abbot snarled as he whirled on Dez. "What have you done?"

"I couldn't let this happen," he said, shifting in turn. Horns jutted out from his auburn waves. "This is wrong."

Maddox gripped the knife. "You're too late."

I glanced down to where wet warmth was rapidly spreading. Aw, Hell, this was so, so crappy.

"I'm going to enjoy killing all of you." A blast of hot wind shot from Roth and blew through the warehouse, pinning Abbot against the wall.

Several of the Wardens moved in, protecting their clan leader. Using the distraction, I summoned every ounce of energy I had in me and forced the muscles in my legs to work. I pushed to my feet.

Donn grabbed for me, but I dipped under his arm, ignoring the pain that lanced through my stomach and zapped between my temples. Taking a deep breath that hurt, I prepared for what would most likely turn out to be an ass-whipping of epic proportions, but everything had seemed to freeze. Even Abbot appeared rooted to the spot he stood in.

Roth stood in his true form now, legs spread wide and shoulders back. I'd forgotten how he looked when he shifted. Fierce. Scary as Hell. His skin was shiny like obsidian and his wings reached farther than any Warden's, arcing gracefully in the air. His smooth head was thrust back, fingers lengthened into claws.

Again, I was struck by the similarities between demons and Wardens. The only difference was their coloring and the lack of horns on a demon's head.

Roth smiled in a way I'd never seen him smile. Malice and righteous anger rolled off him in waves. An avenging angel came to mind, one that was ready to do some major ass kicking.

He took a step forward, his eyes starting to glow orange. "Get ready, I'm about to rain down some brimstone and fire on your asses."

And he did.

A smell of sulfur poured into the warehouse, and then the balls of orange light surrounding Roth's hands shot up, slamming into the Warden closest to him. The Warden went up in flames, screaming as he tried to stop the fire. Within seconds, it engulfed him. He staggered back against the warehouse. The fire spread.

Cayman intercepted two Wardens as Roth shot forward, slamming his fist straight through the chest of another Warden, pulling out what looked a lot like a heart. Cringing, I saw him toss the organ and whirl on the next, catching a Warden with a brutal jab to the throat.

Roth was a badass, a...scary badass.

A fierce wind kicked up, spreading the flames as a loud crack shook the warehouse. The roof groaned and shuddered, then peeled off as if someone had opened a can of sardines. Clumps of charred rock mowed down two of the Wardens, taking them out of the game.

Good God, was this all Roth?

Roth was cutting a clear path toward me. Intent on that, he didn't see the Warden coming up behind him. I shot forward, my legs shaking. "Roth!"

He turned as Donn spun toward me. He threw out his arm, catching me around the neck before he tossed me back several feet. I hit the floor with a grunt and lifted my head. The fire was climbing the walls inches from my face. I jerked back, pushing against the floor with my bare feet.

Hands suddenly gripped my shoulders, hauling me to my feet. "I got you," Dez said. As he turned me around, I saw Donn lying facedown. Dez snapped the chains, releasing the collar around my neck and wrists.

A Warden let out an ear-piercing scream as I met Dez's gaze. "Th-thank you."

He nodded. "You cannot go back to the compound. Do you understand?"

I thought that was pretty evident. "You'll b-be in so much trouble. Jasmine and the twins—"

"Don't worry about us." Dez's eyes narrowed and he

launched into the air, landing beside Nicolai. Together they forced the other Wardens back.

Roth was heading straight for me, but there was one Warden between us.

Abbot dropped down in a crouch, and Roth shot up, his wings spreading out. I didn't know what provoked me, what pushed me forward, but the last bit of energy burst through me.

I threw myself in front of Abbot, coming between him and Roth. Chest heaving and face covered in ash, I raised a shaking hand. "No."

Roth landed no more than a few inches in front of me, the edge of his razor-sharp wing narrowly missing me.

Air stirred behind me. Abbot was rising, his expression mirroring that of Roth. My eyes met his for an instant, and even surrounded in heat and fire, my insides went cold. I knew why I had intervened, most likely saving Abbot's life. In his rage, Roth would've taken him out, but Abbot had raised me and that…that meant something to me.

Even if it meant nothing to Abbot.

Ignoring the pain in my chest, I staggered back a step, colliding with Roth. His arm circled my waist, steadying me.

"You've been touched by the hand of God," Roth spat at Abbot as his arm tightened around me. "It won't happen again."

Powerful muscles in his legs pushed us both into the air. We flew up high, so high that when my gaze dipped down, nothing remained of the warehouse but a shower of sparks and flame.

CHAPTER THIRTY-THREE

Things really stopped tracking once we were in the air, leaving the warehouse behind. I was flickering in and out like a bad lightbulb.

Roth landed at some point on a rooftop, quickly followed by Cayman.

"We can't go to the Palisades," the infernal ruler said. Over his shoulders, the city twinkled like a thousand stars. "They obviously know where you live."

"Yeah, I'm going to have to agree with that." Amber eyes locked on to mine like a lifeline. "I need you to hang in there for me. Okay, shortie? I'm going to get you fixed up."

"I see…souls again," I announced, because for some reason it seemed important to point that out.

Roth's smile was weak and all wrong. "You do? That's real good to hear, baby. Real good. We're going to get you comfortable in a few. Just hold on."

I was vaguely aware of wind rushing over me once more. This time it didn't feel like seconds to get wherever we were going. It was an eternity and then two more years before we landed and then were inside a toasty warm home. I wanted to ask where we were, but my tongue was lazy.

Roth's heart was pounding as he strode across a dimly lit room and then he laid me down on a bed that smelled of li- lacs. As soon as he straightened, a shadow moved off his arm and onto the bed, dots forming together.

Bambi slithered up the bed until she reached my hip. She raised her head, resting it on my thigh. Something tender pulled at my heart when her forked tongue whizzed out, her way of saying hello.

"Open your eyes, Layla."

I thought they had been. I blinked them open.

"How are you feeling?" Roth asked, smoothing a hand over my damp forehead.

I took stock of how I felt. "I don't...hurt so much."

His features tensed as if he'd been delivered a blow. "That's good." Pulling back, he looked over his shoulder. "Cayman?"

The other demon stepped forward, easing my arms to my sides. The humor that usually danced in his eyes was absent. "Bloodroot," he said, running his fingers over my hands. "It's still in her system and it's why she's stuck. She won't be able to shift either way until it's completely out."

How had he known?

Cayman must've read the question in my stare. "I've been around a long time, sugar, and I've seen just about everything."

I was going to have to take his word for it.

Roth's fingers brushed over my cheekbones. "These are claw marks. Cayman, these are *claw marks*."

"I know, bud, but not the most important thing going on right now." He peeled the hem of my shirt up. "This...this is problematic."

A hiss radiated from Roth. "Iron."

"Yeah." He pressed down with hands I barely felt.

I took a shallow breath. "I think...I think I'm dying."

"No," Roth said fiercely, as if his words alone could prevent the inevitable. "You are not dying."

"She's in bad shape," Cayman said. "The bloodroot has been in her system for a while."

Wrapping his hand around mine, Roth shifted closer to me. As he spoke to Cayman, he didn't pull his gaze away from mine, and that was good, because somehow it was anchoring me there. "I hadn't been able to get in touch with her for three days. I thought she was avoiding me again." He looked stricken. "I texted and called but…"

I wanted to tell him that there was no way for him to have known, but it was Cayman who spoke those words as he withdrew his hands. "This isn't good."

"No shit," snapped Roth. "I know that, but we need to fix this."

He shook his head. "She can't heal, Prince. Do you understand what that means? This wound is deep. She may only be part demon, but the iron is doing its thing, and if she were human, she'd be—"

"Don't say it," he snarled, his golden eyes becoming iridescent. "There has to be something."

Cayman stood, retreating into the shadows as if he was giving us space…giving Roth privacy. I opened my mouth, but blood seeped out. Roth was quick to wipe it up and then he cupped my cheek carefully.

"I won't let this happen. There has to be…" His eyes flared bright and then he looked over his shoulder. "What if she feeds? Could that help?"

"I don't know." Cayman's voice reached us. "Couldn't hurt."

"Find me someone. Anyone," he ordered. "I don't care who, just do it now."

"No," I croaked. Drawing on energy, I forced my lips to

move. "I've already done enough damage. I won't...feed. No matter...what."

Frustration twisted Roth's face. "You need to. You're going to. I don't care how much you object. I won't let you die."

It seemed weird that he'd fight this so much considering he'd been sent topside to take me out if I proved to be the cause behind the mess, but now wasn't the time to figure him out. My chest rose sharply. "Don't do this to me. Please. Please...don't make...me do this. *Please*."

He shook his head. "Layla—"

"Don't...do this to me."

His face contorted, skin thinning, and I realized he was close to shifting. He leaned in, pressing his forehead against mine as he took both of my hands in his. "Don't make me sit here and watch you die. *You* don't do that to *me*."

Sorrow rose in my throat, nearly overcoming me, and although his words knocked me off-kilter, there was nothing I could do. I may not know how I'd taken the other souls, but I was not going to actively harm anyone else.

"Do you want to die?" he asked quietly. "Is that what you want?"

"No. I don't want to, but I won't damn another...person to Hell...so I can live."

A shudder rocked through Roth and he drew in a ragged breath. "Oh, Layla," he said sadly. "I can't let this happen. You can hate me when all is said and done, but you'll be alive."

My heart tripped and I started to protest, but Cayman spoke. "Wait. There may be something else."

Roth straightened, looking over his shoulder. "Details. Make it fast."

"What about the witches?" he said, coming closer to the bed. "The ones who worship Lilith. They may be inclined to do something to save her daughter."

Roth's eyes widened. "Do you think they'd have something?"

"Who knows what those freaks are capable of, but it's worth a shot."

"Go," he said hoarsely. "Give them anything they want if they can help her. Anything."

Cayman hesitated for a moment. "Anything?"

"Go."

And then Cayman was gone. Poof. No more. Roth turned to me. "If this doesn't work, I will bring someone in here and you will feed."

I started to argue, but as my eyes met his, I knew there was no point. So did Roth. If the thing with the witches failed, there wouldn't be time to do anything else.

Roth's chin lowered and he drew in a breath as he raised my hands to his lips, pressing a kiss against each knuckle. "Your hands are so cold."

I blinked slowly. There were so many questions I wanted to ask him, but each breath I took required a lot of energy.

"How did this begin?" he asked, raising his tortured gaze to mine.

"Zayne…Zayne kissed me," I whispered, and watched his eyes dilate. "He'd done…it before, and nothing happened then, but…"

His mouth worked. "So because the idiot kissed you, they accused you of attacking him?"

I closed my eyes, focusing on my words. "It's more…than that, but Zayne…he's okay. Now."

"To be honest, I don't give a shit about him right now."

I would've laughed if I could.

"Open your eyes, Layla."

It took longer this time to do that. "I'm…tired."

He swallowed hard. "I know, baby, but you need to keep your eyes open."

"Oh…kay."

A small smile appeared, more like a grimace than anything. He brought my hands to his lap, holding on tight. "You said he kissed you before and nothing happened?" When I nodded, he swore under his breath. "I should've known."

I wasn't really following that part.

"*Bambi.*" Understanding flickered across his face as he glanced to where the snake was curled beside my hip. "I knew she had bonded with you as a familiar. That's what I wanted from her, so she could protect you if necessary, but I didn't know she'd do so on that kind of level. But it makes sense now. You can see souls again, right?"

"Yeah."

"It's because of her. She's not on you now, but when she was, she bonded with you, she changed your abilities and affected them. Familiars can do that, and I imagine even more so for half demons. I thought she would only make you stronger. I didn't know she could affect your ability to control taking a soul."

I closed my eyes as that sank in. So it hadn't been my feelings for Zayne preventing me from sucking out his soul like some kind of cosmic love shield. It had just been Bambi—a demonic familiar. Disappointment was a fierce knot in my stomach, but at least now I knew how it had been possible for me to kiss him. And it explained why my abilities got wonky. At least, for the most part. Maybe Bambi's powers had also warped my feeding, enabling me to take the souls of Dean and Gareth. It made sense, especially since I hadn't gotten sick after feeding off the woman at the club, but felt it afterward with Zayne. The only difference was when Bambi was on me and when she wasn't. And with what happened to

Maddox and the windows—it could've been Bambi affecting my powers again. Or it could've been what Abbot had feared, that my powers were simply changing anyway. And that would mean there was no wraith at the compound, and I guess that was good news.

If that was the case, then if Bambi had never bonded with me, none of this would've happened. I couldn't be mad, though. Bambi had saved my life that night with Tomas. What I didn't understand was why Roth had wanted Bambi to bond with me.

"I would've forced you to keep her if I'd known," Roth said quietly. "I would've never let you leave that elevator if I had known the full extent of how Bambi was affecting you."

Surprised, I looked at him. He sat back with an honesty in his gaze that hadn't been there before.

"Damn," he said in a low voice. "I've made a complete mess out of this."

Cayman suddenly popped back into the room, and Roth eyed him intensely. "Please tell me you have something."

"I do." He approached the bed, and in his hands was a small vial. "There're no guarantees, but this was the best they could give me and you don't even want to know what I had to promise to get this."

"I don't care what you had to promise." Placing my hands gently on the bed, Roth rose. He took the vial from Cayman.

"Oh, you're probably going to care later. But that's something to talk about when it's water under the bridge, right?"

Unease formed in my belly, but Roth had already unscrewed the vial. "What is this?" he asked.

"Some kind of concoction that will reverse the effects of the bloodroot and should, technically, kick her body's natural healing into high gear." He paused. "They said it will make her sleep and not to fear if she slips away."

Roth nodded as he sat beside me again. If this was some kind of trick from the coven, it really didn't matter. I was growing more and more tired, and quickly. I felt a stab of cold terror because I knew I was seriously dying. And I really didn't want to die. I let Roth raise me enough that he could pour the contents of the vial down my throat.

I gagged. The stuff tasted like warmed over death, but Roth kept it to my lips, rubbing his thumb up and down my throat, forcing me to swallow it all. "I'm sorry. I know it tastes bad, but it's almost over."

When it was all gone, he laid my head back on the pillow.

"If this doesn't work, I will take out the entire coven." A muscle thrummed in Roth's jaw. "I hope they are aware of that."

"I think they are." Cayman retreated once again as Roth turned his attention back to me. "I'll go make myself...uh, scarce for a while."

Roth didn't acknowledge him. Instead he shifted and stretched out beside me. My legs felt like lead had fused to the bones. My head turned slightly and my gaze met Roth's. I could see that he was thinking the same thing I was.

Maybe Cayman and the coven's witchy brew had been too late.

"I just want to hold you right now." His voice was gruff. "That's all I want."

My chest squeezed. If this was it for me, that's what I wanted, too. I didn't want to go out alone. It was more than that, but I could barely process what that meant. My lips formed the word *okay,* but it took too much energy to speak.

He wrapped his arms around me and his body was pleasantly warm. After a few moments, I could no longer keep my eyes open. Fear eased off as a smooth, rolling peace washed over me. If this was dying, it wasn't so bad. It really was like falling asleep.

Roth's arms tightened around me as he curled his body around mine, tucking my legs between his and my head under his chin. He drew in a breath. I took the next one and slipped further into the darkness.

"Layla?"

I wanted to respond, but I was beyond answering. The void beckoned and there was no denying it.

"Can you hear me? I want you to know something," he said, his voice hoarse and thick and sounding so very far away, but full of urgency. "I love you, Layla. Do you hear me? I've loved you since the first moment I heard your voice and I will continue to love you. No matter what. I love you."

CHAPTER THIRTY-FOUR

Coming out of the void was a process of epic proportions. My fingers twitched at my sides. My toes curled. The sweet scent of something spicy and wild floated around me. From the moment my brain started churning to when I opened my eyes, I wouldn't have been surprised if it had taken hours.

I blinked and found myself staring at a broad chest. A naked chest. A naked male chest. My thoughts were fuzzy about everything, but I had a general recollection of everything that had gone down. Had I died? Because this wasn't really a bad afterlife. But no, the deep, steady ache in my body warned me I was very much alive.

My hands were tucked against a hard stomach, resting near the head of a beautifully scaled green dragon.

Roth.

One of his arms was draped over my hips and the other was under my shoulders. His hand was buried deep in the mess of my hair. His chest rose and fell steadily. I could feel Bambi on the other side of me, stretched out. What an odd...sandwich to be a part of.

No matter what. I love you.

A tingling heat swept over my cheeks and cascaded down

my neck. That had to have been my imagination throwing those words at me. Demons didn't love like *that*. Not even ones like Roth, who could pull off some very un-demonlike things. But I remembered the sound of his desperation.

I lifted my head just a little. Thick dark lashes fanned his cheeks. His lips were slightly parted. As he slept, there was a youth and vulnerability in his features that were never seen while he was awake.

He looked like an angel.

I didn't know how long I lay there and stared at him, but it was probably enough time to certify me as a total creeper. The time was useful, though. I was alive and other than the soreness in my body, I had the sense I was fine. The bloodroot was out of my system; the wound in my stomach had healed for the most part. I'd be up and kicking around in no time.

But everything had changed.

So much so that I couldn't really even grasp how different my life would be from this moment on. There was no way I could go back to the compound. I didn't want to, not after what Abbot had done to me—the cage, the warehouse downtown. No way. And if Nicolai and Dez hadn't intervened, I would've died…and that was what Abbot had wanted. Like my real father, he, too, wanted me dead. Yeah, that stung and the bite lingered. But I couldn't dwell on it.

I *refused* to dwell on Elijah or Abbot anymore.

School? That was gonna be a no-go. With or without Bambi, it was too much of a risk. I couldn't take the chance of infecting anyone else, especially when I still had no idea how I was doing it. I didn't know what I was going to do, but I knew I couldn't stay here. The Wardens would be after me. So would Hell once it got out that it had to be me behind it all. And the likelihood of ever seeing Zayne again seemed slim, and that tore me up, as if I'd been stabbed all over again.

I could barely remember a time without him and now I'd face however long I walked this Earth without seeing him again, and that…that was going to kill me, especially knowing what I had done to him. The only thing I could hope for was some real confirmation that he was okay. Everything about my life had changed, but somehow I would survive. I would have to.

Roth's lashes fluttered and then they swept up, revealing golden orbs that were bright with relief. He opened his mouth and then wet his lips, but he didn't speak. We stared at each other, and in that moment and in that bed, locked in a tight embrace, it was just us and nothing else.

Then he lifted his hand from my hip, placing the tips of his fingers against my cheek. "The claw marks have healed," he said. "There're just faint pink lines. Who clawed you?"

There was no way I was telling him.

In the silence, he drew the tips of his fingers down to my neck, causing me to shiver. "The chain left a mark."

"Yeah," I whispered.

His nostrils flared. "I will kill them all."

I believed he meant that. Reaching up, I wrapped my hand around his wrist. "I don't think that's…necessary."

"They did this to you." His lip curled up. "I think it's completely necessary."

Lowering my hand, I shook my head and started to tell him that I was okay, but in reality, I was far from it. Yes, I was alive and breathing, but okay wasn't in my dictionary.

"The stuff that the coven…gave us? Did I hear Cayman right?" I asked instead. "Is something owed to them now?"

One dark eyebrow rose as he moved his finger to the curve of my collarbone. "There isn't one ounce of my being that gives two shits about that right now."

A surprised laugh escaped me. It sounded dry and hoarse. "All right."

"I'll deal with that later."

Then he was staring at me again, in the same way he had when he opened his eyes. I found that my breath caught and the muscles low in my stomach tightened. My response confused and even frightened me, because I'd fallen into that stare before and barely resurfaced.

But he was the first to look away. "Want to try to get up?"

I cleared my throat. "Yeah. I could...I could clean up."

That needed to happen. My clothes were soiled and clinging to me. God only knew the last time I'd showered. Roth helped me sit up after shooing Bambi away. She crawled her way up to the head of the bed and watched us. Once I had my legs pitched over the edge of the bed, Roth froze.

He was standing, his hands on my arms, and then he was suddenly on his knees in front of me. Concern spiked. "Roth—"

"I'm all right." He closed his eyes as he slid his hands down to mine. "I honestly didn't know if what the witches gave us would work. I thought when you closed your eyes..." He cleared his throat. "I didn't know if you'd ever open them again."

A knot formed in my throat and all I could do was squeeze his hands.

He shook his head. "All I could think of were all the lies I've told you and that you were going to die not knowing the truth."

I thought of those words I'd imagined and my heart stumbled. I opened my mouth, but he leaned in. Letting go of my hands, he did something I'd never expected.

Roth placed his head in my lap, much as Bambi had done earlier, and let out a weary sigh.

My hands froze above his head. Tears welled up in my eyes and I wasn't sure why. I lifted my gaze to where a sliver of daylight streamed underneath the blinds, casting a halo over Roth's back.

"When I returned topside and went to the compound to speak to the Wardens, Abbot met me outside first, before you came out."

This was nothing new, but I sensed there was more.

"Abbot warned me off before I even opened my mouth, before I could even tell him why we were there," he said, his voice quiet and flat. "Not from his property, but from you. And you know, I got that. I could understand why he wouldn't want you around me. After all, I am the Crown Prince of Hell, not the kind of guy who's welcomed into homes. Particularly a Warden's home."

As he spoke, I lowered my hands to his head, sifting my fingers through his hair. A deep emotion stirred in the center of my chest, tightening my throat.

Roth turned into the caress like a cat nuzzling, seeking more petting. "But it was more than that. Abbot knew then what was happening with you, or what could happen after Paimon's ritual. He thought my influence would aid that process along, that I would bring out the demon side in you. And I think…I think he knew I'd never be able to do what I was sent to do. He didn't want you with me—he didn't want us together."

Inherently I knew *together* wasn't us being in the same room, but more—deeper and intimate. My fingers stilled. "What… what did he do?"

Another sigh rose from him. "He told me not to even think about pursuing anything with you and at first I laughed and I told him that wasn't going to happen. From the moment I was pulled from the pit, I was coming for you and not because I was ordered to—not because of what you'd think. Abbot's threat meant nothing, but…"

My chest rose and fell sharply.

"But he knew…he knew how to get me to stay away." Anger edged his tone now. "He didn't threaten me. He threatened you."

"Oh my God…" I pulled my hands back, pressing them to my lips. Obviously I knew Abbot was so not a friend now, but even then?

"He said that he would…he would take you out to keep you away from me." At the sound of my sharp inhale, he cursed under his breath. "He meant it, Layla. And I wasn't willing to risk it. Those things I said to you that night…I didn't want to say them."

I stared at his bowed head, mouth working behind my hands, but there were no sounds. There were so many things Roth had said to me since he'd returned—vague statements that didn't make sense until now.

He lifted his head then, staring up at me. "And I sure as Hell didn't use you to ease my boredom, Layla. Nor did I want to push you away, but I couldn't be the reason for you to get hurt. I *wouldn't* be."

"Oh, Roth…" I whispered. This…I never expected this to be the reason why Roth had done a one-eighty when it came to how he felt for me.

"I wanted to be with you, but…"

He'd tried to protect me. A hole opened up in my chest, just as shocking as the wound that was now healed in my stomach.

"I'm sorry. It was all for nothing in the end, but I can't undo it." He tilted his head to the side as he watched me. "I know this doesn't change the hurting I put you through. I just wanted you to know the truth and that I…"

I tensed, waiting for him to finish what he was saying and wondering if it would be those words I thought I'd heard him say before I'd slipped away, but he didn't. He studied me as if he never expected to see me again.

And then something occurred to me and I had to ask. "Was…was Zayne out there when Abbot said these thing to you?"

His amber eyes churned a dozen dizzying shades of gold. "Does it matter?"

"Yes," I whispered. It totally mattered if Zayne knew why Roth had turned away from me, if he had known the truth and hadn't told me.

He didn't answer for a long moment and a prickle of apprehension formed at the base of my spine. "It doesn't change anything, Layla. Not really, because no matter what, he…he would've done the same thing if he was in my position." A begrudging amount of respect filled his gaze. "I know that."

Too much was spinning around in my head. I sat there for a few moments, absolutely dumbfounded. My brain was fried. Completely.

Roth smiled a little as he rose, taking a hold of my arms. "Come on. Let's get you cleaned up."

I was officially on autopilot as he lifted me. My first step was a fail. My legs were wobbly, like a newborn colt's.

"I got you," Roth said, propping me up. "Always."

Always. The word bounced around inside of me like a Ping-Pong ball. After guiding me to the bathroom, he left to retrieve fresh clothes from the bedroom. It was a nice bathroom—large with a garden tub and separate shower stall. I caught a glimpse of myself in the mirror. My eyes were too large in my pale face. Zayne's claws had left behind faint pink scratches. A bruise the color of a strawberry circled my throat. I peeled the clothes off and got my first look at the wound.

I shuddered.

The patch of skin above my navel was healed, pink and

puckered. If I'd been human, I would've bled out before Nicolai and Dez had intervened. Hands shaking, I peeled off the dirtied clothes, all of them, and turned on the shower. I stayed under the water until my legs started to tremble, which was only a few minutes.

All of the grime, sweat, blood and things I didn't want to even think about had washed off. On unsteady legs, I wrapped a towel around me and tried to soak up most of the wetness from my hair. I gave up after a few seconds.

There was a knock. "Are you decent?"

"Yeah."

Roth came in with a small bundle in his hands. "It's a pair of my sweats and a thermal."

"Thanks."

He glanced over at me and his stare lingered until my ears turned pink. Running a hand through his messy hair, he turned and walked back into the bedroom. "I'll wait out here. Let me know when you're ready."

Exhaling slowly, I changed into his clothes and was immediately enveloped in his scent. Roth returned, helping me limp back to the bed. I was so tired that by the time my head hit the pillow, I knew I wasn't moving again for a while.

Roth sat beside me and pulled out a phone. "I'm going to order some food. You need to eat."

I wasn't hungry, but the offer was nice. I glanced around the spacious bedroom. It was elegantly furnished. "Whose house is this?"

He glanced up from whatever message he was texting on his phone. "You know, I don't know who originally owned it, but it's demon property these days. Sometimes I come here when I want to get away from the city. So does Cayman."

A huge part of me didn't want to know what had happened to the original owners. "Where are we?"

Tucking his phone into his pocket, he rubbed his hand across his bare chest. "We're over the river—not near the compound. On the other side, into Maryland. We're safe here. No Wardens will find us."

Ugly and distressing thoughts crept into my head and I shook them out. "Where's Bambi?"

"She's currently wrapped around my leg. Thought you could use the space."

"Oh." I fiddled with the edge of the blanket. When I glanced up, he was watching me again. My breath caught.

Roth leaned over my legs. "The food will be here soon. Why don't you rest for a little. I'll wake you when it gets here."

I was exhausted, but sleep would be evasive. "I can't."

He was quiet for a few moments. "What are you thinking?"

"Too many things," I admitted, staring up at a ceiling. "I'm not going to be able to stay here."

"You can stay here as long as you want."

My lips pulled into a small smile. "Thank you, but you know...you know I can't. I have to leave. I don't know where, but I need to go somewhere...where I'm not around people or Wardens. At least until I figure out how I'm infecting people."

"You tell me when and where you want to go, and we'll go."

My gaze swung to him. "You can't go with me."

Roth frowned. "And why not?"

"You've been ordered to take me out. If you leave with me, then wouldn't that be putting a bull's-eye on your back?"

He arched a brow. "Do I look like I care? Besides, I'm pretty sure I've already disobeyed direct orders from the Boss. And there's no way I'm letting you run off by yourself. Hell no. You need someone with you. You need help."

"Roth—"

"Look, you're not doing any of this by yourself. The mess

you're in is partly my fault. I wasn't up front with you about a lot of shit." His jaw jutted out. "And I know things are... screwed up between us. I know that. Even if you tell me you'd rather hump a Nightcrawler's leg than forgive me, I'm still going to be there with you."

I pushed myself onto my elbows. "You're going to go against Hell—against your boss?"

He grinned as he shrugged. "Yes."

"Why would you risk that?"

His eyes met mine. "You know the reason. Deep down, you know."

CHAPTER THIRTY-FIVE

It took another day and a half for my body to get back to normal. During that time, Roth became a sidekick of sorts. As was Cayman. The two kept me entertained while forcing me to stay in the bed.

I ended up watching every Will Ferrell movie there was.

The three of us talked plans about where to go from here. From what we could gather, I had to have been repeatedly around those affected since I obviously hadn't been kissing any of them. That made sense for those who'd passed already that we knew about—Dean, Gareth—but not as much when it came to the lady from the Palisades and those who were nameless and faceless to us. A lot didn't make sense, but who could we ask?

It felt good—a relief—to have some sort of plan, even though it wasn't the most detailed or thought-out, but in the quiet moments, when Roth was gone or Cayman was passed out in the recliner, I couldn't help but think about all I had lost.

And I had lost a lot.

Even though the Wardens had turned on me in the end, they still had been my clan and the closest thing I'd ever had to a family. I'd lost Zayne, but if I were honest with myself,

I knew that had happened long before the fateful kiss. In reality it occurred when I allowed a relationship between us to start, because I'd known how it would end. With Zayne getting hurt. And now our friendship and what we had between us that ran deeper were gone, and he must despise me since I'd fed off him. He had to be repulsed, because he'd trusted me and I had betrayed that trust on a level that went beyond kissing another boy.

I'd almost killed him.

The hurting from losing him hadn't eased, and I doubted that it ever would. It was like losing a limb.

And my friends? Sam? Stacey? They were out of my reach, too, and I didn't even know if I had also infected them and they just hadn't shown symptoms yet. Not knowing that haunted me. God, so much was messed up.

In those dark moments, like now, I wanted to curl up in a ball and pretty much devolve into something entirely useless. I was seventeen and my life, in a way, was virtually over. Maybe I had a whole new life waiting for me, but it was one I'd never, ever planned on.

Roth strode into the living room, carrying a bowl of cheese puffs. He dropped onto the couch beside me, took one long look at me and then popped a handful of the cheesy goodness into his mouth. Only he could manage to eat something so messy and still manage to look sexy doing so.

Damn demon.

Things…things were tense between us. A lot had been said and a lot was still unspoken. One way or another, he'd laid it all out there for me and I wasn't convinced that those painfully beautiful words he'd spoken had been a product of my imagination. I just didn't know what to do with those words, if I should trust them or even allow them a place in my heart. Because my heart and my head were so messed up right now.

"What's up?" he asked, reaching into the bowl and with-drawing a rather large puff.

I shrugged a shoulder as I glanced over to where Cayman was staring at the TV screen. *Elf* was on.

Roth offered the cheesy puff to me. I took it, flicking it into my mouth. Crumbs dropped into my lap. Sigh. He didn't say anything and I knew he was waiting.

I wrapped my arms around my legs and rested my chin on my knees. "I want to see Stacey."

His lips slipped into a frown. "I don't think that's a smart idea."

"I need to see her and Sam. I need to make sure I haven't infected them," I explained. Cayman was now, surprisingly, paying attention to us. "Now that I can see auras again, I'll be able to tell."

"Speaking of seeing auras," Roth began, "I want you to take Bambi back. She may make your abilities go wonky, but she does make you stronger."

I wanted to take her back, too, and maybe I would, but not until we discovered whether she was causing my soul-sucking ability to go to terminator levels. "I will eventually, but I think being able to see souls is important."

"It is." Cayman stretched like a cat. "But going to see your friend is stupid. The Wardens—your clan—will be expecting that."

I held my ground. "They could be, but I need to see Stacey at least. She's my best friend. I need to know if I've hurt her somehow. I...I can't go without knowing."

Cayman rolled his eyes. "Sometimes I wonder if you are part human."

"Shut up," Roth said to him, scrubbing a hand down his jaw. "Okay. I get it. We'll do it, but we have to be fast and we have to be careful. And then we need to figure out where we're going."

Relieved, I loosened my hold on my legs. If only I could see Zayne, but that wasn't possible. That would never be possible.

Across from us, Cayman sighed. "Speaking of places to go. I hear Hawaii is pretty chill. I don't know about you guys, but I could use a beach vacation."

We went to Stacey's house the next day, a Friday. With her mom not being home and her little brother in day care until at least five in the evening, we were able to sneak into the house and wait for her there.

By sneaking, I meant that I scooped up the extra key Stacey always left under the huge potted palm tree on the back patio and we let ourselves in.

I breathed in the faint scent of apples and pumpkin, committing the smell to memory. Stacey's mom had a thing for wall plug-ins that always made her house smell like a toasty fall afternoon.

Roth trailed behind me and I had a feeling he was checking out my ass. The clothing that he and Cayman had "picked up" for me wasn't stuff I'd normally wear. Dresses, skintight jeans that I had to lie down to put on, leather pants and a whole slew of second-skin sweaters.

Today I wore a pair of white jeans and a black sweater that made me feel as if I was seconds away from stripping off my clothes and finding the nearest pole.

I glanced over my shoulder and Roth raised a brow as one side of his lips slipped up. "Can you walk in front of me?"

He chuckled deeply. "Not in this lifetime."

Shooting him a quick glare, I hurried into the living room. Stacey would be arriving any moment and with some luck, Sam would be with her. Both Roth and I figured it would be safer not to tell her I was coming, and we'd circled her neighborhood a half a dozen times before parking three blocks down. Roth had felt that his Porsche was too noticeable, so he'd borrowed Cayman's car.

Which was a vintage Mustang. Yeah, real inconspicuous there.

I sat on the edge of the couch, clasping my hands together.

Roth lingered by the stone gas fireplace. "Want to be naughty and make out on their couch?"

My mouth dropped open.

"Or we can do it on the kitchen counters." He winked. "Of course, bedrooms would not only make us naughty, but also very dirty."

Heat swept over my cheeks, and he laughed. "You should see the look on your face."

"You're a pervert," I said, fighting a grin.

Roth shrugged. "Of all the things someone could call me, that's hardly the worst."

"And probably the most true," I muttered.

He laughed again.

From the front of the house I heard the front door open and I lurched to my feet. I started forward, but Roth beat me to it. He was at the entrance to the living room before I'd taken a step.

Stacey shrieked out in the hallway. "What the—? Roth, you scared the crap out of me!"

"Sorry," he drawled smoothly.

"Where have you been? Where's Layla? How did you...?" She trailed off as she appeared in the doorway.

I smiled when I saw her, suddenly weak in the legs. It was relief...sweet, beautiful relief. Her aura was there, like it had always been—a soft shade of green. Not a pure soul by any means, but she was okay. I didn't understand how since I'd been in constant contact with her, but she was normal and that was all that mattered.

Her backpack thumped off the floor as she spotted me. "Oh my God, Layla, where have you been? I've been so worried!" She rushed forward, but I raised a hand, warding her off. She stopped short. "What?"

"Don't come too close. I'm...well, I'm not sure it would be safe for you to do so."

She frowned as she glanced at Roth and then me. "Why wouldn't it be safe to be near you? And where in the Hell have you been? Everyone has been worried. Sam thinks you got kidnapped by those Church people and Zayne has been—"

"What about him?" Roth cut in, stepping close to Stacey. His voice had dropped. Tension dripped off him.

Stacey's eyes widened as she took a step back. She swallowed hard. "He's stopped over a few times, asking if I've heard from Layla. That's all."

My heart pounded against my ribs like a wild animal trying to escape a cage. "How...did he seem okay?"

She looked even more confused by the question. "He seemed normal. Just really worried and upset. Like me." Her eyes darted over to Roth. "What's going on, guys?"

"When was the last time Zayne came by here?" The fact that Roth wasn't referring to him as Stony proved the direness of the situation.

"He stopped by yesterday, around this time. He's been stopping by every day since—"

Roth swore as he turned to me. "I told you this was a bad idea. We need to leave."

"Wait!" she screeched, stomping her foot. "No one is leaving until someone tells me what is going on!"

"We have time," I told Roth. "No one is busting down the doors right now."

"Yeah, right now." He faced me, shoulders stiff. "I know you don't want to think this and while I don't think he would intentionally ever harm you, I can't say the same for the others who'll follow him. Who've probably been following him every time he comes here."

"I do think that, Roth. I'm not stupid. I know we need to leave soon, but Stacey deserves to know what's going on."

"Damn straight," she piped up. "Crown Prince or not, how about sitting down and shutting the Hell up?"

Roth's brows climbed his forehead and then he laughed. "It's a good thing I like you."

"Everyone likes me," she retorted. Then, taking a deep breath, she looked at me. "What's happened?"

"You might want to sit down for this," I suggested.

For a moment she looked as if she'd argue, but finally she sat. I gave her a quick rundown of what had happened, not offering too much detail on the cage or torture parts. That wasn't anything I wanted to relive. By the time I finished, she was pale and shaken.

"God, Layla, I...I don't know what to say. I want to give you a hug, but you're going to freak if I get that close, aren't you?"

I bit down on my lip. "I don't know exactly how I'm infecting people, but it...it has to be me."

Tears filled her dark eyes. "No. I refuse to believe that. It's not in you, even if you don't know how it's happening."

I smiled at her, really wanting to hug her. "Thank you, but..."

She shook her head. "It doesn't make sense. Why aren't I infected? Or Sam? You're around us more than anyone else."

"We don't know," Roth said. "But that's something we're going to try to figure out."

Running the back of her hands under her eyes, she sniffed

and then dropped her hands to her lap. "What are you going to do? You can't just leave."

My stomach ached. "I have to, Stacey. At least until I figure out how I'm doing this."

"What about school? You won't graduate. High school, Layla."

"I think she knows that," Roth replied drily. "But thank you for pointing it out."

Her mouth trembled. "I'm sorry, but that's just a big deal. What will you do with your life? How will you—"

"She'll be fine," Roth said firmly.

I sighed. "I don't know yet. Maybe I can get my GED and take online college classes until I figure this out."

Stacey stood from the recliner, shaking her head. "That's not right."

No. It wasn't.

She started to pace. "There has to be something we can do. This cannot be your only—"

Roth went rigid as though concrete had been poured down his spine. He swore as he whipped toward me. I was already on my feet, because only one thing would cause that reaction.

"What is it?" Stacey asked, looking around.

"There's a Warden nearby—close," Roth answered.

My hands curled in as static danced over my skin. "What time did you say Zayne usually comes by?"

"Around this time, maybe a little later." Her eyes widened. "He would never hurt you, Layla."

"I know," I said, and I hoped we were both right. I had no idea how Zayne would view me now after I'd hurt him.

"A Warden will know we're here. He'll be able to sense us." Roth turned, his features sharpening. "This will—"

A door crashed open and Stacey shrieked. It came from the back of the house, the same one we'd entered through and *locked* behind us, as if we'd been tracked right up to the door. But I knew Zayne was ridiculously skilled when it came to picking locks. And I knew it was him. The faint winter-mint scent teased my senses.

Roth was suddenly in front of me, but I stepped around him. I wasn't going to cower or hide. Just as my heart leaped in my throat, a shadow fell across the entry to the living room and then Zayne was standing there.

I had a feeling if a hundred people were in the room, he still would've found me immediately. His gaze locked on to mine, and the first thing I noticed was his aura. It was still white and beautiful, but it had dulled a little, like a lightbulb about to go out. And he looked terrible.

Dark smudges crept under his eyes like a faint ink stain. Stubble covered his usually smooth cheeks and there was tension in his jaw. Had I done this to him when I'd taken a piece of his soul?

Zayne stumbled as he took a step toward me, and it was as if he couldn't move any farther. "Layla," he said, the one word sounding broken. It was like a bow snapping. Some of the tautness in his body seeped out. His shoulders sagged.

"Were you followed?" Roth asked.

All he did was stare at me, his face pale and his chest rising in deep breaths.

A low growl emanated from Roth. "Were you followed?"

Stacey took a healthy step back. "I feel like I need to get out of the way."

Zayne shook his head. "No."

His answer did nothing to relieve Roth. "How can you be sure?"

"They don't have any reason to follow me," he said, and then he blinked. "God, Layla, I...I'm so sorry."

Taken aback, I placed my hand against my chest. "Why would you apologize? I hurt—"

"I know what they did to you." He finally looked at Roth. "Whatever you did, however you helped her, thank you. I can never repay for you that. Ever."

Whoa.

Even Roth looked a little knocked off his game by that. There was no smart-ass response. All he did was nod in return, and then Zayne's gaze returned to mine. He shook his head, and my chest tightened.

A knock on the front door raised the hairs along the nape of my neck.

"That wouldn't be a Warden, would it?" Stacey asked. "I doubt they'd knock, right?"

Zayne didn't take his brilliant teal eyes off me. "They wouldn't knock, but I'm telling you, I wasn't followed. They think…they think she's dead."

Roth's lips curled, revealing fangs. He started toward Zayne, and I knew that even though he was aware that Zayne hadn't been responsible for anything, he wanted to shed blood over it—any Warden blood.

Reaching forward, I wrapped my hand around his arm. "Don't. You know this isn't his fault. Don't fight him. Please."

He eyeballed Zayne as if he wanted to finger paint with his entrails. Finally, he turned sideways and leaned in so that when he spoke, his breath danced along my temple. "Only because you asked. Only because of that."

Zayne closed his eyes. The knock came again.

"Uh, I'm going to go answer that," said Stacey, and then she mouthed, *awkward*.

Roth pulled free. "I'll go with you." As he strutted past Zayne, he cast him a look of warning. "Don't make me regret the fact I'm letting you continue to breathe."

A muscle popped in his jaw, but Zayne kept his lips sealed. Once Roth and Stacey were out in the hall, I took a breath I didn't need.

"I...I don't know what to say," I whispered, curling my arms around my waist. "But I'm sorry for hurting you. I didn't mean to. I know that doesn't make it okay, because what I did was so—"

"Stop," Zayne said, and his voice cracked. "Stop apologizing, Layla. None of this was your fault. You don't understand. So much has happened." He broke off, taking a step forward. "I don't care what you did to me or what has happened, but it's not you. It can't be."

"Zayne," I whispered, pleaded really.

"There is a wraith at the house," he continued, and I blinked, unsure whether I heard him right. "It's Petr. Geoff caught it on camera not too long after what...God, what my clan—your clan—did to you...." He swallowed thickly and I swore his eyes got misty. "They think you died. Even Nicolai wasn't confident that he got Roth there in time, but I knew you weren't dead. I would know in here." He thumped his hand against his chest. "I would know if a part of my heart was gone."

I sucked in a breath as the voices in the hall grew closer and then Stacey and Roth had returned. Behind them was a tall and slender Sam, and the air whooshed out of my lungs as if someone had drop-kicked me in my chest.

My knees shook as I took a step back and my brain didn't want to process what I was seeing, but there was no denying it. In my chest, my heart cracked wide-open.

Zayne's brows knitted as he focused on me. "Layla?"

The room spun a little. I was vaguely aware of the way Roth was moving, angling his body toward mine so that he was standing beside me, but every ounce of my being was focused on Sam

He stood in the doorway and cocked his head to the side, his expression elusive and a bit curious. Everything about him looked normal. Normal by the "new Sam" standards—his artfully messy hair, his stylish clothes and the shiny confidence he wore like an expensive pair of designer jeans. Sam had changed.

But it wasn't normal at all.

His smile spread, causing his eyes to twinkle. "Layla? Are you okay?"

The tone of his voice was now like having someone drag nails down my skin. I drew in a breath and suddenly—oh my God—suddenly I understood. It all made sense in a sickening way. I just couldn't see it until now.

"I know," I whispered, horrified.

Confusion marked Stacey's features as she folded her arms. "Know what?"

"Ah," Sam cooed softly. "The light dawns. About time, too, because I was seriously beginning to doubt your intelligence, *sister*."

Ice blasted into the room as understanding swept through Roth and he growled low in his throat.

Sam's gaze flicked to where Roth stood, but he appeared wholly unaffected by the violence rolling off the Crown Prince. But I was blown away and if I thought my world had shattered earlier, I'd been wrong. It was smashed to pieces now.

There was no aura around him. Nothing. Like with Roth and all demons, there was just a vast, empty space. But with Roth, that was expected. Not with Sam.

Sam had no soul.

Oh, but it was more than that. A human didn't just lose their soul. They either had one or they didn't, and if they didn't, they were dead—wraiths. Only something inhuman could rock the no-soul glow. Or something totally possessed.

Zayne had just said there had been a wraith at the compound. It had been Petr doing those things. Not me. And the crone's words resurfaced. We had perceived everything she'd said wrong. What we'd been seeking *had* been right in front of us the entire time and it had been someone who'd always been around me, who mostly had contact with the same people I did. At one point I'd even said it when I'd discovered that the lady in the Palisades had died—that the only other option was that the Lilin was following me around, but I had disregarded that idea, immediately believing the worst of myself.

Paimon's ritual had worked that night that now felt so long ago. It had never been my virginity that had been the key to the spell. Cayman had hit the nail on the head when he said it only had to be a carnal sin. My blood had been spilled that night, it had burnt through the floor, and there had been a cocoon in the basement of the school, which was a part of the ritual—my blood needed to be spilled.

Bambi had affected my abilities, but only for the good, I realized. She hadn't caused me to suck out souls by being around other people. She had helped me, because all the terrible things hadn't been me, but I felt no relief.

"Everyone, including your clan and the *loves* of your life, thought it was you." Sam laughed, and that laugh sounded like his. It *was* his, but what was behind his skin wasn't the boy I knew. "Even you thought it was yourself. And that's kind of sad, actually. Takes low self-esteem to a whole new level."

"Sam," gasped Stacey, pressing her hand against her breast. Blood drained from her face. "What are you talking about?"

His pupils bled into his irises, turning his eyes into shards of obsidian. His features remained the same. No. Sam hadn't lost his soul. He wasn't possessed. It was worse than that, because what stood in front of us wasn't Sam anymore. It hadn't been for a while now.

Sam was the Lilin.

★ ★ ★ ★ ★

THE DARK ELEMENTS *saga continues with*
EVERY LAST BREATH,
coming soon from Jennifer L. Armentrout
and Harlequin TEEN.
But before then, YOU can help decide Layla's future.
Visit www.thedarkelementsseries.com for details!

Meanwhile, read on
for a special bonus scene from Zayne....

"MAY I?"

Layla actually ran from me.

I stared at the door, clamping down on the instinctual urge to give chase. That baseline desire was there, inherent because it was what Wardens did whenever something ran from us, but there was a far stronger reason for the need that had nothing to do with what I was.

Or with what Layla was.

And I really didn't care about what she'd been doing in my father's study at this moment.

She hadn't really run from me, but she had left me, and I didn't like it, couldn't remember a time when she'd ever done so. Not before him—before Roth came into the picture.

Yeah, I didn't like any of that crap.

Pushing my hair back from my face, I exhaled roughly in the silent room. The image of Layla in her bra formed in my thoughts with little to no effort. Just like every other freaking second of the day since I'd seen her.

God, she had been... She was beautiful. Not like it took me seeing her like *that* to realize it—I had for a long time now.

My gaze flipped to the ceiling.

It took me less than five seconds to make it from the study

to her bedroom. I didn't knock, just pushed the door right open, and there she was. Perfect timing.

Minus the cardigan and socks, she wore nothing but shorts and a thin tank that should've been outlawed. Heat kindled beneath my skin as I eyed her, but not like it did right before I shifted. Ah no, this was a different kind of burn—a hotter, deeper one.

I stepped through the door, folding my arms across my chest.

Her arms twitched as if she wanted to move them. "What do you want now?"

The fire in her tone lacked real reprimand. If anything, she sounded more…confused. Bewilderment lingered in the air around her, and that confounded me. "Nothing," I said, and before I could stop myself, I strode to the bed and dropped down. Stretching out, I patted the space next to me while my heart pounded in my chest. "Come here."

"Zayne…?" The confusion increased as she stared at me, rosy lips parted. "You're being annoying tonight."

I was.

Totally knew it, but I couldn't… I couldn't stay away and I was so damn tired of trying to. "You're annoying every night." I smacked the bed again. "Stop acting so weird, Layla." When she didn't move, I raised my brows at her. "You coming?"

Five seconds. If she didn't move within five seconds, I would leave.

Layla moved.

Exhaling softly, she climbed into the bed beside me, and swallowing suddenly became difficult. We'd done this a million times, but tonight felt different. Everything was different.

I needed to clear my head. "Nice shorts," I told her.

"Can you not talk?"

A soft laugh rolled out of me. "You're in such a mood to-night. Was it the sugar-cookie dough?"

She rolled onto her side, and our mouths were lined up. Rarely did she allow herself to get this close and I wondered if she even realized she had. I looked up at her and our gazes met and held.

Without warning, I thought about the first time I realized what I felt for Layla ran deeper than what my father intended—what the entire clan wanted. It had happened on March 23, in the evening while we practiced evasive techniques in the rooms under the compound. She hadn't been paying atten-tion that whole evening. I knew she hadn't been, because she had kept focusing on my...well, on my mouth while I was instructing her. For a while, I'd known she was looking at me differently, and I had been doing everything to not think about it, acknowledge or deal with it, because I had believed it was wrong. Not because of her being half demon or what she was or was not capable of, but because I had always been in charge of keeping her safe. And her not-so-sly lingering looks and the way she'd flush sometimes were *not* safe.

But after training, she had done something she'd done a thousand times. She'd threaded her fingers through mine and squeezed, and as our eyes met that night, I didn't even know what happened. Our entire life together played out in my head in a matter of seconds, replaying our entwined history. And as I squeezed her hand back, I wasn't thinking about anything except how that tiny squeeze felt like a kiss. And that feeling had scared the shit out of me, because I had wanted that then.

It was almost two years ago.

And I still wanted that.

Layla broke away, shifting onto her back.

Did she feel it between us now? The history? How our fu-ture was changing and there was nothing any of us—not my father, the clan or anyone—could change? Nothing that Roth could change? Or had it changed, at least for her?

At once, panic poured into my chest. What if it *had* changed for her because of him? What if it was too late? As much as I loathed the very idea of it, part of me could understand. Maybe I'd waited too long. I'd taken her attraction for granted—her beauty, her kindness, her unwavering faith in me. I'd taken everything about her for granted.

My mouth was dry. "What's going on, Layla-bug?"

"Nothing," she said, her voice barely a whisper.

"Bullshit." I rolled onto my arm, lifting up so I could look at her. Wrong move. Maybe a right move. There was barely any space between us, and as my gaze drifted over her flushed cheeks, I followed the blush to the low neckline of the tank top she wore, the tips of my fingers tingling with the need to touch her, to—

I blinked and my vision cleared again, telling me I was really seeing what I was seeing. It hadn't been the first time I'd noticed that Bambi liked to rest in a place the demonic familiar had no business being.

And it also wasn't the first time I'd found myself jealous of said demonic familiar, and how messed up was that?

Oddly though, as my gaze tracked over the curve of the snake—the curve of her breast—there was no denying the beauty of that damn tattoo.

"She really likes putting her head there, doesn't she?" My voice was rough to my own ears.

"I guess it's soft for her." Her chest rose in a sharp breath, enticing me further. "God," she groaned. "Sometimes I need to—"

I pressed the tip of my finger on her chin, and a deep hunger rose inside me, clawing at the muscle and skin. The power

of the need unsettled me. "That would make sense." I wanted
to… Hell, I knew what I wanted. "I bet it is a…soft place."

Forcing my gaze away, I focused on the chain and ring that
rested against her flushed skin. I lowered my hand, drawing
my finger over the cool links. "Why do you keep this necklace?"

A moment passed. "I…I don't know."

Lie. I knew why she did. It linked her to her mother. It also
linked her to that bastard pain-in-my-ass prince.

He had no place here, I decided as I followed the length
of the chain around the delicate bones of her collar, down to
the smooth band of the ring. I paused for a moment, pulse
pounding way too fast.

What I did next wasn't the smartest thing. I was sure that
damn snake wasn't fond of me, but I had no control at all as
my finger skated over Layla's skin and then toward the very
edge of Bambi's head.

Half expecting the familiar to rise off her skin and bite me
in my face, I was shocked when Bambi shifted, gliding up
toward my touch.

It struck me then that I was touching her—touching the demonic familiar—and my skin was on fire. A shudder worked
its way up the taut lines of my body as I lifted my gaze to hers.
Those pale, haunting eyes entranced me. They had for a long
time, and now I saw something I'd never seen in them before.
A fire. I traced around the snake's nostrils, surprised by the
texture. This…befuddled me, too, dragging a small grin out
of me. It wasn't so much that it was rough, but I could definitely tell that the snake was there, an entire separate being
adhered to her skin.

"It doesn't feel like I thought it would. The skin is just
slightly raised, but it's really like a tattoo." I had this need to
point that out, which was probably as stupid as banging my

head against the wall, because I was sure she knew that. That she'd touched the tattoo before.

I bit back a groan as *that* image took root. Another one I'd never get out of my head.

Layla's lashes drifted shut and her lips parted even more. God and all the demons in Hell, I knew her mouth had to be the sweetest thing ever.

"Does she like it?" I asked.

After a moment, Layla nodded.

The words were out of my mouth in an instant. "Do you?"

Her eyes flew open, and she watched me as I followed the curve over the swell of her breast, to the fragile lace of her top.

I wanted—no, needed to see all of it, all of who Layla was now, but I waited. What I asked pretty much laid it all out there, I thought. If she said yes, then she had to know how I felt about her, which was something I'd never really felt for anyone else before. Sure, I'd known the razor-sharp edge of lust, but with her that lust mixed with something far more potent.

But if she said no, then I would get the Hell out of here. As much as it would kill me, I swore I would.

Layla didn't say no.

"Yes." It was a whisper, but it was like thunder to my senses, rattling every cell and organ inside me.

I breathed deeply, unable to wait. Like a kid who'd been staring at presents under the Christmas tree for weeks, I couldn't contain the anticipation. I held her gaze, seeking out any hesitation as I asked, "Can I see the rest of her?"

Her mouth opened, but there was no sound as a long, torturous moment passed between us, and then Layla nodded.

It was freaking Christmas morning.

My hand shook as I reached for the strap of her top, and I hoped she didn't see that. I slipped the strap down to her wrist, keeping my gaze trained on what I was doing, delaying what I desperately wanted. I moved the other strap to her slim wrist and then threw up a prayer of thanks before I shifted my feverish gaze.

Air punched out of my lungs, and my arm suddenly felt weak, like I wouldn't be able to hold myself up for much longer. I followed the line of Bambi, but I wasn't really seeing it. I was seeing Layla, committing every beautiful square inch to memory.

"Layla…" It was all that I could say.

Never in my life had I seen such beauty as this. The demonic tattoo and the heaven that was Layla's body made for a startling combination.

Unable to stop myself, I continued down the path of Bambi, over the sweetest swell. Layla moved, arching her back as I trailed Bambi's length, all the way to where her body curled around Layla's rib cage. Between the way she felt, the breathy sound she made, and how she rose up as she pushed her shoulders into the bed, I was going to lose my freaking mind.

Who cared?

I'd already lost my heart and my soul to Layla.

ACKNOWLEDGMENTS

Layla and crew wouldn't be here without Margo Lipschultz's awesome editing powers; Natashya Wilson, head editor in charge; Jennifer Abbots, the publicist with the mostest and also another JLA; and the wonderful team of people, from copy editors to booksellers, behind the series at Harlequin TEEN—thank you.

Thank you to K. P. Simmon for being the second publicist with the mostest and to Stacey Morgan for keeping my head on straight. To my awesomely awesome agent, Kevan Lyon—you rock. And Taryn Fagerness and Brandy Rivers—you guys rock my socks off.

The following people have been there for me, one way or another, and I'd probably go insane if it wasn't for Laura Kaye, Molly McAdams, Tiffany King, Tiffany Snow, Lesa Rodrigues, Dawn Ransom, Jen Fisher, Vi (Vee!), Sophie Jordan and, wow, I could keep going, but I'm sure this is starting to bore everyone.

Last but most important, thank you to the readers. Without y'all, none of this would've been possible. At all.